Their client was in danger, but not from them...

Just as Ed tromped into the sunroom, they heard a scream followed by a splash.

"Susan!" he yelled then lumbered through the French doors and across the patio. Both designers dropped their brushes and jumped up to race behind him.

As they reached the pool, they saw Susan face down in a dead-man float. Dropping his towel, Ed jumped into the water, his giant splash swishing Susan farther from the edge. He swam with far more determination than skill, reaching his wife and grabbing her.

His frantic fumbling defied Cara's entire lifeguard training and she thought they both go under. "Flip her over," she cried, shedding her sandals and diving into the water.

"Tow her this way," Maggie called.

Cara instinctively took over the rescue, bringing Susan to the side where Maggie waited. Together with Ed helping to boost Susan, they hauled her out. As Cara worked on their client, Maggie called nine-one-one. Ed kept asking if his wife was all right and sticking his face in the way. Cara shooed him off as she tried to clear the water from Susan's lungs and get her breathing again.

Finally, Susan sputtered, spitting some water and starting to breathe on her own. By the time the EMTs arrived, she was still unconscious, her head bleeding, but her pulse felt stronger and she was breathing shallowly.

"It's all this construction stuff." Ed motioned around widely as the paramedics lifted Susan onto a stretcher. "What's this?"

"Oh, no." Cara blanched as she saw the oily puddle next to a tipped over can of linseed oil. "It's no wonder she slipped." Her horrified stare met Maggie's. *What had they done*?

Design Duo, best friends, and business partners, Cara Fazio and Maggie Ross redecorate and design, discovering a trail of bodies along the way. Danger lurks in the nooks and foundations of homes new and old. Ripping into walls often means ripping apart secrets, and spilled secrets sometimes means murder. When a killer threatens their client and their reputation, Maggie and Cara are forced to switch from designers to detectives. But can they sort through the faux clues to find real ones and solve two murders in time to prevent a third?

KUDOS for *Faux Fatality*

In *Faux Fatality* by Karen E. Rigley, Cara Fazio and Maggie Ross are interior decorators who get side tracked easily when trying to keep their wealthy client alive. Someone is out to get her, and the decorating duo are determined to protect their client, who has also become a friend. Not exactly experienced detectives the two amateurs jump to the wrong conclusions, run afoul of the law, and struggle to figure out the clues, until they think they know who the guilty party is. Along the way, we are treated to some hilarious, as well as suspenseful, moments, and some handy design techniques. The story is cute, fun, entertaining, and it will keep you on your toes, trying to figure out who the killer is. All in all, it makes for a great read. ~ *Taylor Jones, Reviewer*

Faux Fatality by Karen Rigley is the story of a serial predator, a tale that is much too common in reality these days. This killer wants something and is determined to get it, systematically killing people, or attempting to kill them, with little regard for who gets hurt. Enter our two intrepid heroines, Cara Fazio and Maggie Ross, interior decorators and amateur detectives. When someone tries to kill their new client, a wealthy Texas heiress, Cara and Maggie go to work to both figure out who the killer is and prevent him or her from harming their client. While decorating a sun room and designing a backyard pool and grotto, they sift through clues and lay traps to catch a killer, staying just this side of the wrong side of the law and frustrating law men in two counties. Filled with handy decorating tips that I can't wait to try in my own home, *Faux Fatality* is also a fun who-done-it with charming characters and an intriguing plot that will keep you turning pages from beginning to end. ~ *Regan Murphy, Reviewer*

FAUX

Fatality

Karen E. Rigley

A Black Opal Books Publication

GENRE: MYSTERY-DETECTIVE/WOMEN SLEUTHS

FAUX FATALITY
Copyright © 2016 by Karen E. Rigley
Cover Design by Jackson Cover Designs
All cover art copyright © 2016
All Rights Reserved
Print ISBN: 978-1-626945-39-5

First Publication: OCTOBER 2016

Published by Black Opal Books **http://www.blackopalbooks.com**

DEDICATION

I dedicate FAUX FATALITY, *the first mystery in my Design Duo series, to my daughter Erica and to my dear friends Bonnie K. Winn and Ann Miller House for buoying me up and their unending support.*

Chapter 1

Three months ago, Mercerville, Texas:

John Lawson heard a rattle then rustling sounds from the outer office. He didn't glance up from his notepad. "Aimee, that you? Forget something?"

The blast of a nine-millimeter gun pierced his forehead, his last words erased as quickly as his life.

❧❧❧

Present day, Houston, Texas:

"Wow." Cara Fazio parked their Mobile Design Duo van under the slate portico of the huge, contemporary house.

"Be sweet if this job generates us more business in this area," Maggie Ross said, staring upward at the row of large windows fronting the street.

"True."

This was their first design job in River Oaks, an old, ultra-wealthy section of town. Lush Houston vegetation landscaped in a spectrum of greens from feathery ferns to a two-wing silver bell snowdrop tree to tall spreading oaks.

Maggie craned her head to see beyond the tall iron gates.

"I hope this Dexter woman isn't a snob."

"She sounded nice on the phone." Cara reached for her portfolio, sharing Maggie's concern herself, but not about to admit it. An Air Force brat growing up, Cara had constantly been the new kid at school, always moving, leaving friends behind—until she turned twelve and they relocated here to Houston.

She'd learned early in life to ignore snobs, along with bullies, without allowing the flicker of a lash to let her hurt show. Now she needed to edge her friend and business partner back on track. Cara slid out of driver's seat. "Best behavior, Maggs."

Maggie tossed back wavy copper-colored hair, the Irish in her green eyes flashing. "Naturally."

Pushing the doorbell, Cara reached to straighten her jacket. Even though her clothes were lightweight cotton, Houston's legendary heat was unrelenting.

"Hello! Welcome." A lively woman in her mid-forties opened the elaborate door. "I'm Susan Dexter." Smiling widely, her hazel eyes sparkled. "You must be the designers."

"We are," Maggie responded warmly, her concern vanished like a magician's rabbit. Cara refrained from rolling her eyes. Maggie could switch emotional directions faster than a puppy chasing a ball.

"Y'all come in. How 'bout some iced tea or lemonade?"

"No thanks," they replied in unison.

"Just had something to drink," Cara explained.

"Okay then. I guess you want to get started." Susan's hands hadn't stopped moving since she'd opened the door. A hand talker, Cara realized. Much like herself.

Maggie bobbed her head. "We do."

Their client's voice dropped. "Between us—the manor doesn't feel like home yet, but that's where you come in, isn't it?"

Before they could answer, Susan led them through the marbled entry hall to the spacious living room, still chatting.

"My husband bought this house for me, but it's so sleek and elegant. Not exactly my thing." Laughing brightly, she sounded younger than a woman did in her late forties. "I need you to help make a little corner of it my own."

"Our pleasure." Cara glanced around the stark contemporary manor. "It's a beautiful place."

"Oh, it is." Susan brushed a wayward lock of highlighted, chestnut brown hair off her forehead. She couldn't seem to stop gushing. Appearing self-conscious, she tugged at her Asian silk tunic. Probably not the treatment its high-end designer intended for the garment. Though her clothes were obviously expensive, the contagious laugh seemed to suit the woman better. "I just need a comfy spot where it feels homey."

Maggie nodded. "Homey and cozy. We can do that, Mrs. Dexter."

"Call me Susan. I know my request for you two to stay here during the renovation is unusual, but I'd appreciate it."

"Workdays it'll be fine," Maggie said.

"Most of the time," Cara qualified, not so thrilled with that aspect of redo.

"Thanks. Saves you hours of commuting in all this awful traffic and it'll be great to have company. I hate it when the house is empty."

"What about your husband?" Maggie asked.

"We're both glad you'll be here. Ed's dedicated to his career. Works hard and he is gone a lot." Susan's expression clouded briefly, then she laughed. "But we're still practically newlyweds and he fusses over me like crazy when he *is* home. We're about to celebrate our first anniversary soon."

"A year can be more than enough," Cara grumbled under her breath before Maggie poked her in the side.

"Oh, don't give up on love." Susan tapped her chest lightly, indicating her heart. "You just had the wrong man. So did I the first time. I swore off men for years, then Ed happened. He's the right guy."

No such thing. Cara kept the thought to herself. "Your

decor is um, lovely, but everything is so—white." The place right out of a sterile, futuristic movie made her wish for sunglasses to block the glare. "Do you want us to add color to the redo area?"

"Yes, please!" Susan exclaimed. "Let me show you the sunroom where you can work your magic."

"Do you have a style in mind?" Cara swung her short dark hair back as she moved to Susan's side. The high-gloss bamboo floors reflected her full figure like a distracting mirror. No escaping her Italian heritage and a few too many pieces of chocolate.

"I'd adore something old world for the sunroom." Susan's forehead creased, her eyes suddenly sad. "Houston's great, but I miss my small town. Mercerville wasn't for Ed, though. He's big city all the way through. To me, it's strange and overwhelming here but nice."

Cara nodded. She remembered how frightening Houston felt at first with all the people, and the maze of freeways stacked up high. It had been far different from every other place her family had lived. Yes, she understood how intimidating the huge city could be for newcomers of any age.

Susan turned, leading them down a second hallway. "My family home is mid-nineteenth century, with lots of European immigrants settled the Hill Country in the 1800s. And you can tell it by the buildings, especially my house. Ed prefers modern. I like antiques and things with history, but—" Susan looked up, her eyes bright again. "We're starting a whole new life, a new future, and we don't need to weigh it down with history."

A controlling husband? Cara snorted beneath her breath. Maggie shot her a warning glance. Cara read her don't-get-on-how-you-can't-trust-a-man-podium glance. And this time Maggs was right. They didn't want to lose the job before they even started.

Reaching a pair of twelve-foot-tall pocket doors, Susan slid them partway open. "I must confess I do miss color, though."

Maggie gasped. "Such possibilities!"

"Yes." Cara felt a familiar sense of excitement building. She loved the beginning of a new design. Her design mode whirred into action. "Maybe a splash of Tuscany or French country, yet keeping a modern edge?"

"You read my mind." Susan pushed a flyaway strand of hair out of her eyes. "Or even something exotic? Like out of the Arabian Nights?"

All three women laughed.

Cara smiled to herself, envisioning their client in such a space. "*Very* exotic!"

As the laughter faded, Maggie's gamine face eased into a familiar expression. *Uh-oh.* Maggie had a sixth sense. Well, actually, a near-psychic talent. One Cara hoped she'd tune out so they could concentrate on design.

"Maggs?" Cara queried, tipping her head in their new client's direction.

"Sorry. Just thinking this project's going to be an adventure. I feel it."

"*Feel* it?" Cara echoed, hoping her friend was psychic enough to get the message and knock off the telepathy. In this economy, their budding business had taken a hit. They couldn't afford to lose a job.

Maggie shook her head. "It'll be great." Taking a breath, she winked. "An absolute vision."

Relieved, Cara watched as the pocket doors opened farther, sunshine spilling through the wall of windows in blinding brightness. This was the good kind of light. "It's fantastic!"

"Such an incredible blank canvas," Maggie agreed, mirroring Cara's enthusiasm.

"Now all it needs is you." Susan beamed at them.

They heard the door open, rushed footsteps, and then a man's voice. "Darling? Are the designers here? Susan, where are you?"

"In the sunroom, Ed."

A pleasant man about Susan's age entered, sweeping her

into a huge one-armed hug. His wide smile included Cara and Maggie in his hearty hello.

Susan smiled, a blush tinting her cheeks. "This is my husband, Ed." Her blush deepened when he pulled her closer against his side.

"We guessed as much." Maggie replied, obviously comfortable around Susan.

Cara smiled and extended a hand, immediately swallowed within his strong grip.

"I want you to give my sweetheart the room of her dreams." His left arm continued to encircle his wife. "She deserves the best."

"Then, we'll do our best." Cara echoed, wondering how much he'd be underfoot.

He smiled broadly. "Good. I'll leave you ladies alone to plan." Ed gave his wife a smacking kiss and strode out as quickly as he'd appeared.

"He can be a bit of a tornado." Susan explained, still flushed.

"You make a cute couple," Maggie replied dreamily.

Her friend was a hopeless romantic. Cara immediately returned the conversation to her own first love, design was a lot more trustworthy than romance. "Do these doors give you access to the entire backyard?"

They all crossed over to the sliding glass patio doors.

"Yes. I was hoping you'd include the patio and backyard as part of the design?"

"Definitely." More work—more money. *Sweet*. Cara stepped out onto an empty patio, buffeted by a balmy breeze. "This has great bones. We can create an outdoor area, all flowing together."

"We should replace the sliding door with French doors." Maggie spun back to Susan, for once harnessing her tendency to swoop ahead too fast. "If you approve?"

Susan clapped her hands. "I *love* French doors."

Grateful her partner seemed to have forgotten her psychic episode, Cara waved a hand in the direction of the manicured lawn. "Maybe a gazebo over there? Past the pool?"

Maggie's unstoppable enthusiasm kicked up another notch. "We can add the furniture pieces and tropical plants to make it a relaxing lanai."

"I love anything tropical," Susan agreed. "We don't have many palm trees in Mercerville."

"You're easy to please, Susan." Cara slid a tiny digital camera from her bag and began snapping pictures of the interior and exterior areas. "We'll come back on Monday to show you our ideas and get your input."

Laser tape measure in hand, Maggie began recording the dimensions. "We'll bring three different plans for you to consider. Provided you like one, we can talk specific materials."

"I'm sure I'll love them all."

Maggie glanced up from the red laser spot on the wall. "We hope so, but we're always willing to reinvent a design, or ditch it and start over."

Delighted with their new client and the design opportunity, Cara snapped one last frame and tucked the camera away in her bag.

"I'm so thrilled to see what you'll do." Susan started walking them back through the sterile manor. "And to be able to transform the sunroom and patio together. It'll seem like a whole different house."

Glancing at the uninviting interior, Cara certainly hoped so. "We should be set to begin the project mid-week."

"And stay here as we planned?" Susan asked on a hopeful note.

"Yes." Maggie grinned. "Quite convenient."

"Are you sure you want to put up with us?" Cara asked uneasily.

Even though Susan had initially agreed to the arrangement, Cara hesitated. These clients were almost newlyweds.

"We want you here." Susan gave them each an impromptu hug. "It'll be so fun. I can't wait!"

c❧c❧

The weekend zipped by as Cara and Maggie brain-stormed, drew sketches, then gathered color and material samples. The phone rang as Maggie straightened the desk and Cara added a final touch to the third design board.

Cara waved toward the desk. "Can you get it, Maggs?"

"Sure." Grabbing the phone, Maggie pushed a button to silence the ringing. "Mobile Design Duo."

"This is Susan Dexter." Their new client sounded distressed.

"How can we help you, Susan?" Maggie threw a desperate glance at her business partner, but Cara's back was to her, raven hair smooth as a cap as she bent her head down in concentration.

"I need to postpone our Monday appointment."

"Why? What's wrong?" Maggie hoped their client wasn't cancelling the job after all their work. They hadn't even gotten a down payment yet.

"I have to go home for a funeral—back to Mercerville."

Maggie immediately felt guilty about her thought. "Oh, I'm so sorry."

"It's not family," Susan explained in a rush. "It's my late lawyer's secretary."

"Good." Maggie felt flustered. "I mean that it's *not* family."

"I know what you meant. Can we postpone until Wednesday? I'll be back by then."

"Sure. No problem."

"It's weird," Susan confided in a near whisper. "Three months ago my lawyer, John Lawson, was killed when a burglar broke into his office. Now someone killed his secretary, Aimee Travis, in a hit and run. This just doesn't happen in my hometown. Ever."

"Wow." Maggie hardly knew what to say.

"In my entire life there's never been a murder in Mercerville. Not even a hit and run accident. Well, except when

Tommy Barns got drunk and hit the barbershop pole. But he confessed to it, the next day, when Sheriff Watt saw the red and white paint on Tommy's pickup truck bumper." Susan took a breath. "Now two people killed there."

"The world's a tougher place…" Maggie tried to wrap her mind around the coincidence. "But a lawyer and then his secretary. That *is* weird." Her sixth sense escalated. It wasn't anything she could put a finger on, but her inner radar was on alert.

"Ed says it proves small towns are no safer than the city." Susan sighed. "Anyway, if you can switch to Wednesday, I'd appreciate it. I can't wait to see your designs."

"We'll be there. At one, right?"

"Yes. Thanks."

"Okay, we'll see you then."

Susan lingered on the phone. "I wish Ed would go with me, but he's tied up with business."

"Too bad." Maggie tended to champion underdogs and right now Susan sounded like one.

"This will only be the second funeral I've attended since Daddy passed away." Susan's voice cracked. "It's so hard."

"I bet." Hearing the pain and remembering how hard losing a father had hit Cara, then to attend another funeral not long after. *Hard* didn't cover it. Maggie nibbled her bottom lip, wondering if she should volunteer to go. "Susan, is there someone else who could go with you?"

"Maybe Uncle Leland, though he's pretty much an invalid now. I doubt my cousins, Roger or Rachel, will go. Not their thing." Susan fell silent as if lost in thought.

Maggie debated going to some hole-in-the-wall town to pay respects for a person she'd never met. But to please a client—especially one who sounded so sad?

Suddenly Susan spoke again. "Forgive my rambles. I'll see you on Wednesday."

Maggie heard a click then the buzz of a dial tone as she stood holding the phone.

"Hey." Cara's dark gaze filled with concern. "What's up? Did we lose the Dexter job?"

"No, just postponed until midweek. Poor Susan." Still feeling a bit dazed by Susan's call, Maggie explained the situation.

Cara's near perfect features creased into disbelief. "That's horrid. *Two* murders in her hometown?"

"A lawyer, then his secretary. What are the chances?"

"Very strange."

"More than strange." Maggie felt storm clouds billowing above the horizon as she crossed over to Cara and helped gather up their samples. "Let's hope murder doesn't follow our client back here."

"Now you're getting weird, Maggs, but it is quite a mystery." Cara caught a green marker before it rolled off the table. "I bet their local sheriff's in a real tizzy."

"Scary stuff." Maggie hesitated. "Maybe we should volunteer to go with Susan."

Cara frowned, her large, dark eyes adamant. "No way. We have a design to work on, remember? We don't even know our client yet, much less one of her acquaintances. It's not as though there's a serial killer loose in the little Hill Country town. A burglary and a hit and run aren't the same."

"Whatever." Maggie tried to tamp down her unrest, but it niggled at her, the same way it had the summer Cara had tripped on a hiking trail and broke her leg. Maggie didn't want to go on that venture. She felt no more positive about a murder spree in their client's hometown. At least it was far from Houston and their job.

"At any rate, I doubt anyone's going to run down Susan at a funeral. Now, can we get back to work?"

One reason for the success of their business partnership was her own impulsive enthusiasm balanced Cara's pragmatic attitude. Maggie knew she possessed dragonfly tendencies—flitting, hovering, and then darting away. Cara was more like a woodpecker methodically tapping at trees and only taking flight to aim toward the next leaf-filled branch. Maggie just wished her inner radar wasn't saying it might be flitting time.

ოოო

On Wednesday, they hauled their stuff into the Dexter manor. Seeming back to herself, Susan fluttered around them. "Can you spread everything out on the coffee table? Or even the floor? Anywhere. Just put those down and show me. I can't wait to see."

They settled on the white leather sectional. "Here's the first design." Cara laid the sketch on the glass coffee table as Maggie pulled out accompanying samples to arrange beside it.

"Oh my! It's right out of a Tuscan painting." Susan devoured each detail of the colorful sketch. "Makes me feel like I'm in Tuscany."

They showed Susan the other design boards. "This second style is French Country and the third is our take on an exotic tropical retreat."

Susan touched every sample fabric then stroked the metal finishes as they explained each design sketch and handed her their samples. "How can I choose between all these beautiful plans? They're heavenly."

"Which design can you imagine yourself in?" Cara asked, leaning forward, wondering which style would win. She and Maggie had made an unofficial wager on Susan's choice. "Think about a quiet afternoon, reading, enjoying your yard."

"The French country is gorgeous, but maybe too old world for Ed." Susan tapped the tropical sketch of vivid color against neutral sand tones. "And this one feels like an island escape, but in a way, the Tuscan's sort of a blend. It has the best of both."

"Then Tuscan it is," Maggie exclaimed shooting a smug grin at her partner.

Cara should have known. Past experience told her that Maggie's sixth sense was, most often, right. "It'll transform this space into your own private haven," Cara added, ignoring Maggie's gloating as she cleared away everything except the Tuscan presentation. "Now we can let your preferences guide the renovation."

Maggie handed several small wooden squares to Susan. "These are different treatments for the focal wall."

"This warm honey color, it's textured?"

"Right." Cara held up a larger example of the effect. "We want the effect of old, painted plaster, aged by years of Tuscan sun."

Susan skimmed her thumb over the texture. "Cool."

Cara and Maggie exchanged a smile. Then Cara placed the selected square on the design board as Maggie passed along fabric swatches in russet, poppy, vibrant reds, earth tones, goldenrod, olive, and various blues. "Here are fabric samples."

"Beautiful. How many do I pick?"

"One for the draperies, two for the upholstery—one print and one solid, and a third for the toss pillows and accents."

Deciding in mere seconds. Susan handed her selections to Maggie. "Now what?

"Here's an option for your focal wall," Cara said. "See? That's the long wall with centered bookshelves designed on the diagonal. Notice their wine rack look?"

"Yes, that one." It didn't take long for Susan to choose a bronze metal finish and window treatments, then they all agreed on classic travertine tile for the floor.

"Perfect for Houston's heat and humidity," Cara agreed, congratulating Susan on her choice.

"It'll feel cool on your feet. And we can install an under-tile radiant heat system for cold spells in the winter, not that they're too many of them." Maggie grinned. "Houston's weather is nothing if unpredictable. But then this room can be your all-year retreat."

"Now for the color of the tile." Cara guided their client

through the selections, explaining the concept of muted earth tones as a background to the deep rich Tuscany colors.

Susan tapped long nails on one. "Neutral like this? It makes me think of a sandy beach."

Cara nodded. "Perfect backdrop for the warm yellows and reds you want, not to mention that gorgeous Mediterranean blue you added."

Maggie picked up a brochure, unfolding it for Susan. "You'll need some type of roof or covering for rainy days on the lanai. To go with this design what do you think of these diagonal slats that you can open or close whenever you want?"

"Those are interesting. How do they work?"

"A remote control just like auto blinds, except it's an awning."

"Sounds easy. That's important." Susan suddenly seemed to wilt. "I'm so glad ya'll didn't mind postponing till today."

Maggie leaned forward in concern. "Would you like me to grab something to drink?"

"I don't want to put you out." Susan waved her hands limply. "We're trying to get someone to help me around the house, but—"

"I'll find the kitchen," Maggie interrupted.

Susan's voice had lost its lilt as she returned the sample tiles to Cara. "Did Maggie tell you about the funeral?"

"Uh huh. Have they found the hit and run driver yet?'

"Not yet. You'd think it'd be easy. I guess the sheriff examined every dark-colored SUV in the area. And came up with nothing. They think it was an outsider who came off the highway."

"Crazy world, huh?"

Maggie easily located the kitchen. Rummaging in the refrigerator, she grabbed a bottle of vitamin-infused water. Unless her inner radar was off kilter, Susan Dexter was still very upset over the situation in Mercerville.

Maggie returned to the living room to hear the tail end of

Cara and Susan's conversation. "Did I miss anything?"

Cara filled in her in on the sheriff's outsider theory.

"Did your uncle go to the funeral with you?" Maggie asked, as she handed Susan the water. She still felt guilty that she hadn't offered to go.

"He wasn't up to it. Joan Gaynor, an old classmate of mine, was there by herself so we sat together."

"That's good."

"I guess." Susan's expression echoed the lack of conviction in her voice.

"Why? Didn't you and your friend have some catching up to do?"

"Joan wasn't exactly grieving about Aimee's death." Susan shifted awkwardly. "I think she was almost glad."

"Why?" Maggie and Cara asked in unison.

"I guess now Joan gets her job back. This is somewhat complicated. Joan had been a secretary at the Mercerville bank for over twenty years. She wasn't ready to retire, but she didn't have a choice." Susan turned to Maggie. "Remember, I told you that Aimee was my lawyer's secretary?"

"Yes."

"After he was killed, Aimee needed a new job. There aren't many of those in Mercerville, so Aimee set her sights on Joan's job. She flirted with the town banker, Elliot Ohlmacher. He fired Joan so he could hire Aimee. Aimee has, uh, *had* a way with men."

"A real soap opera, huh?" Maggie was surprised at all the drama in such a small town.

"We do have a colorful town."

"But you're here in Houston now and ready for a new sunroom." Cara smiled a bit absently while fiddling with their design board.

Maggie knew Cara wanted to get back to business, but Susan obviously needed to talk. Maggie had a reputation for taking in strays and, right now, their client gave off those same vibes.

"There's one more thing." Susan hesitated. "Back home

we have a beautiful fountain in the garden. I wonder if you could duplicate it for the yard here? It'd be perfect with the Tuscan theme."

"Do you have photos?"

"No. I was hoping you two would make a fast trip to Mercerville with me and see it in person?"

Susan was so hopeful that Maggie didn't have the heart to turn her down. "I think we can do that. Right, Cara?"

"Mercerville?" Cara choked, clearly not happy with the turn of conversation. "We have a tight schedule—"

"It would mean so much." Susan sounded both vulnerable and sad. "Please?"

"Maybe we can squeeze it in," Cara replied, reluctantly surrendering. "As long as there aren't any more murders."

CSCS

The marble fountain at Susan's family home was as unexpected as Mercerville itself. Cara had imagined a broken-down, sad little town.

Even here in the Texas Hill Country, many rural areas had deteriorated after the advent of superstores. But not Mercerville. One or two buildings in the commercial center were vacant, but all the others appeared to hold thriving businesses. People seemed friendly, neighborly. Certainly not a place you'd expect to find two murders in as many decades, much less a few months.

Set high on one hill, their client's house appeared to be the largest in the town. Actually, more like a mansion than a house. Surrounded by luscious landscaping, the place wore its age proudly.

Susan grinned at the housekeeper when she opened the door. "Hi, Gladys."

The woman's wrinkled face broke into a huge smile. Her graceful aging made Cara wonder if Susan inherited the housekeeper right along with the house.

Gladys ushered them inside, fussed over Susan, and then smoothed her apron, collecting herself. "Miss Susan, would you like cold drinks?"

Susan queried her guests who both declined. "No thanks, Gladys."

"Sure is good to have you home." The housekeeper smiled fondly again before disappearing through a doorway.

Walking over silk-knotted Persian rugs, Cara and Maggie eagerly trailed Susan. Glancing sideways into the rooms they passed, they both fell silent for a change, appreciating the antique treasures surrounding them. The place was incredible.

Once in her glass conservatory that opened into the huge yard, Susan pointed outside to the fountain. "See?"

They stared at an exquisite angel pouring water from her outstretched, cupped hands.

"Amazing," Cara whispered, stirred by the sheer artistry.

"It's…" Maggie began, her voice trailing off as she stared at the beautiful statue.

"Perfect," Cara finished for her. "I think it'd be best if we take photos and draw some sketches if that's okay with you. It'll take longer, but I think we'll get a better end result."

Susan waved her hands. "It's fine. Ed has business late tonight, anyway. I'll call him and let him know we're staying over."

That wasn't what Cara had meant, but it *would* be late if they returned to Houston that evening. She bit her bottom lip to stifle the protest she wanted to make.

Maggie tilted her head, studying the fountain as Susan left to phone her husband. "It's going to be tough matching that patina."

"Not to mention staying overnight without bringing even a toothbrush."

"Stop grumbling. You know you have one in the van."

"I don't want to have a slumber party in Mercerville."

"You'll survive one night." Maggie walked in a circle

around the fountain. "Can you imagine giving up all this for that antiseptic house in Houston?"

Cara shrugged. "Not everyone has idealistic dreams of settling in a small town hundreds of miles from the nearest Starbucks." She suddenly felt horrified. "I bet there's not an espresso machine in the whole town. How am I going to wake up tomorrow?" Fueled by her caffeine fixes, she wouldn't be worth waking up without one.

"So you'll drink more cups of coffee." Maggie knelt down to splash her hand in the water, and then touched the carpet of mossy, emerald-green that grew around but not upon the fountain itself.

"Great. That'll make for a fun ride home, stopping at every restroom between here and Houston."

"Sweet talk the housekeeper. Gladys, I think? Maybe she'll fix you some double strength coffee. I don't know how you can stand that sludge you call coffee anyway."

"And I don't know how you can put away nearly an entire cheesecake and not gain an ounce. Let's call it even." Cara had always attributed Maggie's metabolism to her sprite-like behavior. Not to mention her apparently slim Celtic ancestors.

Maggie didn't smile, which wasn't like her.

And Cara knew Maggie well. Way before they'd gone into business together. Cara had been the new girl in junior high school, smart and a bit geeky, not-so-cool socially, feeling awkward that she developed too fast and too young. Just the opposite, Maggie was twig-thin with a trillion friends. From day one, they bonded as if kindred spirits.

That first year, when Cara lost her father she was devastated, but Maggie gave her love and comfort. When the next blow hit and Cara's mom remarried, nearly abandoning motherhood, Maggie and her parents practically adopted Cara. Maggie became not only her best friend, but also her *sister of the heart*.

They truly grew up together. Both loved to swim and joined the high school swim team together, taking their team to state and earning swimming scholarships to the same college.

Thanks to Maggie's mother and her encouragement, they also shared the love of design. Together they helped decorate many of their friends' dorm rooms and the sorority house. Although Cara worked as a lifeguard through school, their decorating business had been the next natural step. "What's wrong? The fountain's gorgeous."

"I keep thinking about those two murders. You're right—Mercerville's in the middle of nowhere, not exactly where you'd expect a sudden crime spree."

"Yeah." Cara pondered the implications, realizing more and more how crazy it sounded. "Logically, they probably aren't connected. Sure, the lawyer was murdered—though it doesn't sound premeditated. The robber might've thought no one would be there. That second death could've been just a terrible accident—like they said, someone from the highway who got away as soon as it happened. Makes more sense than a small town serial killer."

Shivering as they gazed around at the lengthening evening shadows, Maggie whispered, "Small town serial killer?"

Chapter 2

Maggie's reaction was contagious. Cara glanced as shadows conquered the waning daylight. With evening falling, the place didn't feel nearly as friendly.

"Killers lurking around Mercerville?" Maggie hugged her thin arms. "You've got me expecting a maniac to spring out from behind the bushes."

Knowing one of them had to stay attached to the planet, Cara adopted her no-nonsense tone. "Maggs, get a grip. I swear your imagination is vivid enough to propel you to the moon without a rocket." Still, Cara didn't mind when Susan returned, flipping on the outside lights.

"Since our overnight stay was sprung on Gladys, I told her that we'd eat out tonight, and then she only has to worry about breakfast." Again, Susan fluttered her hands as she spoke.

Watching Susan's hands, Cara again wondered if they shared at least a partial Italian heritage. Probably not. She couldn't imagine Susan throwing something when she got mad. Cara's own Mediterranean roots sometimes allowed her passionate side to emerge, yelling and letting things fly. Most the time though, she kept her emotions inside, going quiet.

It was Maggie who let her emotions rein free. Happy, sad, mad—you always knew exactly what Maggs felt—and usually that was a sunny mood. Not so for herself, Cara acknowledged as her own grumpiness percolated at the unexpected stay-over.

"Then after breakfast, you can sketch and take pictures to your heart's content," Susan suggested.

"Excellent. We're losing the light now." Maggie flashed an impertinent grin. "Morning will be the best time to work."

Cara frowned. *Overnight and probably an early morning as well.* She wasn't thrilled with either one.

"I thought we'd go to Addy's Diner for dinner." Susan steepled her fingers together. "If that's okay?"

"Sure." Maggie agreed as they followed Susan back through the mansion and out to the driveway.

"Is it the best place to eat?" Cara asked, suddenly aware of hunger pangs.

"About the only place." Susan laughed. "Unless you want pizza or takeout from the taco stand."

"The diner has my vote." Cara slid into the driver's seat of the van. "Just give me directions."

Susan clasped her seat belt into place. "Like anyone could get lost in Mercerville. Just follow this road back down to Main Street and turn left."

It took only a few minutes to reach Main Street, and the diner, where they parked in one of the diagonal spaces out front.

Maggie sighed longingly. "No parallel parking to deal with. Can you imagine that in downtown Houston?"

"Sure easier for me," Susan agreed as they walked from the van to the diner.

"Very retro," Cara commented, scooting into an aqua Naugahyde-covered booth. The rest of the place was splashed in the turquoise color along with lots of pink and black.

"Everything in Mercerville is retro," Susan countered,

sitting down beside Maggie. "Nothing changes much here."

Maggie reached for a menu. "Small towns are that way."

A plump waitress with fluffy gray hair rushed to the booth. "Good to see y'all, Susan. Can I get some drinks while your friends look over the menu?"

"That'll be lovely, Nan." Susan's voice oozed warm familiarity. "You know what I like."

"Strawberry lemonade?" Nan replied with a wink as she scribbled on her order pad. "And, y'all?"

"Iced tea," Maggie replied.

Cara didn't glance up from the menu. "An iced, double latte, please.

"Say what?" Nan's double chin jutted up as she fiddled with her pencil.

"Oh, give me a Coke." Her attitude faded. By the next day, she'd be a zombie from lack of caffeine.

"You had me going for a minute there." Nan shook her head then reached to clear plates from the next table. "City folks!"

"She's quite a waitress." Cara watched her go, silently bemoaning the lack of her favorite evening drink.

"Actually, Nan owns the place," Susan explained. "Addy was her granny."

"So what's good here?" Maggie studied the plastic-coated cardboard menu.

"Everything. It's good old home cooking."

Nan popped back with their drinks before they could make a decision.

"What's the soup today, Nan?" Susan asked. She turned to her companions. "Don't tell Gladys, but Addy's has the most delicious soup in town."

"Carrot dill." Nan's brow furrowed. "But you need more than soup. You're just skin and bones." She wagged a finger. "What would your daddy say?"

A soft pink blush colored Susan's face as she looked at her companions. "Nan's been fussing over me for as long as I can remember."

Cara couldn't squash a touch of envy at the waif-thin women across from her. She'd been crazy to think she shared any sort of heritage with Susan. Cara knew her Italian genes were to blame for her throwback figure to a time when women actually wanted curves. Now thinner was better. She didn't do thinner well.

Since Nan still had Susan in her sights, Maggie spoke up. "I'll have the chicken pot pie."

Nan scribbled on the well-used pad.

Cara shut her menu. "I think a chef salad and the soup."

"Dressing?"

"Oil and vinegar. On the side, please."

"All righty."

Susan nodded. "The same for me. Except blue cheese dressing." She met Nan's glare with a kind smile. "And we'll have some of your yummy cheese biscuits, too."

Apparently, that satisfied Nan who nodded then sauntered away.

Maggie craned her head, looking around the diner. "The colors are kind of a forties, fifties mix. Probably pink and black in the forties then aqua, that was so big in the fifties."

"Originally it was all pink and black." Susan paused. "That's what Daddy said. The seats were covered in some sort of pink material that wore out pretty soon. Naugahyde was the new, durable thing, but the salesman said he couldn't get it in pink the waiting list was months and months. And since the pink was getting grimy they didn't want to wait. The salesman convinced them that aqua would update the place. 'Course it didn't fit in. So Addy started putting in some more aqua, like it'd been done on purpose." Susan shrugged, but her voice filled with melancholy as she spoke of her late father. "It's been this way since I was a kid, so I guess I never thought it looked odd."

"Not odd." Maggie patted her hand. "Unique. Too many chain restaurants these days to suit me. You could be in anywhere, U.S.A. and recognize every chain eatery. Nope, this place has character."

Nan overheard Maggie's words as she returned with a large basket of warm fragrant biscuits. "That's what I've always thought." She handed them each a bread plate then looked pointedly at Susan. "You moving back home yet?"

"No. Actually, these two are designers who are redecorating the Houston house."

"Why'd you need a city house when you have a lovely home right here?" Nan shook her finger again. "You're a Mercer and you belong here in Mercerville."

Cara exchanged a glance with Maggie, suddenly realizing that Susan was, in fact, *lady of the manor.*

Susan glanced down, seeming uncertain. "Uncle Leland's still here."

"He's getting on in years. And you know how we all miss your daddy."

"We do." Susan's eyes filled with tears. "All of us miss him especially, Uncle Leland. You know they weren't just brothers—they were best friends, too." She dabbed at her tears. "I try to get up here to visit him as often as I can."

Nan awkwardly patted Susan's shoulder. "Didn't mean to get you crying. But you could move back, see him all the time."

Cara watched the exchange with interest. Susan had a lot on her slim shoulders.

"Nan, you know it's not that easy. And I'm happy with Ed in Houston." Susan swallowed, trying to reclaim her control. "Besides, Uncle Leland has Roger and Rachel."

"Harrumph. Those two!" With that, Nan threw up her hands and stomped off.

"Sorry about that." Susan reached into her purse for a tissue. "She tends to mother everybody in town."

Maggie took a biscuit then slathered butter on it. "I think it's sweet."

"Are Roger and Rachel your cousins?" Cara asked, wishing she could get away with that much butter, but she'd just end up wearing it on her hips. Still, she took a biscuit to nibble.

Susan nodded. "Uncle Leland's kids. He married late and they're closer to your age than mine. Roger's kinda taken over running the quarry now my father's gone and Uncle Leland's health is failing."

"The quarry?" Maggie asked, buttering a second biscuit.

"It's our family business."

"And you're a Mercer as in Mercerville?" Cara asked. "You could've told us."

"It's no big deal." Appearing uncomfortable, Susan fiddled with her silverware.

Cara took another bite of the biscuit. It tasted good. Maggie had polished off her second one and was reaching for a third when Nan arrived, hands loaded.

"Oh, here comes our dinner." Susan didn't hide her relief. "Doesn't it smell wonderful?"

Cara made a mental note not to bring up the subject again. She couldn't imagine what it felt like to be an heiress, but apparently it wasn't the stuff of fairy tales.

Nan handed around their meals in silence. Within minutes, she was gone. "Oh, dear." Susan pressed a hand against her chin. "I've hurt Nan's feelings."

"No problem." Cara stirred her carrot dill soup, inhaling its tantalizing aroma. "We'll leave a big tip." Maggie kicked her under the table. "Ouch!"

"Be careful, it's hot." Maggie smiled innocently and then turned to Susan. "You'll get a chance to talk to her before we leave and smooth things out."

"I hope so. I don't want to upset her."

Maggie slipped her fork into the flaky crust of the pot pie. "Trust me. I have a feeling that Nan will be all smiles before we leave."

"Really?"

"If Maggs says she has a feeling about something, you should listen." Cara pulled her gaze from the fragrant chicken pot pie and stared at her naked salad then back at Maggie. The designers shared a smile. "I trust her instincts to be right on."

Just as they were finishing their entrees, Nan stopped by to check on them. "Miss Susan, y'all ready for some of my famous peach pie?"

Cara mouthed "No."

But Susan was so enthusiastic about making peace that she ignored her. "Topped with that luscious hand-cranked vanilla ice cream. How can we resist?"

Plastering one hand against her forehead, Cara gasped. *Why couldn't I have lived in the fifties when men supposedly appreciated the Marilyn Monroe fuller figures?*

"You got it!" With a huge grin on her round face, Nan bustled away.

"Pie ala mode," Cara mumbled. "Just what I need."

"Sounds good to me." Maggie dabbed her mouth with a napkin and rubbed her concave tummy.

Cara reined in her temperamental genes. It wasn't Maggie's fault she was maddeningly thin even though she ate anything that wasn't still moving.

"You can't visit Mercerville without sampling Nan's peach pie." Susan's expression brightened. "We should declare it our town treasure."

The peach pie was pure heaven. As Cara savored the last bite, a ruddy-faced man sporting a combed-over bald spot and an outdated three-piece suit approached the table.

"Susan, nice to see you back in town." He extended his hand and practically grabbed hers, pumping it heartily. "Who are your friends?"

"Mr. Ohlmacher, meet Cara Fazio and Maggie Ross. They're from Houston."

"Nice to meet you, ladies." The overbearing man's voice had an arrogant edge and his smile didn't reach his pale, almost colorless eyes. "I'm sure Susan told you I'm the town banker."

"She did mention you." Cara surreptitiously hid her hand beneath the table, not wanting him to pounce on her next. She felt terrible for Susan whose hand was still trapped in Ohlmacher's.

Susan had to wriggle to free herself. "We were just leaving, Elliot. Have a good evening."

He slipped the bill off the table before they knew what he intended. "I'll handle this for you ladies."

"That's not necessary," Cara and Maggie exclaimed together.

"Please, don't bother." Susan reinforced their protest, allowing a shred of irritation to bleed into her voice.

"It's the least I can do." His cheeks puffed out as he slapped his credit card on the check and crossed to the counter. "Consider it payment since you graced Mercerville with your beauty."

Susan's cheeks were flame-red and she did not look pleased. Cara wondered what was up with that. One thing about Maggie she'd probably wrangle the story out of their client before they made it back to the house on the hill.

The silence in the van as they drove away was in direct contrast to their upbeat chatter when they'd arrived. Susan stared straight ahead, every line of her body tensed.

After a few minutes, Maggie did as Cara had expected. "Your banker's an interesting character."

"He's not *my* banker."

Cara glanced into the rearview mirror and saw Susan staring out the passenger window as Maggie made another attempt. "Isn't his bank the only one in town?"

"Yes. I'd rather not discuss it." Susan sounded every bit the lady of the manor. Didn't look like Maggie was going to even dent the steel shell Susan had built around herself.

"Okay." Never daunted long, Maggie tried again. "Mm, that was yummy peach pie."

"Delicious," Cara agreed.

"The best ever," Susan said.

A squirrel dashed across the road. Jerking the steering wheel, Cara nearly flipped the van, but missed the creature. "Too close." She concentrated on her driving, settling the vehicle back on a straight path.

"For the squirrel and us," Maggie squeaked.

"You're a good driver, Cara." Apparently refocused by the change of subject and near squirrel disaster, Susan's melancholy faded. "You know, I'd almost forgotten how scrumptious Nan's peach pies are."

"You guys can talk, but I'm the one who'll be *wearing* that pie on my hips." Cara turned onto Mercer Hill.

Maggie patted her almost non-existent stomach. "You ought to post a sign as you enter town. *Caution: Peach pie and rogue squirrels ahead.*"

Cara winked at Maggie. "For you, the sign ought to say: *Peach pie this way. Eat all you can hold.*"

"Is it my fault that I have a fast metabolism?"

"Wish you could share it with me," Cara muttered under her breath.

Maggie frowned. "Cara, why can't you ever get it? You have those luscious Italian curves other women envy."

"And men desire," Susan threw in. "You're both young, bright and pretty." She looked first at Maggie then Cara. "How come neither one of you is married?"

"Been there, did that." Cara couldn't keep the derision from her voice.

"That's right." Susan pushed back a stray curl. "You told me."

"And I have a *sometimes* boyfriend," Maggie inserted.

Cara smiled to herself. Maggs knew she preferred not to discuss her unsuccessful marriage, so she'd reclaimed Susan's attention to spare her.

"*Sometimes* boyfriend?" Susan sounded confused.

"Uh huh. Sometimes we date and sometimes he disappears for weeks."

"You both just need to find the right guy. My first marriage was an emotional train wreck. I thought Steve loved me, but all he cared about was my money. I learned the hard way when Daddy bought him off."

Maggie scrunched one eye shut. "Wow, that's cruel."

Susan paused. "I finally figured out it was for the best. But I didn't date for years. Just those awkward setups friends thought would help. My heart was *not* into dating."

Cara understood that. "Didn't trust men?"

"Didn't trust my own judgment. Until Ed came along and refused to take no for an answer."

Maggie sighed. "That's so romantic."

"Yeah, yeah." Cara whipped the van onto the gravel drive. "Romance is overrated. A woman needs something she can depend on for happiness."

"What would that be?" Susan asked.

"Chocolate!" Maggie and Cara chorused.

"Oh, you two!"

As they climbed out of the van, someone behind the shrubbery hollered, making both Cara and Maggie jump. "Yoo-hoo!"

A diminutive platinum blonde popped out of the bushes and ran up the driveway behind them, waving wildly until she skittered to a stop inches from Susan. "Thank goodness, you're home! The library fundraiser's a disaster. We need you!"

Cara noted that the young woman's baby-blue sundress appeared to be a size zero. How could any adult be so tiny?

"Sorry, Faith." Susan shook her head. "I can write you a check, but we head back to Houston tomorrow."

"No!" Faith wailed. "It's a mess. Darlene Lawson and the Schmidts are impossible. You're the only one who can control them."

"You have the ladies' group on your side."

Faith clenched her fists and even in the purpling twilight, her face darkened. "Darlene has both of them buffaloed— they know how she gets, so they're just giving in. Of all things, Darlene wants a talent show. And no one's gonna pay to hear Hilda Hicks sing or old Luther play his fiddle and dance a jig."

Maggie smothered a giggle.

"And the Schmidts?" Susan queried, sounding concerned.

"They want to spend so much money on a gala fund raiser that we'll never earn enough back to pay expenses, let alone raise the money we need."

"What if I call them all in the morning?"

Faith looked unsure. "I wish you'd stay home. Things are so much smoother when you're in charge."

"Can't happen." Susan gave the little blonde a quick hug. "Though I miss this place sometimes, and I certainly miss you."

"All right." Dejected, Faith retraced her path back down the driveway, her sandals flip-flopping as she walked.

"That was my neighbor. Sorry, I didn't even think to introduce you."

"She's no bigger than a baby bunny," Cara replied as she opened the back of the van and pulled out their rucksacks.

"And as cute," Maggie added.

Amazingly, the front door was unlocked. *Must be a small town thing.* Cara's nostrils twitched and she inhaled. The scent of lemon oil blended with flowers filled the house. Yes. She saw a fragrant spray of honeysuckle and fresh cut gardenias, which Gladys arranged beautifully in a Chinese vase and set on the entry table. She wanted a closer look at the vase, to see what dynasty it came from.

Susan's concentration remained on her neighbor. "Faith's a sweetheart, but she has a hard time handling some of the stronger characters in town."

Gladys walked toward them from a dimly lit room, her rheumatic bones moving slower now. "Glad you're home, Miss Susan. Can I get you anything?"

"We've talked about this. No need for you to stay up and wait for me. The doctor said you shouldn't be on your feet as much anymore. Besides, your husband needs you more. Poor Arthur and his health."

"He'll live. And you do me more good than doctors," the older woman retorted. She glanced at Cara and Maggie. "I've known this one since she was a bitty mite."

Their affection for each other was evident. *Nice.* Cara didn't have many warm fuzzies from her own childhood.

Her dad, an Air Force major, got deployed overseas for the umptheenth time shortly after they relocated to Houston— only this time he never came home. Then six months later, her mother remarried. Her mom and globe-trotting, career-obsessed stepdad were always away and traveling. At twelve, Cara felt orphaned. From then on, she pretty much was. If Maggie's parents hadn't treated her like family, she wouldn't have had anyone.

"Let's go upstairs and find y'all some nighties," Susan offered.

"No need." Cara shook away old memories to focus on the moment as she held up her rucksack. "We always keep overnight bags in the van."

"You know—*mobile* designers," Maggie added.

Susan led them up the grand staircase. "I never put it together like that."

The first floor of the house was a good two stories high and the lofty walls that curved beside the stairs were lined with an oil portrait history of the Mercer family. Susan paused by the newest painting. "That's Daddy."

Maggie and Cara exchanged a glance. There was no missing the melancholy in Susan's voice.

Cara's hand caressed the smooth polished banister as they ascended the curving grand staircase. This home had so much more character and beauty than the white ultra-modern Houston manor. How could anyone leave this for that?

Reaching the landing, their hostess stopped at a door-way. "Maggie, I think you'll like the rose room." Susan glanced at Cara. "The ivy room adjoins it and should be perfect for you. We always keep these two ready for guests. You okay with sharing a bathroom?"

"No problem."

On their first mobile design job, they'd shared a room with bunk beds and no bathroom. They'd had to climb to the next floor to take a shower.

The first guestroom, the rose room, lived up to its name

with creamy vanilla walls accented by a stenciled rose border of intense rose-red to coordinate with the rose curtains
and satin bedspread.

"This is so pretty." Maggie spun around arms raised.
"Just like a sweet dream."

"Thought you'd like it." Susan looked pleased. "In the
eighteen-hundreds, craftsmen traveled through our part of
Texas and some specialized in stenciling. You'll find it in
lots of homes around here." With a bouncy step, she led
them to the next room and opened the door. "And this is the
ivy room."

Cara stepped into a room decorated in various shades of
green, like an ivy cocoon. "So serene. It's great."

"I hope you'll both sleep well."

"Thanks," Maggie replied. "We'll see you in the morning."

A short time later, Maggie had changed into her cotton-
knit nightshirt when she heard a knock on the door.

Susan looked a tad sheepish. "Gladys has brought me
cocoa every night since I was old enough to drink it. In spite
of the stairs and her age, she made some again tonight—
enough for all three of us. Do you want to join me?"

"Sure, let me grab Cara."

Cara grumbled until Maggie said *cocoa*, then she threw
on a turquoise silk robe that enhanced her Mediterranean
coloring. And curves.

Maggie couldn't understand how Cara remained oblivious to her own beauty. "Come on, our client's waiting."

A study of watercolor pastels, Susan's room was a gen-
erously sized master suite.

"The way Gladys spoils me, you'd think I was still five
instead of forty-eight going on sixty," Susan apologized,
walking past her massive four-postered bed to the attached
sitting room. A gorgeous rosewood fireplace mantle took up
much of one large wall. Positioned invitingly were two cozy
chairs and a chaise.

Maggie immediately claimed the Edwardian chaise. "I've always wanted one of these."

"Well—" Susan hesitated. "I don't want to point out the obvious, but you are a designer. Don't you go to auctions and estate sales?"

"For our clients, but our own place is a bit cramped." Maggie reached for one of the Dresden china cups. "Now that we've turned the dining room and half the living room into our office, there's not space for one more stick of furniture."

"Interesting arrangement." Susan took some cocoa for herself. "Makes sense."

Maggie nodded. "We like being mobile. When we are home, we hang out at my parents' a lot. Mom thinks she has to feed us and loves to hear about our decorating jobs and design projects."

"True story," Cara said with a smile.

"If Mom hadn't been constantly redecorating and dragging us into her projects we wouldn't have caught the decorating bug," Maggie fingered a curl, realizing that her mother was their number one cheerleader.

"Maggie's parents have always been good to me." The cocoa was thawing Cara's inhibitions. Except for confiding in Maggie, Cara remained a private person.

"Sounds cozy." Susan's animation faded as she tucked a taupe silk and tasseled pillow under her chin. "Oh, dear, I don't want to call Darlene Lawson in the morning."

"Why?" they asked in unison.

Cara chuckled. "Maggs, we've got to stop doing this."

Watching them with obvious amusement, Susan smiled. "I like it. You think alike."

Maggie grinned, winking at Cara. "Occasionally."

Cara stirred her cocoa, noticing the family monogram on the spoon's handle. "In design, anyway."

"So what's the deal with Darlene?" Cara prodded, as she settled more comfortably in her spot, sounding fascinated with their client's small town dynamics.

"Well, guess there's no harm since you don't know her, so it's not spreading gossip. Right?"

"Right." Sitting cross-legged, Maggie targeted Susan. "So spill."

"You remember I told you about my lawyer, John Lawson? The one who got killed? Well, Darlene's his ex-wife. She's a real…ah…number. She even accused John of having an affair with Aimee when she first came to work for him."

"Did he?" Maggie thought it sounded likely if Aimee lived up to her reputation. Maybe the lawyer was one more on the list.

"Ha! You kidding?" Susan threw back her head with a laugh. "John Lawson was a sweet old fuddy-duddy who wouldn't dream of flirting, even if Aimee had danced naked on his desk. He was old school and completely honorable. The only reason he hired Aimee was because the secretary he'd had for years retired."

"Then why did Darlene think they were having an affair?" Maggie fingered the velvet upholstery of the chaise. "Is that why she divorced him?"

"I think Darlene just wanted an *excuse* to divorce him. She was fifteen years younger than he was, they never had kids, and she was bored. It was a big deal snaring the only lawyer in town. But after they were married more than a decade, it wasn't enough." Susan leaned forward. "My opinion? She thought that Elliot would marry her once she got rid of John."

"The banker?" Cara asked.

"Yes." Disdain dripped from Susan's voice. "The guy you met at the diner."

"Let me guess—" Maggie mused. "Elliot's got money."

Susan shivered in distaste. "He might have money, but I wouldn't trust him as far as I could toss his inflated head. Not to mention he's a lecher. He was all over Darlene when she was married, but once she was single, he kept his distance."

"I know men like that," Cara said quietly.

Maggie sent her a sympathetic glance. Cara's ex-husband had been such a jerk that her friend vowed never to get involved again.

"Then Darlene tried to get John back." Susan gave them a knowing look. "But he'd wised up. Since he regretted ever marrying her, he wasn't about to make the same mistake again."

"Hmm." Cara glanced pointedly at Maggie.

And Maggie read her thoughts as clearly as though she'd spoken aloud. *Maybe Darlene had been mad enough to shoot him. The "woman scorned" scenario.*

"Now Darlene pushes into all the committees she can and tries to terrorize everyone into doing things her way."

"Your neighbor seems to think you can handle Darlene."

"As much as anyone can." Susan gave the pillow a tight squeeze. "John was the only one who could keep her in line. Once he died…" Her voice trailed off.

"Do you think she knocked him off?" Cara couldn't keep the thought inside, despite Maggie's warning glare.

"Darlene's bitchy, but no killer." Susan paused as she was about to take another sip of cocoa. "Besides, it was a break-in at the law office. The burglar shot John at his desk and then ransacked the place."

"And a few months later his secretary got it, too." Maggie felt a shiver despite the warmth of the cozy room. "Sounds like Darlene had it in for both of them."

"Half the women in town didn't like Aimee, but Sheriff Watt's sure that both perps are outsiders."

"Perps?" Maggie echoed.

"Perpetrators." Despite the serious subject, Susan surrendered a weak grin. "I watch all the crime shows. Ed's gone a lot."

Maggie shuddered. "If I lived here, I wouldn't want to believe there was a killer in town either."

Cara clutched a toss pillow. "There better not be."

"You two are silly. Mercerville's the safest place on earth."

"Uh huh."

Ignoring Cara's remark, Maggie stretched out her long legs on the chaise. "You told us that your father bought off your first husband...well, I was wondering. Do you wish he hadn't interfered?"

"No. It opened my eyes about Steve. Daddy intervened fast and I got that idiotic marriage annulled. I guess that, sometimes, bad stuff happens for a reason. I learned a lot and my life changed. I changed."

"Earlier, is that what you meant when you said that it was for the best?" Maggie persevered.

"If all that hadn't happened, I wouldn't have met Ed. Since he has his own money, there's no wondering about his intentions. He loves me just for myself." She pushed back some flyaway hair. "I could've been miserable. Married to the wrong guy with no chance for happiness if things hadn't gone the way they did back then."

Cara frowned. "That's a good spin."

"But it's true. Steve was handsome and exciting, but he didn't love me. And, that's all I wanted."

Maggie thought of her undependable boyfriend. "Who doesn't?"

"Maybe you're right, Susan." Cara unclenched the pillow. "Life's a tapestry that's intricately woven. Snip the threads and it unravels."

"So true." Susan sounded surprised. "I think you've got a bit of poet in you."

Flushing, Cara shook her head as she stood, their late night cocoa party dwindling to an end. Maggie swung her legs over the side of the chaise, but didn't stand. "Do you sing in the shower, Susan?"

Both Cara and Susan gave Maggie a double take, but Susan smiled. "I prefer bubble baths to showers."

"I guess singing in the tub isn't the same." Maggie knew Cara wondered what she was doing, but she just wanted to end the night on a brighter note for their client. "I confess I might sing 'Beautiful' or 'Who let the Dogs Out' at the top of my lungs."

With a soft chuckle, Susan replied, "I have been known to hum a bit. What do you sing, Cara?"

"Not everybody sings in the shower," Cara objected, folding her hands primly.

"You do." Laughing, Maggie bounced up. "Lately, Cara's been singing 'Jessie's Girl' and 'Gone.'"

"I remember 'Jessie's Girl.' Good song!" Susan hummed the title line.

"One of my mom's favorites," Maggie replied. "As kids, Cara and I used to rock out to it with Mom."

"Heavens, you girls are making me feel old."

"*You* old?" Cara said in deadpan disbelief. Cracking a smile, she and Maggie chorused together, "Never!"

Susan chuckled, her eyes crinkling as she glanced between the designers who joined in the laughter. Instantly, their client's chuckle turned into a yawn. She covered her mouth. "Sorry."

"It is getting late. Enough playing twenty questions, Maggs." Cara grabbed Maggie's arm and tugged her toward the doorway. "We'd better head to bed and let Susan get some sleep."

"If you need anything, let me know." Susan stood, smothering another yawn. "I'm just a few doors down."

❧❧❧

Once in bed, Cara punched her pillow into shape and tried to fall asleep, always a challenge for her in a strange place. *Not the most convenient thing for a mobile designer.* She squeezed her eyes shut. The mobile part had just happened.

When she and Maggie started their fledgling business, they took whatever jobs available—mostly from friends and family—and that had led them back and forth across a radius of several hundred miles. Mobility became a necessity. Now they had packing and traveling in their van down to an art. The upside proved to be a broad base of suppliers and artisans, many far from their home base in Houston. How she longed to drop the mobile aspect of their business, open a real office and settle into one place.

Cara sighed and bunched her pillow again, turning the coolness to press against her cheek. Traveling wasn't so bad, but the downside was *sleep*. Rather, lack of it.

☙❧☙❧

Maggie dozed off the minute her head hit the pillow. In the midst of a dream wandering hand in hand through a meadow with a fantasy man, a noise jarred her awake. The image evaporated, not the sounds. *Thump. Scrape. Clink.*

Miffed and alarmed, she sat up, opening her eyes wide to unfamiliar darkness. *Where was she?* Maggie blinked, remembering the rose room at Susan's place.

What woke her?

She'd heard something. Scanning the dark bedroom, she tried to recreate the sounds in her mind as she listened for more. Throwing off the covers, she got out of bed and padded to the window, peeking out the curtains.

Between tree branches, clouds wisped over a crescent moon high in the sky. A few stars twinkled in the midnight heavens. Below, the tree canopy cast inky shadows, deepening the darkness, making it impossible to see anything.

She grabbed her robe from the foot of the bed and found her way to the bathroom that separated her guestroom from Cara's room.

Turning the bathroom light on dim, she tapped on the ivy room door, pushing it open. "Cara? You awake?"

"I am now," Cara mumbled as she bolted from the bed, and then staggered toward the door. "What?"

Cara's cap of shiny ebony hair now stuck out in wild clumps. Sans makeup, her doe eyes still looked huge, though sleepy.

"Did you hear something?"

"How could I?" Cara reached for her slippers. "I had the pillow over my head trying to sleep."

"Sorry." Maggie scooted past her friend and crossed to the window. "I heard something, but couldn't see a thing out my window."

"What did you hear?" Cara followed, peering out the window alongside Maggie.

"Not sure. Something weird."

"Like breaking glass? Screams? A gunshot?"

"A gunshot? Thanks. That's comforting." Staring out into the thick darkness, Maggie wished Susan had more outside lights. The few she had did little more than illuminate the patio on the backside of the house. "It wasn't any of those noises."

"Then I'm going back to bed."

"What if someone's breaking in?"

"Susan or Gladys—one of them will hear and call nine-one-one."

"What if they don't hear?" Maggie held one hand to her neck, her throat suddenly dry. "Or they're tied up and gagged?"

"Maggs, you've got to rein in that imagination." Kicking off her slippers, Cara hopped back into bed and pulled up the covers. "It's probably a tree branch blowing against the window in the wind."

"There wasn't any wind, remember?"

"Maybe it started up. Go back to bed."

Maggie took one last, reluctant look through the window. "I can't hear anything now."

"That's 'cause there's nothing to hear."

"You think?"

"Maggs, you haven't had any weird feelings about this place, right?" Cara's voice sounded raspy and Maggie felt guilty for bugging her, knowing what a hard time Cara had sleeping away from home.

"Right."

"Then go to bed." Cara turned over, her back to Maggie. "Don't forget to turn off the bathroom light."

"Can I leave the doors between us open?"

"Whatever."

"Thanks." Maggie clicked off the bathroom light, but left the adjoining doors open—just in case.

ဃသဃ

In the morning, Maggie tromped downstairs toward the kitchen. Cara trailed behind, considering bartering her life savings for an espresso.

Maggie sniffed the sweet, cinnamon scented air. "Apple crisp."

"Apple fritters," Cara corrected as they entered the kitchen. Gleaming copper pots dangled from the ceiling over a large center island. Apparently, Susan had updated the kitchen, though she'd kept an old-fashioned breakfast table in one nook.

"Miss Susan, I nearly forgot." Gladys tapped arthritic fingers against her neatly pinned-up gray hair. "I found this on the entry floor first thing this morning. Someone must've dropped it through the mail slot." The housekeeper withdrew an envelope from the front pocket of her apron skirt.

"An invitation?" Susan opened the envelope and took out a square piece of paper. She gasped, her hands shaking as she stared at the paper.

Alarmed at Susan's stricken expression and sudden paling, Cara dashed to her side. "What's wrong?"

Susan stretched out her trembling hand. "Look."

In words of various print, cut and pasted onto the page, it read: *Curiosity killed the cat.*

Gladys's hand flew to her heart. "I didn't realize it was

bad, Miss Susan. Maybe it's just kids playing pranks."
Maggie put an arm around Susan's quaking shoulders. "Of
course. That's what it is—just a silly prank."

"No." Susan bit her bottom lip, shaking her head. "When
I came back for Aimee's funeral, I started asking questions.
Sheriff Watt told me to leave investigating to him. I should
have. I know. But I just couldn't keep it inside and I wound
up talking to a lot of people."

"I can't imagine that this has anything to do with a few
questions." Cara hoped to calm Susan, but she felt the hairs
on the back of her neck stand to attention.

Susan sniffled. "I just thought that people might tell me
more than they'd confide to a lawman, you know?"

Maggie hugged Susan's shoulders. "Makes sense to me."

"Maybe we need to tell your sheriff about this?" Cara
suggested. "Just in case."

Dismay flashed across Susan's face. "We've handled the
note. They won't even be able to take fingerprints from it."

Cara looked from Susan to meet Maggie's gaze. "Those
noises you heard last night, Maggs?"

"What noises?" Susan's dismay was rapidly turning to
fear.

"I'm not sure what," Maggie admitted. "But something
woke me." She hesitated.

Susan's troubled gaze didn't waver. "What?"

Maggie glanced over at Cara, her voice reluctant. "Most
likely, whoever left the note."

Chapter 3

By the time Gladys ushered the local law into the kitchen, Susan was leaning against the kitchen counter, her hands clasped around a coffee mug.

"Howdy, Miz Susan." The rotund, fiftyish sheriff wore a rumpled tan uniform that boasted a shiny star badge. He spared a nod toward Maggie and Cara as he greeted the lady of the manor.

"Sheriff Watt, thank you for coming. It may be nothing…" Susan faltered.

"Let me be the one to decide that." He targeted her with a leveling gaze. "Now what's this all about?"

Susan explained, handing him the square sheet of paper. Holding it carefully along the edges, he examined the pasted-on message. Reaching in his not-so-tidy pocket, he pulled out an evidence bag and dropped the note inside.

The sheriff grunted. "Got you spooked, huh? I told you not to nose around." He scratched his head where his receding hairline began. "Could just be a dadgum joke."

"Or Miss Susan flushed out a killer." A tall, broad-shouldered officer stepped forward, wearing the same uniform in a very different way. Cara sucked in an instinctive gasp as the deputy's midnight-colored eyes swept over her. "We'll need to take fingerprints. Just to rule you all out."

"Sure." Cara savored the deep masculine cadence of his voice, deciding she wouldn't mind at all if he was the one who took her prints. She'd always felt an inexplicable attraction to deep-voiced men. *And this was some man.*

"Sure," Maggie echoed, fluttering her lashes.

She scored a grin that revealed a dimple in his left cheek.

"Of course, Deputy Rice." Susan sounded embarrassed. "Whatever you need."

Cara stared down into her mug at the dark steaming liquid. Why had Maggie earned the deputy's smile when she hadn't? Needing something warm to banish the disappointment, she sipped Gladys's coffee—not too bad. Not her usual poison, but considering the morning's events, it'd do.

"Jake, go get the kit," the sheriff barked. "I'll print the ladies while you check the area for evidence. Be sure to dust the mail slot."

"Yes, sir." The deputy spun on the heels of his cowboy boots, allowing Cara and Maggie a nice rear view as he strode away.

∽∾∽

Within minutes, Sheriff Watt had fingerprinted Gladys and Susan. Grasping Maggie's hand as though it was wood instead of flesh, he rolled her thumb on the inkpad. She wrinkled her nose at his morning breath and wished it were the handsome deputy taking her prints instead. She glanced over at Susan who was washing black ink off her hands while Gladys tsked over the mess.

"Next!" The sheriff released Maggie, who stepped away to let Cara take a turn.

Not wasting a second, Maggie hurried over to Susan. "You okay? This is more stressful than I thought it'd be."

"I feel so stupid. Like I brought it on myself." Susan moved over so Maggie could wash the blotter ink from her fingers.

"Nope," Maggie replied, sluicing warm water over her hands as Gladys shoved a soapy wet rag at her. "Besides, it could just be a kid's prank."

Gladys nodded. "She's right, Miss Susan. It's probably nothing."

"I hope so." Susan looked doubtful as they all reshuffled to allow Cara access to the sink.

"This ink is gross," Cara complained, stepping between them to wash.

Finished labeling then packing his kit, Sheriff Watt joined the women. "Wrapped up here. If Jake's done, we'll be on our way." He scowled at Susan. "You leave the detective work to us. Understand?"

"Yes." Susan sounded chastened. "Please let me know what you find out."

"Deputy Rice," the sheriff boomed, not responding to Susan's request as he stomped out of the kitchen. "Got anything?"

Once the lawmen left, Gladys served the breakfast she'd kept warm. After their delayed meal, Susan stayed inside to make her phone calls.

Walking outside to sketch and photograph the fountain, Maggie warmed under the sunshine bathing her face and exposed skin, not caring that it probably meant new freckles. She inhaled the heady fragrance of blossoming gardenias, her mood lifting considerably. "How fantastic is this place?"

Cara flipped open her sketchpad to a clean page as they reached the base of the angel fountain. "Look over there beyond the arbor arch—see the colorful patch of native blooms next to the formal garden?"

"Wow." A vivid splash of Texas bluebonnets, tiny daisies and Indian paintbrush danced in the breeze. "We have a lot to live up to at the Houston manor."

Cara perched on a wrought iron bench and began penciling the angel wings. "Susan doesn't expect us to recreate the entire oasis, just this fountain."

"This'll be challenging enough." Maggie snapped photos from various angle then close-ups to capture the patina. The angel appeared poised, almost in flight, to hover above the water, her gown falling in graceful curves to anchor the statue to the fountain base while her hands cupped together from extended arms, spilling sparkling water into the pool. "Remember that artist who does those gorgeous sculptures in Natchez?"

"JJ Wicks?"

"Right. Let's give JJ a call and see if he can help us out on this fountain."

"Great idea." Maggie gazed around, inhaling the blossom-scented air. "Seems like its own little world, huh?"

"Peaceful here." Cara penciled in more detail. "Susan must miss the tranquility when she's in the city."

Maggie crouched to get a better angle of the base. "But there she has Ed."

"Hmm."

"Where's your sense of romance?"

"Are you about done?" Cara scowled, a dent appearing above her left brow. "I want to get back to Houston before anything else happens."

Maggie tossed back her head and laughed. "What? You expect another murder?"

Cara glared back.

Taking her time, Maggie adjusted the lens. "Or are you just panting to get back to your espresso?"

"Maybe both."

A little red bird, its eyes surrounded by a brown mask, darted by Maggie. "Oh, how cute!"

"That's a vermilion flycatcher." Susan still sounded stressed as she joined them, but apparently, her beloved garden could recapture her attention. She gestured toward a stunning butterfly soaring past them. "And that's a red-spotted purple butterfly. Over by the crepe myrtle, there's a spicebush swallowtail butterfly."

Cara looked up from her sketch. "You're good."

Susan shrugged, brushing away the compliment. "Not so much. When I was in the Scouts, we worked on a lot of nature badges." A shadow crossed her face as she squeezed herself in a nervous hug.

Maggie frowned. "Didn't your phone calls go okay?"

"I talked some logic into the Schmidts." Susan bit her bottom lip. "But I couldn't reach Darlene Lawson."

"That's too bad." Cara stared back down at her sketch.

"Maybe she slipped out to the store?" Maggie hoped for Cara's sake that it wouldn't cause them to hang out in Mercerville longer.

"I called around." Susan's flyaway hair fell into total disarray as she raked her hands through it. "Darlene's disappeared."

Maggie felt her throat dry up. "You think she's another victim?" She shivered despite the fair weather.

"Or a murderess on the run?" Cara interjected.

"Neither."

Cara arched one raven brow. "Darlene Lawson did have a motive for both murders."

Maggie wanted to kick her. Just what Susan needed to hear.

"No way." Susan shook her head. "Darlene's no murderer."

"You know the woman and we don't," Maggie soothed.

"Besides, there has to be more than one killer." Susan toed the new spring grass. "The crimes have different MOs."

"MO?" Cara repeated, closing her sketchpad to stand beside the others.

"Let me guess," Maggie quizzed. "Those crime shows?"

"Ah, mystery novels," Susan answered sheepishly. "I read a lot, too."

Free hand planted on one curvy hip, Cara tucked the art pad under her other arm. "Maybe the killer likes variety."

"Don't say that," Maggie pleaded, feeling a chill as intense as a dark cloud smothering the warm sunshine.

Susan raked her hair again, her expression troubled. "What's next?"

Cara eyed both women. "Poison."

芰芡芡

In the days after their jaunt to Mercerville, the Houston manor transformation was in full progress. Their crew had laid the tile in the sunroom and replaced the sliding glass doors with French doors. Now, as Maggie and Cara worked inside, they listened to the sounds of their work crew, clunking and hollering outside.

"I'm glad the tile continues into the adjoining lanai and the backyard, even though it'll take us longer." Maggie applied more wide blue tape to the baseboard as she inched around the room. "It'll help create that indoor-outdoor flow Susan wants."

"She has good taste." Cara knelt down, sweeping her hand across a sand-beige terrazzo tile before tugging the corner of a drop cloth to cover it better.

Maggie winked, knowing her partner had guided Susan into picking Cara's favorite tile. "Our clients always have great taste that's why they choose us."

Cara stood, grinning. "So true."

"Maybe this renovation will earn us a design spread in *Tuscan Accent* magazine?"

"Dream on."

Susan click-clacked into the room on high heels, skirting canvas drop cloths and various cans to slide to a teetering stop by Cara. "Darlene Lawson called. She was visiting her sister in Fredericksburg. Nothing mysterious."

"She's not murdered." Maggie approached the other two. "Luckily."

"And she's not on the run," Cara added, deftly scooting an open paint container out of Susan's path.

Maggie grinned, her funky overalls falling off one shoulder. "So it's all good."

Susan reached over to tuck the strap up in a motherly gesture. "Not all good. The sheriff still hasn't got any suspects."

"What about that note?" Cara asked. "Fingerprints?"

"None besides ours." Susan looked gloomy. "We mucked up any prints underneath."

"There probably weren't any," Cara reasoned. She pointed to the open can of paint. "What do you think about this color?"

Swaying on her ridiculously tall, open-backed sandals, Susan leaned over for a better look. "Ohh—it's almost like a sunset."

Cara grabbed Susan's arm to steady her. "No taking dips in the paint."

Maggie wrinkled her nose, gesturing to her own paint-splattered overalls. "I take care of that quota."

"I adore this coral peach." Susan straightened back up, her high-couture linen outfit looking as out-of-sync as the rest of her Houston wardrobe. She seemed much more comfortable in the regular clothes she'd worn while they were in Mercerville. "But I thought the walls were going to be more of a honey shade."

"This is the base coat. Then we'll borrow some techniques from the nineties as we layer colors and finish off with a translucent honey tea wash. We want the walls to look like they've weathered years of paint and sun fading."

"But none of that happens," Cara added, "until we apply the plaster treatment—"

"To give it the texture you liked on the sample," Maggie finished.

"You still talk in tandem." Laughing, Susan glanced at them in turn. "That's teamwork."

"Yep. We tend to finish each other's sentences, too," Maggie confessed. "Some people think it's rude to do that, but it's involuntary with us."

Cara replaced the paint lid then tapped it snug with a hammer. "At least in design stuff."

"Not only design." Susan wagged a finger at them. "I seem to recall other topics when you did the same thing."

"You got us." Maggie admitted. "We've been friends so long it's unavoidable."

A door slammed, followed by footsteps. Ed Dexter hollered. "Hey, sweetheart, you here?"

"The sunroom," Susan called back, a warm glow lighting her face as Ed lumbered toward her.

Cara held her breath as he trampled over the drop cloths, rollers, tools and containers to reach his wife.

"Hey, babe." He dropped a kiss on Susan's forehead before turning to Maggie and Cara. "You ladies look busy. How about I steal my bride away, so you can get back to work?"

Susan squeezed his hand. "Hope you don't mind, but this room'll be pretty colorful when they're done."

He pulled Susan against his side. "Throw red paint at the walls for all I care, sugar. As long as it makes you happy."

Her brow wrinkled in concern. "But you like things crisp and modern."

"It's not about me." Ed studied his wife's face, his brown eyes darkening further with obvious affection. "It's about you."

Maggie sighed aloud. Would a man ever say something that romantic to her? Jarred from her thoughts, she realized they were watching her.

In for the save, Cara replied for them both. "And we aim to please."

"It's going to be wonderful." Susan wobbled on her heels as her husband squished her closer.

"Excellent." Ed gently guided Susan by her elbow, re-navigating through the work area. "Now, what if I take my girl out to dinner?"

"Aren't they sweet?" Maggie asked, a romantic glaze in her eyes as the pocket doors slid shut behind the departing couple.

"I guess. Susan suggested we consider redoing her sewing room. I wonder if she means it?"

"It probably depends on the job we do with this one." Maggie tugged her slipping denim strap back into place, bunching the sleeve of her T-shirt along with it.

"If we want to get the walls textured tonight we'd better get to plastering." With a stubby screwdriver, Cara pried open a tub and handed it over to Maggie. "You get that wall. I'll take this one."

"Right." But Maggie didn't move, locked in a whirlwind of thought.

"Maggs?" Cara prodded.

"I can't get that note out of my mind." Maggie picked up the wrong tool. "Do you think it's the killer?"

"Why would a murderer stick around in Mercerville to send silly notes?"

"Unless they live there." Maggie felt a chill race up her arms and tugged her sleeve down to cover the goose bumps. "Maybe we should make sure Susan stays safe here in Houston. Just in case."

"Safe in Houston instead of her tiny hometown. Sounds backward, huh?" Cara switched the tool in Maggie's hand for the correct one.

"What if whoever it is…well…follows her here?"

"They won't."

"Might." Maggie dug into the container and buttered the plaster gook onto the wall. "You're good at mysteries, Cara. And I love puzzles. Maybe we can help Susan figure things out."

"You do remember the sheriff's warning?"

"That was for Susan, not us."

"Ha!" Cara scoffed, busy texturing her own wall. "Detective work is not my forte."

Unable to forget the note, Maggie made herself get on with the work. But her thoughts persisted in remaining busy as well. *Who sent that note?*

When Cara finally took a break for a swig from her water bottle, she noticed her design partner had outdone her. Maggie's high energy always amazed her. Personally, she could feel her own energy fading. "Maybe we ought to stop for the night?"

"You can start cleaning up stuff, but I want to finish this section."

"How about we work ten more minutes then both clean up?" Cara attacked the wall once more, determined at least to reach the corner.

"Okay."

Cara swished and swirled then buttered on more plaster compound. It was tedious work, but they were both perfectionists.

"Remember how you compared life to a tapestry?" Maggie swirled the skim-coats of plaster across the focal wall, continuing to progress faster than Cara did.

"Yeah."

"Well, I've decided that the *mystery* is a tapestry. We need to weave the threads together to reveal the pattern."

Cara wiped her forehead with the back of her hand leaving a white streak. "Then we'd better figure out how Susan's thread is woven into the murders."

"So, you do agree that Susan's in trouble?"

"It's possible. If she keeps poking around in the cases."

"She's our client. We have to do something."

"Like what?" Cara carefully pushed the plaster against the corner edge with circular squishes and worked upward toward the ceiling.

"I'll think of something," Maggie promised.

"That's what I'm afraid of." Cara hated working on corners or edges when she did faux treatments. And she hated Maggs coaxing her into unpredictable situations. Unfortunately, the plastering was the least troublesome of the two.

A rap on the French doors from the side garden startled her. Before she could turn around, Maggs was scampering toward the door and opening it to admit Al Black, their crew carpenter.

"The other guys already left, but I was still working on the gazebo when I noticed this stuck in the back gate." Dirt-smudged and clearly tired, he shoved a folded paper into Maggie's hand.

He stood just outside the doors, stomping mud off his work boots, impatience carved in his square jaw and the tense set of his stance. "Gotta go. See you in the morning."

"A note?" Cara quizzed, studying their carpenter, realizing that beneath the grime he was handsome. Al pulled off his work gloves, revealing a broad gold wedding band, aborting her thought. He'd recently replaced their crew lead and she didn't know much about him.

"In the gate. Nearly tossed it with the garbage, but decided it might be important." He turned away, clearly done with the discussion.

"Just stuffed in the gate, huh?" Cara didn't know why she pressured him. He clearly wanted to call it quits after a long day.

"Right." He halted and though his back was toward her, she heard him mutter something else, but couldn't make out the words.

"Well…um…thanks, Al."

"Yeah, yeah." He sauntered off, not turning back.

"Bye!" Maggie called after him, shutting the door and locking it before she unfolded the paper.

"Well," Cara said impatiently. "What is it?"

Maggie unfolded the paper to reveal one word: *Stop!*

Cara stared at the familiar-looking cut and paste job.

"Stop what?" Maggie whispered, gazing down at the paper.

"Stop work on the backyard?" Cara suggested, unable to dismiss Al Black's attitude, though he'd done nothing wrong. "Stop the sunroom redo?"

Maggie's posture grew tense. "No."

Cara could see Maggie's sixth sense igniting. She watched her friend, thinking that with those emerald green eyes, pixie-arched brows and wavy copper hair, Maggs had inherited more than a bit of magical sprite from her Irish heritage.

"It's another warning for Susan."

"We can't give it to her." Cara didn't want to court trouble. "We'll zip it up safely in a plastic sandwich bag and put the note away for now."

"But…"

"It's not addressed to anyone. Susan's name isn't on it anywhere." Cara took a breath, reminding Maggie why they were there. "And it's not good for business."

"Okay," Maggie agreed reluctantly. "You're the boss."

"The *boss*?" Cara raised a brow. "Since when?"

"Since you took charge of our murder investigation."

"What?"

"Well, you're bagging the evidence and withholding information from Susan. So obviously, you're in charge."

"Maggs, we're designers—not detectives."

"We're both now, Cara." Hands on hips, Maggie stared hard at her friend. "And you know it."

"I don't think so."

"Since you're the logical one, you're in charge of the clues."

"What clues?" Cara sputtered.

"That's for you to figure out. You're Sherlock and I'm merely Watson."

"I prefer *Miss Marple*."

Maggie frowned. "But she didn't have a sidekick."

"Exactly."

∞∞∞

The scent of azalea blossoms drifted in the light morning breeze. Maggie sipped her coffee as she and Cara explained to Susan how the exterior work was progressing.

"We'll lay stepping stones here in a pathway to the gazebo." Cara pointed out the French doors of the sunroom.

"In a staggered pattern, so it'll look natural."

"Wonderful." Susan glanced across the yard at the kidney-shaped swimming pool. "I wish we could give *that* some natural beauty."

"What?" Maggie questioned, setting her nearly full mug down.

"The swimming pool."

"Do you have anything in mind?" After seeing their client's lovely house in Mercerville, Maggie wasn't surprised at Susan's disenchantment with the plain functional pool and huge bland backyard.

"A grotto." Susan uttered a self-depreciating laugh. "I know that's asking for a lot, but just a more natural look and a bit of safety would be nice."

"Safety?" Cara gripped her own coffee mug, the rich espresso nearly gone.

Susan waved again toward the pool. "To keep that modern look, there aren't any rails or steps."

Maggie shook her head. "It's a new trend, but not a good one."

"Minimalist," Cara added. "I'm surprised it's not a rectangle. But I'm with you, Susan. I like knowing I can grab the safety bars."

"We can create a completely new design." Unable to contain her excitement, Maggie practically jumped up and down. "A Mediterranean garden landscape."

Cara put down her now empty mug. "I think we know what you want." She plucked her art pad from the corner then flipped it open, her pencil instantly dancing across the page.

Maggie wandered over to their stash of candy, popping a chocolate in her mouth. Not just because she was a chocoholic, she wanted to remain quiet while Cara sketched.

Just as Maggie reached for another chocolate to keep from bugging her friend, Cara held the pad up. "We can build something like this that'll blend with the lanai and gazebo."

"Lovely," Susan exclaimed. "And still create the fountain? You can do that?"

"We can." Filching another chocolate, Maggie couldn't resist beaming as though she'd thought of the design herself. "We'll section the yard into each area—yet, they'll all blend together as a whole."

"But those giant boulders?" Susan pointed at the rock formation where a waterfall spilled between the top of rocks. "They'll weigh a ton."

"The boulders and rocks are artificial. They'll look like they came out of your quarry, but won't weigh a fraction of the real thing. We can get them custom-sized and shaped." Cara sketched in some flora and fauna enhancing the grotto effect.

Susan frowned. "I've known about these products, but until now I hadn't considered how much competition they are."

"The real thing is still the first option for most projects and certainly for new developments. We're limited because of the lot. But I can downsize the plans and use rocks from Mercerville."

"No, I don't want to complicate things. I don't know why the fake rocks get to me." Susan blew a soft sigh. "Now that I'm married, I don't have to depend on the family business."

Cara flipped to a blank page in her sketchpad. "We could do something else, maybe a classic bronze water feature instead?"

Susan shook her head. "Wouldn't be a grotto then, would it?" Her smile edged back in place. "And how better to check out the competition?"

"You sure? Because we can figure out a way to use your stone—"

"No. Not everything's about business. I learned that the hard way." Susan's melancholy tone and darkening eyes spoke volumes.

Maggie wondered what had caused the sudden shift in

her mood. "Of course, we'll have to re-landscape the back-yard to incorporate the grotto pool. Add some flowering trees and vines. An arbor—" She paused. "It'll take extra time and expense."

"Naturally." Susan's smile returned.

But Maggie wondered about this new layer of Susan's past they'd uncovered. Since she hadn't expounded on the thought, it might be a bad memory. Or problems at the family business? Trying to be casual, Maggie licked a bit of chocolate from one finger. "What will your husband say about the added cost?"

"Ed's a pussycat. You heard him yesterday—it's my de-cision." Susan stopped suddenly. "I used to make purchases like this without giving it a second thought because it was my money. But, you're right. I'll talk to him tonight."

"You can let us know what you decide." Maggie mental-ly checked their calendar, realizing that they had a light enough schedule to add the additional job. "We have plenty to keep us busy." She hopped up as Susan rose from the so-fa. "The new yard won't rival your home in Mercerville, but it'll be more inviting than it is now."

"I have to make a quick trip back there this weekend." Nerves etched lines on Susan's face as she threaded her fin-gers together.

"Why?" Maggie and Cara asked in unison.

"Uncle Leland's birthday celebration. He's turning sev-enty."

Cara closed her sketchpad. "At least you aren't playing detective anymore."

"I've kinda still been doing that." Susan unclasped her hands. "A few friends from home have called to pass along the local rumors. Then Darlene Lawson told me what her sister, Hannah, saw."

Maggie exchanged a worried glance with Cara. "What did Hannah see?"

"Darlene's sister told her that Aimee—" Susan paused. "You know? The hit and run victim?"

They nodded.

"Aimee used to meet a mystery man at a motel on the outskirts of Fredericksburg. Hannah works at the coffee shop across the way and saw Aimee, in a hat and sunglasses, ducking into the motel several times with some stranger."

"A mystery man?" Maggie's imagination flared to action. "What if he's the killer? A lover's quarrel!"

"Maggs," Cara hissed. Her gaze swiveled to their client. "You promised the sheriff you'd stop nosing around."

"It's not intentional." Susan shifted her weight from foot to foot. "Everyone's just telling me things now."

"Don't listen," Cara advised.

Agreeing, Maggie patted Susan's hand. "When you get home, just let word spread that you don't want to be involved, and they can talk to the sheriff."

"Like that'll work. I can tell you two are city folk." Susan's cell phone rang. Reading the caller ID, her face brightened. "That's Ed. I'll talk to you later."

The instant the door closed behind Susan, Maggie nearly pounced on Cara. "That explains the note! And here at our work site. Susan's still involved—and now we are."

Cara jumped, touching the base of her throat. "Maggs! I almost swallowed my heart. Geez." She reached for her coffee mug, groaning when she saw it was empty.

"But Susan—"

"I thought since she was in Houston with us, the snooping would stop."

Maggie absently twirled a lock of hair between her fingers. "Maybe we should take that note to the authorities?"

"And say what?" Cara reached for an oversize T-shirt, shrugging it in place to cover her clothes. "Can you imagine trying to explain that one-word note to a Houston detective and be taken seriously?"

"We have to do something."

"Like what?"

"Go to Mercerville with Susan this weekend." Maggie ignored her friend's groans.

"She's got Gladys."

"Gladys must be almost ninety! Plus, if we're with Susan, we can better the odds."

"No way. Not back to Mercerville." Cara sank to the floor like a puppet with strings snipped.

"So you don't care if something happens to Susan while she's there on her own?"

"Do we have to?"

"We do." Maggie stared into the backyard, realizing she hadn't thought about the design since they'd discovered Susan's renewed sleuthing. "We'll tell Susan we need more measurements of the angel fountain."

Cara gazed up from her sitting position on the floor. "This isn't a good idea."

"It is. If we want to keep our client from being victim number three."

Chapter 4

M aggie hung halfway off the ladder to cut in along the ceiling line with a paintbrush while Cara rolled coral paint on the long, newly textured wall.

Cara could hear the beat of country music floating in from their crew's boom box and found herself humming. She didn't mind the smell of fresh paint. She liked working with Maggie as they progressed smoothly together, each instinctively knowing when to get out of the other's way.

"Hi!" Susan bounced into the sunroom then screeched to a stop as she saw the paint color. "Wow, that's bright."

Maggie waved her paintbrush from the ladder top. "Don't worry, it'll end up more subdued."

"Remember, this is just our base coat." Cara moved the roller away from the wall then carefully hooked it by the handle over the rim of a five gallon bucket, letting the excess paint drip down the rack inside. "We like to put the darkest color on first. That way it adds more depth."

Maggie climbed down the ladder to join them. "Next we apply and wipe off a creamy mocha to give it a mottled look. We'll barely allow this undercoat to show through."

"The final stage is when we apply the honey tea glaze, we told you about, to mellow and age the patina," Cara concluded, wiping her hands and rubbing at a coral splotch on her wrist with a damp rag.

Susan moved to an unpainted part of the wall to brush her fingers over the dry primer and trace the swirled plaster. "I sure like this texture."

"The walls will really make the room." Maggie swiped at a smear of paint on her chin, missing completely. "Once the furniture and accessories are in place you'll have Tuscan with a modern edge."

"Just like I ordered." Susan's smile crinkled the corners of her eyes.

Cara extended the stained rag. "Here, Maggs." She tapped her own chin to show where the paint was.

"If you can stand a break, do you want to join me for lunch? I made a crab salad."

"Oh, yeah." Cara suddenly realized how hungry she was.

Maggie held out her paint-stained hands. "We'll wash up and meet you in..."

"The kitchen—it's friendlier."

The women perched on stools around the counter bar, chatting as they munched on crab salad and croissants. Maggie paused, a forkful partway to her mouth. "This is yummy."

"I like cooking, but don't do it much anymore. Just Ed and me—and he's gone so much."

"He's not going with you to Mercerville this weekend?" Cara asked, pulling her croissant into tiny pieces to make it last longer. She remembered reading that French women ate slowly, enjoying their food. Satiated, they didn't gain weight.

"No. He has to stay in Houston for a meeting."

Maggie took the opening and ran. "Do you suppose we could go with you? We need some more measurements on the fountain."

"My, yes!" Susan brightened.

"Good." Cara glanced at Maggie, wishing they could just stay in Houston, but resigned to protecting their client. True,

Maggs had dove into this protection thing, but reluctant or not she agreed and needed to make the best of it.

"Girls, this is so great. You have no idea how I dread city driving." Susan closed her eyes and shivered. "Houston's triple-decker stacked freeways. Even four high! They terrify me. Once I get out of the city and hit country roads, I'm fine."

"It can be kind of intimidating." Cara knew the high-stacked freeways freaked out a lot of people—not just transplants from a small town in the hill country like their client.

"It's especially scary when I drive the little sports car Ed gave me. That's why I take the Yukon when I can. At least I've got something around me, you know?"

"Yeah, feels safer."

Maggie nodded. "We can take the van like we did last time."

Susan reached for her glass of iced tea. "Can we leave Friday?"

Cara began to protest, but Maggie waved her off. "Sure, whatever works for you."

Feeling crabbier than the crab in her salad, Cara munched another bite, realizing that they'd lose a day of work, plus probably leave at some ghastly early morning hour. This was not what she had in mind when they'd signed on for the Dexter renovation. *When did our decorating job turn into private eye shenanigans?*

❧❧❧

It was Maggie's turn to drive as they chugged through the congestion to get past the city limits. Even then, they were still on the freeway until they could exit onto a state highway. Strangers to Houston were usually overwhelmed by the massive size of the sprawling city, the endless freeways. Even though she was a native, Maggie had experienced her own daunting moments with the sheer size and scope of the place.

But now she was more daunted by the feeling that they were heading full-throttle into a murder investigation. Part of her thought it was somewhat exciting, but the situation was still scary. The closest she'd ever been to a crime was in front of her TV set. And then she usually had the protective buffer of popcorn to keep the bad guys at bay. Over the years, Maggie had learned to hide her sixth sense from her parents and everyone, but Cara. Others scoffed at her or started treating her weird, but Cara always listened and stood by her. Now murder shook loose a thunderstorm of psychic signals. If only she and Cara could read them.

Despite her reservations, she hoped that coming with Susan added a layer to their client's protection. Luckily, Susan didn't suspect that the fountain measurements were a bogus excuse. Maggie's hands tightened on the steering wheel. *Somehow, she needed to figure out a way to detour to Fredericksburg on their way back, so she or Cara could ask Darlene's sister a few questions.* How to do it without Susan catching on was a puzzle, but she adored puzzles.

With bluebonnets and bright orange paintbrushes in bloom, the ride to Mercerville eased Maggie's tension, but she was glad to swing onto the driveway at Susan's house.

"We're home." Susan paused with her hand on the door handle. "Sorry, still think of it that way."

"Naturally." Cara opened the back door of the van while Maggie hopped out and started toward the house with Susan.

Gladys must've been peeking out because she swung open the door just as they hit the step. "Hello, Miss Susan, we've been waiting for you."

A bent elderly gentleman hovered behind the housekeeper as Susan rushed forward, hugging each one in turn. "Gladys, Arthur, I've missed you two."

Maggie grinned. Susan might be the lady of the manor, but she certainly treated those in her life with warmth.

Susan stepped back, patting the elderly man's arm. "Arthur, I'm so glad you're feeling better. I missed seeing you last time. But I know when your rheumatism flares up it knocks you out flat."

"I told Gladys I would get up just long enough today to say hello."

Susan made a mock face of horror. "Cross her and you'll be out flat a lot longer than a spell of rheumatism."

They both laughed.

Susan turned to Maggie. "This is Gladys's husband, Arthur Potter, our groundskeeper."

"Lovely to meet you." Maggie extended her hand and was shocked when she felt how chilled and frail his hand was. *How could this old guy still be working?* His grip was stronger than she expected, but accompanied by a slight tremor.

Cara bounded inside the house with her arms full. "These are for you, Gladys."

"What's this?" Gladys didn't look pleased.

"An espresso machine, grinder and my special gourmet beans."

"For *Gladys*?" Maggie winked at Susan who laughed. Loaded down, Cara started toward the kitchen.

"Let me get that." Arthur took the box with the espresso machine and Maggie held her breath, hoping it wasn't too much for him.

Gladys reached for the grinder, but Cara handed her the lighter bag of espresso beans.

Once they were out of sight, Maggie turned to Susan. "Those two live here and take care of things?" She kept her voice low. "They're kind of old to still work."

"They're more family than employees. They've been with us forever. This is their home."

Cara returned from the kitchen in time to hear the last of Susan's words.

"We were talking about Gladys and her husband. And I was just saying they've been here for me always." Susan paused for a second, seemingly lost in thought as she ploughed her hands through her flyaway hair, making it even messier. "There's a girl who comes in from town to take care of the housekeeping and Peter Hoffman does the grounds upkeep and gardening. So Gladys and Arthur's jobs are in title only, although they do supervise the others. But Gladys still rules the roost, no doubt about it."

"Let me guess." Cara arched an eyebrow. "Like the cocoa last time, Gladys finds work to do, no matter what?"

"You've got her pegged." Susan smiled at the designers. "Now let's head to the kitchen for some lemonade or iced tea, before Gladys tracks us down with an overloaded tray."

"And Cara can show her how to set up that new espresso machine." Maggie's voice was innocent but her expression was definitely impish. "I'm sure she's waited her whole life for one of those."

As they trailed Susan through the hallway, Cara elbowed her friend, whispering, "Cut it out."

Marching forward, Maggie tossed back her copper tresses. "Next trip you'll probably bring one for the diner."

෴

Sitting on the bench by the angel fountain to take advantage of some welcome afternoon shade, Susan looked up at the designers who were busy taking measurements. "Tomorrow evening is Uncle Leland's birthday party and you're both invited."

"We couldn't," Cara replied, hoping she didn't have to pretend to take many more measurements. The only ones left she could think of doing required climbing up on the fountain. "It's a family thing. You go and we'll be fine here."

Maggie nodded in agreement as she zapped her measuring tape shut with a snap and slid it into her pocket. "We don't want to intrude."

"My uncle wants to meet you. The town's been abuzz about you since your last visit."

Eyes sparkling, Maggie laughed. "We're the talk of the town, huh?"

"You are. Uncle Leland might be mostly homebound, but he loves to keep up on all the news."

"So we're news in Mercerville?" Cara closed her notebook to join their client on the bench.

"*Everything* is news in Mercerville. You two are *big* news because you're from the city and you're so pretty." Susan coughed into her hand. "And *single*—every guy in town seems to be asking to meet you both."

"Meet us?" Maggie plopped down beside them, so Cara slid over to give her some space.

"From the pharmacist to our town mechanic." Susan's gaze shifted from Maggie to Cara then back. "Not that you girls would be interested in our local men."

Cara sighed. "That deputy's pretty hot."

"And then some," Maggie agreed.

"Ah ha! A little competition between you?" Susan teased.

"He likes Maggie," Cara replied, trying not to sound dejected. "He dimpled at her, but didn't even smile back at me."

"He was on duty and we'd botched their evidence," Susan said. "I doubt he was smiling at all."

"Oh, yes. At Maggs."

"Got a bad boy grin." Maggie's voice went dreamy. "Even if he is a lawman."

"He'll be at the party." After Susan dangled the obvious carrot, she added, "Most everyone will be."

"Okay." Cara realized it might give them the opportunity to scope out suspects. "I guess we can go."

"That's wonderful!" Susan exclaimed.

"It'll be fun." Maggie grinned as if she'd just won a contest with no effort.

Cara held back a sigh. They were burrowing deeper and

deeper into investigating when all she wanted to do was decorate.

"The party's best dress." Susan acted a little embarrassed to mention it, threading her fingers together to avoid Cara's gaze. "Maybe we can find something in my wardrobe for ya'll to wear?"

"No problem," they chorused in unison.

"We always pack our *emergency* outfits," Cara added, aware their slim client wouldn't have anything her size, anyway.

Maggie grinned. "Never know what to expect from our clients."

"You think of everything."

"We try." Maggie hopped up from the bench just as a dragonfly dipped toward them. "It's like a magical garden out here."

A warm breeze, perfumed with evening primrose, swept Cara's bangs across her forehead. She brushed the dark hair out of her eyes. She still couldn't imagine leaving this lovely home for the modern, but lifeless, city manor. "We can't recreate these gorgeous grounds, but I think you'll enjoy the changes when we get done with your renovations in Houston."

"Change is good." Susan gazed around, eyes misting. "I miss this, but Ed's in Houston and of course I want to be with him."

Maggie turned toward the house, sniffing the air. "What's that delicious smell?" Susan stood. "Gladys's pork roast, and veggies—it's been simmering all day. Guess we should go in."

Appreciating her friend's clever change of subject, Cara hoped no one else heard her stomach growl. Did she *always* have to be hungry?

☙❧☙

After dinner, Maggie tapped on the adjoining door to the ivy room. "Cara?"

"Come on in." Cara rubbed her shiny raven hair with a towel, her doe eyes sans liner and face scrubbed clean of all makeup. "What's up?"

"Thought we should make a game plan for tomorrow."

"Game plan?" Cara groaned, sinking onto the edge of the bed. "This is *not* a game."

"Just a *plan* then." Maggie shrugged, wishing her partner in crime wasn't so difficult. "While we're here, one of us should stick close to Susan wherever she goes."

"How do we explain gluing ourselves to her?"

"Easy." Maggie curled on the bed, tucking her knees up under her chin. "Now that we're done with the fountain measurements, she has to entertain us."

"*Bogus* measurements," Cara emphasized, scrunching damp hair with her fingers. "We didn't even need to come. Susan's fine here with Gladys and Arthur."

"And what are they? A million years old?" Maggie couldn't help letting her exasperation show. "We've been over this. How much protection can they possibly give Susan?"

"How much protection can *we* give her?" Cara bounced off the bed and crossed over to the dresser, grabbing moisturizer to rub on her face and neck. "What should we do—fend off the murderer with a paintbrush? Or maybe a wicked putty knife?"

Maggie watched Cara's nightly beauty ritual and tried not to sound miffed, though she felt it. "Just our presence will help."

"We can't attach ourselves to her every minute we're in Mercerville."

"We can try." Maggie joined Cara by the dresser and scooped up a fingerful of moisturizer, patting it on her cheeks. Grimacing, she stared in the mirror, comparing her own freckled looks with Cara's sultry beauty. "You have to admit that three women are safer than one alone."

"If there's a murderer here," Cara said, her eyes meeting Maggs's in the mirror. "None of us are safe."

In the morning, Maggie bounded down the grand staircase with Cara taking the steps much more slowly, blinking sleepily. Maggie reached the kitchen several steps in the lead. "Mmm, I smell fresh brewed coffee."

"Gladys tried out the new coffeemaker," Susan announced from a chair in the breakfast nook, a twinkle in her eyes as she sipped from a Blue Willow china cup.

Maggie sniffed the air again. "Ah, she put her own twist on it?"

"Think so." A smile tilted Susan's mouth. "Let see what Cara thinks."

"Thinks about what?" Looking half-asleep, Cara moved toward the gleaming espresso maker on the counter.

"Here let me get that for you," Maggie offered, slipping in front of her. Cara nodded then wandered over to sit down at the table across from their client.

Maggie set the cup in front of Cara and watched her friend's reaction.

Eyes half closed, Cara raised the cup to her lips. "Ugh!" She came fully awake, slamming her cup down on the tabletop with a thud. "What's that stuff?'

Gladys turned off the kitchen faucet, turning and suddenly startled to see the three of them sitting in the breakfast nook. "You got your own coffee? Sorry, I didn't hear a thing with the water running." She smiled, wiping her hands dry and unaware of Cara's reaction. "Didn't see any point in grinding up more coffee beans when I have perfectly good Folgers already ground."

Cara was still sputtering as Susan poured her a glass of orange juice from a pitcher on the table and slid it in front of her. Watching the housekeeper like a disgruntled bear jarred from a winter den, Cara finally choked, "I gave you *espresso* beans. Gourmet ones—my special blend."

"Coffee's coffee." Gladys dismissed the topic then grabbed an oven mitt as she opened the oven to remove a steaming tray of heavenly smelling pastries to welcome the day.

 〰〰

"Look what you got us into," Cara grumbled as she dusted a champagne-gold shimmer just under her brows and checked her eye-liner.

Sharing the bathroom mirror, green eyes guileless, Maggie finger-curled the copper waves framing her face. "What?"

Cara shook her head. "Are we primping for a hot date? Even a girls' night out?" Nearly scorching the mirror, she glared at Maggie. "No way—we're dolling up for a birthday party for an old guy we've never met, in a town we'd never heard of until we got Susan as our client."

"Your point is?"

"A town with a *murderer* on the loose." Cara pressed her lips together and *not* to blot the lip gloss. "That manic could be at this party tonight."

"You are so brilliant!" Maggie grinned, boiling Cara to the near-slugging point. "Then we'll just have to sleuth around and see if we can shake out the killer." With that, Maggie sashayed out of the room and out of the reflection.

"Grr." Cara stared back at her now solo reflection in the mirror, smothering the impulse to stick out her tongue. She was, after all, a mature adult. Still, Maggs drove her crazy about this murder thing.

Once downstairs in the living room, Maggie spun around, the flutter sleeves of her jade green alive with the spin. "Are we over-dressed for the birthday bash? What if everyone's in jeans?"

"Susan said it was best dress, remember?" Cara smoothed her black dress. "I swear this thing shrunk since I wore it last."

"You look lovely," Susan said, breezing in through the archway as her gaze swept over them. "Both of you."

"This isn't too tight?" Cara rearranged the sweetheart neckline to show less cleavage and tried to peer around at her own behind. "I don't remember it fitting so snug."

"Alluring," a young man said, trailing Susan and smiling—oogling—Cara corrected as she observed him.

"This is my cousin Roger." Susan introduced him with affection in her voice.

As he eyed the designers, Cara eyed him right back. *Weak chin, too slim, knows he's handsome*, she thought, while murmuring, "Nice to meet you."

"Susan told us about you," Maggie said, her smile sweet, but curious. Cara knew her friend was sizing the guy up, too. *Is Maggie getting vibes?*

Roger winked at Susan. "Good stuff, I hope."

"Of course," Susan retorted, playfully tapping his shoulder.

"Cuz is far too nice to tell the truth about you, brother dear." A female version of Roger stepped forward. "Hi, I'm Rachel Mercer. Susan has said awesome things about you girls."

"All true, I'm sure," Roger added, trying to reclaim their attention.

Susan laughed. "Enough, you two. Go see if Gladys needs help, wrap a present or pour yourself a drink." She turned from her cousins to Cara and Maggie. "I want ya'll to meet Uncle Leland before the party begins."

Following their client through the beautiful historic home, Maggie felt euphoric. Sure, she adored parties, but also tonight might be the night they discovered the murderer. Besides, that sexy deputy was invited.

"The party's here—not at your uncle's place?" Cara asked, walking beside Susan.

"I didn't tell you? Sorry. I get a bit scattered since Dad passed away." Susan led them into a wing of the house they hadn't explored. "Social events usually happen here. Guess it's a habit I have trouble breaking."

Maggie heard a sadness coloring Susan's words—as if the woman remembered happier days. Probably when her father was alive. "I'm sure your uncle appreciates not hav-

ing all the to-do at his place. If he gets tired, he can just escape and go home."

"Home sounds nice," Cara muttered, drawing a nudge
from Maggie.

Fortunately, Susan missed their exchange. "Yes, he can
be social for a while, but tires easily."

Uncle Leland stood by the fireplace, his suit hung loose-
ly as if he'd recently lost weight, and as he turned his faded
blue eyes his wrinkled face creased with a broad smile.
"Hello, ladies." He held out a hand and Maggie accepted.
"My niece said you were pretty things and she's right."

"Thanks," they replied in unison then looked at each
other in dismay as both Susan and her uncle laughed.

"She told me about that as well," he added with another
chuckle. "I appreciate you young ladies gracing my birthday
celebration."

"Our pleasure," Maggie bubbled, pleased the uncle was
as charming as his niece.

"Yes, happy birthday," Cara said, not looking thrilled.

The doorbell chimed with musical insistence. Susan excused herself, leaving the designers alone with Uncle Leland. "Is she happy?" he asked softly as they all watched her
disappear down the hall.

"Yes, I think so," Maggie answered, surprised by his
query.

"Don't *you* think so?" Cara asked more pointedly, than
made Maggie comfortable.

"Well, her first marriage wasn't the best and Susan's got
such a tender heart—don't want to see it wounded ever
again." He cleared his throat then tapped a cane that Maggie
hadn't even noticed against the stone fireplace. "We miss
her around here."

"I bet you do," Maggie sympathized.

"Party's on!" Roger led an assortment of guests into the
room then began a round of introductions that spun Maggie's head. She'd never remember what name went to what
face let alone any other details about the people.

Cara was experiencing the same problem. How many people did Mercerville hold? They must all be stuffed here into Susan's house. And more came. And more.

The doorbell chimed continuously. As the house filled with people, Cara observed Susan flitting from group to group and person to person radiating gracious warmth. She appeared entirely in her element.

"I don't like it," Maggie whispered.

Looking around, Cara had no clue what triggered her friend's censure. "What?"

"That man by the fireplace—silver hair, quite handsome for his age—"

"Yeah?" Cara spotted Maggie's target wearing a well-tailored gray suit and holding a drink.

"He's staring at our client. Wherever she goes, his eyes follow."

"So? She looks nice tonight."

"Not a flirting gaze—he's got an intensity that vibrates across the room." Maggie scowled. "It's strange."

"What's strange?" Rachel asked, plopping between them.

"The way that man stares at Susan," Maggie replied in hushed tones as she flicked a glance his direction.

"No biggie." Rachel chuckled, swirling the ice in her glass to clink it against the sides. "He always watches her like that. I've noticed it since I was a kid."

"He d—does?" Maggie sputtered.

"Who is he?" Cara asked, thinking Rachel a bit strange as well.

"Just Kirby Ballentine—he's our family accountant and financial advisor." She grimaced, a tiny dent between her brows. "Was Susan's, too—until her new hubby canned him."

"Ed fired him?" Cara couldn't imagine jolly Ed firing anyone. "Why?"

"Why?" Maggie echoed.

Rachel threw back her head and laughed. "Probably the

way Kirby stares at my cuz." She waved, throwing kisses at a cluster of guests just entering, then refocused on Maggie and Cara. "Later—gotta mingle."

As Rachel slipped through the crowd, Maggie grabbed Cara's wrist. "That Kirby guy is weird. We'd better add him to our suspect list."

"Your *what*?" rumbled a deep voice behind them.

Chapter 5

They spun around, Maggie feeling heat flush her face. "Hello, Deputy Rice," Cara purred, while Maggie searched for her voice. "It's a surprise to see you at a party in full uniform."

"On duty," he snapped, his gaze pinning speechless Maggie. "You ladies aren't stirring up trouble, are you?"

"Us? Never." Cara smiled up at the handsome lawman, but his eyes never strayed.

This must be how a grilled suspect feels. Maggie wanted to sink into the plush carpet, but jutted out her chin instead. "We never stir up trouble." At least her voice finally worked, though it sounded squeaky to her own ears.

"Right." He rubbed his square jaw. "Miss Susan is a fine person, and I don't want her to come to any harm."

Maggie's pulse raced from him more than his statement. "You think she's in danger?"

"Didn't say that." His eyes darkened as they roved over Maggie. She tried hard not to flutter her lashes at him, but he made all of her flutter.

"Sounded like it to me," Cara interjected.

"I'm just sayin' we don't have the manpower to offer round the clock protection every time Miss Susan comes to town. Don't encourage her to dig around the investigation."

"We don't," they chorused.

Maggie shook her finger at the deputy. "We told her *not* to ask questions."

"Sure. Right. I heard your *suspect list* talk."

"Susan knows nothing about that," Cara defended, and Maggie knew her friend hated being wrongly accused as much as she did herself.

"What can we do?" she asked, trying to defuse the situation before Cara got cranky.

"It's up to y'all to help Susan stay out of trouble."

"What kind of trouble?" Maggie breathed.

"The kind of trouble that ticks off killers."

Maggie gasped, reeling from the impact of his statement. He'd just confirmed her fears—coming out of a lawman's mouth made it frighteningly real.

"So what do *you* expect *us* to do?" Cara's hand rested on her hip and Maggie knew the move was a warning signal.

"Not let her snoop."

"Like we control her," Cara scoffed.

"We try but—" Maggie began.

He cut her off. "Do more than *try*." His voice dropped as if he realized they might be drawing attention. "We've never had a murder here before—let alone two. I won't allow a third."

"We're designers, not body guards," Cara grumbled.

Maggie swallowed a lump in her throat. "I promise we'll do what we can."

Gaze on Maggie's lips, Deputy Rice chucked her chin. "Do that."

Before she could exhale, he strode away. In long strides, he crossed the room toward Leland Mercer, leaving her in a daze.

"Earth calling." Cara tapped her foot impatiently. "Maggs?"

Maggie shook off the spell and turned back to Cara. "If he's worried then we ought to be."

"Then let's get Susan back to Houston."

"A note came there, too. Remember?"

"It's the best we can do." Cara's expression and tense body language revealed her displeasure.

Fortunately, Susan appeared, tapping her shoulder. "It's time to light the cake and sing. Please join us."

"Be happy to," Maggie agreed, forcing lightness into her voice. This was a birthday celebration and she intended to help celebrate. Forget lawmen and killers—this is a party!

Cara held her breath as candles blazed atop the huge birthday cake. Would the cake catch on fire? And there was no way a seventy-year-old gentleman could blow that baby out. Fortunately some children, surrounding him with giggles, helped him blow. It was impossible for her to tell, who were relatives of the Mercers, and who were merely citizens of Mercerville.

Within minutes, Susan's diminutive neighbor served them each a slice of cake on a paper plate. "Hi. Remember me? I'm Faith."

"Thanks, Faith, the cake looks heavenly," Cara said, thinking it did. It also looked like umpteen calories.

Maggie just started to add her thanks when Faith blurted, "Oh, here comes Darlene. Bye!"

Cara glanced up to see a woman who wore a burgundy sheath dress and clutched a cocktail glass, charging toward them. A slash of scarlet lipstick curved the mouth of a likely former prom queen, who now showed the years—possibility early forties—and a thicker figure.

"You must be the big city friends of Susan."

"Yes, we are." Cara forced herself to smile politely despite the woman's taunting cadence.

Susan appeared next to Maggie. "Yes, Darlene, they are *dear* friends." Susan drew herself up stiffly. "And *everyone* in Mercerville will show them a warm welcome."

This time, Cara smiled for real. The lady of the manor's warning rang clear. *Don't mess with my friends.* It was the first time she'd witnessed Susan's protective streak.

"Maggie, Cara," Susan said, pulling them toward her and

away from Darlene. "I promised Uncle Leland you'd chat with him for a few minutes."

"Our pleasure," Cara replied, eager as Faith had been to escape Darlene.

"Sure." Maggie bounced eagerly, illustrating she was no more pleased with Darlene than Cara felt.

Swish. In one split second, the drink in Darlene's hand exploded into the air, splattering Susan.

"Oh, so sorry," Darlene crooned, blinking her eyes in mock innocence. "My glass slipped."

"Right," Cara growled, disgusted with the woman, who reeked from too much alcohol and couldn't stop grinning.

Cara assessed the damage. Bangs dripping, blue dress damp and spattered, Susan stood, pale, mouth open, totally stunned. "Come on, Susan," Cara coaxed, "Maggs and I will help keep your dress from staining."

"Sober up," Maggie snapped at Darlene, echoing Cara's thought as they whirled away with their client safely between them.

"Thanks," Susan whispered, letting them usher her through the guests and into the quieter section of the house. "Darlene drinks too much."

"No kidding." Cara fumed, wondering how anyone could be so crass toward Susan. She'd never met a sweeter more gracious person than this client

⌒◌⌒

Maggie's *Irish was up* as her dad used to say. She wished she could've tossed a drink right back in that hussy's face. Still, worry engulfed her. If they couldn't keep Susan safe while they stood next to her—how could they protect her *twenty-four/seven* from a killer?

Roger stepped in front of them blocking the grand staircase. "Hey, what's up?"

Susan uttered one word. "Darlene."

"She threw a drink at you?" Disbelief in his widening eyes as he took in his bedraggled cousin. "Did you chuck one back?"

"She should've," Cara said.

"I almost did," Maggie admitted.

"Wow, you two hang tight with Cuz." He teetered back on his heels, Maggie could see he'd had a few too many.

"We do," Cara agreed.

"Don't forget it," Maggie added, not sure why she felt it was important, but determined he knew they had Susan's back.

Upstairs in Susan's bedroom suite, they waited for Susan to change after Gladys had magically appeared to sweep the spattered dress away. "Mind zipping me?" Susan asked, a soft pink coloring her cheeks. "It's amazing getting spoiled after a mere year of having Ed's assistance."

"Oh, that's romantic," Maggie said, wondering if she'd ever settle into a comfortable marriage with a husband handy to zip a dress or fasten a necklace. She shook her head. Maybe in the future, but not now. She did not admit— even to herself—that she'd just envisioned Deputy Rice's broad hands doing just that.

"You look pretty in lavender." Cara cocked her head, examining Susan. "I think I like this dress better than the blue one. "

"Change your shoes though," Maggie added with a giggle, as her gaze fell upon the sapphire blue pumps on Susan's feet.

"Thanks." Susan blushed again. "What would I do without you girls?" She kicked off her offending pumps and slipped on black ones. "I'm not exactly a fashion diva."

"Like *we* are?" Cara said, raven brow arched, but a smile playing over her lips.

"What did Gladys whisper in your ear when she took your other dress?" Maggie couldn't prevent her curiosity as she awaited the answer.

With a grin, Susan replied, "Deputy Rice had escorted

Darlene out of the party and was giving her a lift home in a police cruiser."

"Good riddance." A scowl clouded Cara's face. "You shouldn't have invited her."

"I didn't." Susan recurled her bangs, though they still drooped lopsidedly. "Uncle Leland's party is an open house."

"Glad she's gone." Maggie spoke the thought aloud. The entire evening she'd felt all kinds of vibes zinging around the party. She knew many of the negative vibes radiated from Darlene Lawson.

Susan encompassed the designers in an affectionate gaze then hugged each of them. "I think Uncle Leland's ready to bid his guests farewell. Come say good bye to him. Okay?"

"Who'll drive him home?" Maggie remembered Roger's not-so-sober demeanor.

"Kirby—he's always there when we need him." Susan led them out of her suite and along the hallway, looking back over her shoulder. "We can't trust my cousins not to drink and drive and Uncle Leland's eyesight isn't the best anymore."

"Kirby Ballentine?" Cara shared a glance with Maggie that Susan didn't see.

"Yes. Did you meet him?"

"No. We didn't have the pleasure," Cara replied, succulently.

"Rachel pointed him out to us, though," Maggie said, remembering the way the man had stared at Susan. "Your uncle will be safe with him?"

"Of course." Susan paused, one hand atop the carved banister. "Everyone's safe with Kirby."

"Doubt that," Maggie muttered, still disturbed by his intensity. Cara shot her the *don't let your vibes mess things up* look. So Maggie kept her thoughts to herself.

∽∾∽

"So spill." Hands on her hips, Cara cornered Maggie in the Rose bedroom.

Cross-legged on the bed, scribbling in a notebook, Maggie lifted a moody gaze.

"I got vibes."

"Uh, duh." Cara moved to perch on the corner of the bed, faintly irritated as the mattress dipped with her weight. "Tell me."

Maggie waved the page in her hand. "Murder suspects. I'm putting Kirby Ballentine at the top."

"Why would he knock off the lawyer? Or the secretary?" Cara rested her chin in one hand. "Motive?"

"I don't know—but we'll find one." Maggie scribbled his name with a flourish. "You have to admit the way he stared at Susan was searing."

"Just because he has a thing for our client, doesn't make him a murderer."

"So *you* say."

"May I?" Cara reached for the notebook. Maggie surrendered it, adding the pen. "We ought to make two suspect lists—one for the lawyer and the other for his secretary."

"What if it's the same killer?"

"They'll show up on both lists."

Maggie scooted closer to Cara. "I think Roger belongs on the lawyer one."

"You're down on men tonight." Cara printed his name. "We'll have to discover motives or our lists will be pointless."

"What are you writing now?" Maggie tried to peer at the page.

"Darlene Larson. She does actually have a motive—for both murders." Cara poised the pen midair. "Let's include the mystery lover on Aimee the secretary's list."

"Yes, that no-tell motel guy who Darlene's sister saw." Maggie bit her lip. "On the way home to Houston, we need to make a side trip to Fredericksburg and talk to her."

"Without tipping off Susan." Cara tapped the pen against

the notebook. "We've got to keep our client clueless about our investigating."

"We can do that," Maggie stated—with far more assurance than Cara felt.

"Ok, let's see what we have on our lists so far. On the lawyer: Roger, Darlene and a burglar."

"Burglar?" Maggie tugged her nightshirt to cover her knees.

"That is the current theory."

"A weak one."

"Like ours is strong?" Cara chuckled at her friend's logic. She skipped to the second list. "On Aimee the secretary's list we have Darlene—again—and a hit and run by a stranger."

"Hey, Kirby Ballentine's not on either list," Maggie complained.

"The motive thing."

"So? Suspect lists were *my* idea."

"Okay." Cara penned in his name. "Happy? Kirby Ballentine is now on both lists—a double suspect. Now give me a reason to keep him there."

"I will. And on Roger, too."

Cara sighed. Her friend and business partner was down on men tonight and she knew what triggered it. Maggie wasn't exactly street smart when it came to males. Cara hated to see her get hurt. "Maggs, that deputy may be hot, but his world is centered here in Mercerville. You know that?"

"I know." Maggie nodded then fiddled with the bedspread, avoiding Cara's searching gaze. "He barely talks to me, anyway."

Cara remembered the way Deputy Rice zoomed in on Maggie. "I don't thinking *talking* is what's on his mind."

Maggie perked up, the lilt back in her voice. "Oh, yeah?"

Cara whacked her with a pillow. "You minx. Like you don't notice?"

"I'm sexy, I'm sexy," Maggie chanted, bouncing up to fire pillows back at Cara just like they did as kids.

Between their laughter and pillows thumping, they missed a tap at the door. Susan opened it gingerly as a pillow whizzed past.

Susan's eyes brimmed with laughter though she attempted to look stern. "Oh? Am I interrupting?"

Maggie sheepishly tucked the pillow she was ready to launch back onto the bed.

But Cara let hers fly. Susan snatched it out of the air and flung it back. It missed both girls, hitting the dresser and falling to the floor with a thump.

"Ya'll are so good for me. You're always entertaining."

Cara curtsied, spreading the skirt of her nightgown as she dipped. "We aim to please."

"What's this?" Susan bent to pick up the notebook. "I must've knocked it off."

Maggie swooped it up. "Just some design scribbles. Before our pillow fight we were playing with some ideas."

Susan clapped her hands. "I'd love to see them."

"Ah, they're way too rough." Cara tried to disguise her panic. "We'll work them up better and show you then. Okay?"

"Of course." Gracious as always, Susan acquiesced. "I thought I'd check on you two before bed. Do you need anything?"

"No chocolate?" Cara's question popped out before she could stop herself.

"I sent Gladys to bed." Susan brightened. "We can sneak down to the kitchen and fix our own?"

"Not necessary," Maggie replied, ignoring the pleading face from Cara.

"Let's. It'll be fun. I haven't done that for years." Susan tied the sash of her robe. "Get your robe and slippers, girls. We're raiding the pantry."

Under Susan's direction, Maggie flitted around the kitchen making their hot cocoa. Once they were settled around the table in the breakfast nook, Cara and Maggie sipped their cocoa while Susan chattered.

"I wanted you to meet Joan tonight, but she didn't come." Susan gazed into her mug as if she saw something she didn't like.

"Joan?" Cara queried, surprised there was anyone who hadn't shown up at the party.

"Yes. She was my friend forced into retirement so Aimee could have her job at the bank." Susan turned to Maggie. "I sat with her at Aimee's funeral."

Maggie nodded, answering for both, as they each tended to do. "Yes, we remember now."

Then Susan smiled again, the difference that made to her face was amazing. When she smiled, it transformed her into a beauty from merely attractive. "And several young men were quite disappointed that I hadn't introduced you to them."

"Who?" Cara asked, more than a wee bit interested. Just because Maggs had the deputy cornered didn't eliminate all the eligible bachelors.

"Bobby Ray for one."

"Is he the guy who hit the barber pole?" Maggie asked, dunking a cookie into her hot cocoa.

Cara watched her friend with envy. She shouldn't even be indulging in the hot cocoa.

"No. That was Tommy. Bobby Ray is the town mechanic. He's also Aimee's ex-fiancé.

"Say what?" Cara nearly spilled her mug, setting it down so hard it splashed.

"Aimee didn't sound like the type of female to settle for a mechanic." Maggie's interest lit as well.

"She wasn't. The first better offer and she dumped Bobby like an odd sock."

"So who was the better offer?" Cara mused, thinking this small town certainly had its share of intrigue.

"My cuz."

"Roger?" Cara and Maggie chorused.

"The one and only."

A sheepish expression crept over Susan's face as if she

felt somehow responsible. For what Cara hadn't a clue.

Maggie shot a smug look at Cara, who she knew she'd be in for a 'I-told-you-so' about Roger being some way involved with the late secretary. Cara sighed, concentrating on the last sip of her hot cocoa. *Whatever will happen next?*

Chapter 6

Maggie at the wheel, Susan in the passenger seat and sitting behind them, Cara yawned and stretched. "Coffee. Need coffee."

"We've barely been on the road," Maggie said with a glance in the rear view mirror at her fellow conspirator.

"Don't be cruel," Cara countered. "I'll be worthless if we don't supply my coffee fix."

"I have an idea," Susan volunteered. "We're almost to Fredericksburg—we can stop at the coffee shop where Darlene's sister works."

"Cool." Cara loved it when a plan fell together.

Sneaking another glance into the mirror, Maggie grinned as well. "All right, Susan, give me directions."

Susan wiggled her seatbelt to turn sideways. "This is great timing! The lavender fields are in bloom."

"They are?" with answering excitement, Maggie stole a look at Susan.

"Huh?" Cara leaned forward. "This is important—why?"

"I've been thinking that some lavender planted along the fence line in Houston would be nice. This gives me a chance to show you." Susan practically bounced out of her seat except for her seatbelt tether. "Fredericksburg is famous for the most gorgeous lavender fields."

"I've always wanted to see that." Maggie had obviously forgotten all about the coffee plan.

"My coffee," Cara insisted, trying to bring Maggs back around.

"Yes," Susan agreed. "We'll get your coffee and then we can detour to see the lavender fields."

"Great idea!"

Cara groaned.

"Can't miss this opportunity," Maggie told Susan.

Something in her voice cued Cara, who sank back against the van seat to relax. Maggs hadn't forgotten the ball was still in play.

"Here we are." Susan motioned toward the parking lot. "I hope Hannah is working it'll be fun to see her. She's nothing like her sister."

"Good," both Maggie and Cara breathed.

When they saw Hannah, Cara understood Susan's comment. This woman was a bumblebee, happily buzzing around the tables. Darlene was more of a wasp ready to sting.

"Hey, girl!" Hannah called to Susan the moment they entered. "Be with you in a sec." Pencil tucked behind her ear, blonde-streaked brown hair in a bun, Hannah smoothed her apron with one hand, flipping open her order book with the other. "Haven't seen you in a blue moon, Susan. Thought you were off to Houston."

"I am, we're on our way back there now." Susan gestured at Cara and Maggie. "Hannah, these are my friends. How are *you* doing? Bet that little girl of yours is getting big."

Hannah wriggled her nose. "Tell me about it. Hallie's in sixth grade. Why yesterday that little tyke was barely walkin' and now she's askin' to wear makeup."

"Already?"

"It's them TV shows and the Internet. Grows 'em up too fast." Her frown reversed back to a smile. "Now what kind I get ya?"

"How about two cokes to go?" Maggie raised an inquiring brow at Susan who nodded.

"You wouldn't serve lattes, would you?" Cara asked wistfully.

"Sure thing, hon. This *is* a coffee shop."

"You do?" *Treasure!* Cara felt like dancing on the booth table.

"To go?" Hannah wiggled her pencil between her fingers.

"Not mine." Cara read alarm in Susan's face. "I'm...ah...allergic to lavender. I'll just sit here and savor my drink while the others make their little side trip."

"Are you sure?" Susan asked after Cara rattled off her latte order. "It isn't far, but we'll be gone about forty-five minutes."

"Barely enough time when Cara's on a coffee binge," Maggie interjected.

"She'll be fine," Hannah poked her pencil back behind her ear. "Place is slow and I got a break coming up in a few. I'll keep an eye on her." She chuckled. "This is Fredericksburg not a crime den like Mercerville."

With a tiny gasp, Susan stiffened.

"Just teasin'. Don't get your petticoat in a knot." Hannah winked and Susan smiled back. Not a convincing smile, but a polite one.

Still, Hannah was far nicer than Darlene was. Little digs might be a family trait.

Watching through the window, at the van merging back onto the highway, Cara sipped her creamy latte, licking the sweet foam off her top lip. Mmm. "Nice."

"Here's a cinnamon roll to go with it." Hannah slid a plate onto the table, the fragrant warm stick pastry tantalizing and tempting Cara's taste buds.

"I shouldn't."

"Sure ya should." Hannah wiped her hands on her apron. "Men like women soft and curvy. Not bony sticks like those teen stars. I'm always telling my Hallie that."

Mindful of her mission, Cara motioned for the waitress to join her. "What if we share this? Is it your break?"

"Close enough." Hannah hollered back to the kitchen and the other waitress on duty. Then she scooted into the other side of the booth now vacated with Susan and Maggie's absence. "You met my sis?"

"I did last night." Unsure of what else to say, Cara just left it there.

"Darlene's always been the looker in the family."

"Looks fade. Sounds like you're the one who caught the good luck." Cara glanced pointedly at the wide wedding band with teeny diamonds. "A husband and a daughter—"

"I did get the blessings, huh?" She proudly showed off her ringed hand. "If sis wasn't so mouthy, she might catch a few blessings, too."

Cara cut the cinnamon roll in half. "Are you and your sister from Mercerville?"

"Not a chance. We were born right here." Hannah put hers on a napkin and began to pull it apart. "My big sis didn't want to stay. Until Darlene snatched that stuffy old lawyer there, she used to talk about goin' to Hollywood."

"Mercerville's hardly that," Cara unraveled her pastry, regretting she'd shared it, but it was a sacrifice for the cause. "And now those murders..." She let the statement dangle.

Hannah didn't disappoint. "Scary stuff." She glanced both ways then leaned forward. "I saw that secretary's killer."

"You did?"

"Aimee used to meet this guy at the motel across the way. You know—on the sly. Bet it was a crime of passion. He did it." Still talking, Hannah popped the last bite of her roll in her mouth. "Always knew he was suspicious."

"Wow, did you tell the police?"

"Cops don't wanna hear nothing from me. They want to pretend it's not murder. Call it a hit and run, a stranger off the highway." She brushed crumbs off her mouth.

"What does the mystery man look like?" Cara felt excitement build. Maybe they could get a solid lead on the guy.

"Don't know."

Disappointment washed over Cara. "Don't know? I thought you saw him."

"I did several times. Only he wore a hat and sunglasses and it was always at night or late evening."

"So you didn't recognize him? Could he be from Mercerville?"

"Could be. Maybe not." The door jingled announcing a new customer. Hannah slid out of the booth. "Could be from there or maybe even from here. See across the way." She pointed out the window. "He'd park over there away from the street light at the far side of the motel and they'd always get an end unit."

"Then how did you recognize Aimee?"

"Her fancy Mercedes Benz and the violet and green stripes in her hair?" Hannah chuckled. "You could spot that wild one a mile away."

"Not your typical look around here." Cara actually enjoyed the casual way people dressed in this area. It felt more carefree than in the city.

"That might be changin' if that new community brings money folk. They're sayin' celebrities are fightin' for the fancy new-builds out Mercerville way."

"Really?" Cara asked, feeling totally clueless. She'd seen nothing like that. "In Mercerville?"

"Outside of town hid in the woods by the lake." Hannah tapped her finger against her head. "A cluster of them's going up with swimming pools and hot tubs. Like who needs *hot* tubs around these parts?" She grabbed her order pad. "Gotta get busy."

"Wait." Cara reached out a hand. "What did he drive?"

Hannah stopped a few feet away. "Who?"

"Aimee's mystery man."

"A dark SUV."

So close. Cara sagged back against the booth, the adrenalin rush she'd felt at the onset now completely drained. If only they could identify the mystery man maybe they could at least solve one crime. Now she understood how Maggie got so into unraveling the mystery. Chasing after clues was quite a rush only the letdown when it didn't pan out was no fun. *No fun at all.*

 ප්‍රcrec

That evening in Houston, Maggie stood just inside Susan's new French doors gazing out to survey the back yard. While the sunroom was coming together nicely, the patio and yard remained a mess. Cara had compared it to emptying a closet with all the contents strewn around before it was organized and put back together. Except this was much bigger than any closet and much more complex. The pool remained functional, but the yard was ripped apart, stepping stones partly placed, holes dug in various places and mounds of dirt scattered around. *A disaster zone.*

Maggie pushed hair out of her eyes. She pulled her cotton top away from her body. The sultry heat glued her hair and clothes to her. Not a whisper of a breeze stirred the air this would be a good night for a rainstorm. Unfortunately, neither the cloudless sky nor the forecast held a promise of any relief.

Cara stepped up behind her. "They issued a heat alert. What do you think?"

"We don't want to be responsible if any of the crew get sunstroke." Maggie shrugged, not seeing any choice. "Or heatstroke. I guess we better give them a few days off."

"It'll put us behind schedule, but between the scorching temps and high humidity don't know how much work we'd get out of them, anyway." Cara scuffed her sneakered toe against the terrazzo tile.

"We can wrap up the glaze treatment on the sunroom

walls." Maggie's mood lightened. "I always get excited when the wall treatment's nearly done. Hope Susan likes it."

"She will."

"Good for us," Maggie retorted, feeling better about the whole project.

"Good for her, too." Cara feathered the hair at her neckline upward. "I don't remember it ever being this hot."

Maggie laughed. "Uh, right. I remember the time we wore our bikinis and poured ice over our stomachs to cool down."

"You got me, Maggs. Guess it's happened, but it's so scorching."

"Ah, yeah." Maggie eyed her friend. "At least you don't put Popsicles in the bed anymore."

"Not often."

"We did come up with some novel solutions in our youth."

"Remember the time we drove all the way to Galveston for cooler air and nearly got caught in a hurricane?" Cara plucked Maggie by the sleeve and tugged her back inside. "Let's close up these doors and stop letting the heat inside. Hurray for air-conditioning!"

"As long as we have power," Maggie answered absently, her mind wandering back to other heatwaves.

"Don't borrow trouble."

"Me?" Maggie charged back, "I'm not the doom and gloom person."

"You are sometimes."

"I am not."

"What's going on?" Susan asked, stepping carefully across the canvas drop cloth as she entered the sunroom. "I swear if I didn't know you two were best friends, the way you squabble would worry me."

Cara looked as guilty as Maggie felt.

"It's just this heat makes me cranky," Cara admitted.

"Me, too," Maggie said.

"Me, three," Susan added, sending them all three into peals of laughter.

"What's going on?" Ed asked, halting at the doorway. He immediately triggered another round of laughter as he stood appearing confused. He cleared his throat. "Ahem. Am I missing something?"

"Something but haven't a clue what," Susan finally croaked, trying her best not to laugh.

"Must be the heat," Ed said with a shake of his head. "Susan, are you ready to retire for night? I thought we'd turn in a bit early and maybe watch an old movie."

"Of course, honey. Be right there." Susan blushed as he wiggled his brows at her in some secret newlywed code.

As his footsteps receded, Susan started chattering. "I'm not used to a television in the bedroom and ever since Ed learned I have a fondness for the old classic movies, he picks one out for us to watch at least once a week."

"Sure." Maggie stifled a chuckle.

Maggie and Cara shared the grin as Susan rattled on, obviously embarrassed at what they were thinking. "Really. Tonight I think it's *Arsenic and Old Lace* with Cary Grant."

"That film's cool," Maggie said, remembering watching it with her mom on TV. "That short bug-eyed guy is in it."

"Peter Lorrie," Cara added. "I loved the way they used light and shadow in those old black and white movies."

Susan glanced after Ed and back at them before hustling out of the room. "Well, goodnight."

"Have fun!" Maggie called after her, certain that Susan was up to more than old movies.

❧❧❧

The next morning, pouring tea-tint glaze into her container, Cara let the rich translucent liquid glug out, filling up to the halfway mark. She wore a cotton T-shirt over shorts instead of her favorite multi-pocketed painter pants. "I swear it's as hot in here as outside."

"Not hardly." Maggie shoved her hair back with her arm then took her turn at filling her own container with the glaze. Unfortunately, the glaze was as sticky as the dark honey it echoed. "Still, the temp in here is plenty warm."

"No kidding."

"Susan reset the air conditioning the way they've been requesting," Maggie moved to the far side of the long focal wall. "You know…to avoid any more brown-outs and power shortages than we already have."

"We would have a client who's conscientious," Cara grumbled. She climbed up on her special-order step stool, hung the handle of her paint container on the hook, and then picked up a large sea sponge. "I'm melting and we've barely started."

"Good thing we gave the crew a few days off." Maggie glanced out the warbled glass of the French doors. "They would've croaked working outside."

"I know, I know," Cara dipped her sponge in the glaze, dabbed it on a cloth, and then began sponging the wall from her corner. "I heard all the warnings on the news. It's a red alert with dangerously high heat indexes." She squished the sponge in a random pattern onto the wall. "I just hate to get behind schedule."

"We'll be further behind if our crew ends up in the hospital." Maggie's fingers were already sticky and she wiped them on the damp rag looped over the ladder. "Must be a million degrees out there. Makes me want to jump in the pool."

"A cool dip sounds good—but there's the wreck we've made of the yard." Cara pointed outside beyond the windows of the sunroom.

"Oh, how refreshing." Across the ripped up lawn, blue water glistened, enticing and wet. Sun blazed with blinding brightness. Maggie felt tempted to activate the remote control blinds to cut the glare, but they needed the light while applying the paint treatment. She blinked sweat from her eyes, knowing the blinds might also take an edge off the heat. "A swim would be worth braving that minefield of a backyard."

"The pool *is* still functional," Cara replied, a wistful note in her voice.

"We've got work to do." Maggie turned for a longing glance the direction of the pool then reapplied herself to the job.

"Spoilsport," Cara muttered, renewing her efforts as well.

Maggie smiled to herself, aware her friend and design partner was just as much a work alcoholic. They both felt driven to get this room ready to put together, decorating was the best part of renovation. No matter how tempting a cooling swim was right now.

"How are my favorite designers?" Susan asked, stepping just inside the sunroom. She gazed at the small areas newly muted by the glaze. "It's amazing the difference that top gloss is making on the color."

"More like you expected than the coral?" Maggie asked, gazing down from the ladder and enjoying the pleasure ringing in their client's voice.

"Definitely." Susan waved at both corners where they were working. "It's great!"

She tugged at the throat of her designer tunic. "This room is so hot. You poor girls are working in an oven. I'll adjust the AC thermostat."

"No, we're okay." Maggie saw Cara's glare, but ignored it.

"I could bring in a fan? There's one on the shelf in the front closet," Susan offered.

"That'd be nice." Cara hopped off her stepstool, wiping her hands on the damp rag by her. "I'll go get it."

She bounded out the room. Susan watched her, saying, "I could've fetched it."

"It's okay. Cara's halfway there by now." Maggie's smile reversed as she noticed the flash of concern on Susan's face. "What's wrong?"

"When you said Cara was already halfway there, it made me think of Joan. She mentioned she was practically on her way before the party last weekend, but she never showed."

"Did you call her?"

"Yes. No answer, just voicemail and she hasn't returned my calls."

"Can you phone someone there in Mercerville to check on her? Husband?"

"She's not married. Doesn't have kids." Susan twisted her wedding ring. "Joan's back to work at the bank now Aimee's gone, but I'm not about to call Elliot Ohlmacher."

"Don't blame you," Cara said, bouncing in with a fan. She cleared an outlet where she plugged in the fan. Then she tipped over an empty five-gallon bucket, sat the fan on top, aiming it where it would span most the room and flipped the control on high. The fan whirred back and forth with an oscillating breeze. "Why were you even discussing calling that lecher?"

"Joan's disappeared," Maggie said, answering for Susan, who nodded in agreement looking forlorn.

"Not to worry, it's probably like when Darlene took off to visit her sister." Cara planted herself smack in front of the fan for several minutes.

"No this is different," Susan said softly, wringing her hands instead of using them in gestures as she talked like she usually did.

"Isn't there someone you can call?" Maggie suggested. "Maybe your neighbor Faith?"

"Yes—you're so smart." Susan brightened, turning to hustle away. "If anyone knows what's up with Joan, Faith will. They're both on the library building committee."

With the fan upping the comfort level of the sunroom, Cara and Maggie worked several hours nearly nonstop, before Susan reappeared. Just as they were closing in on mid-wall from both sides and getting ready to swap places, their client entered balancing a tray of glasses. "Break time. Iced tea?"

"Love some." Cara wiped her hands and rushed over to take the tray from Susan and park it on a box.

"Perfect timing." Maggie grinned at Susan. "We were just about to trade places."

"Trade?" Susan surveyed the wall with bright peachy coral now showing in only the center section. "You don't have much left."

"No matter how we try, it's impossible to match the way we each do the glaze application," Maggie began.

"We don't want it to look like each half was done differently, so when we hit the crucial middle zone, we swap sides," Cara continued. "Then when we actual hit midline we both go over each other's side a little way."

"So when you see the wall as a whole it all blends together," Maggie finished.

"Hopefully, a work of art," Cara added, thankful it was nearly complete. She was tired, hungry and despite the fan, hot. She wrapped her hands around the tall frosty glass then sipped thirstily.

"Thanks for the drink." Maggie accepted her own drink. "We need it."

Susan took the last glass, peering at them over the rim. "Left a message for Faith. Her husband was watching the kids while she attended at a fundraiser meeting. He'll ask her to call me when she gets home."

"You don't think anything happened to Joan, do you?" Maggie asked, dropping to sit cross-legged on the floor.

Susan glanced away then back to gaze down at Maggie. "I wouldn't under normal circumstances."

"And two murders in your hometown certainly isn't normal," Cara agreed, not mentioning her own thoughts had stayed to possibly another crime.

"It's not only that," Susan admitted. She stared into her glass, not meeting Cara's eyes.

Maggie leaned forward. "What then?"

"When Joan went back to her job at the bank, she emptied Aimee's things out of the desk." Susan's words quickened. "Since Aimee was suddenly gone—everything was just as she left it—before the hit and run."

"The desk was still full of Aimee's stuff. We get that." Cara wanted Susan to spill whatever she was having trouble spitting out about Joan. Somehow, she knew whatever triggered Susan's roundabout talk was not good.

"You know how I'd been asking around about the deaths?"

"Investigating," Maggie added helpfully then scolded, "You promised us you'd stop."

"I try," Susan defended. "But everyone already knows and keep coming to me with stuff."

Cara tapped her foot, impatience building. "Go on?"

"Joan phoned to tell me she'd found a phone number scribbled on a scrap of paper with the name part torn off. It was Aimee's handwriting."

"I do that," Maggie said, before taking a sip of sweet icy tea.

"Joan called the number you know just curious to see if it was some mystery lover."

"And?" Cara lead.

"It was Sheriff Watt."

"Aimee had an affair with him?" Maggie gasped, her drink sloshing over the side off her glass to drip onto the drop cloth.

"No way!" Cara exclaimed, visualizing the guy. "Yuk!"

"Not lovers. Joan thinks maybe Aimee knew something about John Lawson's death." Susan's breath came quick and choppy along with her words. "Maybe she remembered something. Saw something and decided to report it to the sheriff."

"Makes more sense. Aimee seemed the type to go for money and not a frumpy middle-age small town sheriff."

"Right." Susan sagged against the doorframe. "Joan knew there'd be no romance that direction. It had to be something else—possibly something far more evil."

Chapter 7

"And then there's the box," Susan added as they digested her statement.

"What box?" Maggie unfolded gracefully as a dancer to stand beside Susan and Cara.

"A carved wooden one Joan found in a locked desk drawer, behind some files." Susan's hand trembled slightly as she set her half-full glass back onto the tray. "Joan said that Aimee must've hidden it. It never was there before."

"What's in the box?" Cara asked, surprised by this news.

"Don't know." Susan shook her head then raked fingers through her hair. "Joan couldn't open it. She thought it was a Chinese puzzle box and she was bringing it to me at the party, so I could try."

"Why you?"

"Daddy gave me an Oriental puzzle box when I was a girl and I'd hide my treasures in it." Memories clouded Susan's face and for a moment, a faraway expression saddened her eyes. She shook it off. "Anyway, I told Joan I might be able to open the secret compartments. But there are so many kinds of boxes that it might not be like mine at all."

A cell phone ring chimed. Susan jumped, laughed, and reached into her pocket. "I never get used to these. Oh, it's Faith! I'll be right back." She opened the French doors and bopped outside, clicking the doors shut behind her before the design duo could remind her about the heat.

Maggie shook her head. "Hope she doesn't roast."

"I give her two minutes," Cara said, watching their client perch on the lone patio chair leftover from pre-construction.

"We'll keep an eye on her," Maggie decided as they switched sides and returned to applying the glaze. "She's not used to Houston heatwaves."

A few minutes later, Susan wiped sweat off her brow as she returned inside. "It's sizzling outside."

Cara and Maggie exchanged a knowing look. "You got that right," Cara agreed. "I think you'd better sip some more of your iced tea. You're as red as a fire engine."

"And just as hot." Susan took several swallows before continuing. "Faith says Joan's in the hospital. She had an accident."

"Not another hit and run?" Maggie gasped, nearly flinging her sponge, flicking droplets into the air.

"Nothing like that." Susan took a long sip, draining her glass and setting it back on the tray. "She does have a bad concussion, cracked ribs, and a broken arm, though."

"What happened?"

"Going down her porch steps the night of the party, she tripped on a skateboard."

"Huh?" Cara stopped painting and turned to stare at Susan. "You said Joan didn't have kids—so what's a skateboard doing on her front steps?"

"Oh." Susan paled. "I hadn't thought of that."

Maggie didn't like the unrest settling over her like dank fog. "Maybe someone knew she'd found Aimee's stuff in the desk?"

"Maybe you better try to call Joan in the hospital and see if she has the box. There might be something crucial inside."

Maggie nodded at Cara's suggestion, wishing they didn't have to involve Susan in this, but there wasn't a choice. Susan knew Joan but they didn't.

"Okay." Susan hugged herself, looking more chilled than hot. "I'll go find the hospital phone number. Faith told me Joan's room number."

"Please let us know what you learn." Maggie watched Susan disappear into the hallway then turned to Cara. "Something's way wrong."

"Right." Cara bit her lip. "This is not good, Maggs."

"Not good at all," Maggie echoed.

"Your sexy lawman will not be pleased."

Icy dread stabbing her, Maggie shivered despite the heat. "Neither are we."

"We're almost done. Let's finish up and track down Susan." Cara attacked the last sliver of coral paint, muting it to a swirled honey sheen, then sponged partway into Maggie's area.

"You got it." Maggie mirrored Cara's movements. "Let's hurry."

೧೩೮

Fresh from her own shower, a light cotton sundress thrown on, Maggie tapped on the bathroom door. "Ready?"

Cara whipped open the door. "Let's find Susan."

"Are ya'll looking for me?" Susan asked, walking down the hall. "That's nice, since I was just coming to invite you to join us for dinner."

Cara perked up, but Maggie said, "We don't want to be a bother."

"No bother. I made chicken fettuccini and thought maybe one of you wouldn't mind tossing the salad and the other slicing the garlic bread while I set the table."

"My kind of meal." Cara marched after Susan, who pivoted direction toward the kitchen.

Maggie followed, the design duo trailing their client like ducklings follow their mother. "I dibs the bread."

In the kitchen, Cara chopped some tomatoes to add to the

salad, as Maggie broiled garlic and Parmesan cheese on the bread, while Susan flitted back and forth between the sleek china hutch and the dining room table.

"This is so fun," Susan said, smiling as she tiptoed to reach crystal goblets from the top shelf. "Meals can be so solitary here. This is like a dinner party."

"Let me get those," Cara offered, stretching a few inches higher. She took down two goblets at a time as Susan placed them on the table.

"You don't have to feed us," Maggie said, slipping her hands into oven mitts to remove the fragrant bubbling garlic bread from the oven.

Cara inhaled deeply, her taste buds salivating at the wonderful aromas. "This certainly beats fast food."

"My pleasure." Susan glanced around then dropped her voice low. "I have something to tell you before Ed joins us."

"What?" Maggie and Cara asked together.

"I talked to Joan. She sounds miserable." Susan frowned. "She asked a nurse's aide to bring her the box, but was told all she had with her was an evening bag."

"Not good," Cara said.

"Not all bad. Joan thinks she remembers dropping the box in the bushes as she fell."

"It probably flew right out of her hands," Maggie said, visualizing the fall.

"Anyway," Susan looked around again, her voice quiet. "I asked Faith if she and her kids would mind looking for it in the bushes in front of Joan's house. She promised to go over there tomorrow and search." Susan's hands fluttered as she took a breath. "We can't discuss this in front of my husband. He agrees with the sheriff that I should stay out of it."

Cara's gaze met Maggie's over Susan's head. "You should."

Maggie nodded. "Yes, he's right."

"Maybe this is all nothing." Maggie cheerfully arranged the garlic bread in a basket Susan handed her. "The accident, the box, the sheriff's number—just coincidence." Yet, even as she said it, Maggie sensed it was more than coincidence. And Sheriff Watt wouldn't be the only one ticked. Neither Ed nor Deputy Rice would be pleased with the three of them for pursuing it.

❧❦❧

Cara stretched and yawned, blinking her eyes open to glaring sunshine. Too bad, she didn't have auto-blinds in here, she thought, then realized those blinds were opened by culprit Maggie who stood by the window. Maggie grinned. "Wake up, sleepyhead."

"The alarm hasn't gone off yet," Cara defended, pulling the pillow over her head to shut out the sun and Maggie both.

"And it won't." Maggie ripped away the pillow. "The power's out. I keep telling you to set your cell phone alarm instead of some clock by the bed."

Groaning, Cara grabbed back her pillow, tucking it under her head instead of over her face. "That's why it's so miserably hot? No AC?"

"Air conditioning not working." Slippers flip-flopping, Maggie flitted to the adjoining bathroom door. "Electricity not working. Our crew is not working."

"And in this heat," Cara groaned, tossing off the sheet tangled around her legs. "We're not working."

"We have to," Maggie protested, pausing in the doorway.

"No power means no coffeemaker and no coffee." Cara rummaged through her clothes to find fresh undies and something cool to wear. She found a pink cotton T-shirt and cut-off jeans. Unprofessional, but in these sweltering temps—she didn't care. "Get me to the nearest Starbucks ASAP. Only then can I discuss working."

"We have to get the woodwork trim, baseboards and

ceiling molding painted before they deliver and install the diagonal wine-rack on Wednesday." Maggie used her school-marm voice.

Unfazed, Cara replied, "No coffee. No work."

On the way back, Cara waved toward the home improvement store just before they passed the parking lot entrance. "Stop here."

"Why?" Maggie asked, spinning the steering wheel in time to make the turn.

"You'll see." Securing her coffee in the cup holder, Cara grabbed her handbag and slid out of the van. "Be right back."

Fortunately, the power outage hadn't hit this section of town. Cara made her way to the aisle with electric fans, remembering an ad on TV the night before. She searched the shelves with no luck then finally spotted the item she needed on top. There was an orange and yellow rollaway stair parked mid-aisle. Since she hadn't seen a clerk or even a stock boy since she'd entered the store, Cara rolled the stair contraption over and began climbing.

"Uh, may I help you?" asked a large-size older man wearing a store nametag.

"I think I've got it." She leaned over to grab the box, just as the contraception rolled backward. He caught the stair-ladder, steadying it to save Cara and the box from toppling.

"Miss, we can't allow customers on this."

She smiled down at him, pretending she didn't notice his appreciative glance at her derriere. "Too late."

He quickly glanced away as if caught stealing quarters from a change machine. "At least hand me the box before you try to climb down."

"Here." Not admitting she'd been concerned about trying to balance the box on the way down, she handed it to him and hurriedly climbed off the thing.

When Cara arrived back at the van, she stowed the box in the rear then hopped back into the passenger seat. Cool air blasted at her full force through the vents. "Oh, this air conditioning is heaven. Thank you, thank you, Maggs, for keeping it on. Just coming from the store to the car about killed me."

"Don't joke about killing." Maggie pulled out from the parking lot, soon merging back into traffic. "Besides, if I hadn't kept it on, I would've fried to a crisp waiting for you."

"Southern-fried Maggie."

"Houston-fried, anyway." Maggie exchanged an answering grin with Cara. "So what's the mystery purchase?"

"One of those battery-powered fans."

"Did you get the battery?"

Cara stared at Maggie. "Uh, no. I got flustered when I had to climb this thing and then the guy came and told me I couldn't and then..."

As she tried to explain, Maggie flipped a U-turn and headed back to the store. "I think we'd better try again and read the box to make sure you get the correct battery. I'm not making any more trips. Got it?"

"Got it," Cara replied, feeling more than a tiny bit stupid for spacing off the *battery* part, since that was the whole idea.

ℰↄℰↄ

The new fan blowing back and forth through the sunroom dropped the temperature to a bearable level. Cara and Maggie brushed semi-gloss paint along the baseboard molding, each woman tackling a different side of the room. Cara pushed her bangs out of her eyes. Her hair felt damp wet, her entire body damp, clothes sticking to her uncomfortably—yet she felt almost guilty since they worked in the only room with even a breath of coolness.

"Poor Ed and Susan. The rest of the house must be unbearable."

"I know." Maggie blew a lock of her hair off her face,

and rocked back on her heels. "I heard Ed say something about a swim. Thank goodness the pool is still useable."

Cara stared outside through the windows at the shimmering blue among the trashed torn-up backyard. "The yard isn't. Don't want them to trip in a hole and sprain an ankle or something on the way across the lawn."

"We'd probably get sued."

"Susan's not exactly the sue-crazy type." Cara laughed then sobered. "But I'd hate for them to be hurt." She certainly hoped the crew had put their construction materials away properly. Just the terrain was risky enough.

Maggie followed her gaze. "I wouldn't blame them for braving the obstacle course. That water looks like an oasis right now."

"I'd dive in," Cara agreed, re-dipping her brush in the paint. "In fact, maybe we could request permission for a swim later?"

Maggie's green eyes sparkled. "Sounds like a plan!"

A few minutes later, they heard Ed boom, "Go ahead, sugar! I just want to grab my towel."

Susan padded barefooted into the sunroom, wearing a navy swimsuit with a matching towel tucked under one arm and waving her free hand. "We're going to splash in the pool and cool down. Don't you girls work too hard."

Cara held her breath, stopping to watch Susan scamper across the lawn, hopping over holes and dodging dirt and rocks. She exhaled as Susan made it past the torn up section and onto smooth grass. "Whew! She made it."

"Back to work," Maggie said. "Let's get done and then we can ask for a turn at the swimming pool later."

"You got it." Cara started painting again.

Just as Ed tromped into the sunroom, they heard a scream followed by a splash.

"Susan!" he yelled then lumbered through the French doors and across the patio. Both designers dropped their brushes and jumped up to race behind him.

As they reached the pool, they saw Susan face down in a

dead-man float. Dropping his towel, Ed jumped into the water, his giant splash swishing Susan farther from the edge. He swam with far more determination than skill, reaching his wife and grabbing her.

His frantic fumbling defied Cara's entire lifeguard training and she thought they both go under. "Flip her over," she cried, shedding her sandals and diving into the water.

"Tow her this way," Maggie called.

Cara instinctively took over the rescue, bringing Susan to the side where Maggie waited. Together with Ed helping to boost Susan, they hauled her out. As Cara worked on their client, Maggie called nine-one-one. Ed kept asking if his wife was all right and sticking his face in the way. Cara shooed him off as she tried to clear the water from Susan's lungs and get her breathing again.

Finally, Susan sputtered, spitting some water and starting to breathe on her own. By the time the EMTs arrived, she was still unconscious, her head bleeding, but her pulse felt stronger and she was breathing shallowly.

"It's all this construction stuff." Ed motioned around widely as the paramedics lifted Susan onto a stretcher. "What's this?"

"Oh, no." Cara blanched as she saw the oily puddle next to a tipped over can of linseed oil. "It's no wonder she slipped." Her horrified stare met Maggie's. *What had they done?*

જી心જ

Maggie felt sick. How could this happen? They had such a great crew, careful and responsible. They'd never had a client injured before. Through the thought-storm in her head, she heard Ed saying to the EMTs, "I'm riding in the ambulance with my wife."

"Sorry, sir. It's against regulations. You'll have to follow in your own vehicle."

"Damn the regulations." Ed tracked behind them as they transported Susan over the rough bumpy lawn then navigated through the side gate into the front yard.

"You can't ride with us." The senior paramedic's tone sounded firm. "She's stable. Get your car while we transfer her into the ambulance."

"We'll meet you there," Maggie offered, but Ed frowned and shook his head.

"No. You've done enough."

Though she realized it was his stress talking, alarmed and ashamed, Maggie watched him climb into the little red sports car, revving the engine then gunning down the street when the ambulance pulled away from the curb with lights flashing. The siren wailed as both vehicles careened around the corner.

Still dripping wet, Cara stepped up beside Maggie. "Hope she'll be okay."

"Me, too," Maggie whispered. "If she is—it's because of you."

"Instinct." Cara shrugged. Instead of looking like a drown rat, she looked like an Italian mermaid, but scared.

"You were amazing," Maggie said sincerely, with a flashback to their college days. She'd always loved swimming, but the lifeguard skills all belonged to Cara. "You saved Susan."

Cara twisted water out of her T-shirt. "Not exactly how I intended to take a dip."

Maggie hugged her soggy friend. "Go ahead and jump in the shower while I'll get hold of our crew lead, give him the lowdown, and get him over here."

"I'll give him—" Cara's dark eyes flashed.

"Fine. Save it for Al." Maggie grabbed the towel Ed had dropped and flipped Cara with it. "Go!"

As Cara dashed inside, Maggie remained standing on the pool deck, staring at the elongated puddle of oil. Sunlight tinted it with golden rainbow hue. It appeared so innocent—yet could've been so deadly. Thank goodness for Cara. She and Cara had always admired each other and enjoyed their friendship. They'd formed an instant bond when they met as giggly twelve-year-olds and that had grown with love and respect over the years. Sure, they drove each other crazy, but she couldn't imagine working with any other business partner. But she knew Cara better than anyone and at this moment she felt almost sorry for Al Black. Making sure their crew left the work site cleaned up and as safe as possible was his responsibility. Because of what happened to Susan, Cara would be a dragon.

Maggie hit his number on her cell phone. He answered and despite his sputtering response, she ordered him to report to the house immediately. For his sake, she wished they had a beam-me-up Star Trek transporter and could get him there while Cara was still in the shower. The renovation was already behind and they could *not* afford the time and grief to replace the guy. It didn't take a sixth sense to know that Cara was livid enough to fire him. She dreaded the explosion when the two of them came face to face.

☙❧☙

The oppressive humid blanket of heat made it impossible for Cara to dry off properly. She gave up and got dressed, her mood as ominous as the power outage and heatwave. It was so hot it seemed to suck the oxygen from the air when she stepped back out into the backyard where Maggie was pointing out the linseed spill to Al Black.

"Mr. Black!" Cara marched up to him and let her Italian sling, reaming him out for endangering their client.

He backed a few steps, but Maggie snagged his arm before he toppled into the pool himself. "Honest, boss," he defended. Broad-shouldered and muscular he towered over both females, but there was not an ounce of aggression in his manner. "We didn't leave this by the pool. It was stored over by the gazebo supplies and out of the way."

"Right." Cara wanted to push him backward—one good shove and he'd be in the water. "That linseed can just toddled over to the pool and then tipped itself over for fun?"

He tilted the brim of his baseball cap to shield his eyes from the sun. "Can't say what happened, but it wasn't left lying around."

Cara took immense pleasure in the fact that it still glared into his eyes. "Evidence proves otherwise."

Maggie touched her hand, but spoke to Al. "We've got a major job here to complete. This is a warning—don't screw up again."

Cara read Maggie's attitude and knew her friend was right. As much as she wanted to fire the man, this wasn't a good time. Still, if Susan wasn't okay—

"Consider yourself warned." Taking a deep breath, Cara balled her hands into fists at her side. "We won't tolerate anything like this again, Al. It's your responsibility to make sure the site is safe at the end of each work day. Your job's on the line."

"Yes, boss." He shoved his hands into his jean pockets. "I'll clean this mess up now and check everything."

"This heatwave's supposed to break by the end of the week," Maggie said softly, obviously in her peacemaker mode. "You and the crew report back to the job Friday morning, please."

"Friday," Cara snapped and then stomped back into the house still fuming. A warning was not nearly enough punishment for what had happened to Susan, but it must do for now.

Still, she intended to keep a close eye on him. This was the second time he'd set off her hackles.

She reached into the fridge for a cold drink. The interior was dark and losing the chill. "I've got an idea." She slammed it shut and spun around to Maggie who had followed her through the house and into the kitchen. "Let's go get some ice for the cooler we keep in the van and try to save as much of Susan's refrigerator stuff as we can."

"Great idea!" Maggie sounded relieved to have some positive action.

Cara recalled the way they'd dropped everything at Susan's scream. "We better clean up our paint first."

"Done. Did that and washed up while you were in the shower. Let me grab the keys and my purse first."

Before Maggie made it across the room, they heard the whirr of the air-conditioning and the hum of the refrigerator. "Power's on," Cara said, elated.

The phone jangled to life, all extensions ringing through the house. "We'd better answer it," Maggie said, not attempting to do so.

"Let it go to voicemail." The ringing persisted.

"But what if it's Ed from the hospital to let us know Susan's condition?"

"He'd call our cell phones." Cara hated answering other people's telephones. It felt so invasive.

"No." Maggie shook her head. "Susan has our cell numbers wanna a bet Ed doesn't?"

"Then you answer it."

Maggie scooped the receiver up on the fourth ring. "Hello, Dexter residence, Maggie speaking."

Cara listened to Maggs's side of the conversation. "Hi, Faith. Sure I'll give her a message." Maggie paced back and forth around the kitchen as she often did when talking. "You and the kids couldn't find any box in the bushes?" She halted, her eyes widening. "Just the skateboard, and it's brand new?" Maggie paced again. "You told your son he could keep it?...That sounds logical. Okay, I'll tell her."

"Well?" Cara demanded, not wanting to miss something.

"No box. All they found in the bushes was the skateboard. Her little boy asked if he could have it. She doesn't think anyone will dare claim it and admit they caused Joan's fall."

"What if it's evidence? Fingerprints?" Cara didn't believe for a moment the accident was innocent. No neighborhood kid had just accidently left a brand new skateboard on Joan's front step.

"After Faith and her kids handled that skateboard, it won't have any more prints than the first note did."

"Guess so." Cara agreed, but it niggled at her. "I think Joan might be lucky she survived that fall."

"On your wavelength. At least this time it was only *attempted* murder." Maggie bit her lip, sounding as worried as Cara felt.

Cara stared back at Maggie. "Let's hope the killer doesn't return to finish the job."

Chapter 8

The phone rang again, startling them both. "Your turn," Maggie said, leaning back against the kitchen counter.

Cara answered, half surprised to hear Ed's hello. Wasting no time, she asked, "How's Susan?"

"Fine. Had a few stitches in her scalp and they're keeping her overnight for observation. She wanted me to tell you."

"Thanks." Cara hesitated then added, "We're really sorry."

"Myself as well. I apologize for yelling at you girls." He sounded contrite. "I was just so upset and scared for my wife."

"We understand."

He cleared his throat. "You saved her. And I didn't even thank you."

"Not me. You'd already reached her."

"But I didn't know what to do. If you hadn't been there—" He choked up and Cara felt tears gather in her own eyes.

"We're just happy she's safe."

"Yep." His voice jollied again. "Don't look for me. I'll stick here at the hospital with Susan tonight."

When they hung up, she told Maggie the gist of the conversation.

Maggie teared up, too. "He sure loves her."

"Yeah," Cara replied. "Don't get all mushy. Let's go get some food. I'm starved."

"You're always starved."

Cara sighed, eying her friend's slender form with envy. "Unfortunately, true." Another thought struck her. "Before we go maybe you better call your deputy."

"Why?"

"Tell him about Aimee's box and Joan, so he's on alert."

"I don't have his number." Maggie acted nonchalant, but she didn't fool Cara.

Cara grinned, pointing to the address book by the kitchen phone. "Bet Susan does."

"I'm not calling him."

"Why not?"

"We've been scolded enough today."

Cara couldn't argue that.

Maggie felt guilty about not calling Deputy Rice, but she just couldn't do it. For multiple reasons. Yet if something more happened to Joan, she'd be responsible. She couldn't shake that out of her head. Tossing in bed, she wondered if Cara was asleep in the other bed or if, this time, she was the only one having trouble sleeping. At sunrise, Maggie actually felt grateful to have an excuse to get up and leave the night behind. One thought crystallized. When Susan returned, she'd put whether or not to contact the deputy into the client's hands. After all, Susan knew the players and she didn't.

Cara and Maggie watched from the guestroom window as Ed helped Susan out of the car and ushered her up to the house. As they heard the owners enter, they stayed in the room.

"Should we go see how Susan's feeling?" Maggie asked, wanting to, but torn.

"Maybe we should give them some space." Cara pulled

on her oversized and paint-splattered, but freshly washed T-shirt. "I think we should just get back to work in the sunroom."

"Okay." Maggie knew her friend was probably right. Besides, she still felt a little raw from Ed's lashing after the pool mishap. "I just hope Susan's okay."

"I'm sure we'll find out soon."

Maggie wished she felt as matter of fact as Cara, but unease settled over her as they entered the sunroom and pried open the paint cans. "I think Susan should decide whether we tell Deputy Rice about the box and Joan."

Cara paused, the screwdriver she was using to pop the lid hovering in midair. "Thought we were leaving Susan out of the loop?"

"We can't on that stuff. She's the one who told us."

"Oh, yeah." Cara scowled a tiny dent between her brows. "That lawman's going to be ticked at all three of us."

"But if Joan's in danger I don't want it on our heads." Maggie used a flat stick to stir the paint, making sure the bottom mixed as well as the top. It was a water-based latex semi-gloss for the trim and she didn't mind the smell. She *did* mind displeasing the handsome deputy though. Whether they told him or Susan did, it wouldn't end up a winning situation.

Why couldn't life be simple? Meet a handsome guy, fall in love, maybe even get married and live happily ever after. Instead of meet a guy, get fingerprinted, and interfere with his murder investigation? Not that there could be a future with the Mercerville lawman.

"Maggs!" Cara said with exasperation. "You're dripping paint all over the place."

Maggie noticed she'd over-dipped her paintbrush in the can and dribbled creamy splatters on the drop cloth. "Sorry, I was just thinking."

"Not about the job?" Cara stretched before bending into a squat, where she began brushing paint from the baseboard corner outward.

"Not about the job," Maggie agreed then wiped up her mess and started to paint.

"About the man?"

"About the man."

"Obviously, the man isn't sometimes-there and some-times-not Wes. Has he called or anything recently?" Cara edged along the floorboard a few inches then stopped to await the answer.

Realizing she hadn't even thought about Wes for a while, Maggie laughed. "You mean after that urgent *tele-conference* the night he'd promised to escort me to Tricia Long's wedding and I had to attend alone? Nope." She dipped her brush more carefully this time. "I won't get a call until he needs a back-up date for something. You know how he is."

"I do. Just glad you finally see it, too."

"Afraid the relationship's been convenient for both of us, because if I'd wanted him to commit, he'd have totally disappeared a few years ago." Maggie realized how true her words were as they tumbled from her mouth—and her heart. "He was my back-up while I searched for Mr. Right. And I was just his back-up date."

"Whew!" Cara grinned, her expression relieved as her voice. "I was so afraid you'd drift into something more with him and you deserve so much better than Wes."

"Thanks, pal." Maggie tossed a crumpled paper towel at Cara. She ducked and it bounced off the dry part of the wall. "Back at ya!" Maggie added.

"Hi!" Susan entered the sunroom, walking slower than normal and wearing a bandage on her forehead. "I always seem to catch you throwing things."

"How are you feeling?" Maggie asked, leaping to her feet to rush to Susan's side.

"Slight headache, but I'm good." Her wide smile swept both designers. "It's nice to have the AC working and I'm certainly not going to be tempted by the pool again until the grotto is complete."

Returning her smile, Cara added, "We're terribly sorry about your mishap."

"Sorry?" Susan's voice grew serious. "Ed said you saved my life."

"He'd already fished you out." Maggie listened to Cara, knowing her friend was embarrassed by the fuss, feeling she'd only done what she'd been trained to do.

"Thank you, my dear girl." Susan walked over to Cara and took hold of her free hand. "You were my guardian angel."

That tickled Maggie's funny bone and she couldn't prevent her giggle sputtering out. "That's the first time in my life I've heard *anyone* refer to Cara as an angel."

"True, Maggs." Cara grinned, chuckling. "Maybe I'd better mark this on the calendar."

Susan smiled as if they were children. "Oh, you two!"

"Almost forgot," Maggie said, deciding not to delay. "Faith called. They couldn't find the Chinese puzzle box in the bushes, just the skateboard."

Disappointment clouded Susan's face. "That's a shame. It has me curious."

"Me, too," Maggie and Cara said together.

"Did you tell her about my own little misfortune?" Susan gently fingered her bandage then rubbed her arm, drawing attention to a purpling bruise.

"No, we're leaving that to you." Cara's gaze followed Susan's action. "That must hurt."

"Not badly." Susan patted her thigh hidden by coral capris. "You should see the other bruises. I feel lucky it wasn't worse."

"Telling Faith isn't all we're leaving to you," Maggie admitted, determined to let Susan rule. "If there's a chance your friend Joan's in danger, maybe you should warn Deputy Rice about the box?"

"You're right." Susan frowned. "But I don't look forward to it."

"Don't blame you," Cara replied.

Maggie just nodded. She was glad the pressure had shift-ed away from her.

That night Cara heard a light tap on the guestroom door. "That's Susan," Maggie announced, not getting up as she flipped through some fabric swatches and jotted down several numbers.

"Duh, yeah—who else would it be?" Cara dropped her sketchpad onto the bed and popped up to open the door, al-lowing their hostess/client to enter.

Susan stepped inside timidly, as if it weren't her own house. "Hi! Got a minute?"

"For our favorite client, always." Cara ushered her to the bed since Maggie occupied the Soho chair.

"All the craziness I bring," Susan said as she sagged onto the edge of the bed. "I don't know how I can be your favor-ite anything."

"What's wrong?" Maggie dropped the swatches and rushed to Susan's side, scooting onto the bed to sit beside the older woman, taking Susan's hands in her own.

Not as demonstrative, yet equally concerned, Cara coaxed, "Talk to us."

"After I called Faith back, I decided I'd better tell Uncle Leland about my mishap before someone else did. He sounded so worried. I tried to explain that I'm fine, but he's not an easy man to convince." She sighed, a faraway ex-pression flashing over her face, as Cara and Maggie waited until she continued. "Then I decided you two were right and I needed to tell Deputy Rice about Joan and the box."

"And?" Cara leaned forward, wondering if Susan had re-ceived a blistering or if the lawman would save it for them. She saw Maggie tense awaiting the answer.

"He got mad at first, but listened. Then he asked ques-tions and made notes. He promised to check it out and watch out for Joan the best he can."

"That's all?" Maggie said, bouncing off the edge of the bed to cross to the window, but it didn't hide her mix of re-lief and disappointment from Cara.

"Not all." Susan grimaced. "When he heard that I'd promised Uncle Leland I'd visit to show him I'm fine, Deputy Rice insisted I bring you two along." She wrung her hands in her lap. "Sorry."

"He did?" Maggie spun back to them in excitement. "He wants us back in Mercerville?"

"Afraid so."

"Why?" Cara felt frustrated. *This Mercerville mystery stole way too much time from work and was getting out of hand.* Her gaze fell to the women on the bed, where Maggie's eager anticipation and Susan's hopeful expression arrested her protest.

"The deputy didn't state why just that it's imperative I bring you home with me." Susan gave them each a hug before she headed for the door, her usually quick step slowed from her injuries. "Sleep well tonight."

Once Susan left the room, Cara threw a pillow at the door. As it thumped to the bamboo floor, she grumbled, "That's for Deputy Rice."

"I think it's a great idea."

"You would." Cara retrieved the pillow, started to tuck it back on the bed, then changed her mind. Instead, she curled upon her designated bed, hugged the pillow to her chest, and moaned, "Not another trip to Murderville."

"Mercerville," Maggie corrected.

Cara kept her voice low, but wanted to scream. "We don't have time to go *anywhere*."

"Susan needs us." Maggie gathered up the sketchbook and the swatches, stacking them on the dresser. "Deputy Rice wants us."

"Wants you."

"Is that what this is about?" Maggs leveled a stare at Cara.

"Of course not." Cara felt guilty that it appeared to be about the deputy. "Have either of us *ever* let a man interfere with our friendship?"

"No." Maggie drew out the word into multiple syllables instead of the one.

"It's our *job*. Not the guy. You can make googly eyes at him all you want once we're done. You can fly to Timbuktu with him. Whatever." Cara pursed her lips. "But right now, we need to stay here on site and make up for lost time, not tool off again to the Hill Country."

"We can make it work." Maggie perched cross-legged on the bottom of the bed and ticked the points off her fingers. "The diagonal wine-rack style bookcase arrives in the morning and we can stain it. Al's promised to come install it when it's dry." Two fingers down, she tapped a third and fourth. "Drapery delivery on Thursday. Then our crew reports back to work Friday and they *know* what to do. With his job on the line, Al will keep them on track. Right?"

"I guess." Squeezing the pillow harder, Cara wished she could stop her unease about Al Black. There was something going on with him and she still intended to discover what.

"We'll get Susan to leave for Mercerville on Friday morning." Maggie finished with satisfaction in her voice, "Then we can return Sunday and be back here on the job Monday morning."

"We have so much to do, but I guess it'll work."

"It will," Maggie chirped, but Cara didn't feel nearly as certain.

೧೨೧

"You hit the right turn-off." Susan sounded impressed.

Cara laughed. "I think our van is trained now. It can drive us all the way to your hometown without me steering."

Susan chuckled. Staring out the passenger window, she suddenly exclaimed, "How lovely!"

"Wow," Cara gasped at the view. Under sunny azure sky, vibrant patches of blue, scarlet, violet and gold splashed across the rolling green hills. The colors undulated as wildflowers danced in the breeze.

"Awesome," Maggie cried from the backseat, pressing her nose again the window.

"I forget how beautiful it is." Sadness tinged Susan's voice. "Until each time I return home and it calls to my soul."

"No wonder." Maggie was a Houstonian born and bred. Despite her city girl roots, this stunning landscape stole her breath. "Makes you want to run through the meadows bare-foot and free."

"Not." Cara spun the wheel into the next turn. "Imagine the bees."

"Always the sensible one." Susan chuckled. Then she waved to the driver of a tractor slowly traveling alongside the lane as they whizzed past in the van.

"Do you know him?" Maggie asked.

"Probably not. Out here, we wave at everybody. It's the neighborly thing."

"And I thought they waved at us just 'cause we're irre-sistible," Cara quipped.

"The men certainly think you girls are." Susan's hazel eyes danced with humor.

"What men?" Cara prodded.

"The butcher, the baker, the candlestick maker?" Maggie volunteered.

"Close. Throw in the pharmacist, the mechanic, the shopkeepers, the lawmen—"

"One lawman," Maggie said softly, but her voice still carried up to the front seat.

"Maggs, you can have the deputy—but I get *all* the rest." Cara kept her tone light, winking at Maggie through the rearview mirror.

Susan began to giggle, sounding more like a teenager than a lady in her mid-forties. That set off Maggie who dis-solved into laughter. Cara joined in—glad that Maggs seemed to be over thinking that she shared the hots for

Deputy Rice. Cara just wanted her friend happy. Unfortunately, neither of them had the best luck with men.

At the Mercer manor, they'd barely hauled their things upstairs to their guestrooms, when Susan's voice floated up the stairway. "Girls, we have company."

Maggie and Cara trotted downstairs, but Susan wasn't in sight.

"In the study," she called.

Handsome and resplendent in his uniform, Deputy Rice stood by the fireplace. His gaze met Maggie's. She sucked in her breath, nearly stumbling. Thrilled as she was to see him, she wondered if he'd rip into them. She felt like blurting out "We didn't involve Susan—she involved us." Instead, she stared into his blue eyes and murmured, "Hi."

"Howdy." His gaze whiplashed from female to female to female, landing back on Maggie. "Now you're all together, we need to talk."

"About?" Standing hand on hip, Cara raised one brow.

"I interviewed Joan Gaynor at the hospital to see who, beyond Miss Susan, knew about the discovery of Aimee's box." The deputy twirled his hat in his hands, but kept his gaze on the women. "She told her boss."

"Elliot Ohlmacher," Susan interjected as the designers nodded.

Ignoring the interruption, Deputy Rice continued, "then she showed a few bank clerks who tried to help open the contraption." Frustration carved into his face, he tapped his hat against his leg. "Which in a town our size means—everyone in Mercerville knew by suppertime."

"Not so good," Cara said.

"That's bad," Maggie said, thinking how handsome he looked even when his expression was somber.

"Just what I expected." Susan spoke softly, entwining and untwining her slender fingers. "Things spread like wildfire here."

"Secrets are hard to keep in a small town." The deputy lowered his deep voice another octave.

"True words, Officer." Susan dusted an invisible spot on the fireplace mantel then turned back to him. "If only I could've seen that Chinese puzzle box. I'm sure I could've opened it and maybe found some clue for you."

"Nope. Let *me* find the clues." A vein throbbed in his jaw. "My job—not yours."

"We just want to help," Maggie defended, feeling more unsettled than ever about Joan's "accident" and wishing the box would surface.

"This might be nothing. Or it might be dangerous." His broad shoulders straightened, making him appear even taller. "Just let *me* take the reins on the investigation from here on out."

"You've done such a fine job so far," Cara reminded him, folding her arms across her chest.

"I've put the word out about the box. If anyone knows something, they can report to me. Not you ladies."

"What about the skateboard?" Cara persisted.

"Checked it out. Thousands just like it in stores all over the county."

"Prints?" Susan queried.

"After the rainstorm and Faith's kids, found nothing." He looked sheepish. "Let her boy keep it."

"That's sweet," Susan said with approval.

"Made sense. No point in hoarding it at the station." Maggie studied the deputy's long dark lashes until his tone jerked her back to the conversation. "I want each of you to promise no more snooping, no more interference."

Maggie swallowed, reluctant to agree, but not seeing a choice. "Okay," she replied, but her chin jutted up and her fists clenched at her sides.

"Fine with me," Cara agreed, showing no such reluctance.

"I promise to try," Susan said.

"Don't try. *Do* it," he commanded, obviously not concerned that he spoke to one of the town's chosen. He took hold of Maggie's arm and led her away from the others. "Question for you."

"What?" Maggie tried not to respond to his touch, but it was hard.

"Do you like pizza?" He gazed down at her, his voice gentling.

"Uh, s—sure," Maggie stammered, hoping and waiting.

"Lunch tomorrow?"

"Yes." She wanted to scream it, but keep her excitement in check and her reply cool.

"I'll pick you up here at noon." A quick grin flashed his dimple as he pivoted on the heels of his cowboy boots. He nodded to Cara and Susan, donned his hat and strode out of the room.

"What was that about?" Cara asked, as they heard the front door click shut behind him.

"A date."

"A date?" Susan repeated, eagerly joining them.

"He invited me to lunch tomorrow—for pizza." Maggie could hardly believe it, and she hoped no one else heard the jackhammer beat of her heart.

"How delightful!" Susan exclaimed.

Cara didn't look as pleased. "You accept?"

"Of course, she did." Susan laughed and hugged Maggie. "I love matchmaking. You and the deputy make an adorable couple." She smiled at Cara. "Now who do we find for you?"

"Never!" Cara recoiled in mock horror. "Matchmaker? Be gone!"

Susan appeared suddenly to wilt. She reached out to catch herself by the mantel. "Ohh."

"What's wrong?" Cara and Maggie asked in alarm, both steadying her.

"Trip home took more out of me than I expected." Susan offered them a wan smile, her free hand flying to her head. "I think I'd better wait and go see Uncle Leland tomorrow or I won't be convincing."

"Let us help you upstairs," Cara offered, tucking one arm in hers as Maggie took the other.

"Good idea." Susan let them led her to the grand staircase. There, she released Maggie's arm to place one hand on the banister, allowing Cara to keep hold of her elbow on the other side. "Maybe I'll have an early night and leave you all to your own devices."

"Don't worry we'll keep busy," Maggie assured her, following close behind as they climbed the stairway in case she needed to catch Susan to keep her from falling.

Maggie felt a heavy responsibility weighing upon herself, Cara, and their team. If the crew hadn't left the linseed oil out, Susan would be fine. Thank goodness, it hadn't been any worse. And that Susan possessed such a kind, forgiving nature.

"Did the hospital send you any medication?" Cara wondered as they walked Susan along the hallway to her room.

"Some pain pills," Susan admitted. "But I hate taking meds."

"I hear you," Maggie sympathized, "But you might reconsider just for tonight."

"Then you'll feel better tomorrow." Cara helped Susan settle upon the velvet chaise lounge. "We'll send Gladys up to you."

"Get some rest," Maggie called, as they exited the watercolor bedroom.

Once assured their client was in Gladys's capable hands, Cara collapsed onto the living room sofa. "Now what?"

"We eat." Maggie crossed to a little carved nook, where an old-fashioned telephone sat on a shelf atop a thin phonebook.

"Do they have Chinese take-out?" Cara asked, unable to smother the hopeful note.

"In Mercerville?" Maggie laughed, flipping through the phone book to the slim yellow-page section. "Fat chance. I just wonder if there's a hamburger joint or something close by."

Cara perked up, sitting up straighter. "Every town has a burger place."

"My thoughts exactly. Cheeseburger with fries and a milkshake sounds good about now."

"My expanding waistline disagrees with your choice, but, hey, I'll sacrifice."

"Aha," Maggie held up the phonebook. "Betty's Burger on Main Street."

"Main Street it is." Cara's stomach rumbled. "I'll run get the keys and my purse. You tell Gladys and see if they want to order anything."

"On it," Maggie replied, already dashing up the stairs two at a time.

Cara watched her friend with envy. Maggie's energy never seemed to flag.

෴

After midnight in the Ivy room at Mercer Manor, Cara punched her pillow into shape for the umpteenth time. Finally, she gave up the battle. She hated trying to sleep in strange beds, not that she'd seen her own bed for ages. She crawled out of bed and padded barefoot over to the window. Parting the curtains, she slid open the window to let the fresh country air blow inside, buffeting her nightgown and feathering her bangs. Cara stared out into the night, her eyes adjusting to the darkness.

Moonlight spilled silver through trees edging the far side, illuminating the lush landscaped grounds in eerie relief. Towering trees as old as the house itself held her gaze as leafy branches fluttered in the breeze. A movement drew her gaze lower. Cara froze as a dark shadow appeared to dash from one tree trunk to another. *Real or her imagination?*

Almost afraid to breathe, Cara stared into the night trying to distinguish shapes. She stood transfixed on the area until her vision blurred. She blinked her eyes to clear them. What had she seen? Was someone lurking in the dark—watching the house? Watching them?

Had she really seen anything at all? Would they discover another note in the morning? Or was it far worse—*the killer waiting to strike*?

Chapter 9

With Susan off to Uncle Leland's house and Maggie getting ready for the lunch date, Cara took the van and drove to Addy's Diner. Just for *lunch*, she assured herself, not admitting even in her thoughts that she might do some investigating on the side. After all, they'd dumped that in the deputy's strong hands. Hadn't they?

Yet, the mysterious shadow had haunted her throughout the night. She'd stood by the window for an hour staring into the darkness seeing nothing move. Eventually, she'd gone back to bed, but couldn't sleep, thoughts chasing through her head. When morning dawned, she didn't have the heart to ruin Maggie's thrill since her friend was floating about the upcoming date. And sharing the midnight watcher with Susan—no way! Besides, it might've been pure imagination. A trick of moonlight. Not a *murderer*.

Wonderful aromas assaulted her senses as Cara entered the diner to a chorus of howdy, and hellos from the other patrons. She smiled a return greeting at her fellow customers, recognizing a few from the party, but most totally new to her. The friendliness of Mercerville contrasted sharply with the big city. She'd always considered Houston a friendly city, but if she walked into a diner there probably nobody would acknowledge her arrival. Well, maybe a leer or two.

Instead of the seclusion of a booth, Cara perched upon a stool at the counter. *Just feeling social,* she told herself. Nan swiped a crumb away as she gave her a warm welcome. "What can I get for you, hon?"

"What's good?"

"Depends what you're in the mood for," Roger Mercer said, sliding onto the stool beside her, the inflection in his tone hoping for more than the menu offered.

Ignoring him, Nan tapped her order pad. "Roast beef sandwiches are the deal of the day. Slow-cooked, thin-sliced on white, wheat or sourdough." She rattled on, "Tomato, lettuce, pickle, onion, jalapenos, steak sauce, mayo whatever you want piled on with fries or onion rings on the side."

"Sounds great on wheat no onions. With fries." Cara was glad she'd set the espresso machine herself the night before—with her own *gourmet* beans, so she'd gotten her java fix this morning. She smiled, adding, "And a diet Coke."

"Ditto. Except to-go." Roger stretched his long legs, grinning as he drew out his wallet and pulled out several bills. "Didn't know I'd have such beautiful company for lunch or I'd have changed my appointment, so I could hang around here instead of rushing back to the quarry office."

"Such a loss," Cara said, softening her remark with a polite smile. Just because he was her client's cousin, didn't mean she had to socialize with him. Or like him.

He pretended to peek around her stool at the vacant one on the other side. "Where's your sidekick?"

"We aren't joined at the hip." Cara tried to tap down her sarcasm, but found it difficult. *Why did he irritate her so?*

"Good thing." He winked as his gaze rolled over her. "Your hips are perfect as they are."

"Do you mind?" Cara glared, but he sat unfazed as Nan handed her a drink in a glass and him one in a paper cup with lid.

"So where is your buddy?" he pressed again.

"On a date." Cara swiveled her stool the other way, turning her back to him.

He spun her back. "A date, huh? Anyone I know?" He chuckled. "If it's a fine citizen of Mercerville, of course I do."

"None of your business." Watching him and blatantly listening as she bustled between the counter and kitchen, Nan slammed a paper bag onto the counter. "Here's your order now skedaddle."

"Springing for hers, too." Dropping a wad of bills onto the counter, he thumbed toward Cara with a grin. He picked up his drink and bag, slid off the stool and sauntered out the door.

"Good riddance," Nan muttered as the door jingled shut behind him.

"You don't sound too keen about one of your town sons." Cara didn't have a lot in common with this diner owner, but she felt a kinship over their dislike of Roger Mercer.

"Got that right." Nan slipped a plate with an over-stacked sandwich and home-cut fries onto the counter. "If yer as smart a city gal as I expect you won't waste your time with the likes of him."

"Not in my plan." Cara squished down half the sandwich to flatten it enough to bite. "Just curious—why don't *you* like him?"

"He's been trouble since his wild teen days, but as a *"Mercer"* always landed on his feet. Then there's the thing when Susan lost her pa."

"What thing?" Cara munched a delicious bite of roast as she awaited the answer.

Nan wiped her hands on a dishtowel and leaned down to whisper. "Word is that Roger got in a wrangle over old Tom Mercer's will. Threatened to contest it."

"A wrangle with Susan?" Cara remembered the comradely between cousins and this didn't compute.

"Our sweet Miss Susan?" Nan's multiple chins jiggled as

she laughed at the idea. "Naw, not her—with the family lawyer—the one who croaked."

ᴄ⁄ᴈᴄ⁄ᴈ

Meanwhile at the house, Maggie checked her reflection in the mirror, pivoting this way and that to swing her green sundress with copper and bronze metallic threads across the tufted bodice and edging the ruffle sleeves. She wore bronze wedge sandals to coordinate with her bronze dangle earrings and matching bracelet. *Would the deputy like her outfit?* It hadn't been easy to figure out what to wear for the lunch date with her limited selection of traveling clothes. Maybe that was good if she were home, she'd probably have changed clothes for the umpthteenth time.

She dashed downstairs as the doorbell chimed then stopped and took a breath before swinging open the door. "Hi!"

"You look good," Deputy Rice drawled, the appreciation reflected in his voice and his expression.

"You do, too," Maggie said, the words tumbling out too fast. "Ah, I mean in your uniform and all."

"On duty." He grinned, amusement dancing in his eyes as he gazed down at her and offered his hand. "*You* are my lunch break."

"Oh, okay." Maggie liked the way he opened the passenger door of the patrol car for her, waiting to close the door after she slipped inside, and then again opening the door for her when they parked on Main Street in from of Pete's Pizza.

Inside, Maggie inhaled the scrumptious pizza smells, her gaze lighting on two signs: *Seat Yourself* and *Cash Only*. They made her smile, especially the *cash only,* that one was a rarity in the big city, but here it seemed appropriate and not surprising at all.

The deputy took her arm and guided her around tables

adorned with red-checker tablecloths and red votive candles. Then waited for her to slide into a corner booth. For a moment, she thought he might sit next to her, but instead he took the seat across the table. She told herself that was better, so they could see each other and converse.

"What do you like on your pizza?" he asked, handing her a menu card from between the salt and pepper shakers. "Ladies' choice."

"Anything but anchovies," Maggie replied, tucking the card back into place.

"Brave enough to try Pete's Supreme? Got a dozen toppings."

"Onions, too?" she asked, remembering a girlfriend had told her back in school that if the guy ordered something with onions it meant he didn't want to kiss. *Odd to remember that now.* She told herself it was silly, but waited for his reply.

"We can leave those off."

She smiled, exhaling the breath she hadn't realized she'd been holding. "Sounds good."

When the pizza came, it was better than good. Maybe the best tasting pizza she'd ever eaten. They concentrated on the meal until he suddenly said, "You aren't doing anymore snooping, are you?"

"We haven't even discussed it since you reamed us out," Maggie answered honestly.

"Good. I'm impressed." He took a third slice of pizza then glanced back up at her. "I was afraid you ladies were like bloodhounds on a convict's scent."

"Hardly. If I recall—you *ordered* us to stop. You didn't leave us a choice, did you?"

Pizza slice raised halfway to his mouth, he stared at her. "There's *always* a choice."

Maggie looked down at her plate, ignoring his gaze, in case he could read her reluctance to let go of the investigation.

"So spill."

Her gaze flew back to his face. "Huh?"

"When I overheard you at the birthday party, who was the suspect you were adding to your list?"

"Just someone staring at Susan all night." Maggie felt uncomfortable and wished he hadn't brought up the subject.

"She looked nice. For her age."

"This was different—intense. Filled the room with strange vibes."

He cocked his head, examining Maggie as if she were a piece of evidence. "Who?"

"An accountant guy."

"*Kirby*?" He chuckled, his tone indulgent as if she'd accused the Easter Bunny. "Kirby Ballentine has known Susan Mercer since she was a child. He's their family friend as well as financial planner. He certainly has no nefarious plans for her."

Maggie felt miffed. "How do you know, Deputy Rice?"

"Jake," he corrected in his deep rich voice. "So why do you think Kirby would harm John or Aimee? This is about *their* deaths, correct?"

"We hadn't figured that out. You stopped our investigation, remember?"

"I thought you might stir a rattlesnake from the rocks, but if you were looking in Kirby's direction, not much danger there."

Maggie's chin jutted up. "I'm sure we could've found a connection between Ballentine *and* the lawyer *and* the secretary."

"True. A natural one, though." The deputy was on the verge of laughter again, tempting Maggie to kick him under the table. "John and Kirby worked together for decades and they were great friends."

"Things are not always as they appear."

"Do you know who helped Aimee Travis clear out John Lawson's office after his death? Kirby. That's the kind of guy he is."

"Ted Bundy was a nice guy, too. Ask anyone—except his victims."

"Kirby even helped Aimee haul all the files from the law office into the Garrett Building. He didn't have to do that."

"Files?" Maggie sat up straight, her pulse racing. "Did you check out the files?"

"Nope."

"Why not?"

"No reason. Remember, we thought John's death was a burglary gone bad."

"Do it now."

"Can't. Place caught on fire and burned down."

Maggie nearly choked on her pizza. "And that wasn't suspicious?"

"Not at the time. The building was old, not to code, and a hazard." A scowl carved deep lines into his tanned face. "And Aimee Travis was still alive."

Maggie swallowed. "Now what do you think?"

His eyes darkened to midnight blue as he rubbed his jaw. "Now I wonder if a sinister thread connects all three events."

Thinking of Cara's tapestry theory, Maggie murmured, "Murder unraveled."

೮ාඌා

Back at the diner, Cara pushed her nearly empty plate away, glancing down at the small pile of leftover fries. She had forced herself to leave those alone. They were golden, crisp, a tiny bit spicy, and bad for her diet. "Nan, think I've done enough damage. Check please?"

"Roger paid. Remember? Eat this before I'm letting you leave." Nan placed a slice of peach pie in front of Cara.

"Mmm." The fragrance of cinnamon and warm peach, dominated her defenses, still she slid the pie back toward Nan. "I shouldn't."

"Ya should." Nan wagged a finger at her. "Men don't want a stick. They want a real woman with curves and something to love."

"There's already plenty of me," Cara said with a laugh as Nan shoved the pie back at her.

"You city gals fall for all that movie and TV stuff. But a real man still wants a real woman."

"Maybe just a few bites."

Cara dove into the flaky crust with her fork then tasted a bite of warm peach. She allowed herself five bites before plopping her napkin over the rest.

She felt someone staring and glanced toward the booths lining the window to see a dark-eyed young man in a blue work shirt and worn jeans, watching her intently from the corner booth.

He smiled, flashing even white teeth. She smiled back and looked away just as Nan reappeared.

"Who's that guy?" she whispered to Nan, feeling more cautious than flattered after that shadow stalker last night. Possibly an *imaginary* stalker, she reminded herself.

"Bobby Ray Clemens—town mechanic." Nan sniffed. "If you want someone with a chip on his shoulder, he's yer guy."

Interest peaked, trying to remember something Susan had told them, Cara leaned forward elbows on the counter. "Why?"

"Quite a list including that, ah, *secretary* who got run over," Nan paused to swish off the counter then continued, "She was engaged to Bobby."

"Oh, yeah, Aimee—the hit and run victim." Facts Susan confided flowed back into Cara's mind.

"Yep. They were engaged, but she dropped him for a better mark—Roger Mercer. They didn't last though. He probably learned what a tart she was."

"She made the rounds with the guys, didn't she?"

"Yep. Ruffled feathers. Maybe somebody's wife, or girl mowed her down—not some stranger. Can't say anyone deserves to go that way, but she had enemies."

"Was she involved with that new community I keep hearing about, the fancy places down by the lake?"

"Wouldn't know and don't care."

"New people might help your business," Cara suggested, toying with her straw, thinking the type of people moving in probably would view the diner as a unique throwback. Maybe make it trendy. Oh, how she wished she could tackle decorating some of those homes.

"Shoot, they'll turn their noses up at my place."

"I doubt that. Everything old is new again," Cara added, realizing the truth in that statement. She saw it all the time in design. Everything cycled and came back around.

Nan merely grunted and scrubbed at a nonexistent spot on the counter.

"Thanks for the yummy food," Cara said, sliding the strap of her handbag onto her shoulder. "And thanks for sharing the local color."

"A pleasure, hon. Come back soon."

"Will do," Cara replied, wondering how much fat, carbs, and calories she'd consumed and deciding she better not return to the diner for a while. But the tidbits she'd learned during her lunch? Now those she couldn't wait to share with Maggie.

Cara arrived at the house to find Maggie there, but not Susan. "Hey, Maggs, how was the date with the deputy?"

"Jake is a cool guy." Maggie had changed into more casual clothes, but she still sparkled.

"*Jake*, huh?" Teasing, Cara watched her friend.

A dreamy expression drifted across Maggie's pixie face. "Deputy Jake Rice."

"So how does the deputy kiss?" Cara asked, watching red flare on Maggie's freckled cheeks.

"Who says we kissed?" She stuffed hands into her pockets, looked down at the floor, and shuffled her sandaled feet.

"Hot lips Maggie?" Cara laughed. "Of course, you kissed."

"He kissed me once in the patrol car, just before he walked me to the door."

"Oh la la! I've never made-out in a police cruiser. Was it hot?"

"*Jake* is hot." Maggie glanced back up and smacked her lips then touched her mouth with her fingertip. "Mmm."

"Whew! I can feel the heat from here." Cara pretended to fan herself. "Deputy Jake Rice, Maggs's new conquest."

"I wouldn't say that."

"You don't have to—I just did." Cara thought about what she'd learned at the diner. "Hate to crash you back to earth, but did he discuss the murders?"

"Some." Maggie traipsed into the kitchen and poured a glass of lemonade for each of them. "The guy who stared at Susan, Kirby Ballentine, he worked with John the lawyer and even helped clear out the office after the murder."

"Makes sense. They both handled Susan's family affairs." Cara sipped her drink, pulled a face, then set it on the counter.

"Too sweet, huh?" Maggie dumped her lemonade into the sink and rinsed her glass. "Anyway, the place he and Aimee stored the files—burned down."

"What?" Cara digested the information. "That's suspicious. Did they investigate?"

"No." Maggie wandered outside into the fairytale yard with Cara trailing behind. "Jake says the building was an old firetrap, and Aimee was still alive, so they didn't have a reason to pursue it."

"Does Deputy Rice suspect Ballentine?"

"He should, but he doesn't." Maggie wandered around the flowerbeds, a tiny scowl furrowing her brow. She trailed her hand along the top of chamomile blossoms and lavender plumes to release their perfume into the air. "He could be too close to the players to see the whole picture. But I've been thinking and might have it figured out."

"Tell me?" Cara touched her friend's arm and Maggie turned to her, green eyes serious.

"Remember I promised to find a motive for Kirby Ballentine? Maybe Ballentine was doctoring the books—the lawyer found out—so Kirby knocked him off and torched then the files and the evidence."

"What about Aimee the secretary?"

"She knew too much."

"Bursting your bubble, but why wait three months to take care of her?"

Maggie shrugged. "Maybe he finally realized what she knew? Or she tried to blackmail him."

"A possible scenario but I have another."

"About Ballentine?"

"No what if someone *else* killed Aimee?" Cara settled on the bench by the angel fountain, watching the water shimmer in the sunshine. "Nan repeated that Aimee ditched her fiancé to date Susan's cousin."

Maggie grimaced. "Obviously, that female hooked up with every male in town."

"Not the point. The secretary was engaged to the town mechanic, Bobby Ray Clemens, then dumped him for a richer model." Cara raised a brow. "Could drive a man to murder."

"Ah ha! Kirby did in the lawyer, later the ex-fiancé plows down Aimee. Two crimes—two killers."

"Unless Cuz Roger knocked off the family lawyer."

"Why?"

"Nan told me Roger got in a wrangle with John Lawson over Susan's dad's will."

"Oh, yeah, we heard about that before, too."

"Guess it's time to resurrect our suspect list."

"Both lists."

"Here ya'll are!" Susan called from the doorway then stepped out into the garden to join them. She walked carefully as if still hurting. "What *lists*?"

"Just work stuff," Maggie said with the save. "You know those famous to-do lists of ours."

"I've seen those lists," Susan replied with a chuckle.

"You two should be famous for list making."

"We try," Cara added, scooting over to make room for Susan next to them on the bench.

"How did it go with your uncle?" Maggie asked eager to change the topic.

Susan sighed. "He's still concerned about me, but I'm more concerned about his health. He doesn't seem well."

"He's sick?" Maggie felt a rush of concern.

"Says not, but he looks rough." Susan blinked away the tears visibly gathering in her hazel eyes. "Dad was just about Uncle Leland's age when his heart began acting up. I hope that's not happening to my uncle. I can't bear to lose him, too."

Maggie put her hand over Susan's. "You won't. I feel he's got a lot of years left in him."

"Right," Cara assured their client. "Trust Maggie's instinct. Her sixth sense is amazing."

Dabbing her eyes and offering them a weak smile, Susan asked, "Where were you fifteen years ago when I eloped with my first husband?"

"Probably in seventh-grade math passing notes to Cara." Maggie chuckled, jumping up to pull Susan to her feet. "We need to explore. Didn't we pass a lovely lake just outside of town? Show it to us."

"Wonderful! I haven't been there for ages," Susan said, delight rich in her voice. "Let's get some bread crumbs from the kitchen, so we can feed the ducks."

"Yeah, feed the ducks," Cara muttered, a few steps behind them. "Excitement in a small town."

Always tuned in to her friend, Maggie heard, dropping behind Susan to poke Cara's arm and whisper, "There's been enough excitement—bring on the ducks."

❧❧❧

That night, Maggie padded back and forth barefoot

across the carpet in the Ivy room while Cara sat at the vanity, applying night cream. "Where's the notebook?"

"On top of the chest of drawers," Cara replied, waving white creamed fingers that direction. "You'll find our original suspect lists about mid-book."

"Maybe we should start new ones."

"Why?" Cara finished her nightly ritual and turned to Maggie.

"Whoa! You could scare off guys that way." Maggie laughed at the white froth covering Cara's face like a marshmallow mask, leaving only eyes, mouth, and nose clear.

"If you were a *guy,* I wouldn't be wearing goop on my face."

"Unless you were married to him twenty years and didn't care."

"I'd always care."

"Me, too," Maggie admitted, hoping someday they both could test their theory. "Let's get back to our mission, finding the Mercerville murderer to keep Susan safe."

"Don't forget there might be two different killers."

"If there are two, then who left the skateboard that took Joan down?"

"Aimee's—because it was for her puzzle box."

"Okay, then who left the threatening notes for Susan?" Maggie flipped to the suspect lists. "The same killer—or the other one?"

"Good question." Cara turned back to the mirror and began wiping the cream off her face, her gaze meeting Maggie's in the mirror. "Now we need to figure out the answer."

Chapter 10

"Susan won't be pleased with us if she sees these lists," Maggie cautioned, perching on the foot of the bed.

"Because we agreed to stop investigating and didn't?"

"No. I bet she hasn't stopped either." Maggie studied the list and waved it in the air. "But look, most of our suspects are *her* friends or family."

"I don't think she considers Darlene Lawson a friend." Cara moved to sit on the bed and peer over Maggie's shoulder at the notebook. "Or that banker Elliot Ohlmacher."

"Maybe not them, but we've got Kirby Ballentine, who everyone claims is her old family friend, plus her cousin Roger. That can't be good." Maggie felt strange vibes as she checked over the names, but couldn't focus it onto one person. "And who knows if she's buddies with the mechanic. We do know she's friends with Joan."

"Let's strike Joan Gaynor off Aimee's list, after all Joan was an attack victim herself."

"True." Maggie scribbled Joan's name off then chuckled. "We have that mysterious secret lover of Aimee's. Susan won't object to him."

"He's only on Aimee's list. If you consider both murders, Darlene Lawson has the strongest motive to knock off both off them. We should find out what she drives. Maybe a dark SUV?" Cara tugged her nightshirt to cover her thighs. "My money's still on her."

"But if we're looking for two separate killers, there are a lot more suspects on Aimee's list than on the lawyer's."

"Possibly more Aimee suspects than we imagine." Cara grinned. "According to Nan there might be a slew of wives and girlfriends who were gunning for that little man-eater."

"We might have to uncover their identities, huh?"

"*Maybe*. Right now we need to dig up the dirt on those we already have listed."

"Sounds cool." Maggie closed the notebook, yawned and bounced off the bed. "It's late. Let's call it a night."

"Wait!" Cara said, jumping up to dash to the window. "What time is it?"

"Almost midnight. Why?" Maggie asked, not liking Cara's sudden tenseness.

"Turn off the light and come here. I need to tell you what happened last night, after you were asleep."

Maggie obeyed, flipping off the light and padding over to Cara's side. "I slept through something?"

"Not sure." Cara parted the curtain to peer out in the darkness.

"Explain?" Maggie asked, a chill racing over her arms.

"About this time last night I was looking out the window when thought I saw a shadow dart between those trees on the far side."

"A person?" Maggie tried to distinguish silhouettes of the landscape, but clouds blew across the moon, casting the night in deeper shadow.

"Couldn't tell. I thought so. Afterward, I stood here forever but saw nothing more."

"Why didn't you wake me?" Maggie hated the thought of Cara standing here alone searching the night, watching someone out in the darkness watching them.

"The entire household was asleep." Cara sighed, a dent above one brow. "Maybe I imagined it."

Maggie shivered. "Maybe you didn't."

ɕↄɕↄ

Sunday evening, found them settling back in at the Houston house. Cara fell into the white Soho chair in their guestroom. "Whew! Hope we don't need to go back to Mercerville again."

"I don't mind it at all. It's a beautiful town."

"Beautiful *deputy*, you mean," Cara teased.

"He is that." Maggie buzzed back and forth sorting and putting away her things.

"You know we have to work double-time to make up for our little jaunt." Cara watched Maggie, as always amazed at her friend's energy level.

"No, we don't. The crew's behind on the exterior transformation, but we're still on track with our sunroom reno and patio."

"We're behind on the gazebo and yard, though."

Maggie shook her head. "Nope, our part's not ready for us to do, so that doesn't count."

"Does."

Maggie halted to fold her arms across her chest. "Does not."

"Let's not argue." Cara said, with a yawn. "I'm too tired. Point is—to meet our deadline, we need to work hard and fast."

"Then tomorrow morning, we better start early."

Cara groaned, realizing she'd asked for it.

Monday dawned, hot and cloudless as Cara stumbled onto the patio struck by the glaring bright sunshine. Squinting and armed with her coffee, she said, "Who ordered *three* palm trees?"

"Uh, *we* did. And now we're adding the antiquing glaze to those terra cotta pots. Next we're hanging fabric in the gazebo. Remember?" Already busy at work, Maggie laughed, handing Cara a brush and a can. "You aren't awake yet, are you?"

"Trying." Cara blinked, sipping her steamy cup of heaven. She handed the can and brush back. "Instead of this, let's head to Old Town Spring and hit the antique stores. We still need to find a chaise, urns and some ironwork we could use for the Ruby Glow Passion vine as a trellis."

"You are *brilliant*," Maggie replied, stuffing things into the corner and ready to play. "Shopping trumps work."

Appearing much more awake, Cara grinned. "Come on, let's go to Spring."

Old Town Spring was a fairyland to both designers, but Maggie especially responded to the history-laden atmosphere and the promise of surprise and priceless finds. Feeling blessed to hold a job she loved and shop from designer specialty stores, to auctions, to tiny antique shops such as these, Maggie floated from shop to shop.

A bell tinkled welcome as they entered Ginger's Treasures. Inhaling the unique musty scent, Maggie felt as if she stepped through a portal back in time. She heard voices of history echoing inside her head like whispers from the past. Each touch of her fingers dancing over an object, from the tiniest hand-painted thimble, to marble lion bookends, to the smooth mahogany of a towering antique armoire vibrated with spirits of lives once lived and tales untold.

The designers were browsing through the cluttered assortment of all things old, when a Black Forest cuckoo clock struck as an eighteenth century grandfather clock chimed, giving Maggie a thrill as she pondered who had once had their schedules guided by the beautiful timepieces.

"What about this?" Cara asked, standing by a Tuscan urn of rustic copper.

"It'll work in the sunroom or on the patio, not in the gazebo," Maggie replied, refocused on the job. "Look! There's a chaise lounge toward the back of the shop and several Tuscan style lamps and lanterns."

Cara waved toward the far side where an old wrought iron gate leaned against the wall. "I can see the vines twining through this alive with blooms."

"Oh, yes!" Maggie agreed with escalating enthusiasm. "And see these…"

The day dissolved into unearthing treasure—yet they still returned to the Dexter house by nightfall.

***

Somewhere out in the night, a barely visible silhouette moved from trees and bushes up to the door. Once there, a white square flashed as a gloved hand shoved the note into the mail drop. Mission accomplished, the figure merged into darkness, disappearing into the night shadows.

***

The following morning, agitation apparent, Susan fluttered outside onto the patio, oblivious of the noise and commotion. "Poor Joan!"

"What's wrong?" Cara asked, planting the passion vine arrested as she spun around.

"I thought your friend was doing fine," Maggie added, dropping her spade to rush to Susan's side.

"Joan is. Was. I mean she went home from the hospital yesterday, but she just called and she's freaking out!"

"Why?" the designers chorused.

"Joan was crying and I could barely understand her," Susan said, translating panic herself. "But the killer left her a note."

"Oh, no!" Maggie cried.

"What did it say?" Cara demanded, tingling with bad vibes that obviously echoed Maggie's.

"'Next time you won't be so lucky,'" Susan quoted, skin paling as she sagged back against the French doors for support.

"Did she give it to Jake—I mean Deputy Rice?" Maggie slipped her arm around Susan.

"Yes. He says it matches the other notes. They're testing it for fingerprints and all that now. But Joan is falling apart."

"I bet," Cara said, feeling deep concern that the killer was still lurking.

"Remember how scary it was for us in Mercerville when Gladys found that note? And poor Joan is totally alone. She's terrified!"

Maggie's eyes grew dark and thoughtful. "That's awful!"

"Joan needs to get a dog," Cara announced.

"That's what my Aunt Jane in New Orleans did when her daughter moved out," Maggie said in agreement. "I remember how alone my aunt felt until she got Corky for a companion."

"I suggested that." Susan's voice faltered. "But Joan said if someone was cruel enough to kill Aimee, they wouldn't hesitate to poison a pet."

"So what's her plan?" Cara asked, not seeing a solution, and resumed her project.

"She's decided to move in with her widowed cousin in Florida. I guess her cousin's been bugging Joan to go join her for two years, but I never imaged Joan would leave Mercerville."

"She's running away because of the note?" Maggie quizzed.

"Our hometown's not the same for her since all the Aimee stuff."

"Aimee stuff?" Cara knew the notes were upsetting—but uprooting your home? That was deep.

"Joan losing her job to Aimee Travis, then Aimee's murder, Joan getting her job back at the bank, finding Aimee's puzzle box in the desk there, then her own near-miss accident that could've killed her, too!" Susan took a breath. "And now this note knocked her over the edge."

"Home isn't a cozy sanctuary anymore." Cara sympathized, packing the soil around the roots and sliding the planter box into position before watering it.

"Can't blame Joan." Maggie still abandoned all attempt at work, her attention glued on their client. "I wouldn't feel safe alone in Mercerville now, either."

"What about her job at the bank?" Cara asked. "She just got it back."

"She doesn't care anymore, says it's not the same, anyway, haunted by Aimee."

"Is she giving two weeks' notice?"

"Definitely not. She owes Elliot Ohlmacher no loyalty— not since he replaced her with Aimee." Susan pursed her lips. "Besides, he'll find some young pretty thing to hire."

"Joan just wants to escape," Maggie said. "I understand her wanting to leave all the bad stuff behind and begin anew."

"That's why I promised to help her pack her things." Susan sounded exhausted. "I didn't want another trip home so soon, but what can I do? With Joan's broken arm and cracked ribs, not counting getting over a concussion, she needs me."

Cara froze. *This wasn't good.* "She needs to hire movers."

"She will, but all her personal belongings...you know?"

"Can't someone else help her?" Maggie asked. "Maybe your neighbor Faith?"

Susan shook her head, acting resigned. "Faith would drag along her three little rascals and they'd be more trouble than Faith would be help."

"You aren't up to moving and packing for Joan," Maggie pointed out. "It's our fault you're walking wounded yourself."

"No choice. Friends help friends."

"Isn't there *anyone* else?" Cara asked, her *own* sixth sense warning it'd involve them as well as Susan.

"Not really."

"Then we'll go with you and help," Maggie volunteered just as Cara dreaded.

"I can't ask that."

"We volunteered." Before Cara could protest, Maggie shot a don't-argue glare and added, "Since you're injured because of our crew's negligence, it's only fair."

"With our help, you'll be done in half the time," Cara said, knowing Maggie was right and feeling guilty about Susan's pool mishap.

"If you're sure?" Susan asked on a hopeful note.

"Definitely," they said together.

When Susan left them alone again on the lanai, Cara stuck one side of the wrought iron gate into the dirt and carefully wound the vines through the open grillwork. "Back to Mercerville? This is getting ridiculous, Maggs."

Maggie shrugged. "What else can we do?" She played with untamed vines, re-enforcing Cara's efforts. "With all three of us, we can get done fast and be back here pronto."

Cara watched the tell-tale blush stain Maggie's face. "You just want to see your deputy."

"Maybe that, too" Maggie continued. "At least the killer's focused on Joan instead of Susan."

"Not much comfort in that," Cara disagreed, as they retreated inside to cool off and escape the construction racket. "Since it's luring Susan back to Mercerville and the murderer's lair."

"You're right. I hadn't considered Joan's note taking Susan back there."

"And us," Cara grumbled, not pleased, but determined to make the trip as quick as possible. "I need to discuss some things with Al if we plan to take off again."

"Okay, but go now. If you wait until we're done with this, they'll be on lunch break."

"Good idea." Cara wiped her hands on a rag. "Be back in a few."

Cara stepped back out into the bright sunshine and sultry heat to the racket of her crew working full bore. Raoul's power saw ripped through sheets of lattice sending cedar dust and splinters flying. Craig and Pete were laying the forms for the cement pour. Jim and Tiko hung off on ladders painting the gazebo.

Raoul stopped the saw. "Si?"

"Where's Al?" Cara asked, not hiding her impatience.

He gestured palms up and shoulders shrugging. "Had to go. He had business to take care of."

"Yeah, business *here*!" Cara's foot tapped with annoyance. "So when will he be back?"

"Do not know." Raoul repeated his gesture, this time shaking his shaggy hair and frowning. "He left Jim in charge."

Cara stomped across the lawn to the gazebo, skirting holes and construction clutter on the way. "Jim, where's Al?"

"Something came up—he'll be back in a jiffy." Jim watched her from atop the ladder, obviously surprised by the edge in her voice.

Still, she couldn't tamp it down. "Send him to me as soon as he gets back."

"Yes, Ma'am."

Suddenly, the entire crew began working harder and faster. Cara sighed. She didn't mean to be the bad guy, but Al's disappearing act just added fuel to her frustration with him.

The moment she re-entered the sunroom, she said as much to Maggie.

"Calm down." Maggie turned to gaze at her. "Maybe he's on a supply run, you just said that everyone was busy working."

"No one said he was getting supplies."

"With you acting so ferocious they probably didn't *dare* say *anything*." Maggie shook a finger at her. "You can't go ballistic about our crew lead at this point in the job. We need Al. The men respect him even if you don't. He keeps the guys on track and the work humming along."

"You're right." Closing her eyes and pressing her palm against her throbbing forehead, Cara said, "All this cloak and dagger stuff has me on edge and our vanishing crew chief doesn't help."

An hour later, when Al Black tapped on the French doors, Cara opened it to see him standing on the patio, work hat in hands and head hung down. Even moping, the stubble-jawed contractor looked imposing, tall, big biceps, broad shoulders and chest. Not someone you'd want for an enemy.

"You want me?" He shuffled his feet, steel-toe boots scuffing over the terrazzo tile.

"Where were you?"

He glanced behind at a triangle of paint cans. "Afraid we were getting low on paint for the gazebo, so made a paint run."

Something in his manner didn't ring true, but the cans were there as evidence, plus Cara felt Maggie's stare boring into her back. "Fine. We need to talk." He backed up so she could move past him onto the patio. Closing the door, she shut Maggie off inside while she drilled him outside.

Later that afternoon, Maggie put down her brush. "We'd better wind up since Susan's feeding us."

"She is? I missed something." Cara gathered the brushes, dropping them into a can partially filled with water to await a proper cleaning later.

"Susan came in while you were outside and said she was fixing taco salad and rolls."

"She shouldn't cook for us, especially the way she's feeling."

"Tried that route," Maggie said. "She's expecting us to join her at six."

"Then let's hurry and maybe we can help Susan or at least set the table or something."

They made it to the kitchen twenty minutes early, but when Maggie offered to set the table, Susan shook her head no. "Let's just eat at the island bar here, instead. That dining room's so austere."

"We could fix that," Cara said with a wink.

"Oh, yeah," Maggie agreed. "Whatever you don't like about it, we can change."

Susan tossed a dishtowel onto the counter and tugged Maggie by the wrist. "Tell me what you two think."

She led them into the adjoining dining room of unrelenting white except for a rectangle glass table, ultra-modern hutch and a brushed nickel chandelier that resembled a flying saucer. "You'd have full reign to change anything, but this." Susan halted at the only splash of color, an abstract painting in primary colors.

"This doesn't seem your style," Maggie said, astounded their client wanted to keep it.

"Heavens no!" Susan smiled, the old twinkle back in her hazel eyes. "Not this exact painting. Just one about the same size to hide this." She slid the painting aside and it clicked into place, revealing a wall safe. She tapped in a code and the door slid up like a mini-garage door.

"Cool," Cara said.

"Nice." Maggie was both intrigued and relieved.

"Never had a safe before." Susan fingered through a stack of papers and envelopes. "Here's a few stocks and bonds, our birth certificates, passports, prenuptial agreement, marriage certificate, insurance policies, and *this*." She withdrew a hardback book from under the envelopes then beamed at the designers. "My treasure."

"Is it old?" Cara asked, stepping forward to see.

Maggie could tell it wasn't a dusty collector item. She accepted the book from Susan who handed it over carefully as if it were the Holy Grail. Maggie read the cover aloud, "*Midnite Shadow* by Bessie Denworth?"

"Yes!" Susan clapped her hands in pleasure. "The UK queen of romantic suspense. She's such a neat lady and this was her first novel. She autographed it to me nearly a quarter of a century ago. Wow—time does fly."

"A best-seller novel in your safe?" Cara laughed. "What no stash of stolen jewels or piles of loot?"

"This is better. I love her stories," Maggie said, thumbing through the pages to read the message penned in turquoise ink. "'To Susan Mercer, my number one fan. All the best, Bessie Denworth.'"

"Tell us," Cara invited as Maggie flipped through the book.

Susan straightened the envelopes and papers in the safe as she answered. "I was in college and she was our guest lecturer. Nobody knew who she was. Her first book was hot off the press, but she was a published author and that was enough. After her lecture, it was her initial book signing, she was nervous, but friendly. While I was waiting in line for my turn to have my book signed, I began reading chapter one."

"Must've been a long line," Cara said.

"She was chatty and about our age. By the time it was my turn, I was so engrossed in her book, the person behind had to jar me back to reality. Bessie got such a kick out of that our friendship was born."

The microwave timer dinged. "That's our rolls." Susan accepted her book back, closed it into the safe and slipped the painting back into position with a click.

"I wonder," Cara mused, trailing into the kitchen area behind Susan. "If the Mercerville murders were part of the plot of a Bessie Denworth novel, what would happen next in the story?"

"Another murder," Maggie stated. And as she uttered the words a cold breeze blew past her. Just the air-conditioning, she assured herself—not feeling assured at all.

Chapter 11

The rusty crane clanked, creaked, rumbled and groaned as it attempted to raise the object from the lake. Finally, silver gray burst out of the water, breaking the surface like a metal beast, water streaming from its nose, down the hood and pouring out of all orifices.

◦◦◦

"What's that up ahead?" Maggie asked, her hands tightening on the steering wheel as she squinted through the windshield at a cluster of emergency vehicles and people in the distance.

"You mean that ritzy new development they're building out this way?"

"I keep hearing about that," Cara responded. "This is where?"

"Close. It's in Shady Grove—" Susan began.

"Hey, you guys! I'm talking about a crash or something. Look," Maggie interrupted, frustrated her passengers were chatting instead of paying attention.

"Yes, I see flashing lights! Over there by the lake." Susan leaned forward, zipping her window down to listen for sirens as they sped closer.

"That's not a car accident," Cara said from the rear seat. "It's way off the road and down by the shoreline. Maybe a boat accident? Or someone drown?"

"Hope no one's hurt," Susan whispered.

Maggie watched the scene grow larger and more visible as they approached, until they could make out a Mercerville patrol car, ambulance, state troopers, tow truck and a wobbling tractor crane with something hooked on its chain from the water.

"There's Deputy Rice!" she exclaimed, slowing the van and flicking on her turn signal. "Let's see what's happening."

No one argued as the van rumbled off the highway onto a dirt and gravel turn-off winding down to the lake. Gravel spit from under the tires when Maggie braked the vehicle to a stop, before she flew out of the van to race toward the people. "Jake!"

Cara followed more slowly, keeping watch on Susan, as their client gingerly hiked down toward the shoreline. They reached Maggie just as a surprised Deputy Rice spun to face them. "Did someone call in the supersleuths? How did you get here so fast?"

Maggie's eyes were on the deputy, but Cara watched the vehicle swing free from the water as the crane turned, lifting around, positioning to deposit it upon the shore.

"A fifteen-year-old Mercedes Benz," Cara said in surprise. "I assume this isn't an accident?"

"Most likely not. Some fishermen spotted it this morning." Deputy Rice switched his gaze from Maggie to Cara when he replied. "But it's been down there awhile, probably several weeks maybe longer."

The windows of the silver Mercedes were down, with water and debris sloshing out of them as well as the open trunk as the vehicle slammed, none too gently, upon the ground.

"No body?" Maggie watched the officers swarm the vehicle, doing a cursory search of the interior.

"Thank heavens, not," Cara said, watching them switch to a different type of search as the deputy and several troopers pulled limbs and plants off and scraped dirt enough to check the VIN number.

While the officers called it in, their communications crackling, Susan shook her head. "I recognize the car."

"Whose?"

"Aimee Travis," Susan mouthed as Deputy Rice turned toward them, saying the name aloud.

"That doesn't make sense," Maggie said, "I thought she was victim of a hit and run accident. I assumed a pedestrian hit by a car."

"Right—in town." Susan looked perplexed as well.

"Maybe the killer feared Aimee had some evidence in her car. Anything in it's destroyed after being submerged in the lake." Cara knew that open windows and trunk weren't an accident.

The deputy sauntered back over to them. "The county's sending a CSI crew to process the car. This erases any doubt about Miss Travis's hit and run just being a random accident. It was murder. Sheds new light on everything."

"About time," Cara muttered, "you guys figure that out."

"What's *everything*?" Maggie asked, wondering what information they missed.

Eyes locked on Maggie's, Rice chucked her chin. "This means you ladies need to back off snooping—it's definitely too dangerous."

"There truly is a Mercerville killer," Susan gasped, sounding faint.

"You don't look so good." Cara steadied her. "Come on, let's get you home."

"Dismissing unearthly radar," the deputy said, his hand dropped to hover just above his holster. "Why are y'all back here so soon?"

Maggie caught his midnight gaze again. "The note Joan found—Susan promised to help her pack up."

"Miss Susan isn't in shape to do that."

"Exactly," Cara called back at them as she led Susan back up the trail to the road.

"Susan isn't up to much, so we're going to help." Maggie fell in step beside him as he walked with them up toward the van.

"Joan Gaynor's leaving town?" He took hold of Maggie's elbow to help her navigate some rocks and roots. "I could tell that note scared her bad."

"Worse than *bad*. *Falling apart terrified*. She's moving to her cousin's in Florida."

"Not just a visit? Permanent?"

"Permanent."

He halted. "I took an oath to protect the fine citizens of Mercerville. I'll find that killer no matter what rock he tries to hide under."

"Or she," Maggie qualified.

"Or she." Rice's voice dropped another octave. "Male or female that murderer is going to pay."

"Deputy Rice!" hollered one of the Troopers. "The glovebox was opened, too, but we might have something. Do you want it or should we save it for the CSI crew?"

"Let me take a look," he called back. The deputy turned back to Maggie. "Git on back to Miss Susan's place, I'll catch you later."

Maggie nodded, feeling hopeful. Not paying attention, she almost stumbled over the uneven terrain, barely dodging a bank of bushes before she reached the van. Seeing Cara in the driver seat, Maggie slid open the door and climbed in the back. "He's going to call later."

"Call you or us?" Cara asked, whipping the van back onto the highway and speeding toward Mercerville.

"Does it matter?" Susan queried, watching out the window.

"Does to Maggs," Cara said with a wink.

"I wouldn't grumble if he gave me a ring," Maggie said with a toss of her head, sharing a grin through the rearview mirror with Cara.

"A *ring*?" Susan repeated smiling as she finally caught the humor. "You don't mean that literally?"

"Probably not," Maggie answered, realizing she spoke the truth and glad Susan appeared to be reviving. "But a phone call or text would be nice."

"Does the deputy text?" Susan asked, shifting sideways to see Maggie.

"Everybody texts," Cara said.

"Everybody but *me*," Susan said, a smile lighting her wan face. "Guess I'm a tech-dinosaur."

"We'll have to get you into the modern world then," Cara replied, as she turned the van onto the Mercerville exit and headed toward Susan's old home.

"Hey, that's an idea! What about Aimee's phone?" Maggie said, leaning forward. "Did anyone check her calls and texts after she was killed?"

"Doubt it. I still can't figure out why no one even reported her car stolen," Cara wondered, driving up the hill to Mercer manor.

"Remember they all thought it was a just terrible accident? A hit and run, but not premeditated murder," Susan said in her town's defense.

"Her car?" Cara pressed.

"Aimee's mom and stepdad drove here from San Antonio for the memorial service, then after they packed up her apartment, rented a U-Haul trailer and left." Susan paused, adding, "Maybe they thought her car was just leased. I never heard anyone even mention it."

"Guess they must've been overwhelmed with her sudden death and all." Maggie felt a powerful wave of sadness for Aimee's family. "Such a tragedy."

"They hadn't seen her for several years, which made it all worse," Susan confided softly, her eyes misting.

"That'd make it even harder." Maggie blinked away her own tears.

"*Mercerville* has apartments?" Cara said, obviously her thoughts on a different track.

"Yes. An eight-plex on the north end of town." Susan took a deep breath as Cara parked the van in the driveway. "It used to be a fruit farm."

"Change is the only constant in life," Cara murmured as all three women climbed out of the van. "You go ahead inside, Susan. Maggie and I will grab the bags."

Maggie watched Susan disappear inside the house. Pulling the overnight bags from the van, she kept thinking about Aimee's phone. "I wonder if Aimee's family kept her phone? I'll ask Jake about it when we talk. He might get some clues on what was happening if he can discover her contacts before the murder."

"I bet the police can access her phone records without needing her actual phone," Cara agreed. "It could prove very important."

"Such a shame the locals didn't properly investigate when the crime happened."

"True, Maggs, but remember this isn't the big city where crime is part of life. Murder was unexpected." Cara put the strap of her own totebag over her shoulder and towed along Susan's wheeled bag, moving ahead as Maggie gathered her own tote and the rest of their things.

"It should be so safe here." Inhaling the fresh country breeze, Maggie stood still a moment there in the shade of a towering oak, serenaded by birdsong. With a whooping flutter, the birds flew up and away as if startled. Their wings seemed to whisper *escape*. "Maybe Joan and the birds have the right idea, this place isn't as peaceful as it appears."

"Come on," Cara said, struggling with the front door. "Could use some help here."

Maggie dashed to help then hauled in her own set of bags and items. Once inside, they didn't see Susan or Gladys, so they just carried everything upstairs, leaving Susan's in front of her bedroom door and splitting the rest between their own guestrooms. "The Rose Room is beginning to feel like home," Maggie called through her open doorway as she deposited her gear on the bed.

"Ah, yeah." Cara hollered back. "That's 'cause we're here more than home."

"Hush," Maggie warned. "Susan might hear."

"Might hear what?" Susan asked with a wide smile as she stepped into Maggie's room.

"How at home we feel here," Maggie replied, leaving out Cara's irony.

"That's lovely!" Susan warmly said, giving Maggie a hug. "Gladys will be pleased as well."

"What's Gladys pleased about?" Cara said, bounding into the room. "Did she finally figure out the espresso machine?"

Laughter bubbled through the room. "Hardly," Maggie retorted, "She'll be pleased we feel at home here."

Cara did a double-take then nodded. "Home sweet home—if you subtract murder."

"Gladys has a late lunch ready for us before we go to Joan's place." Susan's hand hit the doorframe for support as she left the room. "Come on down when you're ready."

Maggie watched Susan moving gingerly down the hall. "We can*not* let her pack boxes. What is Joan Gaynor thinking?"

"She's *not* thinking. She's injured and terrified. Her flight instinct has kicked in. I'm almost surprised that she didn't just flee out of here the moment she got the note."

"Joan's roots are deep." Maggie knew the Gypsy life she and Cara had been living was as foreign to Mercerville residents as if they were Martians.

"I have an idea," Cara suggested. "What if we let the two patients sit and sort, then you and I do the hauling and box stacking? Maybe if they're just planted in Joan's bedroom, or something, it'll be okay."

"Sounds like a plan," Maggie answered, leading the way downstairs to lunch.

Mid-lunch, though Cara and Maggie had tried to avoid the subject, the murders came up with Susan saying, "I wonder what Zelda thinks about Aimee's death."

"Who's Zelda?" they asked, exchanging a glance, before flashing back to Susan.

"Elliot Ohlmacher's wife." Susan buttered a crescent roll and Cara watched the melting butter drip down the side.

"The banker's *m—married*?" Maggie sputtered, nearly choking.

Cara refocused on the subject not the roll. "We thought he was a middle-aged lecher."

"He is—likes them young and pretty and single—but he's none of those three things."

"Didn't you once say Darlene thought he'd marry her when she divorced her husband, your late lawyer?" Cara asked.

"Right. She probably imagined he'd dump Zelda for her, but instead he dropped all interest in Darlene," Susan shook her head. "I've always wondered why Zelda puts up with that man."

"Maybe she doesn't know," Maggie said, forking a chunk of meatloaf.

"She knows," Cara stated, remembering all the red flags a cheating husband raised. "She's just pretending not to know."

"Zelda's is not *the bury your head in the sand* type. She's a blunt speaking German, though not the brightest woman."

"He has money, maybe that's enough for her," Cara stated, nibbling her unbuttered roll.

"How can wealth beat love?" Maggie asked with that dreamy look in her eyes that always worried Cara.

Ghosts of her first marriage obviously on her mind, Susan said, "Sadly, some prefer wealth and security. Still, I can't imagine Zelda tolerating Elliot's betrayal. I could see her chasing him with a butcher knife," she added with a laugh.

That drew a stare from both designers and Cara knew Maggie was doing the same thing she was—mentally adding Zelda Ohlmacher to Aimee's suspect list. "If he's always gone after the ladies, I'm sure she knows."

"Maybe not," Maggie explained. "When Uncle Bert cheated on Aunt Jane she went into denial and then ballistic—apparently, he'd had a mistress for a decade and she'd been clueless."

"There are always clues," Cara argued, hating the subject.

"Guess you're right," Maggie agreed. "Later, my aunt admitted that when she thought back there were times she should've been suspicious, but she trusted him. She believed what he told her."

"Men can be convincing," Susan admitted, her tone expressing old pain and disappointment. "Let's talk about something nicer."

"You got it," Cara replied, pushing her plate away before she emptied the whole thing.

Susan glanced at her watch. "We'd better hurry, Joan's expecting us by three."

As they climbed up the porch steps of Joan Gaynor's house, Maggie couldn't help glance in the bushes for the mysterious puzzle box. All the unruly shrubbery would be a convenient hiding spot for an intruder. If it were her place, she'd chop the bushes down and replace them with flowers.

When Susan rang the bell, the door opened a crack, far as the chain would allow. "It's me," Susan said.

The chain rattled before the door opened wide. "Thank heavens, you're here! And with your nice city friends," Joan Gaynor smiled. "Please come inside."

They exchanged greetings, stepping into a pine-cleaner scented, cluttered room. With short-clipped nearly gray hair, wrinkle-lined forehead and long angular features, Joan appeared older than Susan, by at least a decade, though Maggie knew both woman were the same age and former classmates.

"I so appreciate your help." One arm in a cast and moving as if in pain from her ribs as well, Joan led them through her house toward a bedroom in the rear. "I've been here twenty years and have accumulated far too much stuff."

Susan nodded. "I so understand."

Maggie thought of the difference between Susan's ultra-modern Houston house and her warm alive Mercerville home and decided she personally preferred a bit of clutter. Though not all stuffed into a small place like Joan's, this was a bit much.

In the master bedroom, Joan had knickknacks and doo-dads on every surface. With the eye of a savvy auction attendee, Maggie knew some things were valuable and others junk. "Maybe you two could sort, then Cara and I will pack and carry boxes?"

Cara's dark almond eyes surveyed the situation. "We need a plan. Let's sort into three groups: save and pack, throwaway, or give away."

"I see you have plenty of boxes, Joan," Maggie added, "We'll also need permanent marker pens, garbage bags, and packing tape. Do you have bubble wrap or newspapers to wrap and protect breakables?"

"Somewhere. Sorry, I'm so unorganized. This has been such a stressful time."

"No problem, Cara and I are used to packing up things and getting places ready to renovate or decorate, so I'll help you gather what we need." Maggie accompanied Joan as they rounded up the supplies.

When they returned to the bedroom, Cara had cleared an area by one wall. "This should be enough room for now. We will stack the boxes here."

"Perfect." Maggie pointed to the left. "Giveaway donations here and over there the *throw-away* pile."

After a sputtering start, the four women got into the flow and the piles grew. Maggie felt uncomfortable and awkward going through someone else's personal belongings, while they were merely a few feet away. Still, they worked smoothly for nearly two hours when she noticed both older women beginning to fade. Just as she began to say something, her cell phone rang.

One glance at the caller ID and her heartbeat accelerated. "Hi, Jake." She flashed a grin at Cara then wandered out of the room, down the hallway and away from listening ears.

"Hey, how's my favorite city gal?" Deputy Rice asked in his deep voice.

"Happy to get your call," she teased back.

"You busy tonight?"

Maggie glanced back toward the bedroom at the mounds still to do, but she knew Susan and Joan couldn't last much longer and they'd need to start anew in the morning. "I'll be free in a while."

"Good. How about dinner? About seven."

"Are you on duty?"

"Will be off by then."

"Cool!" Maggie realized she'd never seen him out of uniform. Still the mystery niggled at her. "What evidence did you find today?"

"I can discuss some things about the case tonight. Not now."

"Okay." Her mind raced wondering what he would share. Maybe he'd decided that their help might not be all bad?

"See you tonight." A click and the line went silent. Maggie grinned. He was not exactly a talkative man.

As she reentered the bedroom, Cara raised a brow. "Well?"

"Dinner date at seven." Maggie looked at their client and at Joan. "I'm guessing will be done by then?"

"Oh, my, yes." Joan leaned back against a pillow on her bed. "Afraid I'm out of steam."

"Me, too." Susan's complexion had paled and purple shadows made her eyes appear deeper set. "Maybe we should finish up for today and get a fresh start in the morning?"

"We've made a pretty big dent," Cara said, wiping her forehead with the back of her hand.

"Right. We got a lot done," Maggie agreed. Even with

the AC humming, cramming all four women in one room made it feel warm and stuffy and they'd been working hard.

"Then let's call it a night, girls," Joan said, clumsily rising from her reclining position to sit between a pile of books. "I appreciate all you've done." She shifted the sling supporting her cast. "Everyone else tells me I should stay, especially my boss. He's trying to play the guilt card about me leaving him in the lurch."

"After the way he replaced you with that flirt Aimee?" Susan asked in horror.

"I told him I don't owe him a thing and he was lucky I hadn't ever told Zelda about his indiscretions." Joan pursed her lips in distaste.

"So she doesn't know what a creep he is?" Maggie said, feeling sorry for the banker's wife.

"He's still alive," Joan snapped. "If Zelda knew—he probably wouldn't be."

Cara and Maggie exchanged a glance as Susan said, "I doubt Zelda would off her husband, even if Elliot deserves it."

"I saw her angry once when he forgot their anniversary." Joan shuttered. "She stormed in like a furious grizzly, ranting in German. I was glad she was mad at him and not me."

"Interesting," Cara mused, "I still say the wife always knows—eventually."

"Come on," Maggie urged, concerned that talk of the murders would upset Joan. "Let's go, I have a date."

"Yeah, yeah," Cara playfully retorted, "Brag about it."

Susan laughed, sounding tired and strained. "Home then." She gave Joan a careful hug at the front door. "We'll be back in the morning."

"Thanks again," Joan said, waving bye with her good arm as she shut the door.

Susan was quiet on the way back to the house. "You okay?" Cara asked, from the backseat.

"Just thinking I should've invited Joan to come spend the night. I hate leaving her all alone."

"She knows we'll be there in a flash if she calls," Cara assured Susan.

"And so will Deputy Rice." Maggie glanced over at their client. "Joan locked up the minute she closed the door behind us. I heard the locks click and the chain rattle."

Susan sighed. "You're right. Joan will be fine." Twisting a lock of hair, she added, "Life is strange. I've known Joan my entire life, but we've talked more the past month than for a decade."

"That happens." Cara's voice sounded wistful. Maggie wondered who her friend was missing. She tried to recall someone Cara had lost touch with, but came up empty. She made a mental note to ask privately later but right now, she wanted to get back to the house and ready for her date.

"Iced tea sounds good, doesn't it?" Susan asked as they entered the Mercer manor.

"It does." Cara laughed at the alarm flickering across Maggie's pixie face. "You hit the shower and get ready for your date, Maggs. Susan and I will head to the kitchen for a tall cold one."

"You sure?"

"Scoot," Susan said. "Go get ready for your own tall one."

"A tall *hot* one," Cara couldn't resist calling after Maggie who was dashing up the stairs two at a time.

As Cara entered the cheery kitchen with Susan, Gladys hustled from stirring a bubbling pot on the stove over to them. "Glad you're home, Miss Susan. Dinner will be ready in an hour or so."

"Smells heavenly," Cara said, sniffing the air. "What are you making?"

"Chicken and dumplings." Gladys's plump face wreathed in smiles. "One of Miss Susan's favorite dishes."

"Yum!" Cara replied, her stomach rumbling and her mouth watering.

"Bless you," Susan exclaimed, hugging Gladys who awkwardly patted her back in return. "We'll just pour us a couple of glasses of iced tea and get out of your way."

"I'll do it," Cara offered, before Gladys could. "Would you like a glass, too, Gladys?"

"I—I—why thank you, dear," she stammered, obviously unused to someone waiting on her. "That'll be nice."

"Let's all sit in the breakfast nook," Susan suggested, with Gladys trailing her like an obedient sheep.

"Here you go." Cara handed around the slender tumblers of iced tea then took a chair on the opposite side of the table.

"Thanks," Gladys muttered, still looking abashed.

"Thank you, Cara." Susan took a long sip. "I need more than the bottled water you girls thrive on."

"You're wilted," Gladys stated, back to her no-nonsense self as she studied Susan. "You should have a long bubble bath and a quick lie-down before supper."

Cara also read Susan's fatigue. "Good idea."

With their client upstairs resting and Maggie getting ready for a date, Cara wandered outside to escape into the almost magical garden. Greeted by the fragrance of evening primrose, she settled on the bench by the fountain, impressed by the way it always seemed to be shaded any time of the day, though the angel fountain glistened in sunlight. A balmy breeze played with her hair. Blowing out a relaxed sigh, she watched humming birds darting and hovering above the colorful blossom clusters of white, yellow and pink primrose, dancing beside waving lavender plumes and scarlet daylilies.

She reached over to pluck a lily blossom and inhale the sweet perfume. With the trumpet-shaped lily of blood-red held in her hands, she closed her eyes and leaned back her head, letting gentle breezes caress her skin.

A buzz startled her eyes open. Not a bee, but a miniature, ruby-throated hummingbird hovered above the blossom cupped in her hands. Iridescent feathers shimmered with blues, greens and gold in the sunshine as the hummingbird dipped into the blossom for the nectar. Cara barely dared to breathe, afraid to frighten the tiny bird. *What an amazing creature*, she thought, watching its wings beating so fast they blurred. Exquisitely beautiful, it hypnotized her. She stared while trying to keep her hands still and the flower upright. Never had she been so close to a hummingbird before, just wait until she told Maggie!

∽✺∽

Maggie liked her deputy in civilian clothes—those jeans fitted his form nicely—revealing muscular thighs and a nice butt. Moreover, that shirt he left unbuttoned enough to tempt any female and itching her fingers to undo just one or two more. She shook away the wayward thought and tried to concentrate on what he said as they entered the Fredericksburg Inn.

"Thought this might be a treat for you something different," Jake said as he slid back a chair to seat her.

"Definitely this inn has great atmosphere." She enjoyed his Southern gentleman manners. He was so different from her usual dates and made her feel extra feminine.

"Besides, here we can talk in private without all Mercerville gawking and straining to listen." His dead serious expression emphasized his statement.

"Even nicer then." Maggie smiled, thinking he was handsome enough to star in a movie and make the women swoon. Every single girl in Mercerville, as well as their mothers, probably thought she was poaching on their territory.

After they placed their order, he rubbed his chin and leaned forward. "Finding Aimee Travis's car altered the entire hit and run case. No doubt it's murder—probably premeditated." His voice dropped lower. "Sheds new light on things we thought weren't important."

"Like what?" Driven by curiosity, Maggie found herself whispering, though they were at a corner table away from other customers.

"A single young woman's unfortunate demise compels you to not sully their reputation." Embarrassment colored his face and he dropped his gaze to fiddle with his napkin and silverware. "That's not fitting."

"What? Did the secretary have a night job as a stripper or something?" Maggie hoped he wouldn't clam up now. She was dying to learn whatever was making him so nervous.

"No, Ma'am." He glanced away, so she reached out and covered his hand.

"Don't leave me hanging," she coaxed, determined to unearth the information. "Please explain."

"Whatever I tell you stops here." He targeted her with an intense gaze. "Except, I guess for your buddy in crime-busting."

"I promise." Maggie shutdown a thrill as he turned his hand to clasp hers within his strong solid grip, his thumb absently caressing her palm.

"Back when this all happened," Jake cleared his throat then plunged ahead. "It didn't seem pertinent to the investigation when the coroner discovered Miss Travis was four months along."

Chapter 12

"Aimee was pregnant?" Maggie gasped, wrapping her mind around all the implications.

"Shh!" Finger to his lips, he glanced around the room. "Trying to protect her reputation."

"Sorry." Maggie thought of all the possible fathers and it truly made her head spin. "Did they run paternity tests or can you that early?"

"Don't know if they could've. Didn't consider it. Felt it was none of our business."

"But that pregnancy might be why she was killed."

"I realize that now, but it's too late. I'll just use detective work to figure out who was responsible for her condition. Maybe the guy didn't even know."

"Or maybe he did." Maggie took a sip of her lemonade, thinking. "It could be anyone she hooked up with so many men."

"I reckon they've been a few." He looked so embarrassed about the delicate subject that Maggie pitied him. His shy side was quite appealing.

"A few? I know several possibilities and I never met her."

"Like who?" he asked with a keen stare.

As she met his gaze, an awful thought struck her. "Ah,

Jake, you weren't one of Aimee's conquests, were you?"

He suddenly relaxed, throwing back his head with a rumbling chuckle. "No way."

"Good." Her breath whooshed out with relief.

"Aw, your Irish is showing." He chuckled, a teasing gleam replacing the intensity in his midnight eyes. "You're *jealous*."

"Am not," Maggie sputtered. "I just meant that would screw up your investigation— conflict of interest and all."

"Sure." Laughter alive in voice and manner, he grinned. "Just the *case* —no personal interest?"

"Right." Her chin jutted up in defiance. Still she felt relief as the waiter swept their plates onto the table with flourish. "Just the case," she emphasized when her date's attention diverted from her flaming cheeks to their dinner.

After a few bites, she asked, "How did you know I'm part Irish?"

"Let's see." He pretended to count on his fingers. "Your flame red hair, your dreamy expression, when you seem to float off into a land of leprechauns and rainbows, nearly magical emerald eyes, and your flash-fire temper."

"I don't have a temper," Maggie argued, flattered by much of his description, except that.

Without a word, he leaned back, grinning and staring. She felt her cheeks warm and pretended to eat. They continued to keep the banter light throughout the meal, never referring again to the late secretary and her condition at the time of the murder. As thrilled as Maggie was to be dining with the handsome deputy, part of her was restless, anxious to share the latest thread of their mystery—Aimee's pregnancy. Just wait until she told Cara!

⁊ᔖ⁊

"You waiting up for me?" Maggie asked, her eyes crinkling up at the corners as she laughed.

"Not really." Cara yawned and stretched, dropping her paperback mystery onto the chair. "Just reading awhile to unwind. How was the date?"

"Great." Maggie peeled off her date outfit and tugged on her nightshirt, then before heading to their shared bathroom, she perched on the foot of the bed. "Guess what happened?"

"He kissed you." Cara teased her friend, sensing excitement vibrating through Maggie.

"Besides that. About the murders." Maggie leaned forward. "I think Jake's decided to include us in the loop."

"Susan, too?"

"No. Just us." Maggie's voice dropped to a whisper. "He volunteered some important info tonight."

"What?" Cara felt her own pulse racing faster, but still wouldn't admit, even to herself, that the challenge of solving the mysteries sparked it.

"Aimee was pregnant."

"Whoa! That sheds new light on motives."

"We have to keep it secret. Jake's being a gentleman and trying to protect her reputation."

"Ah, a little late for that." Cara bit her bottom lip, her head swirling with thoughts. "Who was the father?"

"That's the big question. And did he know?" Maggie mused.

"If so," Cara wondered aloud, "Did Aimee attempt to use her pregnancy to get the guy to commit?"

"Or maybe she hid the pregnancy?" Maggie suggested.

"How far along?"

"Barely four months. Apparently, she didn't even show."

"Happens." Cara nodded. "Lucy didn't show until she was far into her fifth month, remember?"

"True, when we threw her the baby shower." Maggie grinned. "But Jen did *way* earlier. She looked like she swallowed a basketball."

"We're about the only ones from our old gang who haven't started families, yet." Cara tried to push away a wave of melancholy and concentrate on the mystery. "Anyway, we need to figure out who the baby's father was and if that led to Aimee's murder."

"What if Aimee was involved with someone new and the father-to-be was a former lover?" Maggie grew pensive. "You know how a new barn cat tries to kill kittens from another sire?"

"Sheesh," Cara grumbled. "I hate that image. Besides, he doesn't take out the mama cat."

"Still, it could mess up a new romance if she was preggers from an old one."

"Or if the father-to-be was already married..." Cara began.

"Like the banker," Maggie interjected.

"It could mean big trouble, so maybe he..." Cara continued.

"Or his wife Zelda," Maggie added.

"Decided to eradicate the problem—and Aimee," Cara concluded, before Maggie could interrupt again.

"Both creamed by the hit and run," Maggie reiterated, obviously enjoying their verbal duel.

"Touché." Cara always had fun bouncing design ideas off Maggie. Now it spilled over into their mystery clue brainstorming. "What if the father was the late lawyer, John Lawson? Susan said he and Darlene never had kids. Maybe Aimee expecting his baby was the last straw and Darlene ran her down?"

"Doubt she'd tell Darlene she was pregnant. Aimee seems the type to use the pregnancy to get what she wants—probably a man, marriage or money."

"Or all three." Cara wandered to the window, parting the curtains to stare into the darkness. "What if Susan's cousin Roger was the father? Aimee could've used her pregnancy as leverage to get him to marry her? That would make Aimee and the baby part of the Mercerville royal family."

"And be blackmail if he'd already broken off with her."

"People have killed for less." Clouds shadowed the moon, cloaking the night. Cara hugged herself, hoping no watcher-in-the-woods lurked tonight—if there had ever been one. All this mayhem played havoc with her imagination.

"Maybe it was Kirby Ballentine, the financial advisor, who got in over his head with the hot young secretary?" Maggie rummaged through her bag, found their notebook and flipped to the suspect list. "Kirby tried to extract himself and she played the baby card, pushing him too far?"

"So he ran over her?" Cara shook her head as she turned to face Maggie. "You do *not* trust that accountant, do you?"

"No more than you trust Darlene." Maggie laughed. "Well, we won't figure it out tonight, since we haven't even made it down to Aimee's mystery lover on the list, let alone any not-known-yet angry wives, or significant others, irate because of Aimee and their man."

"It gives us lots to consider, doesn't it?" Cara rescued her paperback from the chair. "I'd better get back to my own room and let you get ready for bed."

"Thanks for waiting up," Maggie called over her shoulder as she reached the bathroom door.

"I didn't," Cara returned, but they both knew she did.

At Joan Gaynor's place the next morning, Maggie whirred into gear. "Cara, want to go finish the bedroom and bathroom with Susan and Joan, while I start on the kitchen?" She winked at Joan. "I know what needs to be done in kitchens."

"Good idea." Cara knew they could wrap up their part in just a few hours and the rest they could leave for the movers. "Let's get busy." She hustled the older women back into the bedroom, letting them sort and chatter as she packed, boxed and bagged.

Their words flowed past her until she heard Aimee's name. "Um, what did you say about Aimee. I missed it."

"That if life had turned out differently, Aimee might've been my cousin-in-law," Susan replied, folding a rose-red chenille bedspread and laying it upon the pile of bedding to save.

"Huh?"

"When Aimee and Roger had been dating a few months, Rachel called me all upset one night, saying she was afraid her brother was falling in love. She called Aimee a gold-digger," Susan blushed. "And a few other things."

"I bet." Cara dropped the charity bag to give Susan full attention. "Then what happened?"

"I guess he wasn't as smitten as she thought, because next I heard they were broke up and Aimee was taking over Joan's job."

"That hit me out of the blue," Joan said, distress etching deep lines in her long face. "I'd been instructed to put any calls from Aimee Travis straight through to my boss and she phoned constantly. I thought it had something to do with that new development outside of town. Had no idea that all the while she was angling for my job."

"Then Ohlmacher canned you?" Cara said, disgusted with the banker and Aimee.

"He gave me the choice of early retirement or being laid-off. Said the bank was downsizing." She snorted. "Lies. He just wanted to hire that tart."

"Did your boss and Aimee have an affair?" Cara asked, thinking about the baby secret.

Joan cleared her throat, the fingers of her good hand thumping a jewelry box. "I know they, ah, met for lunch frequently and often he barely returned before closing."

"Poor Zelda!" Susan exclaimed.

"This was while Aimee dated Roger Mercer?" Cara wanted to create a timeline of relationships.

"No wonder my cousin dropped her!" Susan interjected.

"Seems like it went on for a quite some time, so I imagine so." Joan moved her jewelry box to the pack and move pile. "It might have even begun while she was engaged to the mechanic."

"Bobby Ray Clemens is a good mechanic and a nice-looking young man," Susan said. "He works for his uncle at the garage we've gone to forever."

"Even after Aimee dumped him for your cousin?" Cara asked, watching Susan and noticing how wan she appeared. Good thing they were almost through, just some bathroom stuff and the linen closet left.

"That's not my business and won't change where I take the car." Susan continued, "This is what I know about Aimee. I've learned from Rachel and others that when Aimee moved here from San Antonio a few years ago to work for John Lawson, she first hooked up with Bobby. Maybe around the time of the break-in when John got killed, Aimee started dating Roger."

"So Aimee's not a local?"

"Heavens no!" Joan said, acting offended.

Joan's reaction persuaded Cara that she'd pumped them enough. "Let me empty the bathroom linen closet while you two do the medicine cabinet. Okay?" Feeling an urgency to finish up and leave Mercerville and the murders behind, she carried piles of towels and bedding from the linen closet, depositing stacks on the bed. "We're almost done."

On cue, Maggie appeared in the doorway. Hair a bit mussed, but looking pleased as a cat in a knitting basket, she grinned. "Hey, kitchen's boxed and labeled, cabinets wiped out and counter top shined. What can I do in here?"

"Super Woman strikes again!" Cara teased.

"Amazing," Joan sputtered. "You did all that so fast?"

Susan smiled proudly. "Didn't I tell you these two are fantastic?"

"That you did," Joan agreed, awe in her voice.

A half hour later, Joan walked them to the door, profusely thanking them. "I cannot express how much I appreciate all your help. The movers will take care of the rest in the morning."

"I'll miss you," Susan said, her hazel eyes misting as she hugged her old classmate with a one-sided hug to avoid the slinged arm and injured ribs.

"We'll keep in touch." Joan patted Susan's shoulder. "It's not like you still live here in town, anyway."

"I'm here plenty," Susan replied, releasing Joan as Maggie and Cara edged toward the front door.

Cara suppressed the urge to comment, knowing if she said they all three practically lived here now, it'd get her in trouble with Maggie. Instead, she held the door open, saying, "Bye, Joan. Have a nice time in Florida."

"Bye," Maggie echoed, cleverly drawing Susan outside into the warm sunshine along with them.

Once they were all three settled in the van, Susan exhaled a long breath. "You girls must be anxious to get back to Houston."

"Are you too tired to make the trip back?" Cara asked, concerned about the client, but also concerned about any more delay.

"I might catnap on the ride," Susan admitted. "Let's stop and get our things at the house. Gladys prepared a late lunch for us to eat before we hit the road."

"Food always sounds good," Cara responded, aware of hunger pangs and glad to know they weren't completely skipping the meal.

"I hope Joan will be safe." Susan pushed a wispy lock of hair off her face then leaned her head back against the seat.

"Just one more night in Mercerville, then she'll be out of the killer's reach," Maggie replied quietly, leaning forward so Cara and Susan could hear.

"I know," Susan answered. "She'll be fine."

"We hope," Cara whispered to herself.

ೞೞೞ

Darkness purpled the night sky as they arrived back at the Houston manor. Once inside, Susan excused herself to find Ed, so Maggie and Cara beelined to their guestroom. "What a weekend," Maggie said, plopping her gear by the dresser.

"We're putting a new spin on *mobile* with this job," Cara

grumbled, stashing her things back into the bathroom. "We need to plant ourselves in one place."

"Talk to me," Maggie said, aware something was up with Cara, who had appeared pensive the entire drive back to Houston.

"About what I gleaned from Susan and Joan on Aimee's love-life?"

"About whatever you want." Maggie watched Cara unpack with her back facing her. She knew if she pressed too hard, Cara would clam up. This way maybe it'd gradually spill out once she got talking.

"Timeline's all convoluted. It's possible that Aimee was involved with up to four guys overlapping that conception time frame. Probably the murdered lawyer's out of the equation though."

"Yeah, I tend to agree."

"Darlene still stays on both suspect lists." Cara stated, turning to glance around and shoot a don't-argue glare.

"Fine, as long as Kirby Ballentine stays on the lists, too." Maggie kicked her tote bag out of the way and closer against the wall. "So who are the four possible sperm donors?"

"The ex-fiancé mechanic, cuz Roger, the banker, and the mystery lover—unless we add Kirby to make it five."

"So we're back where we started."

"Yep." Cara gathered up her lotion, body wash and nightwear, but paused outside the bathroom door. "Unless some new guy throws his hat in the ring or there's a shady underside to that lake development thing and Aimee was in on it."

"More intrigue? That's all we need!"

"Hmm, could the mystery lover be an old flame from San Antonio? Apparently, she'd only been in Mercerville two years."

"Possible." Maggie didn't want Cara to stop talking and shower, yet. She still hadn't discovered the cause of Cara's melancholy mood. "Old flames can burn hot."

"Or turn to ash," Cara wandered back into the bedroom, dropping onto the edge of the bed, still holding her stuff.

"This about your ex?" Maggie sat next to her, hoping whatever was bugging Cara would finally spill.

"No." Cara shook her head, her dark almond-shaped eyes sad. "Remember in college when I had that thing with Justin Reed?"

"Sure, you two were inseparable. We were juniors. He was a senior and a chemical engineer. He was a great guy and I thought I'd be maid of honor before long."

"Almost happened, but you know me. I blew it." Cara closed her eyes a minute. Maggie waited in silence until she spoke again. "When Justin's roommate let it slip that Justin had bought a ring and was going to propose—I panicked."

"You were right not to jump into marriage if you weren't ready."

"*Right*?" Cara whispered, pain in her voice. "Instead, I waited for King Jerk and eloped the day after my graduation. Because he was *exciting*, I married Mr. Wrong. Maybe Justin was my Mr. Right and instead I broke his heart. Now I don't even know where he is. If he ever married. Anything."

"Regrets get us nowhere." In all their years of friendship, she rarely witnessed Cara like this. "We don't get do-overs. We just have to plow forward."

"Aimee was only a few years younger than we are and now she's dead along with her unborn child. Maybe because of a wrong choice." Cara stood back up and headed into the bathroom. "We don't always get second chances. Maybe I blew my one chance at real love."

"Cut it out!" Maggie couldn't believe her *never wave the flag of surrender* friend was sounding so defeatist. "Cara, you're smart, beautiful, talented, and one day you'll meet the right guy. Aimee's life is over, but *yours* isn't. I *know* you have a wonderful future. I feel it!"

"Yeah, yeah, yeah," Cara said before disappearing into the bathroom, but Maggie caught the smile steal across her face. "If Maggs feels it—it must be true."

"Now that's the old Cara," Maggie told herself, relieved they had things out in the open. Their conversation with Susan about *losing touch with someone from the past* floated through her head. Maybe Justin Reed is who Cara felt sad about. They'd lost touch after they broke up and he graduated. Where did he return? To Virginia? Maggie wasn't sure, but she didn't want to ask Cara. Hopefully, now the subject could just ebb away like a seashell at high tide.

~~~

July morning sunshine radiated brightly through sunroom. Thankful for the air conditioning, Cara slanted the blinds to dim the glare. It wasn't as scorching as that dangerous heatwave a few weeks back, but it was definitely Houston hot. "What were we thinking, Maggs, to schedule the crucial part of our outside job midsummer?"

"Just happens that way. Not the first time," Maggie replied, measuring the windows before placing the custom order for the taupe shadow-panel sheers. She began punching in the phone number when they both heard a rat-a-tat-tat on the French doors. "You get that?"

"Sure." Cara opened the door to a blast of heat as Al stood outside.

"Update for you," he said, as Cara stepped outside on to the patio, closing the door behind her.

"Shoot." Cara tried to tap down the displeasure Al Black always triggered.

"The artificial rock delivery's pushed to next week." He turned, gesturing toward the pool. "Works out better for us. This way we'll be ready to install them immediately."

"Okay," Cara tapped the toe of her sandal, fighting mixed feelings about the rock delay. No matter what, her crew always seemed to make things work. So far Al kept to that, she reminded herself. "And?"

"Gazebo constructed and painted. You can put up the fabric when you want, but I won't advise it until we get the messy stuff done out here."

"Right." She could tell he had more, so again she said, "And?"

"Everything else is on schedule." Still he stood, jamming his hands in his pockets and watching her through puppy dog eyes.

"Al, what is it?"

"You know that note I found and gave you?" He glanced around nervously, right hand fiddling in his pocket. "Found another one jammed in the back gate on Friday but you were gone."

Cara froze. This wasn't what she expected. She extended her hand and, instead of dropping a note in her palm, he strode over to the edge of the patio to pick up a dented lunch box. Opening it, he shifted a sandwich, banana, and an apple then dug under a napkin, finally lifting up a soiled envelope. "Sorry. I stuffed it in here Friday."

"Ah, t—thanks," she stammered, grabbing it and rushing back inside.

"What's wrong?" Maggie asked, glancing up at her. "No on-site disaster while we were gone, I hope?"

"Note." Cara's hands were shaking as she withdrew the note from the envelope and unfolded the paper.

Maggie looked over her shoulder, reading the cut and paste missive aloud: "'Next time you won't be so lucky.'"

"Exactly the same message as Joan's warning." The enveloped slipped from Cara's grasp to flutter to the floor.

Maggie retrieved it, holding it by the edges. "Yuk, it smells like tuna and bananas."

"Spent days in Al's lunchbox. Don't worry about prints. It's a lost cause like the others."

"I'll go get a sandwich bag," Maggie volunteered. "You probably want to save this one like the other note Al found?" She halted in the doorway. "I assume we hide this from our client, too?"

Cara nodded, still staring down at the words. Did this mean Susan's fall into the pool wasn't their fault? Not Al or their crew screwing up? Had the killer somehow *arranged* Susan's accident the same way he'd done Joan's? Or had the killer heard about the mishap and decide to use it to frighten them?

Either way, this proved Houston was no safer than Mercerville.

Chapter 13

That's kind of strange," Maggie said as she marked the spots for the curtain rod brackets above the west wall windows.

"What?" On her stepstool instead of a ladder and stretching to tiptoe, Cara mirrored Maggie's actions on the opposite wall at the east end.

"That it's Al who found the note again—why not Raoul or Jim or Tiko?"

"Guess he checks the perimeter before leaving." Cara still didn't trust Al Black—she felt him hiding something. Maybe Maggs was finally keying into her suspicions? "Or he planted them both."

"Why?" Maggie sounded perplexed. "Besides, we never told him about Susan's first note, so how?"

"Unless he's the killer."

"He didn't know either victim, so you don't make sense."

"Did you know he moved here from San Antonio?" Cara climbed down off the stepstool to the floor, setting down the tape measure, pencil and bronze bracket. "Now we've found out Aimee lived there, too."

"Along with two million others. Even for you that's a reach."

"What if he's her old flame and is the mystery lover who she held trysts with in Fredericksburg?" Cara envisioned the scene, both of them wearing hats and sunglasses to hide their identities. "Then something went wrong. They had a blow up? Maybe Al found out about the other men."

"So he kills her by vehicle homicide in *Mercerville*?" Maggie shook a finger at Cara. "Talk about farfetched—and *you* say *I'm* the one with a weird imagination."

"I'm just sayin'." Hands on hips, Cara glared back at Maggie. "It's possible."

"Anything's possible," Maggie retorted. "That doesn't make it so."

"Well, I'm going to talk to him right now!" Cara stormed out the French doors into the construction zone of the Dexter's backyard, hollering, "Al!"

"Not here," Pete said, yelling over the buzzing jigsaw. "Think he took an early lunch."

So angry that she didn't dare spit out the words in her mouth, she stomped across the lawn over to Jim. "I need Al."

"Left me in charge until lunch." Down on his knees, digging with a hand spade, Jim looked up at her. "Doubt if he'll be gone long, ma'am."

"Where did he go?"

"Not sure." Jim removed his hat to back-arm the sweat off his brow. "I'll tell him you want to see him when he gets back."

"Do that." Cara marched back inside, not stopping until she stood face to face with Maggie. "Al's disappeared again—and *you* don't think he's suspicious?"

୧୬୧

When Al tapped on the French doors, Maggie smiled and waved at him, glad that Cara was in the kitchen fixing iced tea. "Come in, Al. We missed you earlier."

"Yeah. Heard you wanted me?" He glanced around as if expecting Cara to materialize with a hatchet attack. "I had to pick up some supplies and then grabbed lunch."

"Maybe for the next while, you'd better check in with us before you leave the jobsite. Okay?"

"Okay," he replied, hurrying back outside.

"Whew," Maggie whooshed, "Disaster averted. Now if I can keep Cara distracted until she calms down."

"What disaster?" Susan asked, standing in the inner doorway, looking curious.

"Just a delay on the artificial rock delivery," Maggie fibbed, telling herself that part was true—just not the current crisis. "But this will work out better, anyway. They'll arrive next Thursday and our crew should have everything ready."

"Ever since ya'll told me about them, I've been so excited! I know Cara thought I'd want boulders from my quarry, but only because I hadn't considered this possibility. It sounds much more fun!" Susan's animation was infectious, her hands flying as she spoke and eyes sparkling.

"Simpler for sure." Maggie laughed. "We're glad you're pleased. It's easier to use the lightweight made-to-order sized ones."

"I can't wait to see and touch them and watch you install them. Where's Cara?" Susan glanced around the room just as Cara stepped up behind her.

"Fixing iced tea." Cara held a glass in each hand. "I should've poured one more."

"No thanks, I'd float away. Just drank a soft drink." Susan stepped into the sunroom, allowing Cara to move past. "This room gets prettier every day."

"That's our job." The designers exchanged grins as Cara handed Maggie a glass and patted her stepstool with her left hand. "Come sit, Susan. How are you feeling?"

"Better than I thought I would." A wide smile curved her lips as she sat. "You two must be frazzled, yet you've been working away like troopers all day."

"We're getting to our favorite part," Cara began.

"Almost time to bring in the details," Maggie explained, her enthusiasm catching fire as she twirled around, "the fabric, furniture, artwork and all the accents that create the room."

"If only we were that far along outside," Cara added.

"You're close. Maggie told me the fake rocks are coming soon. I can't wait to see them!"

"Really? We've been feeling guilty about not using your quarry stone."

Maggie nodded. "It's super you're fine with the manufactured ones."

"Actually, I'm so curious to learn all about those imposter boulders." Susan folded her hands in her lap, an odd expression on her face. "I'd like to ask you two a favor."

"You're the client. Your wish is our command," Maggie said, wondering what Susan wanted. Hopefully, it wouldn't be a major change in the design—not at this stage.

"Oh." Susan's hands fluttered back to life. "It's not your work."

"What do you need?" Concern inflected Cara's voice.

"Saturday is my birthday. Ed is taking me out for a special dinner Friday, but then he's got an important conference over the weekend."

"We'll be happy to celebrate with you Saturday," Maggie offered, glad it was something simple and totally understandable. After all, Susan didn't know anyone in Houston, yet.

"We can treat you to lunch," Cara suggested. "Or even a movie?"

"It's not that simple." Susan's cheeks reddened and Maggie held her breath. She knew what was coming. "My cousins are throwing me a little get-together back home and Ed doesn't want me to travel to Mercerville alone."

"He's right." Maggie ignored Cara's hiss. "You shouldn't drive that far until you're all better."

"Anyway," Susan twirled a wayward strand of hair.

"Roger's extended an invitation to you both and I'd be delighted if you'd join me, plus that would solve my, ah, transportation dilemma."

"We can do that." Maggie didn't dare glance at Cara, but she felt strongly Susan shouldn't be alone on her birthday—not here and not in Mercerville.

"You're sure it's okay?" Susan turned to look at Cara. "I feel like such a wimp, but I'd truly adore your company."

Cara nodded yes, but her strained expression and that dimple above her brow signaling displeasure transmitted *no*.

"Sounds fun," Maggie said quickly, hoping her friend could handle one more trip to the Texas Hill Country. "We love parties!"

"Wonderful!" Susan clapped her hands together and then gingerly scooted up off the stool.

"This'll be a great birthday!"

"Just great," Cara mouthed.

Fortunately, Susan had turned back toward Maggie and didn't see, so Maggie smiled warmly. "Birthdays should be fun."

The moment Susan left the sunroom and her footsteps faded away, Cara groaned. "If this is a bad dream—please wake me."

"You're tough. You can handle it."

"I don't think we're charging near enough for this job," Cara muttered. "Murder, mayhem and Mercerville were not included in the price."

෴

"Fun time!" Maggie waved around the room. "Ready to hit the art gallery and then go select the final accessories for this sunroom and lanai?"

"Should we take Susan along with us?" Cara asked.

"She's not up to it."

"Up to what?" Susan asked, teetering on platform sandals as she entered the sunroom, catching the doorframe for balance.

"Shopping for the finishing touches for the room," Cara volunteered, "We still need a few items."

"Like what?"

"A few paintings, a metal sculpture, a Tuscan tapestry to echo the colors of the area rug we found—" Maggie began.

"I saw the perfect tapestry!" Susan beamed. "It has the same color palette as that gorgeous rug."

"Where?" Cara asked.

"Online." Susan's cheeks pinked. "I discovered some surprising deals on Tuscan tapestries and I fell in love with one."

"Cool!" Maggie said, pleased.

"Oh?" Cara said with skepticism.

"Do you want to see?" Susan's eagerness drew them both into following her into the harsh white living room where a laptop computer sat on the coffee table. "It'll take just a minute to boot-up, but I can find the tapestry quickly. I saved the link into my favorite places."

"When did you find it?" Cara asked, curious, but not sure at all about Susan making such an important selection on her own.

"Restless last night when Ed was snoring." Susan gave a soft laugh. "So, I snuck out into the sitting room and did some window shopping online."

A few clicks of her mouse pad and she turned the screen to Cara and Maggie. "See?"

"Wow." Cara examined the exquisite pattern, threads woven into a scene of Tuscany vibrant with Mediterranean blue, golden yellow, sage and olive greens, and splashed with poppy and wine reds. "Is this authentic?"

"Yes," Susan proudly replied. "Pretty, isn't?"

"Pretty?" Maggie stared at fabric spun into an artist view through a vine-twined stone archway of a Tuscan hillside and the sea beyond. "It's gorgeous!"

"You'd think we'd designed the entire room around it,"

Cara admitted, realizing she shouldn't have doubted Susan's taste.

"Then I can order it?"

"Yes!" the designers chorused.

"It's perfect," Maggie added, grinning. "Now we better live up to your standards with our own choices."

Susan laughed. "You two always do." Her gaze rested on Cara. "May I ask you something, a silly personal question?"

"Shoot," Cara replied, wondering what Susan had on her mind this time.

"I'm still getting used to my name being Dexter after a lifetime of being a Mercer." She coughed into her hand. "Except for a brief moment during my doomed first marriage. Anyway, Fazio is your maiden name, right? Not your ex-husband's surname."

"Definitely," Cara responded. "I didn't want anything that belonged to him, especially to be saddled with his last name."

"What was it?" Susan asked, her voice gentle.

"King."

"That's why she refers to him as King Jerk," Maggie said with a wry expression Cara understood.

"Not the *only* reason why," Cara deftly returned, motioning at the computer monitor before guiding the conversation back to the tapestry. "How long before delivery?"

"Ten days. It's shipped from Italy."

"That'll work. We'll hang it last," Maggie said, obviously calculating in her head. "The final artist touch."

"We need the dimensions to plan around," Cara informed their client. "But, Susan, you found a treasure."

"I did, didn't I?" Susan gave a hiccupping giggle. "After I order this I think I'll take a nap."

"A nap?" Cara said, puzzled.

"It's Friday and since I didn't sleep last night, and Ed's taking me out to dinner to celebrate my birthday this evening, I'm getting a bit light-headed. Need a little nap before he gets home."

"Good idea." Cara noticed Susan's hand shaking slightly as tiredness clouded her eyes.

"I seem to wilt easily since my mishap."

"No wonder," Maggie consoled, helping Susan up from the sofa. "You can order the tapestry later. Let us help you to your room now."

After they settled their client safely in the master suite, Cara whooshed out a sigh of relief. "I still wonder if Susan's fall was our crew's fault—or something more sinister."

"Me, too." Maggie shoved a wayward curl off her forehead, but it stubbornly bounced back over her brow. "Guess we'll never know the answer."

"Maybe we'll find some answers at the party in Mercerville tomorrow night." Cara bit her bottom lip, remembering the newest warning note.

"I thought you didn't want to go." Maggie watched her with open curiosity.

"I don't." Cara stared right back. "But since we are going, we might as well make the trip useful."

"Uh huh." Maggie gave her a knowing grin.

"Cool it, Maggs. I need to do something to keep busy while you make moon-eyes at the deputy."

"Like that's the *only* reason," Maggie charged back, too smugly.

๛๛๛

Maggie viewed Uncle Leland's house as a sister version of Susan's Mercerville home—not quite as exquisitely decorated, but almost identically built with the same craftsmanship of artisans from a different age.

She sipped her champagne, peeking over the top of her crystal flute to watch for Jake. Susan had promised he'd make an appearance.

"Interesting birthday bash—not nearly as many guests as

her uncle's shindig." Cara gazed around the room *people watching*. Something they both loved to do.

"Susan told her cousins to keep it subdued."

"Subdued or *dead*?" Cara quipped, just as Roger and Rachel waved at them, crossing the room to join the designers.

"Hi," Rachel bubbled. "Isn't this just the pits? Elevator music and nobody fun."

"I have someone fun," Roger stated proudly glancing down at a petite raven-haired, honey-complexion beauty standing beside him. "This is my date, Gabriella Clemens."

"Nice to meet you, Gabriella," Maggie began to say as a young man, definitely not dressed for the party, but with the same dark eyes and coloring as Roger's date, burst into the room aiming right for them.

"Gabby!" The guy grabbed Gabriella's arm. "What are you doing with this creep? You're going home with me." Anger discharged from him like lightning shooting from a thundercloud.

"I'm *not* going anywhere with you." Her obsidian eyes narrowed as she jerked away, reeling him backward a step. "Just leave."

"Not without you." He glared down at her, teetering close enough that Maggie smelt the whiskey on his breath and noticed his eyes were bloodshot. Roger stood in silence, but slipped an arm around his date's shoulders as if claiming his territory.

"You're making a scene," Gabriella snapped.

"Big deal. We don't belong at this hoity-toity party." He reached for her arm again, but she slapped his hand away. "Dammit, Gabby. Get out of here before he tries to buy you off, too."

"Bobby, get lost!" Gabriella pushed at his chest. "You're disgusting."

"Come on, baby," Roger said, turning her and guiding her across the room without a glance backward.

"Hey!" Bobby hollered, stepping forward in a fighter stance. "Get your hands off my sister or I'll kill ya!"

"Not happening." Deputy Rice hooked his arm before he could follow. "Clemens, you need to sober up."

"Hell, man," he protested as Jake marched him toward the front door. "You don't understand."

"I understand plenty," the lawman growled, his voice low enough to only reach Maggie and Cara's ears. "You can leave now or spend your night in the drunk-tank."

"What kinda choice is that?" Bobby slurred, Jake's strong hold keeping him upright.

"The only one you've got, pal," Maggie heard Jake respond as he marched the party-crasher out the door, not releasing hold as he kicked the door shut behind them.

"Roger's date is Bobby Ray Clemens's sister," Cara whistled, watching their exit. "Who'd a thought?"

"There isn't exactly a huge dating pool in this town," Rachel admitted, reminding Maggie she remained standing beside them.

"Isn't Bobby the mechanic who was engaged to Aimee, the hit and run victim?" Maggie shook her head to take it all in. She'd waited for Jake to show, but didn't expect it this way.

And now the man was gone again. She didn't even get to say hello.

"Same guy." Rachel looked disgusted. "When Bobby Ray's not drinking he's not bad. But drunk—he's as bad as his daddy."

"*Mean* drunk?" Cara clarified, exchanging a glance with Maggie, who knew she was upping him higher on the suspect list.

"Is that why Bobby dislikes your brother? The Aimee thing?" Maggie asked, realizing someone had turned up the music, during the altercation, and she had to speak louder to be heard. Something about smooth Jazz did not work with volume blasting.

"Hey, bro, turn down the music," Rachel called to her brother, apparently feeling the same way.

Roger waved, taking Gabriella's hand and keeping her

close as he moved to the stereo. Most guests continued to mingle quietly as if nothing had transpired. Once the volume muted to reasonable, Rachel answered. "Those boys have been fighting ever since they were fifteen and got in trouble together."

"They used to be *friends*?" Cara said, surprise ringing in her voice.

"Best buds from grade school until sophomore year of high school. Those two were always getting into trouble together."

"Friends?" Maggie repeated, not sure how this fit into the equation.

"There's no love lost now," Cara pointed out. "Hard to believe they ever got along."

"They were inseparable." Rachel grabbed a glass off the tray as a waiter walked by them. She took a gulp then added, "Those two were wild, though my dad tried to claim it was just mischief, sometimes it was worse."

"Like what?" Maggie asked, bad vibes zinging like invisible darts. She glanced over at Susan who appeared oblivious to the turmoil, sitting beside her uncle with a cluster of well-wishers surrounding them.

"When I was ten and they were twelve, they painted skulls on the water tower and got caught smashing pumpkins on the Walker farm. Then they stole a hay wagon, broke out windows of the school and vandalized more stuff than I can remember. It kept escalating. Then I was thirteen when they set Parker's barn on fire. Killed a prize mare and stallion. The sheriff arrested Bobby, but Daddy somehow got Roger off. Sent him away to military school until he graduated."

"What happened to Bobby?" Maggie asked, thinking it unfair if they were punished differently.

"Arrested, despite being a juvenile. Kicked out of school, though he claims to this day he dropped out." Sadness dropped over Rachel's pretty face. "His dad beat him in a drunken rage. Poor kid. He tried to hide, but I saw his split lip, black eyes and broken nose. Never healed exactly straight. Goes for emotionally, too."

"That's horrible," Maggie exclaimed. She didn't condone the boys' actions, but what happened to Bobby was wrong.

"It was." Rachel glanced around the room, probably anxious to move on to other guests and a better topic. "Roger came home at holidays and for a few months before college, but their friendship died the night of the fire. Bobby Ray's hated him ever since."

"Don't blame him," Cara said.

"Susan told us he works at his uncle's garage as a mechanic," Maggie recalled, still hurting for the wronged youth, yet realizing it was the adults' fault, not Roger—he was a kid back then. Not in control of their fates.

"A *good* mechanic." Rachel sighed. "Working usually keeps Bobby out of trouble."

"The bad blood between him and your brother, does it apply to you, too?" Maggie asked, sensing an underlying caring to Rachel's words.

Startled, Rachel's eyes opened wide. "I don't hate Bobby Ray if that's what you're asking."

"Not what she meant," Cara interjected. "Question is does *he* hate you?"

Rachel stirred her drink with her fingertip to make the champagne swirl, then she sucked it off her finger. Finally, she replied, "Bobby was my first kiss. If life were different, I wouldn't mind repeating that kiss—bet he wouldn't either."

"He is good-looking," Cara said. "I thought so when I saw him at the diner one time."

Rachel nodded, looking dejected head to foot. "He's got a sweet side, too. But since his sis and my brother hooked up, he isn't even civil to *me*, anymore."

"Does he fix your cars?" Maggie asked. "Susan said your family has always gone to his uncle's for repairs."

"We do, but not Roger. If it's his car, I drive it there in

case Bobby is at work. He usually is. Then we all pretend it's for me." She sounded even sadder. "That used to work—maybe it won't now that he hates all things Mercer."

"When Bobby drinks, he has a bad temper," Cara observed, echoing Maggie's thoughts. "Could he be dangerous? Really hurt somebody?"

"I don't think so," Rachel answered, avoiding their gazes. "Oh, there's Josie and Tess. Gotta greet them. Catch you later." With that, she escaped.

"What do you think?" Cara asked, as they both watched Susan's cousin merge into a group of guests.

"I think," Maggie responded, wishing Jake would reappear as she turned toward the front entry. "Bobby Ray Clemens is a dangerous man."

Chapter 14

Stars studded the moonless night sky, as a lone figure dressed in black stealthily moved from tree to tree and bush to bush toward the target. Only an occasional gleam off the tool belt or crunch of brush revealed the trespasser's presence. But *tomorrow*—tomorrow, everyone would know of this midnight visit. *Tomorrow will be life changing for more than one.* With an evil smile, the intruder amended the thought—perhaps *life-ending.*

෴

The next morning Cara and Maggie loaded their bags along with Susan's into the van for the ride back to Houston. "Too bad you didn't get any time with your deputy this weekend."

"At least we got to chat awhile when he got back to Susan's birthday party."

Cara chuckled. "Like he *chats.*"

"Sorta." Maggie grinned, prancing back toward the house as Cara slid the van door closed. "For him he was downright chatty last night."

"About?" Cara watched her friend unable to miss the

lively animation Maggs always exhibited when she discussed the sexy lawman.

"Stuff." Maggie's hand flew to her cheeks before she added, "Bobby Ray Clemens for one thing."

"That guy was pretty wasted last night. Did Deputy Rice drive him home?"

"No. I asked that, too, but he said the mechanic lived at the bottom of the hill, so he threatened Bobby Ray with jail if he even thought about returning." Maggie paused, her hand on Susan's front door. "Then Jake watched while Bobby staggered down the hill and into his place."

Cara stepped up beside Maggie. "Anything mentioned about the murders?"

"Not much. Don't you think we ought to tell him about the two notes we got in Houston?" Maggie looked troubled. "I almost did last night, but wanted to talk to you first."

"Maybe. But not while Susan's around. She'd go into shock if she knew the killer tracked her there." Cara felt a surge of guilt. "And that we've been hiding it from her. We might even get fired."

"She wouldn't do that," Maggie defended.

"Hmm, the only thing consistent since we took on this job—is *nothing* goes as planned." Cara thought about event after event from Susan's postponement at the beginning to all that happened since. "Besides, Susan doesn't need added stress. Right?"

"Right," Maggie replied as she turned the doorknob. "Let's see if she's ready to go. For some reason I feel a sense of dread settling over Mercerville. I'll be glad when it's in our rearview mirror."

"Me, too," Cara agreed, shaking off a dark cloud of her own.

"There you are." Susan greeted them inside the entry. "Gladys told me you were loading the car. That's sweet. I could've carried my own."

"No problem," Cara responded, thinking Susan looked a lot better. Maybe her birthday party was worth this trip.

"We ready to hit the road?" Maggie asked, practically bouncing on her toes with impatience.

"Ready," Susan said, snagging her handbag, a leather purse packed heavy enough to rival Cara's own.

As the door clicked shut behind them, Cara hoped they were closing the Mercerville chapter. "I'm driving," she announced, flipping her keychain. "Let's go."

They piled into the van and it practically purred as she started the engine. *Even their vehicle was ready to leave Mercerville*, Cara thought, smiling too herself.

Clouds gathered warring with the sun. "Looks like we might be heading into a rainstorm," Maggie said, peering out the windows as they passed through town toward the highway.

"Oh, dear!" Susan exclaimed. "I left my raincoat and umbrella in the hall closet."

"Should we go back for them?" Cara asked, wondering if they'd ever make it past the city limits sign.

"It's okay." Susan sounded wistful. "I can buy new ones in Houston."

"Are you sure?" Maggie asked, leaning forward as far as her seatbelt allowed. "It'll only take a few minutes."

Driving along smoothly and almost out of town, Cara held her breath as Susan hesitated.

"Well, I should have two sets anyway. One for each house. Just never got around to it."

Cara pressed the gas pedal speeding forward as they crested a hill, leaving Mercerville behind. She could see the lake glimmering blue ahead on the left. They were nearing the area where Aimee's Mercedes Benz had been towed out of the water.

"I'm not sure you're up to shopping yet," Maggie persisted.

Cara bit her lip, wishing Maggs would hush.

"Houston shopping is a bit intimidating," Susan agreed. "I hate to inconvenience you girls though."

"No problem," Maggie cheerily replied. "Right, Cara?"

"Uh, yeah. A pullout overlooking the lake is about a half mile ahead. I'll turn around up there."

"That's where we stopped when they found Aimee's car," Maggie said. "Looks a lot more peaceful now."

"The lake is so beautiful and calm. It's hard to imagine anything bad ever happened here," Susan agreed softly.

Cara let off the gas, slowing as she turned into the turn-off. She hit the brakes. *Nothing!*

"Stop!" Maggie yelled as the van rumbled off the road. "What are you doing?"

"No brakes!" Cara grinded the emergency brake to no avail.

Mouth dry, heart in her throat, Cara frantically shifted gears, jamming it into reverse. Too late. Gravity prevailed, plunging them over the edge, bumping down the bank, the lake rushing at them.

"The bushes!" Maggie cried.

"Right!" Cara aimed toward the bushes. Praying the van wouldn't roll as the vehicle angled on its downward rampage. If the shrubbery could at least slow them before they propelled into the water, they had a chance.

With a grinding crunch, the van slammed into the thicket. Force of impact bit her seatbelt into her body, Cara fought trying to steer, desperate to control the vehicle. With a rip, the undercarriage hit a huge rock jutting up from the ground. *Pifftz.* Airbags inflated, whomping her body, stealing her air. Now she couldn't see out the windshield. Feeling helpless, she still fought. Crushing, scraping, tearing and bumping they crashed through the bushes as the van propelled toward the lake. Just as the front tires splashed into water, the engine died. The van shuddered to a stop.

"You two okay?" Maggie croaked from the backseat, her voice thready.

"Superb." Cara wrestled the airbag, trying to see Susan. "Susan?"

No answer. "Susan!" the designers cried in unison.

Terrified, Cara struggled out from the driver's airbag,

climbing out of the van. "Maggs, phone for help. I'll go around and check Susan."

"She's got to be okay," Maggie whispered, grabbing her cell, not wasting a second to call.

Cara sloshed through the shallows, thankful the van hadn't gone deeper and praying Susan would be all right. She could see through the passenger window and her heart nearly stopped. Blood dripped down Susan's face and her purse wedged between the airbag and her forehead. With a burst of adrenalin strength Cara wrenched the door open.

Feeling Susan's throat for a pulse, Cara shoved away the airbag as best she could. It was like a living thing enveloping them.

"Jake and the EMTs will be here in minutes," Maggie said, sliding her phone away as water ebbed and splashed around their ankles. "Susan?"

"She's unconscious, but has a weak pulse. We need to stop the bleeding." Cara peeled off her T-shirt, pressing it against Susan's forehead. "It looks like her purse turned into a projectile."

Sirens wailed in the distance. Maggie rummaged in the van and grabbed Cara a shirt out of a totebag. "Here. We need all their attention to be on rescuing our client, not on you and your lacy bra." She reached to take over applying pressure on Susan's wound. "Put your top on quick. I see flashing lights down the road."

છ૭૯૭

The patrol car screeched onto the turnout. The car door slammed. Jake ran and skittered down the bank toward them. An ambulance whipped to a halt beside the police cruiser and soon EMTs picked their way more carefully down the hillside, carrying their equipment and a stretcher.

"You okay?" Jake asked, grabbing Maggie by the shoulders as she and Cara moved out of the EMTs' way.

Maggie nodded, staring up into his eyes. She was aware

of the paramedics administering to Susan, taking vitals, giving oxygen, and slowing the bleeding, yet she couldn't tear her gaze from Jake's. Stirred by the concern he radiated, she couldn't prevent the flare of joy that this dynamite deputy actually cared about her. "S—Susan's h—hurt," she finally stammered.

"Miss Susan's in good hands." Gaze not wavering, he kneaded Maggie's shoulders. "What about you and Cara? Do you need to be checked out?"

"Don't think so. Susan's unconscious." She glanced back at the van, where the EMTs were carefully transferring Susan to a stretcher.

Susan coughed suddenly, pushing the oxygen mask away to ask weakly, "Where are you taking me?"

"Your choice, ma'am," one paramedic answered. "To the hospital at Fredericksburg or to Doc Hudson at the clinic here in town."

"He's my doctor," Susan whispered. "I want to go to the clinic."

"You need a hospital," Cara protested, stepping up to the stretcher. "Not a small town clinic."

"She's right," Maggie added, full attention riveting back to their client and the medics. "Susan needs scans, MRIs and all that."

"We have them." Jake drew her attention back to him. "Thanks to Susan and her family's generosity, Mercerville now has a state-of-the art-clinic with all the fancy equipment."

"Right," a mustached EMT agreed. "As of last year our clinic is one of the best in the county."

"You sure?" Cara demanded. Though disheveled, shook-up and stressed, Maggie sensed Cara's total focus on their client's health.

"It's a fact," the other medic stated as he fastened the straps, readying to transport Susan on the stretcher up to the ambulance. "Enough talk. We've got to get her there immediately."

"Wish we could ride with her," Maggie said.

"Good idea," Jake responded. "One of you can ride in the back with her and the other upfront."

"Isn't it against regulations?" Cara asked, sharing a glance with Maggie as they both recalled Ed's clash with paramedics.

"Hal?" Jake's voice rang out deep and firm. "Gerry! You guys take these gals with you to the clinic."

"Sure thing."

Cara's brows raised, but she smiled.

Maggie grinned back, realizing there were certain advantages to small town ways. "Wait!" she said as they'd hiked partway up the hill. "What about the van?"

"Probably not drivable. I already called Sunrise Garage for a tow," Jake answered, holding her elbow as he assisted her over the uneven terrain.

"All our stuff?" Cara asked, hesitating halfway.

"I'll throw it in the cruiser before the tow-truck arrives. I'll take it to Miss Susan's place then pick y'all up at the clinic."

"That's sweet." Maggie gazed up at him, nearly tripping in a tire rut left by their van.

He caught her. "My pleasure. Glad to help."

"Thanks," Cara said, cresting the hill to scramble onto the pavement.

"I want to ride in the back with Susan," Maggie volunteered. "You ride up front with the driver?"

"You got it." Cara paced the paramedics, waiting for them to hoist Susan into the back of the ambulance before she circled to the passenger door.

Deputy Rice leaned down to give Maggie a quick kiss on the lips, then he took hold of her waist and boosted her up into the ambulance behind the stretcher and the medic. "See you at the clinic later."

The driver slammed the rear doors shut before Maggie could reply. She perched beside Susan, trying to hang on as the ambulance, siren blaring, rumbled onto the highway and back toward Mercerville. Maggie's head whirled and, if she closed her eyes, she re-lived the crash. *Not good.* She opened her eyes to watch Susan, who'd relapsed into semi-consciousness, occasionally moaning, but mostly quiet.

What a morning! Maggie breathed thanks and added a silent prayer that their client would be okay. At least Susan's bleeding stopped and a bandage covered the newest wound—inches from her healing one. Hopefully, Susan was like a cat with nine lives and could bounce back strong and healthy again.

"She's stable." The medic said as he reached over to adjust Susan's IV line. "Another minute and we'll be at the clinic. Doc's waiting for her."

"Would the hospital have been better?" Maggie couldn't resist asking.

"Doubt it." He shifted to turn toward her. "We can life-flight her by helicopter if necessary. I think she's best off in Doc's care. He knows her and has all the needed technology."

"Okay." Maggie's hand flew to her head. "I'm a bit dizzy myself."

"No wonder. It's miracle you didn't plummet deep into the lake. This could've been an underwater rescue—or worse—victim recovery."

"Cara's driving saved us." Maggie bit her lip, realizing the truth of his words.

"Lucky ladies." The medic twisted his thin moustache. "Been keeping your guardian angels too busy from what I hear."

"Especially Susan's," Maggie replied, hoping they wouldn't need luck or angel protection to keep her safe anymore. If only Jake could catch the murderer and they could all breathe again.

∽∾∽

"It's pouring now." Cara stared out the clinic window at

the falling rain, glad they made it inside before the Texas heavens began to weep.

"Thank goodness the rain waited. Susan didn't need to get wet now." Maggie paced back and forth across the waiting room. "I wish we'd hear something."

"It feels longer than it's been. Remember they're taking x-rays, running scans, hopefully all the tests she needs."

Maggie glanced around the caramel, ivory and taupe colored waiting room where the furnishings were modern and clean, but not fancy. Nothing like she'd imagined to find at a clinic in such a small town. "This place is nicer than I expected, so maybe they do have everything."

"Hope so." Cara spun as she heard a door at the far side open.

"You Susan's city friends?" asked a plump older man as he entered, peering at them over his thick glasses. His white coat and dangling stethoscope labeled him the doctor.

"Yes. How is she?" Maggie asked, rushing toward him.

Cara joined her. Head thumping a painful pulse, she awaited his answer, hoping for the best, fighting fear of the worst. This was her fault. She'd been the driver.

"Well, we checked her over inside and out and I stitched up her head." He scowled at them. "Inches from another wound—also recent."

"She fell into the pool in Houston," Maggie explained, obviously feeling as guilty as Cara. The doctor's glare didn't help.

"I've been treating Susan since she was a wee girl and she's had more mishaps the last few months than during her entire lifetime." He cleared his throat. "I can't talk for city folk, but in my opinion, she'd be a lot healthier stayin' put in her home here and not gallivanting back and forth to Houston."

"The brakes failed," Cara defended, feeling awful.

"It wasn't our fault," Maggie finished.

"Not blamin' anybody. Just sayin' you're fortunate her head's as tough as her pa's was."

"So she's okay?" Cara asked, relieved and hopeful.

"Will be. She can go home now she's all patched up." He shook his stethoscope at the designers. "But no traveling farther than up the hill to her house for at least three days."

"It'll take that long to get their van fixed," Deputy Rice said, striding across the waiting room to join them.

Cara hadn't even noticed him enter, but apparently Maggie had. Maggs's eyes were on the tall lawman's every step. "Three days?" Cara calculated in her head. That meant they couldn't leave until Wednesday. The rock delivery was scheduled for Thursday morning. She hadn't thought there was that much damage to the van.

"That's with them doing a rush job on your vehicle." The deputy leveled a gaze on her that she imagined sent his subjects scattering, but she glared back.

Maggie intervened. "We do appreciate the mechanics putting us as a priority." Her pixie face puckered into a frown. "I can't understand losing the brakes."

"Not everybody stays on top of vehicle maintenance like they should," tutted the doctor.

Cara's hackles rose. She hated being accused of something she didn't do. "The brakes were fine. We just had the van inspected last month."

"True, license renewal, inspections, the whole package and it passed with flying colors," Maggie agreed, not looking any happier than Cara felt.

"I've already asked them to check the brake-line," the deputy added, in a matter of fact tone. "We'll know more tomorrow. Right now, how about we get you ladies back to Miss Susan's place where Gladys is waiting."

"That's as far as I'm lettin' Susan go," Doc huffed, before disappearing back through the door. "No gallivanting to Houston with you city girls," he called back at them.

"Sorry about that," Deputy Rice said, addressing Maggie. "Doc Hudson's gruff, but a great doctor."

"As long as Susan will be all right," Maggie replied, smoothing her wild copper curls, freckles stark against her pale face. "This has been a miserable morning."

"Tell me about it," Cara muttered, wishing for a brief moment that someday, a man would look at her with the same concern and affection she witnessed as Deputy Rice studied Maggie.

"Don't you think it's time we told Jake about the Houston notes?" Maggie shot a pleading glance at Cara, who shrugged.

"Why not?" Cara realized they were way over their heads. "If someone tampered with our brakes—it might be the same person who left threatening notes at the Houston manor."

"What?" Susan gasped, standing in the doorway, leaning against Doc for support.

"We didn't see you," Maggie apologized, her eyes wide.

"Tell me what's going on," Susan demanded in her rarely used *lady-of-the-manor* voice.

Cara sighed. "Deputy Rice is having the brakes checked out to see why they failed."

"We don't know if it was sabotage," he stated, calm and authoritatively. "Just routine."

"And the notes?" Susan persisted, for all her injuries, sounding just as authoritative.

Maggie unzipped the side pocket of her purse and withdrew two plastic sandwich bags containing the notes. She stuffed them into the deputy's out-stretched palm. "Here. We didn't know what to do with them."

Susan went limp, collapsing as they rushed to her. The doctor kept her upright until Deputy Rice lifted her into a waiting room chair.

"She can't handle all this danged nonsense," Doc announced, taking her pulse and listening to her heart. "Couldn't you discuss it out of my patient's earshot?"

"Hey, we didn't know you guys were here," Cara defended, as she bent to retrieve the bags Deputy Rice had dropped.

"Where else would we be?" Doc scolded. "It's my clinic."

Cara gave up on reasoning with the doctor as Susan moaned, blinking open her eyes. "Is this a bad dream?" Susan whispered.

"Very bad," Cara replied, deciding it certainly was.

❧❧❧

The next morning, with Cara inside on her cell phone to suppliers, Maggie relaxed in the garden with Susan. The phone conversation last night with Ed, telling him about the accident and his wife's condition was not something Maggie ever wanted to repeat. But today dawned a new day. Acting cheery, she and Gladys settled Susan in a lounge chair by the fountain. So instead of the bench, Maggie sat in a patio chair at her client's side. "Nice that the rain cleared. The way sunlight sparkles off your fountain is gorgeous."

"It always calms me to spend time out here. I enjoy the scent of the flowers, the birds singing and even the bees buzzing."

Maggie inhaled the perfumed air as sunshine warmed her skin and a breeze danced her curls. She patted down her hair, noticing Susan's hair fared no better and stuck out in places.

"It is peaceful."

"Did the killer really leave us notes in Houston?" Susan asked, shattering the peace.

"Uh, yeah," Maggie admitted, feeling uncomfortable. The way she explained this might cost them their client. And at this late stage of the job. *Where was Cara when she needed her*?

"Why didn't you show me?" Susan started to sit up, but her hand flew to her head and she eased back against the lounger.

"Your name wasn't on them. No name was." Maggie met Susan's gaze, adding, "We were trying to protect you."

"I'm stronger than I look," Susan insisted, though she looked ready to blow away in the breeze.

"We know, but you were so stressed. We just couldn't add to it." *So far, so good.* Maggie crossed her fingers.

"How many notes did you hide from me?"

Oh, oh. *Not so good.* "Two. Only two."

"What did the notes say?" Susan didn't sound pleased or mad, just weary.

"They were cut and paste like the Mercerville ones. The first read *STOP*." Maggie took a deep breath then continued, "The second was just like Joan's: *Next time you won't be so lucky*."

Susan gasped, practically turning green. "This was after my pool accident?"

"Right. Only we didn't get it until we got back to Houston after helping Joan."

"Where were the notes?" Susan's eyes clouded, her voice wavering. "*In* my house? The killer was inside my own home?"

"No!" Maggie exclaimed, afraid she was handling the discussion all wrong. "Outside. At the far edge of the property. Our crew chief found them jammed in the back gate."

"The same person found *both* notes?" Susan asked with an incredulous expression and hands flying. "At the same time?"

"Weeks apart maybe even a month or more," Maggie replied, realizing they might have good reason to suspect Al Black, after all. It *was* quite a coincidence. Maybe this time Cara was more tuned in that she'd been.

"How does your head feel?" Maggie asked, desperately trying to change the topic.

Susan fingered the bandage on her forehead. "Hurts. Maybe more than the last time."

"Did you know your purse hit you?"

"It did?" Susan said in surprise. "I remember sitting my

handbag on my lap, instead of leaving it on the floor like I usually do."

"I do that, too, sometimes to dig out my keys or a lip-gloss." Maggie tried to steer the conversation on a new subject once again. "I wonder how your friend Joan likes Florida?"

"Adores it. I got a phone call from Joan this morning," Susan said, a tiny smile curving her lips. "She loves Florida."

"That's great." Maggie sincerely felt pleased.

"Yes. Joan declared she should've made the move years ago. She's even dating, nearly every night."

"Dating?" Maggie exclaimed, "Every night? That's more dates than I've had all year."

Susan twinkled. "Apparently at her cousin's retirement community, *Joan* is the hot young chick."

"Imagine that," Maggie replied, eager to tell Cara.

"Yes, imagine that," Susan repeated with a soft chuckle.

A ruckus sounded from the house. A man yelling above Cara and Gladys's voices, doors slamming.

"What?" Maggie's head swung round to see Ed burst out through the patio doors into the garden.

"Ed!" Susan gasped, again sitting upright, but staying that way.

"Susan, we're leaving. I'm taking you home."

"You can't," Maggie protested, jumping to her feet.

"I want her home safe with me." Ed clomped toward them. "Mercerville's dangerous."

"She's safe—she has us all around her," Cara stated, trying to reason with him as Gladys hovered beside her, wringing a dishtowel into knots.

"Safe?" Ed purpled, sounding ready to bulldoze through anyone between him and his wife. "After a crash into the lake nearly killed her?"

"The doctor says she can't travel yet," Maggie intervened, planting herself in Ed's path though he outweighed her by a ton.

"No hick doctor is going to dictate where my wife recovers. I'll take her to a real doctor in Houston." He sidestepped Maggie to reach Susan. "Come on, sugar. We're going home."

"If you're sure," Susan replied, trying to get off the lounger.

"Here, Sweet cakes, let me help you," Ed offered, his voice softening as he bent toward her.

Maggie had to admit that Ed handled Susan gently as he half-assisted, half-carried her into the house. Then he turned back to them. "Please, get my wife's bags for us."

Maggie grumbled right along with Cara as they marched upstairs like truculent children to gather Susan's things. Gladys fretted, making sure they rounded up all Susan would need. Remembering the forgotten items that triggered their turn around before they lost the brakes, Maggie added the raincoat and umbrella before they went out the front door.

Who knows? she thought. *Maybe the brakes would've gone out on the top rung of a Houston triple-decker freeway, killing us all. Blessings can come hidden. Yesterday, Susan wanting her rain-gear might have saved all our lives.*

"Thanks." Ed stashed the bags into the rear of the Yukon.

The windows were up, so they couldn't talk to Susan, still Maggie called past Ed into the vehicle. "Take care, Susan. We'll get to Houston as soon as we can."

Ed slammed the rear door shut, turning to them. "For your safety, you two shouldn't hang around this town. If my wife isn't safe here, no one is." With that, he hurried around to the driver's side, got in, and gunned the engine.

Maggie watched the Yukon whip around and shoot down the driveway, sending dust and gravel flying.

"Will Susan be okay?" Faith asked, popping out from the bushes. "I heard that Doc ordered her not to travel."

"Ed's just in a protective mode, concerned about his wife and wants her safe under his wing," Maggie replied, trying to convince herself that the drive back to Houston wouldn't harm Susan.

"I guess," Faith said, her baby blue eyes huge. "I don't really know him."

"No loss," Cara quipped.

"Ignore Cara." Peacemaker kicking in gear, Maggie smiled at Faith. "Ed can be so sweet with Susan and I've never heard him ever raise his voice at her."

"Saves his grumpiness for us." Cara brushed dust off her jeans.

"We do irritate him sometimes," Maggie admitted.

"Well," Faith drawled, a knowing expression on her face, "Maybe he doesn't like sharing Susan with you."

"Huh?" Cara said, lifting her hands palms up with a shrug.

"I get it," Maggie replied. "You may have something there. They are practically newlyweds and we've been underfoot."

"Plus Susan appreciates your friendship. She told me how much your company means to her." Faith flashed a quick grin. "You know some husbands want *all* the attention."

Maggie considered Faith's insight. "Good point. Maybe when he's around, we'll give them more space."

"This is outrageous." Cara scowled, the tiny dent above one brow alerting Maggie. "Susan's going back to *Houston* and we're stuck here in *Mercerville*."

Chapter 15

"You're staying in town awhile?" Faith squeaked, sounding way too pleased.

"No choice. Our van's in the shop," Cara replied, turning to Maggie with a sudden thought. "Unless we rent a car?"

"I checked. None to rent here. We'd have to go over to Fredericksburg and our insurance won't cover it. Besides, we *need* our van."

"And you'd have to return here to get it once it's fixed," Faith pointed out. "Which means another round trip to and from Houston and back again."

"You're right," Cara reluctantly agreed, seeing the logic of the diminutive blonde.

"Maybe you'd like to come over for lunch?" Faith beamed. "I just live next door, the baby's down for her nap and the boys at school."

"Sure," Maggie said, ignoring Cara's glare.

"Nothing fancy, just tamale pie casserole." Faith dimpled at them. "Leftover from last night. But it's good."

"Okay." Actually, it sounded very good, Cara admitted to herself. Now Susan was gone it felt awkward to hang out at the Mercer house and they especially didn't want Gladys waiting on them. No way.

"I'll dash inside and tell Gladys," Maggie offered, before taking off into the house.

"This is so nice!" Faith took Cara's hand, startling her.

The action was done in childlike innocence. Yet, in the city, *almost strangers* usually respected personal space. Of course, this wasn't Houston and they did *know* Faith. Still, Cara subtly withdrew her hand to brush her hair out of her eyes. "Are you sure you want us to crash your lunch time?"

"I'd just be grabbin' a bite over the sink. This'll be much more fun!" Faith parted the hedge between bushes. "I'd better check my sleeping angel. You two come on over when you're ready."

"Will do," Cara agreed, as always amazed by the neighbor's tiny size. She must not eat much of her own cooking.

"No need to knock. Just come on in the kitchen door. See ya in a few!" With that, Faith slipped through the hedge, branches flipping closed behind her.

A few minutes later, shimming through the hedge proved easier for Maggie than Cara. "Hey, Maggs, wait up."

"This reminds me of summer camp," Maggie laughed, plucking a wild flower as she stopped to give Cara time to catch up.

"Why, because you're quicker?" Cara asked, plucking leaves out of her hair.

"No, because your jeans are dirty." Maggie sashayed, across the grassy patch to Faith's sidewalk that curved up to the house.

"Faith said to use the kitchen door." Cara rubbed at a stain on her knee then gave up and trotted toward the side entrance. "It's this way." Maybe Maggie was faster, but she was better with directions.

Maggie fell in step beside her as they skirted a flower garden. "This lunch might be useful."

"Definitely—I'm starved."

"Besides the food." Maggie dodged a calico cat as it dashed across their path. "We might learn more about some of the suspects from Faith. She's a talker."

"Okay, but let's not be obvious about digging. The last thing we need is word getting around that we're snooping again. I don't want to see another threatening note."

"Right." Maggie reached the kitchen door, hand raised to knock. "Susan can't handle any more of those."

"Neither can we." Cara let Maggie knock despite Faith's invite to just walk in. Small town unlocked doors, even with a murderer prowling about, simply floored her. If she lived here in Murderville, she'd use every lock and alarm system available.

"You're here!" Faith exclaimed, a golden-haired cherub on her hip. "This is Angel, she woke up just in time for lunch with us."

Maggie reached out and touched the tot's teeny hand. "You're a cutie, just like your mama."

The child smiled then buried her head against Faith's shoulder. With one hand, Faith unlatched the highchair tray and sat Angel down. With a deft movement, she snapped on the tray and sprinkled Cheerios across it. "This will keep her busy while I nuke our dinner."

"What does she eat?" Cara asked, eying the tot, not used to sharing a meal with children. "Does she throw food?"

"Not much. Dumps her bowl sometimes, but usually she's too busy eating to play with it." Faith bustled around the galley kitchen setting plates, napkins and silverware on the pine table. "I'll give her some finger food. She ate her lunch earlier."

"Can we help you?" Maggie offered, standing beside the highchair as Angel jabbered, cramming Cheerio after Cheerio into her mouth and pushing some around the tray like a toy car.

"Nope. Sit and take a load off." The microwave dinged. Faith removed a scrumptious smelling casserole. "Oh, one of you can grab a couple of cans of soda pop from the fridge and get me one too, please."

Cara collected three Cokes from the refrigerator and put them on the table then picked a chair farthest away from the highchair. "This is a cute house." She gazed around at the sunny yellow kitchen and gleaming white countertops. "How do you keep it so clean? I mean with kids and all."

"Clean?" Faith laughed. "Don't look too close." She slid the casserole dish onto a trivet on the table. "Dig in."

Cara didn't need to be asked twice. She spooned the tamale pie casserole onto her plate, inhaling its tempting aroma. "If this tastes as good as it looks, I'll be in heaven."

Maggie took a bite of Cara's before dishing up her own. "It does! Yum!"

"Oh, yeah," Cara said after her first taste. "This is what I'm talkin' about." She glanced at Faith. "I'd weigh a million pounds if I cooked like this."

"Like you ever cook anymore," Maggie countered.

"I never have time. Besides, I haven't seen our kitchen for months."

"Enjoy not cooking while you can," Faith advised them. "Once you get married, you'll go nuts trying to figure out what's for dinner every night."

"Chinese take-out." Maggie winked at them.

"Doesn't work often enough," Faith replied good naturedly. Angel flipped a piece of cereal at them. "Especially once you have kids."

"Makes sense." Maggie put a clean spoon onto the highchair tray. "Can she play with this?"

"Ah, she'll probably throw it on the floor." Faith smiled a *proud Mommy* smile as Angel promptly chucked the spoon over the side of the tray. "Her favorite game is you-pick-it-up."

"That'll teach me." Maggie laughed. "She's such a doll."

Cara saw a gleam in Maggs's eyes. For one brief second she wondered what would happen to their business when one of them married and started a family. She shook off the thought, knowing they'd deal with that when it happened. If there was one thing their partnership proved, it was they could adapt to most *anything*.

"Just wait until the boys run in here whooping and hollering to get her screaming and wanting to get down and play with them. She won't look as cute then." Faith passed around a basket of rolls. "Angel can be a little devil when she wants something."

"Can't we all?" Cara responded. At that moment, Angel hit her with a Cheerio and all three women dissolved into laughter.

Midway through lunch, Maggie launched her questions. "Faith, our van's at the Sunrise garage. Are they any good at repairs?"

"Best place in town." Faith giggled. "Only place, only mechanics in town."

"Bobby Ray Clemens and his uncle?" Cara interjected, joining the game.

"Yep. They're really good. I think Bobby'll take over the garage one day." Faith tore off a piece of roll and put in on the tray.

"Doesn't he have a booze issue?" Cara asked, nibbling on her own roll.

"What if he gets drunk and messes up our van?" Maggie mentioned, understanding the direction to lead the conversation.

"He hardly drinks anymore." Faith noticed their exchange and added, "Oh, I heard about Susan's party. We couldn't go because this little one had a teething fever. But Bobby doesn't fall off the wagon much. He's nothing like his father."

"His dad's an alcoholic, right?" Maggie asked, knowing the boy must've had it tough. That didn't make her forget his anger though. Mean drunks were dangerous.

"His dad *was*. Died in a car wreck a few years back—drinking and driving, you know," Faith explained, popping another piece of roll in Angel's mouth.

"We witnessed the scene Bobby made at the party, so it makes us nervous about him repairing our van." Maggie watched Faith closely trying to detect any hesitation.

"You got that," Cara emphasized.

"You can trust Bobby Ray's work. His uncle trained him to be one of the best mechanics in the state." Faith jumped up and began wiping off her tot's face and hands. "I'd just as soon have him work on our cars as his uncle." She twinkled at them. "Besides, he's cuter!"

Cara raised a brow. "Ladies' man?"

"Not really. The girls like him. But he's not a skirt chaser, as my hubby would say."

"We heard he was engaged to the secretary who got killed?" Maggie queried, trying to dig subtly.

"Not hanging out in the single scene since my marriage, so I find out through the rumor mill, but seems that Travis girl went through guys like a speedboat cuts through water. I know Keri, Bobby's former girlfriend. She had nothing nice to say about the outta towner who stole her man."

"No one says much nice about Aimee Travis." Cara finished off the last bite of tamale. "Right, Maggs?"

"Nothing to us, anyway," Maggie agreed, springing up to help clear the table.

"Not to speak ill of the dead," Faith confided, whisking dishes over to the sink and rinsing them off. "But not many folks around here will miss that dead secretary—no females, at least."

"As in wives and girlfriends?" Cara prodded, adding silverware to the dirty dish pile.

"Anyone in particular?" Maggie added. "Maybe the banker's wife?"

"Zelda?" Faith asked, startled. "She's scary."

"We haven't met her."

"You're lucky." Faith took Angel out of the highchair, again attaching the tiny moppet to one hip. "If Zelda Ohlmacher's on any committee, I won't be. Disagreeing with her—well, you might as well skip in front of a semi."

Maggie's cellphone chimed a funky ring. "Excuse me," she said, glancing at the calling number and wandered toward the kitchen door.

"Can we help wash the dishes? " Cara asked, wondering if Maggie's call was the deputy.

"No thanks. I'll stuff them in the dishwasher later." Angel started to fuss as she tugged on a lock of her mommy's flaxen hair. "This rascal needs to be changed."

"Cara," Maggie exclaimed. "We need to meet Jake at the house. He's got news on the van."

"Lunch was delicious," Cara said, glad for an excuse to escape before the diaper thing.

"Bye, sweet girl." Maggie tickled the baby's chin. Angel giggled then buried her face in Mommy's shoulder again. "And, Faith, thanks for feeding us."

"Sure. Drop by anytime. It's nice to spend time with grownups." Faith hugged them each, not exactly pleasing little Angel. Or Cara. "See ya later."

"Bye," Maggie called as they hustled out the door. Once outside, she put a hand on Cara's wrist. "Jake is already waiting for us at Susan's place and he sounds tense."

"What's wrong now?" Cara muttered, tangling with the hedge once more.

The patrol car was parked in the drive, but the deputy was nowhere in sight. Feeling odd just to walk in as if they had Susan with them, Maggie rang the bell.

Gladys opened the door wide and shooed them inside. "None of that nonsense. Miss Susan wants you to make yerselves at home here during your stay." She motioned a hand toward the entry table. "There's the car keys in the bowl. I have instructions to leave the car at your disposal, too."

"Fine. The car will come in handy," Cara said, "but we don't want to put you out. No cooking for us or waiting on us."

"Yes, ma'am." Gladys nodded, not entirely convincing, but Maggie's gaze met the deputy and she missed the rest of Cara's exchange with Gladys before the housekeeper disappeared down the hallway.

"Howdy." His midnight eyes held Maggie's, sending her

a message that if they were alone he'd take her in his arms.

Cara stepped forward. "What's so urgent, Deputy Rice?"

He swiveled his attention to include both designers, switching to what Maggie termed his *on-duty* mode. "Mechanic's report reveals a cut brake line and tampering with the emergency brake. No accident." He scowled, his brow creasing as his rubbed his jawline. "Sabotage."

"Thought so," Cara said.

"Me, too." Maggie hated their fears were confirmed, but they knew their van and kept it in top condition.

"Neither one of you's surprised?" He sounded taken aback as if the firework he lit had fizzled. "Someone tried to kill you—or Miss Susan."

"We survived." Maggie put a hand on his forearm, feeling the strength beneath his shirt.

"If that's the extent of your earth-shattering revelations, I'm going upstairs and call our crew. Hopefully, things are going better in Houston," Cara said then tromped up the stairway, leaving Maggie and the deputy alone.

"Duty calls. Can't stick around." He fiddled with his hat. "But I'm off duty this evening. There's a good fish and chip place down the highway a ways. What if I take you and Cara there to dinner?"

"Sounds great." Maggie felt an internal flutter, but smiled calmly up at him.

"About six." He searched her face for a moment then added, "Then you two can tell me whatever else you're holding back on the case. Since asking—or ordering you to stop your own investigating does me no good, guess we might as well put our heads together before anything else happens."

"Sure." Maggie nodded, watching him and wondering how this would go down with Cara.

He dipped his head to press a butterfly kiss upon her lips. "Glad you're okay. Later."

Maggie stood staring after him as he strode out the door.

Upstairs, she found Cara in the Ivy guestroom. "Jake invited us to dinner tonight."

"Us?" Cara laid her phone on the dresser and turned to Maggie. "I'm not date crashing. You go."

"He invited us both."

"I'll accept Susan's offer and borrow the car to go to the diner." Cara grinned. "I can sample the Monday special."

"What's that?"

"No clue, but probably packed with calories and carbs." Cara smoothed her hands over her curvy hips. "Just what I need, huh?"

Maggie laughed. "You can't fool me. You just want to quiz the locals again. I think mystery busting's gotten into your blood."

Cara pressed a finger to her lips. "Shh. Even if it's true, I'll never admit it."

"We've got several hours to kill," Maggie said, going to the ever-present sketchbook. "We might as well work on the Devereaux design plan."

"Right." Cara crossed over to a leather case to dig out their colored pencils. "If events continue as they have lately, we might be off this job and starting that one sooner than we planned."

"Not going to happen," Maggie replied.

"You hope," Cara retorted.

Just before six, Cara already gone, Maggie heard a rat-a-tap on the rose room door as she applied her makeup. "Come in."

Gladys peeked inside. "Miss Susan phoned with a message for you."

Maggie dropped her eyeliner, turning to the doorway. "What? Is she all right?"

"Didn't sound too chipper to me." Gladys stepped inside the room, looking worried. "Miss Susan says to tell you and Cara that they arrived in Houston safe. She's not feeling so good, so the mister is fixin' her tea and toast and then going to tuck her in for an early night."

"Now Susan's home, she should be just fine," Maggie assured the housekeeper, hoping she spoke the truth and Susan had weathered the journey okay.

"H—home?" Gladys sputtered, wringing her apron. "*This* is her home—not some city house." The housekeeper shuffled out the door and down the hall mumbling, "She oughtta be here with me carin' for her properly. Tea and toast! What kinda nourishment is that?"

Maggie smiled at her own reflection in the mirror, knowing that Gladys's sentiment was echoed all over Mercerville. They all felt Susan belonged there and not in Houston. It was sweet how loyal they all were to Susan.

Just as she slicked on her lip gloss, doorbell chimes drifted upstairs. Unable to stifle her excitement, Maggie grabbed her purse and a cotton sweater then dashed downstairs to throw open the door.

Tall and handsome in faded jeans and a muscle shirt instead of his uniform, Jake greeted her with his usual, "Howdy." He looked around behind her. "Where's your partner in crime?"

"Cara's not joining us," Maggie answered, as he took her elbow to guide her down the front steps to his truck.

"That so, Irish?" Reaching the passenger side, he flashed his devastating dimple at her, drawling, "What a shame."

❧❦❧

Usually a booth or corner table person, Cara found herself again aiming for the counter stools until she heard someone call her name.

"Hey, Cara!" Rachel waved at her from a side booth. "Come join me."

"You here alone?" Cara asked, sliding onto the seat across from Susan's cousin.

"Was meeting a friend, but she just sent a text to cancel." Rachel sipped on a straw stuck into a strawberry shake, glancing around. "Where's Maggie?"

"With the deputy." Cara opened the menu. As much as she loved Maggie, they weren't glued together, but in this town everyone seemed to assume they were. "A date."

"Oh, yeah, I heard they had a thing going." Rachel cocked her head, eyeing Cara. "I also heard you drove into the lake and my cuz got hurt again."

"You heard right."

"Thought I'd drop by to see her after dinner."

"You can't." Cara closed the menu. "Ed took her back to Houston."

"What?" Rachel nearly knocked over her shake. "Doc will be furious. He doesn't want her traveling yet!"

"I know," Cara said. "Ed came to get her, so Susan went with him." She shrugged. "We had no control over the situation."

"That's rotten."

Cara felt she'd disappointed Rachel. Feeling uncomfortable, she changed the subject. "What do you know about the lakeside community being built by the lake?"

"My friend's one of the contractors. He says it'll be very upscale, high end finishes, top appliances, really pricy stuff."

"Who is the developer?" Cara squashed down an excitement bubbling inside and told herself she was just making small talk.

"I can't remember, but I have a card in my bag. Ian passed out a stack when he got the job." She rummaged through a fringed leather, hobo bag and eventually extracted a shiny blue card. "Here. I have no use for it."

"Thanks. Just curious," Cara replied, a gossamer idea forming as she pocketed the card.

Order pad in hand, Nan appeared. "Know what you want, yet?"

"Steak sandwich and onion rings," Rachel answered, then they both looked at Cara.

"Sure. Sounds good. And one of those," Cara added, pointing at the shake, deciding why not?

Everything here was a gazillion calories, anyway.

"You got it." Without scribbling a word, Nan poked her pencil back behind her ear and bustled away.

"Remember at the party when you said Bobby Ray hates all things Mercer?" Cara asked, once they were alone again.

Sadness cloaked Rachel's face as she cautiously replied, "Yes, why?"

"Our brakes were tampered with," Cara hesitated then plunged forward, "And Susan is a Mercer."

"Bobby wouldn't hurt her!"

"You positive about that? He had both the knowledge and opportunity *and* he was so furious that night."

"Isn't he the one *fixing* your van?" Rachel asked, playing with her straw and not denying Cara's statement.

"Apparently," Cara answered, unable to disguise her concern. "We're just *thrilled* about that."

ຄາຄາ

Maggie pushed her fish and chips around her plate, unable to stop thinking about the car crash and the murders. She must be crazy, sitting across the table from a sexy hunk lawman and thinking about other stuff instead of him. Finally, she stabbed a fish chunk and nibbled it.

"What's wrong?" Jake studied her in concern. "Don't you like it?"

"It's good. Excellent fish. Great chips!" Maggie picked up an English-style chip to prove it. "Yum."

"Enough." Jake chuckled then reached out and snatched the chip away to pop into his own mouth. "You're overdoing it, Irish."

"It is good." Maggie took a pile of chips, transferring them onto his plate. "But I'm just not hungry."

He placed his large hand over hers to stop her from adding more. "Tell me what's up?"

"Trouble brewing," Maggie whispered. "That old saying

fits." Her gaze flew up to meet his. "I feel it in every fiber of my being, Jake."

"The bad stuff is behind you now." He turned her hand in his, rubbing his thumb gently across her palm. "I'll see to it."

Realizing her knight in cowboy armor was no match for a universe in turmoil, Maggie replied, "Wish life was that simple."

"Are you withholding more evidence from me?" A vein throbbed in his muscular neck.

"We gave you the notes." Maggie withdrew her hand as he stopped the thumb caress. "The only thing else we have is suspicion."

"Who do you suspect?"

"Who *don't* we suspect might be a simpler question." Maggie twisted a curl, glancing around the eating place and glad they weren't in the middle of Mercerville. "The only one we've eliminated is Joan Gaynor, between the note she received and moving to Florida—"

"Joan was on your list?" he said with disbelief.

"Aimee Travis did steal her bank job away," Maggie defended.

Laughing, the deputy leaned back in his chair. "I don't think that fine lady even swats flies. No wonder you gals have to par down your list if you suspect the likes of her."

Chin up, Maggie retorted, "We have a very efficient list. Two in fact—one for each murder and several of our suspects are on both."

He sobered, scratching his jaw. "Maybe we ought to compare lists, Irish."

"Can do." Maggie twisted the curl, fretting about the van. "Cara and I need to get back to the Houston job-site. We need our van repaired."

"Workin' on it. Have Bobby Clemens and his uncle full steam and there's no better mechanics in Texas."

"Did Bobby know John Lawson, the lawyer who was killed?"

"Everybody knew John. Small town. He was our only lawyer."

"So he represented Bobby?"

"Nope." Jake grinned, flashing that dimple. "Just the opposite."

"Please explain?"

"Young Clemens got in a bar skirmish a few years back, but the guy—Hal Peabody, a clerk at the hardware store, wouldn't fight. Bobby got madder. He's an ornery drunk."

"Tell me about it," Maggie said, recalling the party crasher.

The deputy rocked back in his chair, lost in thought as he spoke. "Keith threw Bobby out of the joint. Too drunk to think, Clemens jumped in his decked-out pick-up truck, rammed Hal's sedan, then took off."

"Where does the lawyer come into this picture?" Maggie asked. *A hit and run triggered by drinking and explosive temper—the same ingredients that caused Aimee's demise?*

"Hal Peabody sued for damages. John was his lawyer. Bobby didn't have money, so he lost his truck. He loved that pick-up, used to go four-wheeling every weekend." Jake grew thoughtful. "Now he drives an old heap. That boy holds grudges."

"Grudges can be poison," Maggie replied, discovering one more thread in the murder tapestry, a possible motive for the mechanic. She mentally added Bobby Ray Clemens to the lawyer's list, which placed him on both. *Another double suspect.*

She squeezed her eyes closed. *And he was repairing their van. How scary was that?*

ᥱᢙᥱᢙ

"That's it!" Cara stormed out of the ivy guestroom and through the hallway with Maggie a half step behind.

"This is why I didn't tell you after my date last night that the mechanic had a grudge against the murdered lawyer. I knew you'd want to do something crazy."

Cara spun around, Maggie nearly crashing into her. "We're partners, Maggs. That means sharing."

"I did share, this morning." Maggie and Cara resumed their trek down the hallway. "This is a bad idea. You can't confront a murder suspect alone."

"Tag team won't work. You're out and I'm in. The guy flirted with *me* in the diner that time, plus the entire town knows you and the deputy are an item." Cara tapped the toe of her sandal.

"That matters? Why?"

"Like a killer's going to loosen up around a lawman's girlfriend?"

"You might be in danger. We didn't bargain on this," Maggie protested.

"Sheesh!" Hands on hips, Cara rolled her eyes. "What could happen to me at Sunrise Garage on a Tuesday morning in Mercerville?"

"All these bad vibes floating around and you ask that?" Maggie scrunched her face in frustration, both hands dragging through her wavy curls. "It's my fault. I coaxed you into searching for clues, but *not* this way!"

"If I can trick Bobby Ray Clemens into admitting something, Deputy Rice can arrest him, then we can get back to *design* instead of playing detective." Cara gestured at the hem of her peach sundress. "This short enough? I want to look alluring."

"You always do." Maggie shook at finger at her. "I still don't see how you can record the conversation on your cell phone without him knowing."

"That's why I love my phone. It fits in my hand, hardly noticeable."

"What if he does notice?"

"I'll pretend I'm getting a text. No big deal," Cara replied, ignoring her friend's panic.

They reached the top of the stairs as Maggie grabbed Cara's arm. "You can't do this."

"I can, Maggs." Cara shook her arm free. "And I will."

Chapter 16

Maggie watched Cara circle in the Mercer towncar then drive out the long driveway just before a silver Camaro turned onto the drive. *Who?* Whoever it was they'd be disappointed to discover Susan was not home in Mercerville, but back in Houston.

The Camaro braked to a stop. Roger Mercer jumped out, dashing up the steps to Maggie. "Hi! Was that Cara? Glad I caught one of you."

"You want us—not Susan?" Maggie still didn't trust Susan's cousin. After all, they had him on both suspect lists for Aimee's and the lawyer's murders.

"Right." He smiled a charming grin and Maggie noticed his eyes were the same hazel as his cousin's. "Dad sent me to invite you girls over for dinner since my cuz has vacated the premises."

"That's nice, but we couldn't impose," Maggie replied, startled that Susan's Uncle Leland would even think of them.

"Won't accept no for an answer. Dad's orders." Roger's hands flew just like Susan's as he talked. Must be in the Mercer genes. "Nothing fancy, just me, Dad, and Sis dining on the best chicken enchiladas you ever tasted."

"Does sound good," Maggie answered, wondering what

Cara would say and certain the menu might persuade her since they both adored Mexican food and Tex-Mex dishes.

"Great! We'll pick you up about six." Roger bounded back down the front steps. As he open the car door, he added, "Later!"

Maggie watched him race away in the Camaro. Had she made the right decision? Would Cara mind that she accepted the invitation? It might help them investigate Roger. They'd have to do it subtly though, so he'd have no clue he was a suspect.

She only hoped Cara was being as *subtle* confronting the mechanic.

∾∾∾

Sunrise Garage looked right out of a fifties movie as Cara spotted it on the fringe of town isolated by the ranches and farmland. Abandoned ancient gas pumps stood as rusty sentries guarding the building. The office was glassed on two sides, allowing her to see through the windows that it was empty, though papers scattered over the old desk. Gravel crunched under her tires as she parked the car in a spot in front of the office door. Deciding there was no point entering a vacant office, she carefully picked her way around the side to the open garage doors. The pungent odor of oil and grease hit her as she scanned the repair dock for anyone.

"Hello? Anyone here?" Her voice echoed in the silence, then she heard the whirr of an industrial fan accompanied by the clanking of a wrench before a squeak as the mechanic wheeled out from under her van.

"My uncle's at lunch," Bobby Ray Clemens began from his prone position, wrench in his right hand and wiping his grimy brow with the other. "Can I help ya?"

"Yes," Cara wore her perkiest smile, tugging her sundress just enough to draw his eyes. "It's our van you're fixing. Thought I'd see how close to done you are."

"Right. The city chicks." He jumped to his feet, looking intrigued. "Afraid it won't be ready until tomorrow."

"No sooner?" Cara said, not having to feign her disappointment.

"Afraid not." Bobby was bad-boy handsome, even grimy and unshaven. He had his sister's dark eyes and hair, but both in a rough masculine version. With his square muscular build, his ragged and ripped muscle shirt, he showed off biceps and abs any pro-wrestler would envy. Fighting down her vulnerability, Cara recalled the bitter menace from his drunken rage at the birthday party. She did not want this man for an enemy. He loomed large and dominating as he moved forward, closing the distance between himself and Cara.

"Ah, okay." She took a step backward, wishing more traffic traveled the road or that another business—or even a house or two were close by. It felt as if they were alone in nowhere land, just Cara and this hulking, wrench-welding murder suspect. Remembering why she'd come here, she took a deep slow breath and batted her lashes. "I confess I'd hoped the van would be fixed by now."

He stopped, his eyes raking her head to sandals, lingering on the curves between. "Never want to disappoint a pretty girl, but we've been working our as—" He switched words. "—*butts* off. You're lucky we had the parts or it'd take a week."

"We do appreciate it." Cara couldn't figure out how to question him without him catching on. She could already hear a defensive note replacing his flirtatious tone. This was not the time or place to back a potential killer into a corner, or she might end up the next victim. "I should go and let you get back to work."

"Just a minute," he said, latching her arm with a strong grasp of his free hand.

She stiffened then forced herself to relax and smile. He couldn't know they suspected him. "Yes?"

"There's a honkytonk up the highway. Would you like to go for a drink tonight?"

"That's kind of you to ask," she replied, knowing from his sensual stare kindness did not trigger his invitation. "But I can't tonight. Maybe next time we're in town," she said, to prevent it from sounding like a rejection.

Eyes narrowed and expression darkening, he released her, raising the wrench in his other hand. "Workin' stiffs aren't worthy of city types?" he spit out.

"I don't date *strangers*—no matter their occupation," she quipped, not letting him know she quaked inside as she stood there.

Hating the fact she didn't even have anything useful on her cellphone, Cara spun around to sashay away. Acting far braver than she felt, she bargained that even if he were a killer, he wouldn't attack her from behind. Bobby didn't appear the cowardly type—more an in-your-face than a be-hind-your-back guy.

e∕∂e∕∂

"You turned your back on a murder suspect who was holding a wrench?" Maggie gasped, unable to contain her horror. "He could've bashed your brains in!"

"I'm here and fine." Cara eyed her friend. "Bobby just yelled, 'Your loss!' at me as I left."

Maggie raked her hands through her curls. "You are impossible or crazy, Cara."

"Hmm, *Crazy Cara* has a nice ring to it." Cara grinned and tossed the notebook at Maggie. "I bet you would've done the same thing. It was a clever way to escape. Now we need to go over our lists."

Maggie grunted, but flipped through the notebook to find their lists. "Got them. Now what?"

"Deduction time is chocolate time." Cara tossed Maggie a piece of her secret stash.

"Great idea. Brain power." Maggie popped her entire piece in her mouth.

"We need to think of some questions for Roger tonight." Cara nibbled slowly on her chocolate as she stared out the rose room window down into the garden. "When you're facing a suspect your mind goes blank and you can't think of a thing. So we need to have a topic plan."

"Good idea." Maggie found a blank page, her pencil poised. "So what do we need to know from cuz Roger?"

"About the baby."

"You didn't blurt out the baby thing to Bobby Ray, did you?" Maggie asked in alarm. She hadn't seen it, but knew Cara had deleted her phone video since the mechanic exchange had been a bust.

"Of course not." Eyes flashing, Cara's hands flew to her hips. "I can be subtle—besides, I never got to even steer the conversation around to the dead secretary."

"Just checking." Maggie scribbled onto the notepad. "That's a delicate subject and I promised Jake it stops with us. We can fish, but not let on a clue that Aimee was preggers when she was murdered. Okay?

"I *know*." One brow raised, Cara eyed Maggie. "I keep secrets quite well, if you recall?"

Maggie squirmed uncomfortably, remembering several secrets that her best friend and business partner had kept for her over the years. Since they were kids, when Cara vowed to keep her mouth shut, she always honored it—no matter what. "You're the best at secrets. It's just that this murder stuff is new to us both."

Grumbling in disgust, Cara said, "So let's wrap up the mystery part and concentrate on design. Thank goodness, we can get back to the job in Houston tomorrow. I'm going crazy here."

"Crazy Cara, crazy Cara," Maggie chanted, winning a reluctant smile from her friend. "Now let's figure out a few points to weave into our conversation with Roger and then get ready for dinner."

☙❧

Mid-dinner, Cara forked a bite of chicken enchiladas with an appreciative moan. "Mm, these are wonderful!"

"Juanita's recipe," Rachel replied, "Dad coaxed it out of her before she left."

"Best cook we ever had," Uncle Leland said, his angular face crinkling with a smile. The smile faded and his hand shook slightly as he lifted his fork. "How she married that no good Clemens was beyond me, still, she stayed on until Bobby Ray was born."

"Y—your ex-cook is the m—mechanic's mother?" Maggie sputtered.

"And Gabriella's," Roger added. "That's where my girl she gets her looks."

"Heck with looks," Uncle Leland said with a guffaw that sounded stronger than the elderly man appeared. "Her *cooking* was divine."

"Still is and she's teaching Gabby," Roger said, obviously smitten.

"Let me get this straight." Cara glanced around the table. "Your former cook is Juanita, who married Clemens senior, now deceased, and they had two children: Bobby Ray and Gabriella."

"So her kids are…" Maggie picked up the ball, turning to Roger who sat on her left. "Bobby the mechanic and his sister who's dating you."

Rachel laughed, dabbing her ruby lips with a napkin. "Small world, huh?"

"It certainly is in our town," Uncle Leland agreed, again shaky as he tipped his glass to his lips.

"Great town," Maggie nodded.

"Everyone in Mercerville's been so good to us," Cara said, sneaking one more enchilada from the serving platter. "You inviting us here for dinner is very kind."

"Wouldn't dream of letting you girls be on your own and

I'm certain Susan would expect no less hospitality from us," Leland Mercer told the designers, sweeping a warm smile between them.

"Southern hospitality thrives in Mercerville." Smiling back, Cara pushed her nearly empty plate aside. "Susan's neighbor, Faith, fed us lunch yesterday."

"Faith Donovan, now Faith Pruit." Rachel wadded her napkin and tossed it by her plate. "She got married right after high school graduation and has been having babies ever since."

"We didn't meet her boys, but we saw the newest addition, an adorable baby doll named Angel," Maggie said, not faking the spark in her eyes.

Cara groaned inwardly, hoping her friend hadn't caught baby-fever.

Rachel pursed her lips and gave a fake shudder. "Three kids and Faith's just my age."

"At least she's not an old maid like you, Sis." Roger grinned, his tone teasing.

"Since when is twenty-three old?" Rachel countered. "You should talk. You're a quarter of a century old." She grabbed a snap-pea, launching it at him.

"None of that!" Leland commanded, as his son dodged the pea. "No food fights at the table!" He took a shallow breath. "And in front of guests."

Cara and Maggie laughed, enjoying the casual sibling skirmish. Aware they needed to return the conversation to babies, Cara said, "Does that mean you're ready for daddy hood, Roger?"

Alarm replaced the humor in his expression. "Not ready for that, yet."

"You better marry first." His father shook a bony finger his direction. "Mercers have a reputation to honor and you two better respect our responsibility."

"Don't be so stuffy, Dad," Rachel said. "We're not in the Victorian era."

Always the peacemaker, Maggie changed the topic. "Our

van will be ready tomorrow. I'm going to miss everyone here in Mercerville."

"Especially one deputy," Cara said to ride her.

Maggie blushed, but they had accomplished the conversation turnabout as Rachel said, "Turning Jake Rice's head isn't an easy achievement. Every girl in town's tried and failed."

"Yep—even my sis," Roger gloated.

"You dated Jake?" Cara and Maggie both blurted.

"No," Rachel answered haughtily.

"He wasn't interested," Roger expanded, ribbing his sister once again and this time receiving a killer glare.

"Well, dinner was scrumptious, but we have to go." Cara could sense Maggie wanting to ask more about Jake, but that wasn't a good game plan. You don't ask a woman scorned about the guy who shut her down. "We've got packing to do."

"Thanks so much," Maggie told Uncle Leland as they bid their goodbyes.

"I'll run you home," Roger volunteered though Rachel had driven them over.

"Nice," Cara said, relieved it wouldn't be his sister—too tempting for Maggie to give the girl the third degree.

Misunderstanding, Roger winked at her. Cara bit her lip on her ready retort. She'd riled enough murder suspects for one day.

The next morning, Maggie tapped on Cara's door, calling, "Come on, Jake's downstairs waiting to take us to pick up the van."

Dressed and ready, Cara opened the door. "I hope it's fixed right. It makes no sense to have the repairs done by the same guy who might've sabotaged it."

"Jake made sure that Bobby's uncle checked everything out before he signed off on the repairs, so we're safe. No worries."

"No worries," Cara echoed as she followed Maggie down the stairs. "That's a laugh."

They waved goodbye to Gladys who stayed on the porch as Jake stashed their gear in his police cruiser.

"You two ready to roll?" he asked, opening the passenger door for Maggie then the back car door for Cara.

"More than ready," Cara replied, glad this was not a Houston police car where all types of felons had been hauled to jail in the same backseat.

Bobby Ray Clemens was nowhere in sight when they arrived at Sunrise Garage. Instead, his uncle, Paul Clemens, a wiry man with leather skin, Roman nose and gray-streaked brown hair greeted Deputy Rice with a handshake.

Paul Clemens looked nothing like his handsome nephew. Maggie felt an instant liking for the man as he had them sign some paperwork then handed over the keys to their van.

"Looks good," Cara said, circling their vehicle. "But how does it run?" She touched the front fender that showed no sign of the wreck. "And how well does it stop?"

"Purrs like a warm kitten and stops like a dream," Mr. Clemens answered, opening the driver's door while the deputy transferred their things into the van. "Here you go, young lady."

Cara froze. Just for a second, but long enough for Maggie to read that her friend wasn't quite ready yet to take the wheel of the van, retracing the exit which lead to their crash. "Hey, I've got the keys, I'll drive." Maggie slipped past Cara and onto the driver's seat.

The deputy slid the side van door shut. "Wait a sec, Irish." Hardly noticing Cara walking around to the passenger side with Mr. Clemens as an escort, Maggie's full attention fell on Jake. Blocking with his body, he leaned in so she couldn't close the driver's door. She inhaled his masculine scent, her gaze locked on his midnight eyes and those sexy lips. His mouth captured hers for a brief, but scalding kiss. It only lasted a heartbeat.

"Take care, Maggie."

She blinked as the door slammed and he was gone.

"Wow, on a hot meter you just exploded the top off," Cara said, staring at her.

"Uh huh." Maggie touched her lips. "He's one hot deputy."

"Well, he lives in Mercerville, and we don't, so can we finally escape this town?" Cara fastened her seatbelt. "Please, Maggs?"

It was late afternoon when they arrived at the Houston manor. Ed wasn't around, but Susan gave them hugs. "Missed you two." She giggled into her hand, her gaze a bit unfocused. "Put your bags in the guestroom and come talk to me."

Susan wandered off in the direction of the kitchen. Cara exchanged a glance with Maggie. "Do you think she's been drinking?"

"I've never seen her drink before, maybe a glass of wine once with dinner." Maggie hauled her gear through the white landscape and into the guestroom. "I wonder where Ed is?"

"Who cares?" Cara shrugged as she dumped her things on the Soho chair. "Maybe we'll luck out, and he'll be off on a business trip for a few weeks."

"One can hope." Maggie perched on the edge of the bed. "I guess we'd better go find Susan. Maybe we can get her to eat something. I swear she's tipsy."

"Tomorrow is the rock delivery. She'll be excited about that." Cara started unpacking and placing her makeup on the dresser.

"It's so cool Susan didn't make us use real stone from her family quarry." Maggie added some of her own items. "Those boulders would've killed our budget."

"And our *crew*," Cara said, disappearing into the adjoining bathroom with shampoo, shower gel and toothpaste.

Ten minutes later, they found Susan in the kitchen, perched on a barstool, spinning around.

"Where's Ed?" Maggie asked, glancing around as if he might appear any moment.

"Oakville, no Dallas, no…" Confusion clouded Susan's face. "I can't remember. He told me this morning before he left." She swirled around on the stool again.

"Have you eaten anything?" Cara asked, reaching out a hand to stop Susan's spin.

"Cereal." Susan cocked her head. "Want some?"

Maggie was already rummaging through the fridge. "What if I fix us an omelet? We can add cheese, green peppers, and mushrooms."

"No mushrooms," Susan stated with a frown.

"No mushrooms, no problem." Maggie cracked and whipped the eggs as Cara chopped the peppers, parsley sprigs and grated the cheese. Together they had the omelets ready within minutes.

"Smells good," Susan said, eating normally, making Maggie wonder if she'd imagine the tipsiness. "And tastes even better."

"How are you feeling?" Cara asking, watching their client just as keenly.

Susan's hand flew to the bandage on her head. "Almost better." She smiled at them. "Much better now you girls are here."

"Trust me, we're glad to be back in *Houston*," Cara said with emphasis on Houston.

"The artificial rock arrives in the morning," Maggie interjected, not allowing Cara to expand and slander Susan's hometown.

"That's nice."

Susan didn't seem interested. Concern niggled at Maggie as she observed Susan's bland expression.

The designers looked at each other in alarm. Maybe their client did want her *own* stone. Maggie sighed. *Too late now…*

❧❧❧

The next morning brought glaring sunshine and controlled chaos. In the midst of the artificial rocks and boulders delivery with a half dozen guys hauling a mountain of fake stone into the backyard, Al approached Cara and Maggie. "Got to take off real fast."

"What?" Cara cried, doing a double take at their hulking crew chief.

"Now?" Maggie asked in astonishment.

"Urgent business."

"*This* is urgent business," Cara stated, her entire being set to blow.

Reading the signs, Maggie tried to tamp down the fireworks. "Can't it wait?"

"Not if I'm going to live." Chagrin dropped over his expression and he looked trapped.

"You *won't* live if you walk off the job now." Cara tensed, ready to lash out.

Maggie touched her arm in warning, trying to defuse the tension. "Al, it has to wait."

"Hell." Al swept off his hat, his puppy dog eyes tormented. "I'm damned either way."

Cara glared up at him, fists clenched at her sides. "Take off now and you're fired."

"Please, I need this job."

He focused on Maggie, appearing so miserable that a wave of sympathy flowed over her. This was partly her fault. She remembered telling him to let them know first whenever he left the jobsite—otherwise he might've have slipped out unnoticed in all commotion.

"What's so urgent?" Maggie asked, sensing this was a man torn.

"Wife's expecting. It's our first. Pregnancy's makin' Brianne crazy." He took a breath and continued. "If I don't get her fish tacos and chocolate pudding quick, she'll fall apart."

"Just take it to her after work," Maggie replied, digesting his explanation.

"Nope." He sounded so morose, it was almost comical.

"She'll call me every five minutes crying and screaming until I get there, then when I get home she'll either throw it at me in a rant, cry her eyes out or not speak to me for days. Been there, done that. Can't live with her either way."

"Huh?" Cara stared wide-eyed at him. "The pickles and ice cream thing's why you've been disappearing?"

"Yep." Head hung in shame, he dropped his voice real quiet. "Please don't tell the guys. The crew will lose all respect for me if they hear the wifey's got me runnin' and fetchin' like a hound dog."

"They'll understand," Maggie soothed, as Cara stood with her mouth open.

"No, ma'am." He straightened up, putting his hat back on over his wavy brown hair. "I can't run your crew if they're laughing behind my back. A leader needs respect to get the job done."

"This entire time has been about food cravings?" Cara murmured, remaining dazed.

Maggie glanced around the yard as the mountain of artificial rock piled higher and higher by the back fence. Everything did appear under control. "Okay, Al, take off now, but get back here fast."

"Thanks." Relief lightened his step. "I'll make up the time. Always do." With that, he strode out the gate and immediately they heard his pickup engine gun to life.

"You thought Al was a killer." Maggie laughed, watching Cara still assimilating the news. "And the poor guy's just a henpecked husband terrorized by his hormonal wife."

"If he feeds his wife fish tacos and chocolate pudding in the same meal," Cara retorted, arms folded across her bosom, "he *is* a killer."

༻✿༺

True to his word, Al made it back quickly and soon was barking orders and helping the crew assemble the artificial stone to see how they should fit to form the grotto. Cara watched, still absorbing the pregnancy-craving angle. Guess she'd have to cross him off their suspect list. "I can't believe Susan's not out here to witness this. Remember she said she couldn't wait to see and feel the fake rocks?"

"And to check out the competition." Maggie bit her lip. "You don't think she's drinking again today?"

"I don't think it's alcohol." Cara shielded her eyes while trying to watch the crew stacking and arranging the stone according to the design plan. She knew Al wanted to test match the diagram, before setting them permanently in place. "I think she's on pain pills."

"But Susan doesn't like pills," Maggie protested. "Besides, Doc doesn't seem the type to over-prescribe medicine. I doubt he gave her enough to still be taking any."

"Ed threatened he'd take her to a *real* doctor in Houston, maybe he did, one who prescribed pain pills." A boulder toppling from its place nearly knocked into Al, momentarily distracted Cara, then she glanced back at Maggie.

"Guess that makes sense." Maggie twisted a curl and nibbled on her lip again. "She's taking too many or too often. Something."

"How's this?" Cara suggested, "Let's order pizzas. We don't want the guys to take a long lunch break and we've got paper plates in the van. Then we can take some pizza inside to Susan, feed her, and see how's she's doing?"

"Great thinking!" Maggie grinned, the lilt back in her manner. "You order the pizza while I make a drink run. Bottled water and Cokes for all."

Just as Maggie returned and stashed the drinks along with fresh ice in their big work cooler on the patio, her cellphone be-bopped her favorite rock song. "Hello?"

"Maggie? This is Faith," said a little girl voice.

"Hi, Faith" Maggie replied in surprise.

"Hope you don't mind. Jake, ah, Deputy Rice gave me your number."

"That's fine." Maggie had no idea why Faith was calling.

"I've been trying to call Susan all morning on both the house phone and her cell. She doesn't answer. I'm worried."

Faith sounded frantic. Maggie remembered one time when she and Cara were on a decorating job in Virginia and Mom had accidently left the ringer off on the phone. Mom and Dad didn't answer for two days. Distressed, Maggie finally called a neighbor to check on her parents. That sense of panic she'd experienced washed back now as she talked with Faith. "Susan's inside. I'll get her now, Faith. Hang on."

Maggie tracked through the sterile mansion room by room, finally discovering Susan asleep in a recliner in the entertainment room with the giant screen television flashing jungle scenes, sound on mute. She shook Susan's shoulder. "Wake up, Sleeping Beauty."

Susan stirred, stretching as she blinked her eyes open at Maggie. "Is it morning already?" she asked groggily.

"Almost noon." Maggie handed her phone to Susan. "Faith's on the line for you."

"Okay. Thanks." Susan gazed at the foreign cell phone a moment then put it to her ear. "Hello?" She listened for a minute before saying, "I'm fine. Sorry. I didn't hear it ring."

Maggie wandered around the room, trying not to eavesdrop, noting the entertainment room had foam-back white draperies. Black-out curtains in white, who'd a thought? Maggie shook her head. The only time she'd seen a place done in this much white was the ice palace scene in Dr. Zhivago. An old movie she used to watch with Mom and Dad. And *that* place had more warmth!

"Maggie, Faith wants to talk to you again," Susan said, holding out the phone.

"Thanks." Before answering it, Maggie said to Susan, "Cara and I ordered pizza, do you want to freshen up and join us?"

Susan struggled out of the recliner. "Sure."

Maggie headed back toward the sunroom, going out to the patio and yard that way, as if her body was programmed with an internal GPS. "Hey, Faith, you wanted me?"

"What's wrong with Susan?" Faith sounded nearly as concerned as before. "I told her the trouble we're having with the benefit dinner menu. Darlene insists on serving turkey. Who wants turkey midsummer? Plus, it's a pain and a mess to cook. Do you think Darlene would cook it? No way!"

"Ah, about *Susan*?" Maggie said to steer the conversation back.

"Whoops. Didn't mean to rant," Faith said sheepishly. "Anyway, when I explained to Susan, she just said *okay*. I waited for her solution—Susan always has a solution—*nothing*."

"I did wake her from a nap."

"A nap?" Faith exclaimed. "Susan taking a nap? She's like a whirlwind always busy, never stopping."

"I can picture that," Maggie said, recalling Susan's usual demeanor.

"So finally I suggested ham for a main dish." Faith's voice dropped. "She just said *sure* and *bye-bye*. I had to holler to catch her just to ask to talk to you before she hung up on me. She's acting strange."

"We think it's just pain meds." Maggie agreed with Faith, but didn't want to say much. "We'll keep an eye on Susan and take care of her."

"Please do." Faith sounded ready to cry. "We miss her so bad. Susan left a big hole in Mercerville when she moved away."

Maggie hurried outside and told Cara what had transpired, concluding, "So we aren't the only ones concerned about Susan."

"Not surprised. Here's the pizza now—told them to deliver to the back gate. Let's get food to the crew and go inside to our client." Cara headed for the gate where a pizza girl stood waiting, balancing a stack of pizza boxes.

"Pizza!" Maggie announced as they found Susan twirling on a kitchen stool again. "Grab some while it's hot."

Cara passed around paper plates while Maggie opened a pizza box where they'd combined several types of pizza. Susan selected a piece of Hawaiian pizza, Maggie mushroom, olive and sausage as Cara grabbed a plain pepperoni slice.

"We never eat pizza." Susan munched delicately on her slice. "Ed doesn't like it."

"But *you* do." Maggie grinned, pleased that their client was digging in.

She swore Susan had lost weight and the woman was already slim enough.

Cara must've been thinking the same thing, because she said, "Did you eat anything this morning, Susan?"

"Probably." Susan licked her fingers then took another slice of pizza.

"That's a yes or no question," Cara pressed, sharing a startled glance with Maggie.

Maggie had the feeling that Susan hadn't licked pizza off her fingers since she was a small child. Her manners were impeccable. Pills or booze, Susan was on something.

"This is yummy."

"It is," Maggie agreed. "Ah, do you want a drink with that?"

Susan giggled and Cara sighed. "Maggs meant water, iced tea, or maybe a soda?"

"Lemonade." Susan's wide mouth curved into a smile. "I like it sweet."

"We've noticed," Cara dryly replied, opening the fridge. She ignored the pitcher of lemonade and grabbed the tea decanter. "Oh, look, iced tea, chilled just the way you like it."

Maggie grinned, understanding Cara's hope that the caffeine might help sober up their client. "I'll get the glasses."

"I can pour," Susan offered, licking her fingers again.

"No, that's okay—we've got it," Cara replied, not filling Susan's glass all the way to the top as if she poured for a child who might spill.

"Are you taking some medicine?" Maggie asked, tossing away any pretense with impatience.

"Yes. Just like the doctor ordered." Susan peered into her glass. "This lemonade looks funny."

"It's tea," Cara corrected. "What doctor? Doc Hudson?"

"No." Susan shook her head, her flyaway hair sticking out wilder than usual. "The other one."

"Here in Houston?" Maggie decided Cara must be right about the meds.

"Yes." Susan flicked a mushroom off her third piece pf pizza, flipping it onto the pristine countertop. "I like Doc better."

"We do, too," Maggie said, realizing he'd never get Susan pumped up on drugs. He'd be horrified to see her now.

After Susan polished off her last slice of pizza, she tilted on the stool. Cara caught her. "You okay?"

"Just sleepy."

"How about we help you to your room and you can catch a nap?" Maggie asked, thinking that would be the safest thing for their client.

"Thank you," Susan murmured as Cara helped her off the stool.

They barely got her onto the huge king bed, before Susan conked out. Maggie tucked a silky white comforter around her then noticed Cara sweeping two medicine bottles off the nightstand.

"What are you doing?" Maggie whispered.

They never touched a client's personal items.

"These are the culprits." Cara unapologetically trotted out of the room with bottles in hand.

Maggie scurried after her. "You can't take those."

"We need to see what's she's taking if we're going to take care of her." Cara took the bottles into their guestroom and clicked on her laptop computer. It was in hibernation mode, so it flashed to life. Cara handed the bottles to Maggie. "Read the spelling of these to me and we'll see what they do."

Cara typed in the first medication. "This isn't a pain pill, it's an antidepressant."

"Oh, not good!"

Maggie spelled out the other one.

"Even worse. This is a tranquilizer. *One* is bad—*both,* awful." Head in her hands, Cara muttered, "Maggs, this is all our fault. Susan hearing us about the Houston notes after our crash sent her over the edge."

Chapter 17

Maggie checked the bottles. "These aren't real strong and the doses are low. The antidepressant prescribes one pill in the morning and one before bedtime." She peered at the other bottle. "This says taken as needed not to exceed two in twenty-four hours."

Cara's fingers flew over the keyboard. "But look—you shouldn't take them together. It can be deadly. Yet, the same doctor prescribed both." She scrolled down side effects. "If we can find this out online, the *doctor* should know better."

"Both warn not to take with alcohol. Or with sleeping pills." Maggie shook the bottles. "These are half empty."

"Let me see those." Cara snared the medicine and dumped the antidepressants onto the dresser.

"What are you doing?" Maggie cried catching one pill before it toppled off.

"Counting." Cara slid them to one side by twos, doing a silent count. "Just as I feared. The bottle should contain forty. Seven should be gone if taken as prescribed. Eight at most. Sixteen are missing."

"Susan's taking a double dose!" Maggie scooped the pills back into the bottle. "No wonder she's acting weird."

"Not done." Cara repeated the count for the other bottle.

"This is dangerous. Sixteen are missing from this one, too. The bottle only contained thirty and now there's twelve left. Both meds were prescribed Monday and we know it had to be late afternoon by the time they reached Houston and saw a doctor here."

"She'll kill herself."

"Not on our watch." Cara took both bottles and marched toward the bathroom.

"No, Cara." Maggie whisked the bottles out of her hand. "We have to put the meds back."

"We need to flush them down the toilet."

"These types of medications can't be stopped cold turkey. Susan needs to be weaned off them under a doctor's care." Maggie felt tears gathering in her eyes. "Or we might screw Susan up worse."

"You sure?" Cara asked as Maggie nodded.

"Maybe we should call Ed to let him know about this?"

"Right, and have him blame us?" Cara snapped. "Besides, what happened when we phoned him after the crash and told him about Susan? He packed her home and found the jerk doctor who got her on these."

"What can we do?" Maggie asked, keeping her voice soft as they neared the master bedroom.

"Not sure, but we'll think of something." Cara stopped at the doorway where they could see Susan still sleeping. "She's safe right now, so let's get back to work."

"Guess we're adding nurse to our detecting and design duties, huh?" Maggie whispered.

"We *undercharged* for this job." Cara scowled, pivoting toward the sunroom, not waiting as Maggie tiptoed into the master suite and replaced the bottles on the nightstand.

☙❧❧

The designers supervised as Al and the crew set the grotto, building the surround and the mountain cliff, adding the diving board midway. Flowing from the cliff pinnacle, the waterfall—meant for effect, not climbing—would cascade from the tiptop.

Cara snapped photos as they progressed. "It's looking awesome, isn't it?"

"It is." Maggie grinned. "We're so good." Her grin dipped into a frown. "Wish our client could appreciate this. It's her vision we're creating."

"She will." Cara turned off her camera and slid it into her pocket. "We'll help her get back to her enthusiastic self."

"How?"

"I'm still thinking," Cara replied, knowing there was always some solution. Discovering *what* it was would be the challenge.

Maggie squinted toward the lowering sun. "Tomorrow morning we have the electrician scheduled to do the patio, grotto, pool and the rest of the exterior lighting out here."

"And then we can refill the pool. Imagine the shimmering blue water in the grotto—"

"The rockwork will be set that fast?"

"Yes, that's why Al's using that stinky resin adhesive. It's sets faster, harder and is better for underwater than cementing them with concrete."

Maggie pinched her nose. "I hope the smell goes away."

"It will once it's dry." Cara laughed. "Well, guess that's one part of the reno Susan can be grateful to miss."

Evening approaching, the crew began cleanup under Al's watchful eye as Cara's stomach rumbled a dinner alert. "We should feed Susan."

"Okay. I'll go find her. Maybe we can just run and grab something?"

"Smart thinking—won't hurt to pry her out of the house." Cara snapped a few more photos with her wafer thin digital camera. The transformation from generic pool to grotto today was remarkable.

She felt sad that their client, who'd been so excited to see the process, slept the day away in a drug fog. It was their fault Susan had gotten to this state and their duty to correct it. But how?

On the way back from the burger bar, Susan rode in the passenger seat, jumping as her purse rang.

"That's your cell," Maggie said.

"It is?" Susan rummaged through her handbag, finally pulling out a blue cellphone. "It stopped ringing," she said in dismay.

"Just check messages or missed call," Cara said, glancing over from the driver seat.

"I'm not sure how," Susan replied, her voice mingling apologetic with frustration as she punched buttons.

"Here," Maggie said, reaching up from the backseat. "Let me."

Susan handed over her phone. Maggie whistled. "You have a dozen missed calls. A lot of them from Faith. One from Gladys, but the last two from your husband."

"Oh, dear." Susan looked confused. "How do I call him back?"

"Here," Maggie handed the phone back as it rang Ed's number.

"Ed?" Susan said cupping her hand over her phone. "I'm on the way home. We went for burgers." Cara and Maggie tried not to listen, but confined in the van, they couldn't help it as Susan added, "I feel okay. You won't? Okay. Love you, too. Bye-bye."

Susan fiddled with her phone, shutting it and dropping back into handbag. She sighed, "Ed's delayed. He won't be home tomorrow, not until Sunday night."

"Sorry." Maggie sympathized, wondering how they could leave Susan totally alone this weekend. They had planned to go back to their own place after the workday today, until Monday morning. "You must be disappointed."

"Why the delay?" Cara asked.

Susan's sad eyes turned to gaze out the window. "Some workshop conference and they need him as a last minute fill-in on the panel."

"The weekend will fly by," Cara assured her, obviously not in sync with Maggie.

"Here we are home." Maggie said, scrabbling out the van to assist Susan. "You must be worn out."

"I am." Susan accepted a helping hand as she admitted, "Ever since the car wreck, all I want to do is sleep."

"Meds might contribute to that," Cara muttered.

Not catching the irony, Susan said, "One makes me sleepy, but the other one's to pep me up."

"Oh?" Maggie queried, trying to sound casual as they entered the house. "Do you want us to help you to your room?"

"Whatever for?" Susan asked as if they hadn't done so earlier.

"Okay." Maggie replied, turning toward the guest quarters. "We've got some paperwork to do, so we'll see you in the morning."

"Thanks for dinner," Susan called as she aimed the other way.

Cara caught up to Maggie tugging her shirt sleeve. "Shouldn't we say something to Susan before she takes her bedtime dose?"

"Say *what*? 'Susan, dear, we snooped in your room, stole your medications, and played with your pills?' You want to get us fired right before our job's finished?"

"B—but," Cara sputtered, "At least we should warn her she's double dosing."

"How do we do that without confessing?" Maggie kept walking. "Besides, maybe Ed used some of those pills—or put them in a pill holder or something. We have no proof Susan took all the missing ones."

"The way she acted, she must have," Cara defended.

"Maybe she forgot to eat with her medication, or took them too close together. She acted fine tonight," Maggie answered, throwing herself into the Soho chair. "We're judging without all the facts."

"I hope you're right." Cara stared into the dresser mirror

meeting Maggie's gaze in the reflection. "Or it's on our heads."

৫৩৫৩

Maggie saw the electrician wave her over as he climbed out of deep pool section of the grotto, wiping sweat of his face with a bandana hanky. "The pool lights are installed, but I can't finish the lights along the path and the gazebo until Monday. Family emergency and I gotta run."

"We're putting water in the pool in a few hours," Maggie protested.

"Go ahead. That section's complete, but even the installed patio and grotto lights won't work until I finish up Monday. Juice is off to all this area until then." He mopped his face again then packed up his tools. "Sorry, but I'm out of here."

Cara dashed across the lawn to join Maggie. "What's up?"

"He can't finish until Monday." Maggie surveyed the backyard, realizing that he had the exterior lighting three quarters done. Still, this would put them behind schedule again.

"Why?"

"A family emergency."

"What next?" Cara grumbled, stomping back toward the house. "Guess this means we can't fill the pool."

"Yes, we can. He said to go ahead. He's through with that area."

"Thank heavens! Al has to check water depth and make sure it's all good." Cara halted, turning back to Maggie. "Have you seen our client today?"

"No. Have you?"

"No, but I heard her singing when I ran in for a bathroom break."

"Singing?" Maggie repeated in surprise. "That's nice."

"Uh, don't think so." A brow raised, Cara tapped her

foot. "She was singing *Wind Beneath My Wings* and gig-gling."

"Better than crying," Maggie said, hating to admit it sounded like their client might be over-medicated again.

The house phone was ringing as they entered the sun-room and just kept on ringing. "Susan will get it," Maggie said, hoping she stated a fact.

The insistent ring persisting then finally stopped. "See?" Maggie added, but before she could finish her sentence, the ringing renewed. "Maybe Susan's in the shower."

"Maybe she's oblivious," Cara countered.

Maggie wandered into the kitchen, noticing the caller ID. "That's Gladys."

"Why don't you answer it?"

"Why don't you?" Maggie charged back just as the ring-ing stopped. "Maybe Susan got it."

"Doubt that." Cara rubbed her stomach. "It is lunchtime. We might as well hunt her down and see if she wants to eat lunch with us."

They tracked Susan down in the media room, asleep in the recliner again. This time the television was on a talk show. Cara clicked it off as Maggie shook Susan's shoulder. "Hey, sleepyhead."

"Oh, hi," Susan said with a broad grin. "Is the show over?"

"Yes and it's time for lunch. We brought extra sub sandwiches," Cara offered, her arms crossed as she gazed over at Maggie and Susan.

"You're always feeding me," Susan said, stretching and trying to get out of the recliner while it was still in lounge position. "I should cook for you."

"You can, but not today." Maggie snapped the chair up-right and Susan scrambled free.

"Gladys called," Cara said circling the recliner to stand beside Maggie.

"How nice!" Susan cocked her head. "What did she want?"

"Don't know," Cara added. "We thought you answered."

"I didn't hear it." Susan smiled. "I'll call her back."

"Good idea." Maggie led through the white mansion into the kitchen where Cara took a foot-long sub out of the fridge.

The phone jangled back to life. Cara picked it up off the counter and handed it to Susan.

Susan wandered around the kitchen, chattering on the phone as Cara divided sub into three sections and Maggie poured them iced tea. Susan put the phone down, announcing, "That was Gladys."

"We guessed as much," Maggie replied, smothering a giggle, though she knew she shouldn't be amused.

"She said that a package from Italy arrived." Susan sounded confused. "Why would I get something from Italy?"

"Isn't that where you ordered the tapestry from?" Cara asked, suddenly interested.

Maggie passed napkins around. "I thought you were having it sent here."

"I meant to, but sometimes I forget and use my old address." Susan perched on a stool and daintily unwrapped her sandwich. "I must've put down the Mercerville one instead."

"No problem," Cara replied, looking smug. "We can all go to Mercerville this weekend to get it."

Maggie did a double take, putting a finger in her ear as if clearing it. "Did I hear you say we're going to Mercerville tomorrow?"

"Sure." Cara smiled and winked. "Maybe we'll drop by and say hello to Doc while we're there."

Grinning back, Maggie nodded. Things did happen for a reason. The tapestry delivery worked to their advantage—a perfect excuse to get Susan help.

With so many projects nearing completion and the pool refilling, the afternoon whizzed by, not giving them time to think about Susan until their crew had cleaned up and headed home. Evening shadows lengthened as Cara and Maggie shut the French doors of the sun room.

"Long day, huh?" Cara said.

"Should we check on Susan?"

"Will you?" Cara flexed her shoulders. "I want to hit the shower first."

"Okay," Maggie agreed, "but you owe me."

"Deal," Cara returned then touched Maggie's arm. "Are you in sync about the trip back to the Hill Country?"

"Sure. Just surprised." Maggie twisted a curl. "You did spring it on me."

"I know, but it was like one of those cartoon lightbulbs going off in my head when she told us about the tapestry delivery screw-up."

"I'm still absorbing it's *your* idea—the way you hate going there."

"It's the right thing to do." Cara pushed a hand against her forehead. "We'll take Susan and her meds to Doc Hudson in Mercerville."

"*You* are voluntarily choosing to go to Mercerville." Maggie still felt amazed.

"Cut it out. Doc will know what to do for Susan."

"What about Ed? What if he gets home before we return?"

"We'll deal with him later." Cara smiled to herself, imaging his reaction when he arrived home to find the house empty and a note saying they'd gone to Mercerville. "Susan is our client, not him."

"You got that right," Maggie said with complete agreement.

○◞◠◜○

Brainstorming and sketching out the placement of furniture and planters for the patio, the designers bent over the dressing table together, using it as a makeshift desk.

Maggie yawned. "Wow, I didn't realize it was so late.

We'd better hit the hay if we're taking Susan to Mercerville in the morning."

Cara glanced at the clock. "Midnight already?"

"Oh, no," Maggie exclaimed, as she plugged in her cell-phone charger. "I must've left my phone in the sunroom. I've got to charge it. Be back in a sec."

Barefooted, she dashed through the dark house by instinct, barely noticing the sunroom doors were already slid apart. Just as she entered the room, she heard a splash and glanced over to see the French doors to the patio standing open.

"Cara! Get out here!" she hollered, dread flooding her as she ran pell-mell outside. Racing across the patio and across lawn to the pool, lighting nonexistent except for a shrouded crescent moon, Maggie charged toward what appeared to be a giant water lily in the pool. But it was a body—their client! Susan floated face up in the water, her lavender night-gown ballooned around her body. Maggie dove in, sluicing through the unheated water.

"Maggs, what's wrong?" Cara ran onto the patio calling out into the darkness.

"Susan's in the pool." Maggie swam up to within reach of their client. "Help me get her."

Maggie towed Susan to the edge, boosting the older woman up as Cara bent down to grasp under her arms and hoist her out. Maggie scrambled out after, helping Cara lay her gently down. "Is she unconscious?" Maggie asked, trying to catch her breath and shivering.

"No," Cara announced with an odd expression while checking Susan. "I think she's asleep."

"Asleep?" Kneeling next to them, Maggie rocked backward in disbelief. "Sleepwalking into the pool and not waking up?"

"Apparently. She's soaked, but seems to be fine—no water in her lungs, no injuries, and her breathing's regular."

"The meds?" Maggie said, watching the even rise and fall of Susan's chest beneath the sodden nightgown and struggling to understand how Susan could sleep through it all.

"Guess so."

A slight breeze gusted, whipping Maggie's hair and squeaking the back gate. Her gaze riveted toward the gate, swinging to and fro. "Look!" Maggie pointed to it. "You don't think—the *killer*?"

Cara jumped up, running to the gate, looking out, then latching it shut. "Nobody. The guys probably just neglected to check it."

Maggie shivered from the inside out. This chill had nothing to do with being soaked. Something far more sinister triggered a chill she couldn't ignore.

👁👁👁

To Cara's amazement, they hustled their client inside supported between them, got her reasonably dry and into a fresh nightgown, then back in bed without Susan waking. Such heavy sedation. Could she be adding sleeping pills to the mix? At least Susan hadn't crashed into the rocks when she walked off the edge into the pool. She wasn't injured. She hadn't drowned. Thankfully, Maggie had heard the sleepwalker fall into the water.

If Maggs hadn't made that nocturnal visit to the sunroom to fetch her charger, Susan could be dead. Before they left the master-suite, Cara swiped the medicine bottles off the nightstand. This time with no protest from Maggie. Cara shuttered, hugging herself. Morning and Mercerville couldn't come too soon.

👁👁👁

As Cara turned the van onto the Mercerville exit, she drove straight to Doc Hudson's clinic instead of Susan's house. "Doc made us promise to let him check you over.

You know how he worries about his patients."

"Oh, okay," Susan agreed, having been extremely quiet the entire trip. Docile and subdued, she climbed out of the van and followed the designers into the clinic.

Doc Hudson stood by the front desk checking a chart as they entered. "Hello, Susan," he said with his voice gruff, but manner gentle. "I've been waiting for my favorite patient."

"You have?" Susan allowed him to shepherd her toward the doorway to the exam rooms.

"Let's see how your head's healing and if those stitches have dissolved."

Cara sidled up to him and slipped the medicine bottles into his hand. He nodded then took hold of Susan's arm as they disappeared into the back with the door closing behind them.

"Thank heavens," Maggie whispered, standing beside Cara. "She's in his hands now."

"The Tuscan tapestry going to Mercerville instead of Houston gave us the perfect excuse to get Susan here." Cara wandered over to look out the huge picture window. "Blue skies, no rain in sight today. So different than our last visit to this clinic."

"That was a nightmare. I don't even want to think about our last visit here." Maggie paced up and down the carpet, pivoting and retracing her steps.

A receptionist and a nurse returned to work at the front desk, but no patients entered. Glad they were almost alone, Cara joined her friend, tracking along beside Maggie. "Maggs, I thought a murderer on the loose was the worst problem we faced on this job—but turning sweet Susan into a drug addict—"

"I know, I know," Maggie responded, stopping at the far end of the room with Cara. "But that swinging gate last night spooked me. What if the killer saw Susan sleepwalking and pushed her into the pool? He could've finished her off if I hadn't run outside."

"You imagine the killer was there last night?" Cara frowned. "Just because of an unlatched gate?"

"Think about it. He's been stalking both Susan and Joan, leaving notes, watching—but now Joan's gone, and there's only Susan left."

Chapter 18

Doc Hudson ushered Susan through the door back into the waiting room. "Susan is healing fine," he announced. "And I'm sending her some mild medication to take *one* once a day. Gave her enough samples to see her through."

"Her other pills?" Cara queried, holding her breath.

"Not necessary anymore. In fact—" He cleared his throat then added, "—she's promised never to take them again. Or any other pills unless I *personally* give them to her. Right, Susan?" She nodded and he patted her hand. "Run along with your friends now."

"We're out of here," Cara said, smiling her thanks at the small town doc.

"Goodbye, young ladies. Try to behave." He waved then picked up a chart in dismissal.

Once they were back in the van and on the road, Susan's purse rang again. This time she caught it in time to answer the call. "Uncle Leland!" she exclaimed, "You've never called my cell phone before." She shifted uncomfortably in her seat. "You called the house for two days? Something must be wrong with my phone."

Rolling her eyes, Cara glanced back at Maggie through the rearview mirror.

Susan ended her call, turning to Cara with a request. "Please take me directly to my uncle's place instead of home. He's all worked up and worried about me."

"No problem," Cara replied, driving past their normal turn. "His place is the hill two streets over, right?"

"Right."

Unsure about the detour, Maggie chewed her lower lip. They still hadn't crossed Roger off their suspect list and now they were delivering a vulnerable Susan into her cousin's lair.

Maggie's sixth sense was so overloaded, she was unable to decipher if the dark cloud billowing around them grew darker and more threatening here in Mercerville than she'd felt it in Houston. Either way, she intended to remain on high alert.

Rachel threw the door open, giving a Susan a warm hug and ushering them all three inside Uncle Leland's huge regal home. Through the entryway, Cara could see into the study just off the grand staircase. There, Roger stood chatting with Kirby, the accountant/financial advisor.

Roger glanced over. His manner revealed surprise, instantly transformed by a cocky grin. "Hey, Cuz!" He sauntered over to join them at the base of the staircase. "Didn't expect to see you."

"We're glad you came." Rachel gave Susan another squeeze. "Dad's been driving us crazy worrying about you."

"He's been upstairs roaring like a lion," Roger added, taking the other side of Susan who hadn't said a word. "We'd better get you up there and show him you're still kicking."

Between the two cousins, they hustled her up the stairway. Susan threw an apologetic glance over her shoulder. "I'll be back down in a minute."

"Take your time." Maggie waved cheerfully.

Cara noticed Kirby still standing by the fireplace as he intently watched Susan climb the stairs. The woman displayed difficulty keeping up with her cousins.

"Hello, Kirby, isn't it?" Cara said crossing over to him and extending her hand. "I'm Cara Fazio." She motioned to a reluctant Maggie. "And this is Maggie Ross."

"Susan's city friends," Kirby said with a smile curving his mouth, though his eyes still followed Susan until she reached the top and disappeared from view. His gaze switched to the designers. His eyes were gray-green, his features even and he'd aged handsomely in the manner of a silver-haired Gary Grant. "Nice to meet you, Cara." He released her from his firm handshake and took Maggie's hand. "And you, Maggie."

Body stiffening, Maggie pulled her hand away quickly, making Cara wonder if her friend had gotten bad vibes. She knew Maggs was ultra-suspicious of this man, still usually politeness overruled vibes. "Are we interrupting business between you and Roger?" Cara asked to cover up Maggie's lack of manners.

"We're done. I'd dropped by to have him sign a few papers." He motioned toward a file sitting on the mantel. "But he did and we were just chatting."

"About?" Cara said, disguising her curiosity with a flirtatious tone and a glance through her lashes.

He appeared oblivious to her charms. "Susan, actually," he replied, his gaze stealing back to the top of the stairway. "We've all been concerned about her."

"Join the club," Cara replied.

"Susan didn't even tell me hello. That's unlike her. She's always gracious." He suddenly stopped talking, full attention back on the staircase.

Stepping carefully, hand clinging to the banister, Susan descended, watching each stair as if it might move.

"Susan?" The trio exclaimed, all moving toward the staircase to meet her at the bottom.

"I wanted to dash downstairs to tell you that I promised to play a game of chess with Uncle Leland." Susan smiled wanly, one hand remained on the banister. "I'm afraid my dash has disappeared with my energy."

Kirby grabbed her by the shoulders, startling them all. "Are you sick?" he demanded.

"I'm fine," Susan responded, staring up into his eyes.

"You're not fine." His hands stayed clamped on her shoulders, but Susan didn't struggle, just continued their eye contact.

"You got that right," Cara muttered.

"Susan, what's wrong with you?" His intensity set off Maggie's internal alarm. She itched to pull Susan away, to somehow get between them and protect her.

"She's had an accident—several," Maggie told Kirby, moving as close to them as possible. She then added, "Doc Hudson just examined you, right, Susan?"

"Yes," Susan nodded as Kirby released her.

"What did Doc say?" Kirby appeared embarrassed as if he'd suddenly realized he had hold of her.

"I'm healing well. It just takes time." Susan's voice was soft, yet there was an inflection Maggie couldn't identify. "Anyway, I came downstairs to ask if you if you'd be a dear and show Maggie and Cara the quarry or maybe take them for coffee while I spend some time with my uncle?"

"My pleasure," he replied, though Maggie knew better.

Susan turned to Maggie. "Unless ya'll would rather go to the house without me?"

"No way," Cara said. "I've never seen a rock quarry."

Maggie nodded. "Coffee and rocks—can you beat that?"

Susan giggled. "Not the type of *rocks* girls prefer." She flashed the diamond of her wedding band.

Kirby blanched, stepping back, allowing enough space for Maggie to move between them.

She took hold of Susan's hands. "You sure you'll be okay if we leave you here?"

"Of course. Why ever not?" Susan said with confusion.

Cara snagged Maggie's wrist. "Come on, partner, let's sight-see *and* get me a caffeine fix." She turned to Ballentine. "If you're game, Kirby?"

"Certainly," he replied, a polite smile on his lips.

Maggie sensed he was as reluctant to leave Susan as they were, yet she felt sure it was for a far different reason.

Cara sat in the passenger seat of his white Lexus, curious about the man who set off Maggie's signals, yet seemed innocuous. She wasn't a bit curious about the quarry. Kirby remained the real draw.

"Which first," he asked, "Coffee or the Mercer Quarry?"

With a shrug, Cara replied, "I'm for coffee. Rock quarries don't fascinate me."

"Coffee it is," he responded, hitting the gas pedal aiming through town. They sped along with Kirby making polite small talk.

"The quarry has been in the Mercer family for five generations," he said. "Times have been rough on and off, but they always keep it solvent somehow."

"I got that impression from Susan once." Cara watched a few puffy clouds gathering as she gazed out the passenger window as Kirby watched for a parking spot.

"Did they have to lay off employees?" Maggie asked.

"At times. They always tried to avoid that, but sometimes things got tough. Not just for the employees—the Mercers have fought a lot of battles to keep it afloat and profitable."

"Does Susan's uncle still run it?"

"No. Handed over the reins to his son. All the responsibility's on his shoulders now. Rachel sometimes helps in the office, but Roger's proven to possess excellent business sense."

"He does?" Cara asked, her surprise evident.

"Yes. Leland and I are impressed." Kirby's voice lowered, his hands tightening on the steering wheel. "In the past, Roger didn't always display that potential."

"We've heard a few stories," Maggie said, not expanding on it since Ballentine remained on their suspect list right along with Roger. She felt powerful vibes whenever Kirby was anywhere around Susan. And who knew what had transpired between him and the murder victims? Maggie's pride had stung when Jake had scoffed at her for suspecting the financial adviser, but until Kirby convinced her otherwise, he stayed on her list.

Then Cara spoke. "Kirby, what do you know about that new development outside of town?" She shot a side glance at Maggie, who couldn't figure out why.

"I think it's a great thing to infuse life into town. Should generate business for the locals. You've probably noticed some of the vacant buildings on Main Street?"

"One or two," Maggie replied, "but nothing like most of the small towns around here."

"Better, but not good. We're losing our young people to the cities. They go off to college and don't come back since there's not enough opportunity here." Kirby slowed, searching for an open parking spot. "One of the developers is an old college mate of mine, Shawn Mann. He has quite a vision for Shady Grove and the clientele it'll attract."

"Are all the places alike?" Cara asked, showing real curiosity, again puzzling Maggie.

"No. Just the opposite. A variety. He's building hacienda-style, colonial, rustic cabin, alpine, adobe, modern, English cottage and even Mediterranean."

"So who does the interior design?" Cara wondered, intense concentration on her face.

"I can check."

Now Maggie understood Cara's fishing expedition. Always business first.

As they parked in front of the diner, Kirby's cell phone rang. He glanced at the number then said, "You two go on inside and grab us a booth. I need to take this."

As they slid into an aqua and gray booth, Nan waved hello. "Be with you gals in a sec."

"I like Kirby," Cara told Maggie. "He's nice."

"People think most murders are nice, until it gets to the killing part," Maggie replied, not about to be fooled.

He entered the diner, spotted them, and strode over to the booth to take the empty side opposite the designers.

"Thanks for waiting. That was Susan. Roger convinced her to stay for dinner and she wondered if I'd entertain you."

"That's not necessary," Maggie protested. "You can just drop us back at our van."

"Wouldn't dream of it," he said, flipping over the menu to read the daily special clipped over it. "We're already here and it'll be my pleasure to treat you to dinner. Please consider yourselves my guests."

"Do you think it's wise?" Cara asked, turning to Maggie.

"Dinner with me?" Kirby said confusion apparent.

"No. Leaving Susan alone over there," Cara blurted, feeling embarrassed. She hadn't realized how it sounded to him.

"Why not?" Taken aback, his gaze swept between them. "She's in the bosom of her family."

"It's just that Susan's fallen victim to a series of mishaps and isn't feeling herself lately," Cara babbled.

"We, ah, promised Doc we'd keep a close eye on her," Maggie added.

"Can't imagine a safer spot for Susan. Her uncle and cousins adore her." He dropped the menu, his keen gaze locked on the designers. "What's up?"

"We've heard rumors about the cousins—the bad blood between them and Susan," Cara confided, feeling more uncomfortable by the minute.

"That's crazy!" Kirby laughed in what appeared to Cara, genuine surprise. "Roger disagreed with John Lawson, their lawyer, on the wording of a stipulation or two. He's never been at odds with Susan. More to the point, she babysat the cousins when they were little and is one of the few who actually *likes* Roger and Rachel. Most people pretend to just because they're Mercers."

His natural response sounded refreshing and honest. In fact, the more Cara spent time with Kirby, the less she viewed him as a suspect. She intended to make that clear to Maggie as soon as they were alone. He did *not* belong on either suspect list.

After dinner, Kirby returned them to Uncle Leland's place, but he declined to go inside. "Give Susan my best," he said before bidding them goodbye at the front door.

"Wonder why he didn't want to come in with us?" Maggie charged as if it were a crime.

"He said he'd finished his business with Roger," Cara defended. "He was being polite, not wanting to intrude."

"So *you* say." Maggie flipped her hair back as she pressed the doorbell, sending chimes ringing.

Roger opened the door to greet them with, "You should've joined us for dinner."

"We weren't invited," Cara replied, allowing a smile to soften her statement.

"Technicality," Roger tossed over his shoulder as he ushered them inside.

"Besides, we had a nice dinner with Kirby Ballentine."

"Good man," Roger said. "Got a bum deal from Susan's husband—when he fired Kirby right after the wedding, it surprised us all."

"Where's Susan?" Maggie demanded, looking around.

"Upstairs." Roger stopped beside the mahogany and leather bar. "Dad conned her into another game of chess and Sis is out with friends." He grinned. "Guess you're stuck with me."

"Susan is, um, feeling okay?" Cara had hoped they could just grab their client and run.

"Actually," he eyed them. "Cuz is doing better now than when she first arrived."

"The meds are wearing off," Maggie blurted before Cara could stop her.

Cara frowned. That was Susan's personal business and who knew how trustworthy Roger was?

"Meds?" Roger spun back to face them. "Susan hates pills."

"We know." Cara sighed. This was their client's family.

"The accidents lately have taken a toll on your cousin physically and emotionally," Maggie admitted.

Roger sounded stumped. "Doc Hudson is an old fogey about dispensing drugs."

Cara exchanged a glance with Maggie, who nodded. "Not him," she explained. "Ed took Susan to a Houston doctor."

"Ed, huh?" Roger slammed a fist on the bar counter. "He'd lock her away in a tower if he could."

"True," Cara grumbled, earning an elbow poke from Maggie. "Tell us about it."

"So you aren't fans, either?" Roger selected a bottle of wine from the wine rack behind the bar. "Want to join me in a drink?"

"Espresso?" Cara asked hopefully.

"Nope. Sorry." He showed them the Chardonnay. "Wine?"

"No thank you," both designers replied.

Cara added, "We need to stay sharp."

"Why?" Wine pouring aborted, Roger glanced between them, a quizzical expression on his face. "This have anything to do with my cousin's wellbeing?"

Cara raised a brow then plowed forward. After all, if Roger was the murderer, he knew about the stalking, the notes, and the brakes. If not, he was family and deserved to know. "We're afraid Susan's in danger."

"No way," Roger protested, nearly spilling his wine. "Who'd want to hurt *her*?"

"Whoever killed your lawyer and his secretary."

"A killer is drugging my cousin?" Roger exclaimed, practically vaulting over the bar to land beside Maggie.

"You've got it all mixed up," Maggie replied. "I'm afraid the med thing might be our fault. We were trying to protect Susan, but ended up upsetting her after she was injured and already shook up."

"And it just kept escalating," Cara continued. "Then Ed took her back to Houston in such bad shape—"

"Which lead to the prescriptions," Maggie finished. "We feel responsible for that part."

"Join the club," Roger confided, "I've done something that'll upset her, too. She'll probably have my head when she finds out."

"Finds out *what*?" they asked together, but Roger's gaze flicked away from them to the top of the stairs.

"There you all are," Susan called as she descended the stairway in her normal graceful way. "I think Uncle Leland beating me at chess, twice in one day, has cheered him up immeasurably." She smiled around at them. "Where's Kirby?"

"He didn't come in with us," Cara answered, "but he treated us to a delicious dinner of a million calories and carbs at Addy's Dinner."

"That's so sweet of him," Susan replied as if she hadn't suggested it, then she chuckled. "I hope none of you minded?"

"No. He's good company," Cara replied.

"How are you feeling?" Maggie asked, glad their client appeared herself again.

"Fine. A bit frazzled." Susan walked over to snag her handbag off the entry table. "Gladys is waiting for us, if you're ready to go?"

"So ready," Cara responded.

"Me, too."

Maggie glanced at Roger who gave Susan a hug as he mouthed, "I'll call" at them while his cousin's back was turned. They had to learn what he was hiding from Susan, and, apparently, he was willing to share.

ᏪᎧᏪᎧ

Back at Susan's Mercerville home, they left Gladys fussing over Susan and escaped upstairs with the bags. Once inside the Ivy room, Cara closed the door and turned to Maggie. "How can we talk to Susan's cousin without her discovering?"

"I have a feeling he's pretty inventive." Maggie bounced as she sat on the foot of the bed. "Your bed is firmer than mine—no fair!"

"As if that helps me sleep." Cara arranged the few things she unpacked. "Whatever happens here we must get back to Houston tomorrow night."

Maggie cocked her head, her green eyes thoughtful. "So Ed won't get mad at Susan and us?"

"Who cares about Ed? He's never mad at Susan and *always* mad at us." Cara pressed her palms against her forehead, trying to dull the throbbing headache. "Our *job*, Maggs. This is a critical stage and we're so close to done."

Maggie nodded and stopped bouncing. Her cell phone be-bopped to life. "Speak of the devil—it's Roger. Does *everyone* in this town have my cell? Why not yours?"

"Just answer," Cara said, knowing the obvious. Deputy Rice was passing along Maggie's number.

"Yes," Maggie answered instead of hello. "Okay. We can do that." Maggie snapped her phone shut and looked up at Cara. "Roger will meet us in the garden after Susan goes to bed. He'll watch for her bedroom light to go off."

"Another night watcher?" Cara flopped into the sage green velvet side chair. "This cloak and dagger stuff gives me the creeps."

"Me, too." Maggie hugged herself, a forlorn expression on her normally bright pixie face. "Something's brewing in the universe and it's aimed for us like a tidal wave."

"We'd better be ready to ride the wave then, Maggs."

છાજા

Wind had blown clouds over the moon, shrouding it and cloaking most of the starlight. The scent of magnolias, roses and night-blooming jasmine perfumed the air.

Maggie and Cara sat on the bench by the fountain waiting for their client's cousin.

They heard a rustle by the magnolias and a "Psst."

"Coast is clear," Cara replied.

"Susan's tucked in bed and asleep by now," Maggie told the bushes.

Roger crept out, a bit clumsily, nearly tripping over the rock border around the daisies. "Hope so. You have to promise not to breathe a word to Cuz. Okay?"

"What's the big mystery?" Cara asked, more annoyance than curiosity in her tone.

Maggie elbowed her friend, hoping Cara would rein in her attitude. "Roger, what is going on?"

"I hired a private eye to investigate Ed."

"Why?" the designers chorused.

"Because my cousin got sucked into an ill-advised marriage once." Roger tugged at the collar of his golf shirt, looking extremely uncomfortable. "And I don't think she's done any better this time."

"She told us about the marriage her dad annulled," Cara said. "And claims Ed is totally different."

"Maybe not so much," Roger replied, circling the patio and keeping his voice low.

"Susan adores Ed and he adores her," Maggie protested, thrown aback by his disclosure. "Why would you investigate him?"

"Don't trust him." Roger scooted over a patio chair and sat adjacent to them. "Ed made his move when Susan was most vulnerable—right after her father's death. And believe me," he said in earnest, "My uncle wouldn't have approved of that whirlwind relationship and quick elopement."

"She's so happy with Ed." Maggie couldn't let go of her first impression of Ed hugging Susan to his side so lovey-dovey. They were the perfect couple and this didn't fit.

"Too many red flags," Roger persisted. "Since their marriage he tries to isolate Susan from us, her family and friends. The whole town, in fact."

"Ah, they live in *Houston*," Cara pointed out. Maggie nodded in agreement.

Voice laced with frustration, Roger stated, "Ed lied about several things."

"Why should we believe you?" Maggie argued, her sixth sense in tatters.

"I'm getting the detective's report in the morning then we'll see who's truthful."

Roger sounded hurt, but Maggie didn't care. For all she knew, Roger was trying to get the spotlight off himself. She remembered the rumors about his break with Lawson after Susan's father's will was made public. Despite what Kirby said, maybe there *was* truth to that, maybe he knocked off the lawyer and the secretary. Now he had sights set on his cousin and to frame Ed while he was at it?

"I'd like to see that report," Cara mused.

"That's a deal," Roger replied, standing and replacing the patio chair where it belonged. "Rachel will collect Cuz and take her off to church in the morning. I'll bring the report here to show you."

"Susan didn't say anything about church," Maggie said, feeling unease about this entire thing, especially going behind their client's back. *Again.* She bit her lip. *It turned out so well the last time.*

"Susan doesn't know yet. Sis will call her in the morning and not take no for an answer." He moved toward the magnolias, adding, "See you in the A.M."

As he disappeared, Cara groaned, "I hate mornings."

"Then we'd better go to bed." Maggie didn't want to discuss Roger. Or Ed. Or anything. She tried to push Roger's words out of her mind, but all the suspicions and theories swirled around like a tornado in her head.

☙❧

In the morning, Cara shook her head in wonder as Rachel hustled Susan and Gladys off to church. Rachel certainly had persuasive powers, even getting the housekeeper out of the house while Arthur was confined to quarters with a rheumatism flare-up.

"Coast is clear," Maggie whispered into her cellphone, reminding Cara of games they played as kids. But this wasn't a game. It was deadly serious.

Chapter 19

Minutes later the doorbell rang. Cara whipped it open to see Roger, flanked by Jake on one side and Kirby on the other.

"Susan's says you two are her only friends in Houston," Roger announced, no boyish grin present. "We have to help her."

So startled to see Susan's cousin bringing the other two men, Cara forgot to even say hello and just backed up to let them enter the house. Never at a loss for words long, and noticing Roger clutching a file folder and Kirby with a briefcase, she finally asked, "Should we go into the kitchen where there's a table if we need it?"

"Sure," Roger said, leading the pack through the house.

The designers trailed the men, Cara feeling strange as if they were all invading her client's home. "We didn't expect a party."

"Jake needs to hear this and Kirby's onboard with me." Roger took a seat at the head of the table, placing the folder in front of him as the others selected chairs around the table.

Maggie's eyes narrowed at his statement, her assessing gaze moving from Roger to Kirby and back. "On board with what?"

The deputy leaned over from his seat next to Maggie and

covered her hand with his. "Mellow out, Irish, let the man talk."

Maggie tossed her head, but left her hand beneath his.

Roger cleared his throat then began, "The PI faxed this report to me this morning and it confirms my fears. Susan's husband is not the man he claims to be."

"Then who is he?" Cara asked.

"A piranha." Kirby growled, face practically as gray as his hair. "We have to protect Susan."

"What is this?" Maggie asked, green eyes flashing. "Are you two teaming up to bad mouth Ed? None of us may like him, but Susan loves him."

"Let's hear what they have to say," Jake soothed again, turning her hand over in his.

Cara watched from where she sat on the other side of Maggie and across from Kirby. "We're listening. Shoot."

"I hated to use trickery to get my cousin out of the way, but it's exactly because of your point, Maggie. Susan won't hear a word against Ed because she does love him. That's why I've tried to unearth facts to back up my position." He swept the table with a sad glance. "Unfortunately, my hunch was right."

"We never should've let it get this far," Kirby said with a groan. "I've been following the money trail practically since the man took control of Susan's finances."

"When he *fired* you?" Cara pointed out, not sure these two could be trusted to rate their client's husband.

"More than that," Roger said, reclaiming their attention. "Ed took over complete control of my cousin's finances and her life." He cracked his knuckles like a fighter before a match. "And he's done this before."

"Done what?" Cara asked, feeling like she was swimming in swamp water and couldn't find solid ground.

"Marry for money?" Jake injected, addressing the other men with a question in his voice. "That's low, but not criminal."

"Unless he knocks off his wives," Cara offered. Maggie

kicked her from under the table. "Ouch! Hey, I was just kidding," Cara apologized, rubbing her leg and witnessing all the varying expressions of horror she'd triggered.

"It's no joking matter," Maggie scolded. "Besides, Ed has his own money."

"No," Kirby announced, tension carved in his face and the line of his body. "Ed has no funds beyond hers. It's all a sham. It took me awhile to dig past all the layers of deception he has in place. The man's clever, incorporating various companies in different states and countries. But ultimately his business is a shell holding corporation with no assets."

"Right." Roger nodded, his cheerful manner vanished today. "The detective's report revealed the same thing. I'm afraid Cuz has been suckered again."

"Impossible." Still struggling with this new direction, Maggie protested, "Ed bought the Houston house as a gift for Susan using his own money."

"No—he used her money," Kirby corrected, speaking slowly as if the weight of the situation rested upon him, wounding his soul. "This is my fault. I let her down." He flexed one fist then stared at the table top. "I should've trusted my instincts and immediately checked into the man, but it blindsided me when Susan eloped so soon after losing her father. Then she let Dexter fire me, so I thought my personal feelings tainted my judgment."

"Susan made her own choice, Kirby. We don't control what others do." Maggie's heart wrenched at his agony. How could she have suspected him of murder? He obviously cared deeply about Susan. Yet, Maggie felt mystified. How could this all be true? Could Ed Dexter be the gold-digging cad they were claiming? Had she misread the powerful vibes from Kirby? She just couldn't realign her thoughts to match this new reality.

Roger thumped the file on the table. "If I would've done this before Cuz married, she wouldn't have given the man a second look." He targeted Kirby, voice kind. "If we're claiming blame, I'm guilty, too. Like you, I didn't trust Ed, but Susan seemed so happy. I should've investigated him then."

"Unless Miss Susan files charges when she learns this," Jake said, scooting his chair back and standing. "I don't see why I'm needed here."

"How about fraud?" Kirby open his briefcase, pulling out a stack of documents and computer printouts. "Theft? Embezzlement?" He went grayer, expression haunted. "And possibly violence." He hesitated, "I fear John Lawson as Susan's attorney stumbled on to some of Ed's maneuvers."

Maggie and Cara both gasped, "No!"

Jake sat back down. Hard. "Say what?"

The missing thread, Maggie realized with escalating horror. "The lawyer's dead—so is his secretary."

"Gets worse." Kirby's voice cracked. "Dexter's not only going through Susan's money without her knowledge, but she's wife number three. Possibly, wife one and two are dead."

"A real black widower!" Cara exclaimed, looking as stunned as Maggie felt. "I was just kidding before—stupid me."

Maggie felt worse than stunned, she felt sick, and frightened for Susan. "For real?" she whispered, meeting Kirby's troubled gaze.

"Unfortunately—yes."

"That's why it's so urgent to get Susan away from Ed," Roger told them, pulling pages from his file and sliding them across the table. "So far this is only a preliminary report. He'll get me the detailed one in a few days. Plus he's searching death and insurance records now."

"This is all conjecture." Face grim, Jake scribbled some notes. "You don't actually *know* what happened to Ed Dexter's wives? Maybe he just divorced them?"

"No divorce records so far. Been searching public records online, but finance is my field." Kirby waved three papers, each with an official seal. "Marriage number one in

San Diego fifteen years ago. Number two seven years ago in Maine. Susan's here in Houston."

"Not easy even for my private eye. Don't have any social security numbers or addresses, plus his first wife was a Sarah Johnson and his second a Mary Black." Roger tapped his file. "Unfortunately, names which are far too common and on opposite coasts. It's taking time to weed through all the possibilities." His cellphone buzzed and he checked it. "Sis texting to warn me they'll be here in ten minutes."

"Better go," Kirby said, pushing back from the table.

"Wait," Roger requested. He handed the file to Jake. "You look this over. Sis and I will take Susan home with us for lunch with Dad. Why don't you guys do tacos in the park away from prying ears?" He met the deputy's eyes. "This is urgent. Susan needs protection."

As Roger left, Kirby refilled his briefcase then addressed Cara. "You ladies are welcome to ride with me. No need to take three vehicles."

"Yeah, piling the four of us all into my police cruiser might look strange," the deputy said, rubbing his jaw. He turned to Maggie. "On the other hand, they're used to seeing *you* with me."

"Fine," Cara said, preferring a Lexus to a patrol car. "I'll go with Kirby and we'll meet you two there—wherever there is."

"We better hurry. Don't want Susan to catch us." Maggie popped up and snared the deputy's free hand, dragging him away.

At a slower pace, Cara and Kirby followed them out of the house. Once inside his Lexus, Cara tapped Susan's cell number, who naturally did not answer, so she ended up just leaving a message. "Susan, Deputy Rice stopped by and is taking us for tacos. Let me know if you want us to bring one back for you." Cara grinned at Kirby as he started the car. "That'll set her free to accept lunch at Uncle Leland's."

"Clever." As he drove, Cara could see the tension rigid through his shoulders. Despair and determination warred across his face. "I hope there's something in Roger's file combined with what I've gathered that will convince Susan to leave Ed now."

"Won't happen." Cara shook her head. "She loves that man and will demand rock-solid proof to get her to even *listen* to a word against him."

"How do we keep her safe until then?" Kirby asked, anguish ripe in his voice.

He parked next to the patrol car—the only other car at the entrance to a woodland park of grassy areas and towering trees. Unable to answer Kirby's question, Cara let her nose lead her toward a picnic table sporting a pile of tacos and burritos.

"We just grabbed food from the taco stand on the way here," Maggie announced, passing around napkins as she sat thigh to thigh beside Deputy Rice.

Cara couldn't help wonder what would happen to that relationship once they completed the job for Susan. The designers had no other link to Mercerville. Would Maggie and the deputy drift apart or somehow stay connected? If he hurt her friend, Deputy Rice would have Cara to reckon with and she was fiercely protective of those she loved.

"The money trail and reports in your briefcase, Kirby," Rice queried, getting right to the point. "Did you obtain that information in a legal manner?"

Embarrassment crept over Kirby. "Not exactly. Since I've been fired as Susan's financial advisor or even her accountant, I'm no longer authorized to access her accounts and that's where I got onto the track of Ed's deception."

"Afraid of that." The deputy took off his hat and laid it on his bench. "You know I'm duty-bound to go through legal channels."

"Had to do something. I'm responsible." Dropping his head to his hands, Kirby broke down, confessing, "I've loved Susan for so long." Voice cracking, he continued, "I've always felt I'm far too old for her, so I never stepped forward." He groaned, glancing up briefly, but long enough for Cara to see the tears gathered in his eyes. "But now this has happened and sweet Susan's in danger. If I'd admitted my feelings, perhaps she wouldn't have been vulnerable to a predator like Ed Dexter."

"Sorry, pal. I never knew," Deputy Rice muttered, his voice grave.

"No one did," Kirby admitted.

"Rachel did," Cara realized, pieces of the puzzle falling into place as she looked over at Maggie who blinked away tears and nodded.

"That's why I got intense vibes off you whenever you were around Susan," Maggie whispered. "But I misinterpreted them."

"I've been hiding my affection for her for so long and now it's too late."

"Never too late," Cara said, not usually moved by what she considered sappy emotions. But this man revealed a gallant romantic side, totally diverse from his reserved efficient persona. If his anguish touched her deeply, no wonder Maggs wiped a tear or two.

Maggie sniffed back a tear, swallowing a lump in her throat as she absorbed his compelling confession. She'd so misread Kirby. As she thought about his interactions with Susan. It fell into place—his deep affection, the love and longing intensity. Even Rachel's casual comment that he'd always watched her cousin that way.

Suddenly, Kirby straightened. "I hope Susan still has her prenuptial agreement. It also contains a stipulation that Susan's inheritance reverts to her family if she dies first. The original document on file with John, her late lawyer, no longer exists. It was destroyed in the freak fire where the law records were stored."

"We saw the prenup," Maggie said. "In Susan's safe at the Houston house."

"Well, the just envelope," Cara corrected, "Susan said it contained the prenup."

"Make sure the document's still inside," Kirby advised,

squeezing his eyes shut for a moment. The designers exchanged a glance, both wondering of a way to look into Susan's safe, when Kirby groaned, "He'll get rid of it before getting rid of her."

"No more killing, not Miss Susan, not anyone," Deputy Rice declared, addressing Kirby. "I'll take the material you and Roger gathered and launch my own investigation through legal channels. That rattlesnake must've made slip-ups and I'll nail him."

"But how do we protect Susan now?" Kirby had pulled himself together—somewhat—to recapture his businessman demeanor.

"Ed can't harm her while we're at the house with them," Cara said, realizing that meant weekends there, too. Not that they'd spent a weekend home for weeks.

"We'll be so underfoot," Maggie added, "he won't be able to breathe without one of us hearing."

"If anybody can do that," Deputy Rice said, actually grinning. "You ladies can."

"This contains the dirt I dug up on Dexter." Kirby slid a flash drive across the table to the deputy then stood, grabbing his briefcase. "Find something to hang that scumbag."

Jake slipped the thumb drive into his pocket. "Count on it."

Kirby glanced at his watch. "Unfortunately, I have a meeting in twenty minutes. Cara, may I drop you back at the house?"

With a shake of her head, Cara finished munching her bite of taco and swallowed. "No thanks. I'd better go with these two in case Susan beats us back there."

Kirby handed each designer one of his business cards. "Please keep me informed about Susan." Voice thick, he added, "Keep her safe."

❧❧❧

Dishtowel in hand, Gladys greeted them at the front

door. "Miss Susan should be home shortly. She says to tell you she's all packed and ready to go."

Maggie sniffed the air. "Mm, something smells delicious, Gladys."

"Raisin bread," she replied, sounding none too pleased. "Sending some with Miss Susan." Mumbling about nutrition and common sense, the housekeeper shuffled into the hallway leading to the kitchen.

"It does smell good," Cara said, "Maybe Susan will share with us?"

"Lucky you," Jake replied in his deep voice, then his gaze met Maggie's and she smiled back.

"I'm going to run upstairs and finish packing." Cara's wink at Maggie easily translated into *I'm leaving you two alone*. With that, Cara headed up the grand staircase.

Maggie wandered over to the huge picture window to gaze outside. Jake stepped up behind her, wrapping his arms around her and pulling her back against him. "Pretty day."

"It is." Her pulse fluttered as she felt his solid strength, then he turned her to face him.

"Don't feel right about letting you go to Houston. Dexter's dangerous and if he catches a whiff of your suspicions, he might lash out like a wounded cougar."

"He won't. We'll be fine." Maggie felt lost gazing up into Jake's eyes and warmly encircled in his protective embrace as his hands kneaded her back.

"Better be." He stroked her cheek with his thumb. "I have a buddy on the Houston police force, Tom Bitner. I'm going to bring him in on this."

"Do you think you can find solid evidence?"

"If it exists, I'll find it." The deputy released her and stared out the window. "I'll have Roger file a complaint that the business funds or estate money is being siphoned. That will give me a legal right to lodge an investigation."

"So you'll use the info Roger and Kirby supplied for a guide," Maggie said, hoping her deputy would find something fast.

She knew that, in reality, she and Cara were little defense for their client.

"Count on it." Jake's gaze swept back to Maggie as if reading her thoughts. "We'll grab that rattlesnake before he can strike."

ෙංෙං

"I drove home last time," Maggie told Cara, tossing her the keys as Susan settled into the passenger seat.

"But I drove up here," Cara began to protest as she caught the keys. Maggie shook her cellphone and tipped her head their client's direction. "All right, Maggs, jump in the back."

Cara glanced into the rearview mirror as Maggie sent and received text after text on her phone. Probably from the deputy. Maybe also Susan's cousin. Susan appeared oblivious to the chimes and sounds of Maggie's exchanges. She probably thought Maggie was playing a game on her phone. They had tried to show Susan how to do that.

"If you're sleepy, feel free to nap," Cara told Susan as the woman yawned for the second time.

Susan stretched her arms, yawning once more. "I'm fine, but I should sleep well tonight."

"Wish I could," Cara muttered, unable to stop her words in time.

Maggie popped up, "Cara always has trouble sleeping."

"I have some sleeping pills—" Susan offered.

"No!" the designers chorused, then Cara scolded, "Doc made you promise to only take the medicine he gave you."

"Will do." Susan nodded. "And I did promise Doc I'd throw all the other pills away—but it's shame to waste them if someone else needs them."

"Not into pills," Cara said, stealing a side glance at her passenger. "Dump them."

"Right, get rid of all the meds except the ones Doc sent

you," Maggie seconded from the backseat, her phone chirping, but she ignored it.

"I wonder if Ed will be waiting for us?" Susan queried, gazing out the window. "I tried to call him after church, but my cell phone's dead."

"Guess we'll find out in a few hours," Cara responded, wondering the same thing except for a much different reason.

When they arrived at the Houston house, Ed was prowling the place like a caged mountain lion and he pounced instantly. "Where have you been? I've been worried sick! Can't you answer that damn cell I gave you?"

Susan paled, taken aback. Maggie and Cara each moved forward to flank their client as Susan stammered, "I—uh—left you a note."

"This?" He waved a paper in their faces. "Some odd scribbles about you going to fetch a tapestry from Italy? Makes no sense."

"The Italian tapestry she ordered was delivered to Mercerville," Cara explained, stepping between them, her dark eyes flashing.

"I'm sorry," Susan said, still looking stunned and staring at Ed through wide eyes, as if she'd never before been the target of her husband's wrath.

She probably hadn't been, Maggie decided as Ed's demeanor underwent an immediate change. He beamed and pulled his wife into a bear hug. "No matter—you're home safe now."

"Yes, I'm home," Susan said, her voice unsteady.

"I apologize for my outburst, dear. I was so worried about you. Frantic, but you're here and fine." He took her hand, leading her toward the master wing. "Come along and you can tell me all about it."

Cara opened her mouth to protest, but Maggie touched her shoulder and shook her head, placing a finger to her lips.

"Remember your lamp that had a short and wouldn't

work?" Ed told Susan, his voice carrying as they walked away. "You know how I like to fiddle with electrical gadgets, well, I fixed your lamp. Let me show you that it's good as new."

"Hope he doesn't electrocute her," Cara said. "We need to get her away from him."

"Not tonight, Cara. Time to back off." Maggie felt certain of that. "I'll leave Susan's bag here. They can get it later. The tapestry we can unload in the morning. Let's take our stuff to the guestroom."

"But Susan—" Cara objected.

"She'll be fine. He knows we just witnessed his blowup so he'll be syrup-sweet awhile."

"Better be." Cara trekked toward the guest room. "We can't follow them into their bedroom."

Once in the privacy of the guestroom, Maggie pushed the door shut with her foot before she deposited her gear. "Susan just had a glimpse of Ed's true colors. Maybe that'll help when we're trying to convince her."

"Hope so. I hate leaving her with him, even with us in the same house." Cara looked troubled—the tell-tale dent above one brow.

"Me, too," Maggie replied, "But he won't risk a thing after that scene. Susan's probably safer right now than she's been in months."

"Maggs, ever thought about opening a design studio and planting in one spot?"

"Then we wouldn't be the Mobile Design Duo," Maggie countered.

"But we could sleep in our own beds at night."

"I don't like all these trips to Mercerville, either," Maggie answered. Her cell chirped signaling another text message. She read it then passed it over to Cara.

"Roger's sending us the final detective's report as soon as he gets it?" Cara said as she read. "We haven't even read the preliminary one."

"But we can." Maggie removed the laptop from the soft-sided case, opening it to hit the power button. "He already emailed that one. That's what some of the texting on our trip back was about. I gave him our email address."

"The other messages were between you and your deputy?" Cara asked, already moving so she could see the computer screen.

"Uh, yes." Maggie barely glanced at Cara's knowing expression. Instead she busied herself to bring up Roger's email. "Here we go."

"Look," Cara said as she scanned the screen. "In the email note Roger admits he had gone through his and Rachel's email exchanges between them and Susan, making notes of where and when Ed was away on business."

"He also gave the detective info on the Mercerville murders," Maggie whistled, "just on impulse, not because he saw a connection at that time."

"He has good instincts." Cara looked over at Maggie. "Maybe you're not the only one with a bit of psychic ability?"

"Like mine's worked right, lately?" Maggie still couldn't believe how off track she'd been. "Let's check out the report."

"Wow," Cara said as they scrolled down. "This reveals fact after fact blowing holes in Ed's itinerary and alibis."

"While on a supposed business trip to New York at the time of Lawson's murder, Ed was racking up credit charges for gasoline in the Texas Hill Country," Maggie read aloud, a chill sweeping over her. "And the night before Aimee's hit and run, Ed received a speeding ticket in their dark blue Yukon just outside of Fredericksburg."

"I think I'm going to be sick," Cara groaned, pressing her temples. "You know what this means?"

"Ed did murder them both!" Maggie's mind spun, spewing over facts possibilities. *Insane.* As dread crept over her, she had to restrain the impulse to run and drag Susan away from Ed. "Kirby was right—the lawyer discovered him embezzling Susan's money—"

"Ed couldn't leave John Lawson alive." Cara's voice grew grimmer. "Even if Lawson wasn't onto Ed, the lawyer had drawn up the prenup agreement and could testify to its existence. In order to inherit Susan's wealth, the document and any witnesses to it had to be dispatched."

"He's a monster!" Since meeting Susan and her husband, Maggie had considered them such an ideal couple. "How could Ed be this duplicitous? This deadly?"

"People aren't always who they appear to be," Cara pointed out in her pragmatic way. "Life isn't always what it seems."

"Too true." Maggie forced herself to continue reading. "See these motel charges on his credit card? Isn't that the Fredericksburg no-tell motel where Darlene's sister had seen Aimee?"

"Ed must be the mystery lover! Yuk!" Cara exclaimed.

"You don't think her baby was his?" Maggie whispered, imaging another blow to Susan.

"Timeline's wrong." Cara scowled, scrunching her face as she figured the math in her head. "Look at the motel dates—she was already pregnant."

"Then it's probably Roger or Bobby," Maggie surmised. "Or someone we don't know about."

"We'll never know now. If the unborn baby wasn't the reason for her murder, guess it doesn't matter. Maybe it's better for Roger and Bobby to never find out."

Maggie pushed the computer aside and grabbed her phone.

"What are you doing?" Cara asked, adjusting the laptop so she could still read the screen.

"Calling Roger. We need to tell him about the mystery man angle."

"For real?" Roger replied when she sprung it on him. Then she heard a gasp. "I'll be damned," he responded as if his memory was pricked. "Aimee dropped me for someone from the city." He sounded flabbergasted. "I suspected her new guy was married—never dreamed it was my cousin-in-law!"

Maggie ended the call, turning to Cara. "I bet Ed had an affair with Aimee to discover how much she knew and a way to dispose of any incriminating files remaining."

Cara nodded. "And if he hadn't been able to steal the prenuptial agreement when he murdered the lawyer, he'd need her to lead him to it."

"Then Aimee knew too much or got demanding," Maggie said, trying to stop the horror film playing in her head. "We need to tell Jake."

"Hit the speaker button. I want to be in on this conversation."

Listening politely at first to their barrage, Deputy Rice interrupted their neatly solved conclusions. "Everything is circumstantial. There is no real evidence that ties Ed Dexter to the murders."

"That's your job," Cara replied.

"Wish I could get my hands on the Yukon." The deputy sounded frustrated.

"Can't your Houston officer friend?" Maggie suggested.

"Not without a warrant. So far we have nothing concrete enough to get one." His voice deepened. "I'll find something. Trust me."

"I do," Maggie answered softly with a glance at Cara.

Cara got the message and headed toward the bathroom. "Need to put my stuff away."

Maggie took her phone off speaker to finish the conversation. "Jake, it's just us now."

"As romantic as that sounds, Irish, we're still quite a distance apart." His voice dropped. "Kirby made a suggestion—let me run it by you."

"What?"

"Would you and Cara be able to meet us partway tomorrow evening for another pow-wow, maybe in Hampstead at the BBQ Grill?"

"Sure. Anything to help Susan."

"Don't let her know or allow Ed to realize you'll be gone any chunk of time." He paused then added, "Will six-thirty work for you?"

"We'll be there."

❦❦❦

"We need proof!" Roger slammed a fist upon the table, startling several diners who glanced over at their back corner booth then returned to the business of eating.

"Keep it calm," Cara told him, reaching across the table to pat his hand.

"We must protect Susan," Kirby said, his voice not carrying past their booth, though sounding just as urgent as Roger did.

"We're staying at the house with her. We know Ed hates it, but until our reno job's finished we'll stick like glue." Maggie flounced her head, chin up in determination.

"What happens then?" Kirby asked. "When you're done?"

"I'll have Ed behind bars by then," Deputy Rice stated.

"You'll have to hurry," Cara admitted. "Things are rolling. We might be done by the end of the week."

"Then we have to tell Susan now and get her away from that psycho," Roger snapped.

"Susan won't even *hear* accusations against the man she loves until we have *ironclad proof*," Maggie reminded him. "Besides, if she let our suspicions slip to Ed—she might end up in worse danger."

"Agreed," Cara seconded, knowing her friend was right on.

"Right," the deputy confirmed.

"True. Susan won't believe us," Kirby replied with resignation, his complexion again cast in gray. "She won't even *listen*."

"Okay," Roger conceded, teeth gritted as he punched his fist into his palm.

"I've got the flash drive, and I'll study the files from the private investigator," Jake informed them. "I've already contacted Tom Bitner on the Houston police force. He'll work it from his end."

Cara could see Kirby remained troubled. "Are you okay?" she asked in concern.

"When this shakes out, I'm wondering what emotional damage Ed's betrayal will do to Susan."

"She's strong," Cara reminded him. "She survived it before."

"And she'll have all of you to help her through," Maggie said. Meeting Kirby's gaze, she added, "You'll know how to be there for her."

"We'd better let you ladies get back," the deputy said, grabbing his hat as he stood.

"You're right." Cara walked out of the barbeque place with Kirby and Roger while Maggie lingered behind with Jake.

Kirby opened the van door for Cara. "Thanks for meeting with us."

"No problem," she responded, giving him a smile. "We'll take care of Susan."

"Please do," he requested earnestly, shutting the driver door before joining Roger who offered her a goodbye salute from the sidewalk.

Maggie stood beside Jake in the entry area between the inner and outer doors. "I have an idea," she said staring up at him, wishing he'd once again flash his dimpled grin, but no one had been smiling much tonight. "Cara and I can convince Susan to let us redecorate her dining room to give you more time."

"Hope you don't need to do that." He placed his big strong hands on her shoulders. "I want you out of there and safe."

"Safe sounds good," Maggie replied. Then she stood on tiptoe and kissed him.

On the way back to Houston, Maggie took a deep breath. "We need to formulate a plan to flush out Ed and keep Susan safe."

"But he's a *murderer*," Cara protested, switching lanes as they hit the Houston freeways.

"We have to prove that. I still can't help suspecting Kirby. It's awfully convenient, him coming up with dirt on the *husband* of a woman he loves," Maggie retorted.

"I'll keep an open mind if you will, Maggs. Meantime we need to expose Ed if he is the villain."

"You're the best about coming up with a plan. Think on it."

Cara fell silent a moment. "Well, it's no secret Ed doesn't like us much. So first, we need to become a thorn in his side."

"Got that covered," Maggie said with a laugh. "I told Jake we can persuade Susan to let us redecorate their dining room and the sitting room."

"Perfect! That will drive Ed ballistic—us in their house for even longer!" Cara joined in the laughter. "Love the way you think, Maggs."

"Aren't we wicked?" Maggie grinned back at Cara.

"And cunning," Cara replied.

Maggie whooshed out a breath. "Cunning enough to catch a killer?"

Chapter 20

While their crew was doing last minute cleanup, planting and landscaping outside, the designers decided to do a final check on the sunroom. "I think we should get Susan in here for approval on where we hang the tapestry. It's the only thing left inside," Maggie suggested, sliding an urn-potted palm over just inches to create a balanced vignette in the far corner.

"Now?" Cara winked, pausing from leveling an old world oil painting on the opposite wall. "Not wait until it's all done with a big reveal for the client?"

Maggie laughed. "As if Susan hasn't been in here and probably the patio, the gazebo, and backyard a half dozen times this morning alone."

Cara eyed the painting, giving it one more straightening tweak. "I'm just glad to have the old Susan back, flitting in and out and curious about everything."

"That was scary. She was so out of it and didn't even notice or care about the artificial rock when she'd been so eager to see the process." Maggie stared at the painting. "Raise the left corner a little."

"This good?" Cara pressed the frame enough to raise it a touch. They used their levels religiously, but when it came to the last touches, they eye-balled it with an artist eye.

"Perfect." Maggie stood, shaking out her arms. "Those palms are heavy. Why did we ever put them in ceramic urns and real terra cotta planters?"

"Ah, 'cause they're Tuscan?"

"Oh, yeah." Maggie grinned, looking past Cara. "Speak of the devil."

The pocket doors slid open, Susan poking her head. "Thought I'd bring you some iced tea."

"Thanks." Maggie noticed the tray in her hands as she balanced three glasses. Susan couldn't have done that a few days ago.

"We were just going to track you down." Cara took the tray from Susan's hands and placed it on a stool. "It's time to hang your tapestry."

Susan selected one of the glasses and sipped before saying, "I hope it's as pretty as it looked online. I never even unrolled it to check."

"It's even better." Maggie and Cara unrolled it, watching the delight play over Susan's face.

"Magnificent!" Susan moved over to finger the beautifully woven scene of Tuscany, vibrant with all the colors they'd incorporated in their design plan for the room. It couldn't have fit better if they had commissioned it. "Oh, here's a lose thread at the bottom."

"Don't pull it!" Cara reached out to stop her. "Or it'll unravel."

"I'll fix it." Maggie grabbed a pair of scissors from her prep-kit. "Let me snip it and tie the threads."

Susan admired the intricate interwoven scene, gushing over the beautiful design and then stood back as the designers—Maggie on a chair and Cara on her stepstool—held the tapestry in place against the long wall between the twin diagonal bookshelves. "Oh, yes!" Susan clapped her hands. "Right there!"

Once the tapestry was anchored and hanging securely, Cara asked, "They're still undergoing the last minute work—but do you want to see your lanai and grotto?"

"Yes, please." Susan pranced to the French doors. "Ed had me on such a tight leash yesterday, I didn't get much chance to peek."

Cara and Maggie exchanged glances. Then Maggie said, "Now remember when we go outside that our crew's still been planting the landscaping today. It's a bit of a mess, but by the end of the week, the transformation should be complete."

"What are they planting?" Susan queried.

"Olive, lemon and cypress trees," Cara said, before opening the patio doors. "And a few palms. Wisteria and grape vines along the fence line—"

"Spider lilies, jasmine," Maggie continued. "Rosemary, lavender, basil and pineapple sage."

"Plus a bit of this and that," Cara concluded, throwing open the French doors. "Just ignore the piles of dirt and the guys digging and planting."

Maggie had imagined their client's reaction when she saw the grotto area and wasn't disappointed as Susan gasped, "Breathtaking!"

"So you like?" Maggie chuckled.

"Love it!" Susan shone like the sunshine. "You've transported me to a Mediterranean grotto." Joy flooded her features as she danced across the lanai tiles and onto the lawn then hopped the stepping stones, exclaiming, "Even more beautiful than I dreamed!"

"You *dreamed*?" Cara asked with raised brow.

"Yes, I dreamed of how it looked, but it was night and hard to see." Susan's forehead furrowed and she pushed hair off her face. "The shape of the grotto and water sparkling seemed so real I felt like floating."

Maggie gasped, realizing Susan was remembering her drug-induced sleepwalk.

"Yesterday the electrician wrapped up wiring and installing the lighting," Cara said her voice matter of fact as she whipped a *don't say it* glare at Maggie. "Let us show you the control panel."

She led them back onto the lanai which remained a work in progress and over to the newly installed lighting controls. "It's hard to appreciate it all in the bright sunlight, but this switches it all on—patio, fountain, stone pathway, pool and grottos, gazebo and the perimeter lights." She played with the different touch buttons. "Or section by section…"

Maggie reached over to tap a few herself. Even in the daylight, they watched the luminous glow of the various lights changing colors. "See these buttons control all the areas individually with a rainbow of colors."

"Fantastic!" Susan smiled warmly at the designers. "I'll have to come out and play with the lights when it gets dark."

"Please wait until we have the work finished," Maggie warned. "We'd appreciate if you don't come out back unless we're with you while there's still landscaping happening."

"Yeah, no more accidents," Cara agreed, folding her arms and tapping a foot.

"Okay," Susan agreed to their relief.

Maggie's phone sang it's music ring. She glanced at the number. "Uh, you two go on inside. I'll be there in a minute."

⁓⊃⋖⊃

"Susan scared me when she talked about playing with the exterior lights at night," Cara confided, powering up the laptop computer that evening when they retired to the guestroom.

"I hear ya," Maggie countered, just as her phone sang out. "Roger, wait—repeat that—you're talking too fast."

Cara motioned at her, so Maggie hit the speaker button to let Cara join in the call as panic ricocheted through Roger's rapid-fire words. "The latest report from my detective. Susan married a monster. We have to save her!"

"Slow down, tell us," Cara said, knowing he could hear her as well as Maggie.

He took a breath. "This report reveals that while living in California, Dexter's first wife died of an *accidental* overdose of sleeping pills on their one year anniversary."

Cara and Maggie stayed silent, listening with dread as he continued, "Seven years later Ed relocated to Maine where his second wife died from an *accidental* fall when they'd been married just over a year."

"As we feared," Maggie gasped.

"Keep talking," Cara prompted, the repeated use of the word *"accidental"* chilling her. Neither death was *accidental*, no more than whatever Ed planned for Susan's demise.

"Using different insurance companies cross country," Roger said, this time his voice edged with sarcasm, "the *grieving* widower collected huge life insurance policies."

"He must find a new target wife every time he goes through the money," Maggie whispered.

"Ready for the kicker?" His voice cracked. "The creep has a mega-policy on my cousin."

"And they've been married a year," Maggie punctuated with emphasis.

"Send us the entire report," Cara requested, realizing they must come up with a plan of their own. They had no time to wait for the deputy to go through legal channels.

"And get it to Jake," Maggie ordered, before ending the call.

"Now we know the real reason for Susan's tranquilizers and drugs. Ed must've been responsible for doubling her dose." Cara sighed. "It wasn't Susan who was hooked. He was finding a way to drug her, but we intervened."

"I hope Jake can do something," Maggie said, pacing the floor. "But our suspicions aren't tangible proof for the authorities and trying to investigate those deaths will take time."

"We don't have time."

"Jake is doing his best," Maggie defended, but she acted as worried as Cara felt.

"Maggs, collecting evidence and trying to get a warrant is great, but it's slow going through legal channels without proof. If we want to keep our client alive, it's in our hands."

"What can *we* do?" Maggie halted, biting her lip.

"We have to trap Ed into a confession."

"That's not going to happen."

"It will if one of us acts as bait. We'll set him up." Cara's mind spun into gear, suddenly all the mysteries she'd ever seen or read flickered through her head. "We know Ed wants us out of the way, so he can knock-off wife number three."

"That's why we'll stick around to guard Susan and drive him crazy."

"Uh-huh. We'll get Susan to agree to the dining room remodel. but then—" Cara felt excitement build. "—we'll make a big fuss about never being able to do a job solo, that we can only function as a team."

"I get it," Maggie said, plopping onto the foot of the bed. "He'll try to get rid of one of us to get rid of both of us, so he has Susan to himself."

"Right."

"That's dangerous!"

"Not if we control the plan." Cara wandered over top the window, gazing out as sunset blasted the sky with orange and violet.

Maggie tore some papers out of their notebook, proceeding to rip them into shreds.

"What are you doing?" Cara asked.

"Since all our other suspects have tumbled off the lists, we don't need these." Maggie grew pensive. "This murder tapestry's unraveled to reveal one sinister thread. The true murder plot has always revolved around *Susan*. She is the ultimate target."

"You're right," Cara agreed. "Susan's lawyer was murdered because he caught onto Ed Dexter. Then Aimee was killed because she knew too much and was the only one left who could incriminate Ed."

"He's cleared the path to eliminate Susan," Maggie stated, voice trembling, "Now, we're the only ones who stand in his way."

ભળભ

"Isn't that great, Ed, honey?" Susan gushed. "This room will be so pretty!"

He merely grunted, "Whatever you want, my dear."

Sitting across the dining room table, Maggie and Cara exchanged a satisfied glance. Though he tried to hide it from his wife, the designers could see how displeased Ed was with Susan's news that they'd stay to redecorate the dining room.

"We're just glad you like our vision for the decor," Maggie said. Playing it up, she emphasized what great team chemistry they have and how they could never do a project solo. "Our design ideas always flow together. We wouldn't do any job if we couldn't work together."

"You make a great team," Susan said with a warm smile.

"More than that—Maggie's my right hand and brain power," Cara slyly added. "I'm useless without her."

"And it's impossible for me to do even the smallest project without Cara by my side." Maggie responded, noting the cruel gleam in Ed's eye. Cara was right, already she sensed him plotting for one of them to be knocked out of the picture, therefore ridding him of both. As much as she disliked Cara's plan, now that they'd set it in motion, if only it'd work without either of them hurt.

Later, outside arranging the patio furniture, Maggie scooted a lounger into position and turned to Cara. "Okay, we're driving Ed to the brink under their feet, practically eating all the meals with them, hanging around constantly and now he's fallen for our *can't do anything solo* routine. What's your secret plan?"

"You won't like it."

"So give," Maggie demanded, refusing to be left in the dark a moment longer.

Cara dropped the hand spade she'd been using on a clay pot overflowing with poppies and rosemary. She met Maggie's gaze. "What do I excel at and absolutely love?"

"Design."

"Besides design."

"Swimming."

"Exactly. That's how we'll sucker him. He hasn't a clue." Cara grinned. "We've seen Ed in the pool. He's a floundering whale. In the water, the advantage is all mine."

A shattering thought struck Maggie. "What if it really is Kirby and not Ed? I mean Kirby does have feelings for Susan and Ed did fire him. How do we know he hasn't fabricated the evidence? Or even paid off Roger's detective?"

"Wrong, but still works. Kirby's twice our age and spends his time sitting at a desk not a gym. Advantage mine."

"I totally trust Jake to keep Kirby in the dark about our scheme, but can we trust Roger?"

"Definitely. Jake, Roger, and Rachel will be in on it. In fact, we'll use them to bait Kirby."

"But he's their friend."

"Yes, and they're anxious to prove his innocence, so they'll help just to show it isn't him."

"I'm sorry I've acted so impulsively, trusting my off-kilter sixth sense about Ed, but I still can't shake suspicions about Kirby. He could've found some way to frame Ed out of revenge."

"Maggs, I'll keep an open mind. We'll set it up to bait either man." Cara's voice dropped. "Just hear me out on this."

"Okay. How does it work?" Maggie felt deep reservations, but Cara wore her don't-challenge-me attitude.

"We'll set a trap—to appear I'm alone and vulnerable. When someone tries to go for me—*wham*!"

"Why you?" Maggie protested. "I'm the one who dives into life without thinking. You're supposed to be the sensible one. Besides, I'm a great swimmer, too."

Hands on hips, Cara tapped her foot and leveled a stare at Maggie. "It's *my* plan. I get to star."

"Not fair. Can't we both do it?"

"No. The killer won't take on two of us. But one female—alone at night—"

"Just you alone with an evil murderer?" Maggie protested, "I don't like this."

"Told you that you wouldn't." Cara touched Maggie's hand. "I'll be fine. On solid ground, I'd never take a killer on, but, Maggs, in the water, he's the one who doesn't have a chance."

"What do I do?" Maggie demanded, feeling bad vibes swirling wilder and closer.

"You're in charge of backup."

c/sc/s

"Now you've done the final inspection of the outside portion of your renovation," Cara teased their client. "We should all celebrate with a test swim in the grotto tonight."

"Wonderful," Susan exclaimed, clapping her hands. "Ed, you'll join us girls?"

"No thanks," he replied, shooting a disdainful glare at the designers.

"We can help you test the diving board," Maggie suggested, "I've been so tempted to play in the grotto pool."

"Me, too," Susan agreed. "Ed, why don't you change your mind?"

"Want no part of it," he grumped with the response they anticipated.

With nightfall descending and Susan in the master-suite to change into her swimsuit, the doorbell rang.

Cara and Maggie let it keep ringing, only coming out of the guestroom as they heard Ed answer the door.

On cue, Rachel whooshed inside. "Where's Susan? I found myself here in Houston for a dinner with a friend, who just canceled, so I'm kidnapping your wife."

With beach robes covering their swimsuits, the designers moseyed into the room. "Hi, Rachel," Cara said, greeting her.

Maggie grinned. "I'll go tell Susan you're here."

Cara and Rachel stood talking with Ed stuck between them. Both woman shifted positions each time he tried to leave, like schoolboys blocking each other's way. "Ed, how rude of me," Rachel said, the moment he finally stepped clear. "You're certainly invited to come along with me and Susan."

"No thanks. I have work to do," he muttered.

"You're a surprise!" Susan rushed into the room, her clothes obviously thrown on in haste and her hair more a flyaway mess than usual. Maggie followed, mere steps behind.

"Cuz, I'm stealing you away to the Garden Spot." Rachel smiled sweetly at Ed. "Your husband declined my invitation to come along."

"Oh, okay." Susan gazed at Ed and the designers apologetically. "Cara and Maggie, please go ahead in the pool. I don't want to ruin your fun."

Ed flashed a blistering glance at them, but plastered on an artificial smile as he turned to his wife. "Run along with your cousin, my love. I've got a report to write."

Maggie began sneezing—one sneeze after another, Cara hiding a grin. Maggs was the best fake sneezer ever.

"Ew," Maggie sniffled. "My allergies." She sneezed some more.

"Bless you." Cara handed Maggie a tissue from her robe pocket. "You having a flare up?"

"Yes." Maggie wiped her eyes and nodded then sneezed again. "Ah-choo! I don't think I can play in the water tonight."

"Then I won't either," Cara stated.

"Oh, no, go ahead," Maggie insisted.

"Please do," Susan said, "It's such a lovely night."

Ed watched through narrowed eyes. Cara and Maggie pretended not to notice as he lingered by the doorway to listen. She knew a slightly different ploy had been fed to Kirby by Roger.

"Guess I could swim alone for a little while," Cara said, hoping she sounded reluctant.

"Should I stay to swim with you?" Susan offered, sounding torn as Maggie sneezed again.

"No, no," Maggie said. "Rachel never gets to Houston. Go enjoy her."

Rachel towed her cousin out the door. "We're out of here."

The door slammed shut behind them. Maggie gave another sneeze for effect as she watched Ed out of the corner of her eye. "Go on, Cara. Play in the water for me. I need to take my allergy medicine."

"You sure?"

"Go!" Maggie ordered then headed toward the guestroom, sneaking a glance back as Ed sidled away with a cunning grin on his face.

With the lights set low to illuminate her way, Cara padded barefoot across the yard to the pool. She slipped her robe from her shoulders, letting it fall onto stonework at the edge of the water. The pool had heated to a comfortable temperature and, as she splashed into the warmth, she savored the buoyant call of the water, for a brief second forgetting her dangerous mission—to lure a killer using herself as bait.

Time for one quick dive. She'd make it look amateurish. She felt him watching.

Maggie waited the promised three minutes and then crept onto the patio, using a strategically placed planter as cover. Cara had insisted it'd be fine, but Maggie wasn't so sure. Maybe her sixth sense had been off kilter lately, but right now, her heart thundered so loud she thought the sound must carry. *If everything goes according to plan, Cara will be safe*, she kept reminding herself, over and over and over.

She held her breath as she watched Cara scale the artificial rocks to the hidden diving platform, which was six feet below and to the left of the top of the waterfall. Suddenly, the torches flashed, the lights flickered then went out.

All the exterior lightning was extinguished, casting the grotto into inky darkness. Maggie gasped. She couldn't see Cara. This was not part of their plan. Was it part of the killer's?

ℰ∽ℰ∽

Unable to see, Cara lost her footing, bumping partway down. She heard a cruel laugh. *Ed.* She knew it!

Catching her, Ed seized her, yanking her up by her shoulders. Stunned, she reeled backward, but his hold cinched. Her water advantage gone, high on the man-made cliff, she felt overpowered by his brute strength. Struggling, she tried to scream. His hand clamped over her mouth.

She bit him, gasping, "You can't get away this!"

"Watch me," he sneered, his breath foul as he drag her higher up the rock formation, making sure she felt the faux rock jabbing and battering her. One hand clamped back over her mouth, his arm locked around her in a vise-grip, he moved agilely for a man of his age and size. Cara knew she'd underestimated his strength. Where was her backup?

He snarled in her ear, "It'll be a tragic accident—you falling, breaking your neck in the very grotto you designed."

Waves of fear assailed Cara as she fought him, trying to wrench free. Immune to her frantic struggles, he climbed, dragging her to the top of the waterfall. As if he enjoyed the torment, he continued, "Understandably, my wife will be overcome by despair and within a few weeks she will overdose on tranquilizers."

Cara bit, this time hard enough he jerked his hand from her mouth. Screaming, she flailed wildly as he tried to throw her off the waterfall. He lost his grip, trying to keep hold of Cara and the uneven fake rock. Sensing his balance shift, she grabbed onto a boulder, kicking harder. She held on fiercely, using her entire body to buck and kick. She felt his hold slipping. He gasped. She kicked again.

Chaos erupted. Loudspeakers blared. Search lights flared with blinding brightness, freezing the scene as Ed toppled over the edge. *Thud.* Cara heard him land on the tiles—not in the water.

Maggie scrambled up the cliff surface, reaching a hand out to Cara. "You okay?"

"A little slow there on backup, Maggs," Cara rasped, barely able to catch her breath

"Was waiting for your signal."

"Power out is also a signal."

Maggie helped her along as they climbed down the rocky area together. Amidst the sirens and people running around, the exterior lights lit. Shaking from the trauma, Cara wrapped a towel over her swimsuit, watching the officials hovering over Ed's body. It was apparent he'd never hurt Susan or anyone else again.

❧❧❧

Susan's Mercerville home was lit with twinkling fairy lights, draping trees, light posts and shrubs all the way up the long curving driveway and then leading like a magical pathway to the front entrance. "Looks like we're almost the first to arrive."

"They went all out for the engagement party, didn't they?" Cara said, braking the van after maneuvering to park. "I heard the entire town is helping throw this shindig."

"A lot to celebrate," Maggie replied, climbing out in a lady-like manner, one high-heeled pump at a time. "Susan's back in their fold and going to marry one of their own—finally."

Cara raised a brow. "Hmm, I thought Kirby was on your bad list."

"That was before he linked us up with the Shady Grove people and found that rental building for us." Maggie tossed her copper waves. "He's really a nice guy."

"I told you that from the beginning when you insisted he belonged on the bad list. You aren't the only one with instincts." Cara tugged the skirt of her cocktail dress down over her hips, until the hem fell into place properly.

Their clothes were not made for such a long drive. Houston to Mercerville. This time for a good reason.

Cara hoped she appeared fresh as Maggie looked as she trotted up onto the front porch a step behind.

"Bad list *before* I learned Kirby was a loyal and lovelorn knight trying to rescue Princess Susan." Maggie had that dreamy look in her eyes as she paused at the front door.

"Still think this happened too fast."

"Kirby swore he wouldn't bury his feelings for Susan any longer or allow her to put herself in harm's way again." Maggie twisted a copper curl around her finger, still sounding dreamy. "Says they aren't getting any younger and shouldn't waste any more time, either."

"Guess he does have a point. Susan's track record is worse than mine." Cara rang the doorbell, listening to the chimes echoing. "Hopefully, she's got it right this time."

The door snicked open. "Congratulations," the designers chorused as the beaming engaged couple swept them inside.

"Thanks. About time, huh?" Kirby replied, standing relaxed, appearing at peace.

"We have something to tell you," Susan added excitedly, her hands flying until she snared Cara's and lead them into the sitting room off the entry. "Come in here."

Kirby slid his arm protectively around Susan's shoulders. "We found the missing Chinese puzzle box. Ed had it hidden inside a boot box at the back of his closet under things."

"Did you get it open?" Maggie asked. She still felt bad she'd so misread the strange vibes he'd always transmitted when it was simply him attempting to cloak his affection.

"Yes," Susan answered. "It was easy—just like mine."

"Don't keep us in suspense," Cara demanded, "What was inside?"

"Pages torn from her journal," Kirby explained, "Aimee had made entries about leaving the office unlocked for Ed the night John was murdered, telling him where the files were stored, and then their secret meetings in Fredericksburg."

"They weren't having an affair," Susan offered, her hazel eyes full of emotion. "He was meeting her to make payoffs. Aimee blackmailed him, but she got scared and thought if she told him she had evidence hidden in a secret box, it'd keep her safe."

"That sure didn't work," Cara said.

"Maybe he thought she was bluffing," Maggie surmised. "Until Joan found that box."

"Unfortunately for Joan, all of Mercerville heard about the puzzle box," Kirby added. "Including him."

"Maggie?" Jake stepped into the room, targeting her as he softly said her name.

"Excuse me a moment." Maggie moved toward him.

Jake took her hand and pulled her out of the room and into his arms.

After capturing her lips with a sweet kiss, he took hold of her shoulders, grinning down at her. "Well, Miss Irish, will I see you in Mercerville again after tonight?"

"There's always a possibility." She searched his face, wondering what the future would hold. A deputy in a small town and a big city designer didn't share much in common. "Cara and I are considering relocating to Mercerville."

"For real?"

"Stranger things have happened."

"Works for me." Jake's eyes darkened and his dimple flashed as his mouth slanted down for one more kiss.

In the sitting room, Kirby winked as Cara rolled her eyes, thumbing toward the doorway where Maggie had disappeared with the deputy. "Romance must be in the air."

Susan smiled contentedly. "For some of us it takes a while to see the real thing."

"If there is such a thing." Cara glanced back at the doorway as Maggie reappeared, glowing pink and her lipstick smeared.

"Oh, there is," Kirby assured them, the expression of his face echoing his words. "Sometimes you just have to sweep the fake stuff out of the way first."

"True love is like a real boulder from my quarry," Susan added, a slight tremor in her voice. "Solid and dependable, not easily tossed aside like the fake rocks."

"Now that's romantic," Maggie said, catching Susan's statement.

"Kirby tells me you girls are renting the old Betsy's Bonnets building to set up your design studio." Susan twinkled at them, giving Maggie the sense that the idea had originally been Susan's.

"That vacant hat shop is the perfect set-up for our studio and office, plus we can live in the apartment above the shop," Cara winked at Maggie. "And we're dropping the *mobile* from our name."

"Will you get enough business here in Hill Country?" Concern flashed over Susan's face as her hands fluttered like butterfly wings.

Maggie nodded. "We think so. We've already lined up several jobs from the new Shady Grove residents, plus we'll still travel to a few select clients."

"But not often," Cara corrected. "Mostly, we'll stay planted right here."

"Enough talk about us," Maggie said, eyeing Susan. "So tell us—how are you?"

"Fine, even better than fine." Susan gazed up at Kirby

and smiled then turned back to Maggie and Cara. "Natural-ly, at first I was shattered by Ed's betrayal. But with Kirby's help, I've healed. Now I'm looking forward to a happy fu-ture."

"The money?" Cara prodded. "Did you recoup any?"

"Thanks to you two and your wonderful designs." Susan poked Kirby in the side, her relationship obviously a far more comfortable one than she'd had with Ed. "Tell them."

"She sold the Houston house, along with its gruesome memories." Kirby shared a smile with his fiancée, love lighting his entire face as he glanced proudly down at Su-san. "Thanks to the renovation, the house resold for two hundred grand over Ed's original purchase price. We also sold the vehicles he bought. Overall, she's out some money, but not as bad as it could've been." He dropped a kiss on her forehead. "She's safe, and that's all that matters."

"Safe and happy. We have something for you," Susan said, leading them toward a leather trunk. She lifted the lid. "The Tuscan tapestry from the sun room."

"You don't have to give us your tapestry," Cara ex-claimed, her dark eyes flashing delight belying her words.

"It belongs with you two," Susan insisted. "And will look beautiful in your new studio."

"Thanks," Maggie said with appreciation, recalling its symbolism.

After all, a piece of fabric wasn't cursed. Just unraveled long enough to solve the case as they separated the faux persona of Ed to reveal his true self—a killer.

Their first case. But not their last, Maggie sensed. Not a psychic observation—just a feeling, because next they'd head to renovate a ghostly mansion. Not that they *looked* for murder. It was just in the design.

THE END

About the Author

Author/poet/designer Karen E. Rigley is internationally published and has won numerous awards for her work. She's a member of Mystery Most Cozy, Sisters in Crime, and the International Women's Writing Guild. Rigley now lives in the heart of the mountain west, after living on both coasts and overseas. She's passionate about mysteries, writing, and design, yet still finds time to enjoy family & friends.